Amanda Stevens is an award[...] novels, including the modern g[...] Queen. Her books have been described as eerie and atmospheric and 'a new take on the classic ghost story.' Born and raised in the rural South, she now resides in Houston, Texas, where she enjoys binge-watching, bike riding and the occasional margarita.

Carol Ericson is a bestselling, award-winning author of more than forty books. She has an eerie fascination for true-crime stories, a love of film noir and a weakness for reality TV, all of which fuel her imagination to create her own tales of murder, mayhem and mystery. To find out more about Carol and her current projects, please visit her website at carolericson.com, 'where romance flirts with danger.'

Also by Amanda Stevens

Digging Deeper

A Procedural Crime Story
John Doe Cold Case
Looks That Kill

An Echo Lake Novel
A Desperate Search
Someone Is Watching

Twilight's Children
Incriminating Evidence
Killer Investigation

Also by Carol Ericson

A Discovery Bay Novel
Misty Hollow Massacre

The Lost Girls
Lakeside Mystery
Dockside Danger
Malice at the Marina

A Kyra and Jake Investigation
The Decoy
The Bait
The Trap

Discover more at millsandboon.co.uk

THE SECRET OF SHUTTER LAKE

AMANDA STEVENS

POINT OF DISAPPEARANCE

CAROL ERICSON

MILLS & BOON

All rights reserved including the right of reproduction in whole or in part in any form. This edition is published by arrangement with Harlequin Enterprises ULC.

This is a work of fiction. Names, characters, places, locations and incidents are purely fictional and bear no relationship to any real life individuals, living or dead, or to any actual places, business establishments, locations, events or incidents. Any resemblance is entirely coincidental.

This book is sold subject to the condition that it shall not, by way of trade or otherwise, be lent, resold, hired out or otherwise circulated without the prior consent of the publisher in any form of binding or cover other than that in which it is published and without a similar condition including this condition being imposed on the subsequent purchaser.

® and ™ are trademarks owned and used by the trademark owner and/or its licensee. Trademarks marked with ® are registered with the United Kingdom Patent Office and/or the Office for Harmonisation in the Internal Market and in other countries.

First Published in Great Britain 2023
by Mills & Boon, an imprint of HarperCollins*Publishers* Ltd
1 London Bridge Street, London, SE1 9GF

www.harpercollins.co.uk

HarperCollins*Publishers*
Macken House, 39/40 Mayor Street Upper,
Dublin 1, D01 C9W8, Ireland

The Secret of Shutter Lake © 2023 Marilyn Medlock Amann
Point of Disappearance © 2023 Carol Ericson

ISBN: 978-0-263-30753-5

1223

This book is produced from independently certified FSC™ paper
to ensure responsible forest management.

For more information visit: www.harpercollins.co.uk/green

Printed and Bound in the UK using 100% Renewable Electricity at
CPI Group (UK) Ltd, Croydon, CR0 4YY

THE SECRET OF SHUTTER LAKE

AMANDA STEVENS

Chapter One

Patches of sunlight filtered down through the murky water as Wade Easton skimmed along the lakebed. His scuba flippers kicked up a cloud of sediment and spooked a flathead catfish feeding on bottom sludge. Wade hung suspended until the residue settled, taking a moment, as he always did, to enjoy the underwater solitude. Overhead, a sunfish swam by, the blue-green coloration striking when the beam from his head lamp hit its scales. For a moment, he swam a few feet below the elongated body in complete synchronization until the fish darted away and became lost in the underwater twilight.

The bottom of the lake was littered with boulders and man-made debris, mostly cans and bottles, but every now and then, he'd spy something a little more interesting, like a lost watch or cell phone. Despite his innate curiosity, he left the items where he found them. He wasn't treasure-hunting today—not that kind of treasure—and he wasn't equipped to pick up litter. That task would fall to another diver on another day. With any luck, his meticulous research would lead him to a sunken high-end speed boat conservatively valued at a quarter of a million dollars. The kind of luxury vessel one frequently admired at a Miami Beach boat show but rarely spotted on a lake in southern Alabama.

The thirty-eight-foot stunner had been reported stolen two weeks ago, just days after the vessel had been brought up from the Gulf and berthed at a local marina. Wade had his suspicions about that theft. His gut told him the boat may have been scuttled with something even more valuable onboard. Possibly cash, possibly drugs, possibly both. He hoped to soon find out.

He moved languorously through the water, keeping an eye on his gauges, though descending to forty feet in a freshwater lake was far less risky than the deep-sea dives he'd once relished. If anything went wrong, he could ditch his equipment and swim to the surface without fear of decompression sickness or nitrogen narcosis. He could literally follow the sunbeams.

However, in his line of work, he'd learned the hard way the danger of being lulled into a false sense of security. He was diving alone, so precautions had to be taken. No one even knew he was back in town, much less at the bottom of Shutter Lake.

A shadow passing overheard startled him. He glanced up, wondering if his empty boat had been spotted, but it was too early for most recreationists to be out on the water. The mist that had hovered over the glassy surface at daybreak was just starting to burn off when he'd set out. The forty-five-minute boat ride had taken him to the far north end of the lake, miles from the condos and marinas that populated the more picturesque southern end. Since the old bridge had been condemned and later demolished, no one came back this way except for the occasional sport fisherman trolling for a lucky spot. If someone wanted to sink an expensive speed boat, nestling it among the abandoned pylons and iron girders would be a good place to hide it.

He checked his air pressure. Still in good shape, and he

had another tank in the boat if he needed more time. Might turn out to be a wasted morning, but for now, he'd keep looking. Wouldn't be the first time a hunch had sent him on a wild-goose chase, but his instincts were more reliable these days. As an independent investigator hired by the kind of insurance companies that covered expensive toys like private jets, sports cars and custom-made speed boats, he'd developed an almost sixth sense for sniffing out fraud.

Not that he needed to do much sniffing in this case. For all the pristine scenery, Shutter Lake had always had a seamy underbelly of corruption. The countless small businesses that catered to an influx of tourists every summer—marinas, bait stores, boat and equipment rentals, repair shops, restaurants, hotels, bed-and-breakfasts, campgrounds, food trucks, dinner cruises, souvenir vendors and so on—provided endless vehicles for laundering the drug money that traveled inland from the Gulf Coast. Those opportunities coupled with the scruples of the man who claimed his boat had been stolen, and Wade definitely had his doubts.

For as long as he'd known Brett Fortier, the man had been an operator, using his charm, looks and family connections to skirt the law. Sinking an expensive boat for the insurance money and then claiming the vessel had been stolen was right in his wheelhouse. All he had to do was live off the insurance money until things quieted down and then dive down and collect the booty he'd hidden onboard.

Another shadow passed overhead. This time Wade didn't bother checking the surface but kept gliding through the water, searching for the spot he'd scoped out using aerial photography and sonar. Might be nothing more than abandoned wreckage from the smashed bridge, but he wouldn't know until—

Hold on.

Something large rested on the bottom of the lake. Adrenaline bubbles gushed upward as he maneuvered around a mound of twisted metal and concrete.

Not a boat, after all, but a luxury coupe. The discovery sent a thrill of alarm up Wade's spine. He recognized the vehicle—or thought he did. Despite the old money in the area and the more recent invasion of new wealth, a Rolls Royce Wraith wasn't a common sight in Fairhope, Alabama, much less at the bottom of Shutter Lake.

Memories assailed him as he approached the vehicle from the rear. Ten years ago, a wealthy woman named Eva Dallas McRae had vanished after putting her affairs in order, packing her bags and leaving a note for her only child, instructing the seventeen-year-old not to come looking for her. She'd fallen deeply in love and wanted a fresh start somewhere far away from Shutter Lake, far away from the obligations and expectations of her family. She'd left behind a devastated daughter, a betrayed husband and an endless wave of gossip and resentment that still simmered in certain quarters of the town to this day.

Wade took a moment to control his breathing. After the initial shock, he was keen to explore. He checked for a license plate, but the metal tag had probably rusted through and fallen off the vehicle years ago. After a cursory search of the lakebed, he moved back up to peer through the rear window. He couldn't see much. A decade of pressure and slime had taken a toll.

Another sunfish swam by, iridescent in the glow of his dive light as he circled the car. He became all too aware of the silence. Like a tomb. No sound at all except for a dull roar in his ears. He told himself he could be mistaken about the owner. No way to know for certain without checking the registration, a difficult task since both front and rear tags were missing and any VIN etchings would be concealed by layers of rust and grunge. Somehow the car had miraculously escaped damage from falling bridge debris only to be slowly eaten away by time and corrosion.

Still, there was no mistaking the flying lady hood ornament—the Spirit of Ecstasy—that remained intact. He swam up to the driver's side, wondering if he could get the door open. Maybe there was some form of identification inside. He grasped the handle as he pressed his face against the glass, trying to get a look at the secrets that might still be hidden inside.

What the...?

He jerked back in shock as another burst of bubbles shot to the surface.

The skeletal remains floated eerily behind the steering wheel, the empty eye sockets staring straight ahead as if focusing on a destination that only the dead could see.

Wade steadied his pulse and moved back in, angling the beam through the glass. He thought at first the seat belt must have kept the skeleton in place. Without restraint, the body would have floated upward. Then his light caught the flash of steel around the left wrist bone.

Sometime before the car went over the bridge, the driver had been handcuffed to the steering wheel.

ABIGAIL DALLAS STEPPED through the French doors and carefully placed the breakfast tray of coffee, fruit and assorted pastries on the glass-topped table before joining her friend, Brie Fortier, at the wrought iron railing that encased the flagstone terrace.

Another day in paradise.

No heels, no suits, no ringing cell phone or long-winded meetings to sit through. What a luxury to step from the shower and don the day's attire of shorts, sandals and T-shirt. Not that the reprieve would last forever. She hadn't returned to her hometown to lounge around the lake for the next few weeks. She was here to pitch in until her stepfather was back on his feet. A lot of hard and unpleasant work lay ahead of her. Not today, though. Not tomorrow, either, but come Monday morning, she planned to hit the ground running.

Breathing in the lake air, she trailed her gaze down the stone steps to the private dock, where a small vessel bobbed against the bumpers. Later, she'd take the boat out for a leisurely ride. The shady cove was still quiet, but the lake beyond was already ablaze with tempting sunlight. By midafternoon, the temperature and humidity would climb so high that anywhere except in the water or under the AC would become extremely uncomfortable, but for now, an early morning breeze cooled the terrace and perfumed the air with oleander. She listened to the gentle rustle of the palm fronds and banana trees and wondered again why she'd stayed away for so long. She was a Dallas, after all. Her ancestors had helped found Fairhope, or so she'd always been told. Her roots ran as deep as Shutter Lake. Yet the night she left town, she'd sworn never to return.

Never say never.

"You hear that?" Brie leaned out over the railing and cocked her head toward the water. A strand of pale blond hair came loose from the bun at her nape and coiled at her temple. Abby marveled at how little her friend had changed in ten years. Still as slender and tanned and gorgeous as the day they'd graduated high school. Still with a furrow of anxiety across her brow, no matter her professional success or personal happiness.

"Sirens," she pronounced grimly as she shot Abby an uneasy glance. "I heard one earlier, too. Sounds like the whole damn police department has been called out."

Abby lifted a hand to shade her eyes as she peered across the water toward Lakeside Drive. "I wonder what happened."

"Some kind of accident, most likely. It's the weekend, so a lot of people are out on the water. You know how that goes. Booze, boats. Boats, booze. Seems like every summer we have at least one major catastrophe."

Abby shivered. "I should be accustomed to the wail of sirens after living in Atlanta for ten years, but somehow the sound seems more ominous down here."

"That's because when you hear a siren in a small town, you know there's a good chance that tragedy has befallen a friend or an acquaintance. Or, God forbid, a loved one." The wrinkle in her brow deepened as if something had just occurred to her.

"What's wrong?" Abby asked.

"Nothing. It's just… I can't help wondering where my brother is right now. I tried calling him earlier. He didn't pick up. Which isn't unusual for Brett. He's never been a morning person. I know it's irrational to worry, but every time I hear a siren, I can't help thinking about the time the police came to our house in the middle of the night. I heard the sirens long before they showed up. I remember lying in bed, shivering from a premonition that had plagued me all day."

"Do you have a premonition now?" Abby asked.

"No…not really."

"Then stop worrying. The accident happened years ago. Brett was a reckless kid with a fast car. He's a grown man now."

"As if anything has really changed," Brie grumbled. "You'd think a near-death experience would have taught him a valuable lesson, but the only difference now is that his toys have gotten even faster and a lot more expensive. My brother is what you'd call an adrenaline junkie, whereas I—"

"You're the sensible twin," Abby said. "You always have been."

Brie winced. "Gets a little old if you want to know the truth. Just once, I'd like to be the carefree sibling."

"Then you wouldn't be you." Abby nodded to the phone clutched in Brie's hand. "Call him again if it'll make you feel better."

"That's the thing. It probably won't. If my call goes to voicemail, I'll just fret even more." She released another heavy sigh. "At some point, I have to quit mothering him. I know that. Like you said, he's a grown man, nearly thirty years old. And he was born two minutes earlier than me, so technically, I'm the little sister. He should be watching out for me."

"Just admit it," Abby teased. "You've always enjoyed bossing him around."

"For all the good it does." Brie's smile seemed strained.

Abby turned to her friend. "What's really going on? It's not just the sirens putting you on edge, is it?"

"Am I still that easy to read?" Brie glanced at her. "I don't want to dump my problems on you. You've got enough on your plate."

"You're not dumping anything on me. I want to help. Just tell me what's wrong."

Brie bit her lip, then shrugged. "It's nothing. Just a client that's been irritating me more than usual. As for Brett, he probably turned off his phone so that he could sleep in. I'm sure he's fine."

Abby didn't press. Something was obviously troubling Brie, but for whatever reason, she wasn't yet ready to confide in her. Fair enough. They'd been best friends in high school and had kept in touch off and on during Abby's ten-year absence, but they were no longer confidants. Rebuilding that kind of trust would take time. "We don't even know for certain there's been an accident," she said. "Could be a robbery or a drug bust. Lydia says there's been a lot of cartel activity around the lake lately."

Brie rolled her eyes. "As if the cartels have even heard of this place. We're a thousand miles from the border, last time I checked. And as for your stepsister, I wouldn't put too much stock in anything coming out of her mouth. Lydia McRae always has an ulterior motive for everything she says and does. Don't you forget that. She'll paint as bleak a picture as she can of this place just to try and keep you from moving back here permanently."

"I don't think she was trying to scare me off. It was just an offhand comment in an email." Abby didn't understand the need to defend her stepsister. The two had never been close, far from it. Lydia had had a chip on her shoulder for as long as Abby could remember. She'd begrudged everything about her father's marriage to Abby's mother, and she'd made no bones about her dislike of her new stepsister. She'd resented Abby's friends, her popularity and especially her inheritance. When they were first introduced, Abby had been excited by the prospect of an older sister, someone with whom she could share secrets and their wardrobes. She'd quickly learned it was easier to avoid Lydia altogether than to try and befriend her. Brie was probably right about motive, but Abby didn't want her to be.

"You've always underestimated her," Brie said. "I've never understood why. Especially after all the hateful things she said to you when your mother left. I've had a few business dealings with her over the years, and I can tell you without a shadow of a doubt, she's still as bitter and unpleasant as she ever was."

"She's been cordial to me so far," Abby said.

"Which makes her even more dangerous. I'll say it again. Don't let down your guard around Lydia McRae, and don't let her get under your skin. She may think she's the boss, but you're in charge. Almost all the real estate holdings belong to the Dallas side of the family, including the house James and Lydia still live in. Your mother was successful before she and James married. Any wealth accumulated prior to the wedding still belongs to her. Just because father and daughter have been running the company for the past ten years doesn't mean they've got a legitimate claim to her prewedding assets. Or to yours."

"It's tricky," Abby said. "Technically, Mother and James are still married. As far as I know, neither of them ever filed for a divorce. As for my claim…" She paused. "I left town, too. I abandoned the business just like my mother did."

"No, you didn't. You went to live with your grandmother in Atlanta. You were only seventeen. No one expected you to step in and fill your mother's shoes at that age."

"I could have come back after college."

"Coulda, woulda, shoulda." Brie gave a dismissive shrug. "You're home now and I, for one, am thrilled to have you back. You know I'm here for you, right? Anything you need, just say the word. I'm a damned good real estate attorney if I do say so myself."

"I appreciate that."

Brie turned and plucked a fresh strawberry from a crystal bowl before pouring herself a cup of coffee and stirring in creamer. "Speaking of your lovely stepfamily, how is James doing?"

"Better than expected," Abby said. "He was released from the hospital the day before yesterday."

"You've seen him?"

"No, but I spoke with him briefly on the phone. I went by the house as soon as I arrived in town, but he wasn't up to company."

Brie gave her a look. "Who told you that? Lydia? You're hardly company."

"You can't blame her for being protective," Abby said. "I'd probably do the same in her shoes. Besides, we'll have plenty of time to catch up while I'm here."

"I guess." Brie picked at the food, then walked back to the rail as she sipped her coffee. "I'm just surprised he was released so soon after a major heart attack."

Abby nodded. "I was, too, but Lydia says his doctors are pleased with his progress. He'll have to take it easy, of course, but that's why I'm here."

"Much to the chagrin of your wicked stepsister, I'm sure."

"I'm not a kid anymore. I can handle Lydia."

"Famous last words—" Brie broke off as a boat with an outboard motor puttered up to the dock. She set her cup aside and leaned over the rail to get a better look through the lush vegetation. "Who could that be this early on a Saturday morning? Are you expecting company?"

"No one but you. I doubt anyone else knows I'm around." They watched as a tall, lean man in damp board shorts climbed out of the boat and looped rope lines around the metal cleats bolted into the dock. He was shirtless and bronzed, his longish hair tousled from the wind.

Brie called down to him. "Hey! This is private property in case you didn't notice the sign!"

He turned to stare up at them. After a moment, he lifted a hand and waved.

"I'm not being friendly, dude," Brie muttered. "Don't wave back," she admonished when Abby lifted her hand.

The man removed his sunglasses and tossed them in the boat while simultaneously reaching for a T-shirt he pulled over his head.

"See? You've encouraged him. He's coming up here." Brie sucked in a quick breath. "Oh, hell no."

"What?"

Her gaze narrowed. "Without sunglasses, he looks just like…" Her voice trailed off on a faint gasp. "Oh, my God, it *is* him! You've got to be kidding me!"

Abby turned back to the newcomer. Her stomach fluttered unexpectedly as they made eye contact. It was him all right. *Wade Easton.* Last she'd heard, he left town sometime after she moved to Atlanta. They hadn't spoken in well over a decade. She rarely even thought about him these days, and she only dreamed about him once in a blue moon. After all that time, what was he doing down there on her dock?

And did it really matter? Maybe he'd heard she was back in town and decided to drop by to catch up. Or maybe he wanted to satisfy his curiosity and assuage his guilt at the same time. After all, she was certainly curious about him. First love and all that.

Brie swore under her breath. "You'd think he'd know better than to show his face around here after what he did to you."

"That was a long time ago," Abby said. "We were kids. Everybody gets dumped in high school. It's a rite of passage. I don't hold a grudge."

"Well, you should. Once a cheat, always a cheat in my book," Brie fumed. "Damned if the rat bastard doesn't still look good."

"How dare he!" Abby said with a chuckle, though her

heart thudded and her palms had started to sweat. She wiped them on her shorts and hoped Brie hadn't noticed.

"He could have at least had the decency to pack on a few pounds and chop off that hair," Brie said.

But no. He was still lean and cut and bronzed, his thick hair curling at his nape. Abby couldn't tear her gaze away and, apparently, neither could Brie.

"How did he even know you were back?" she asked.

"I have no idea."

Brie's voice dropped accusingly. "Please tell me you're not still in touch with him."

"We haven't spoken in years." Abby's nails dug into her palms. The pain surprised her. She hadn't realized her fingers were clenched so tightly. With an effort, she relaxed her hands and clasped them behind her back as the subject of Brie's contempt left the dock and slowly climbed the flagstones steps, disappearing momentarily into the jungle of vegetation that crowded the stairs. As one, Abby and Brie leaned to the right to try and catch another glimpse of him.

By the time he emerged from the oleanders and palm fronds, Abby had managed to recover her poise. She leaned against a wrought iron post, folded her arms and stared down at him.

He paused on the steps to squint up at them. He wasn't yet thirty, but the crinkles around his eyes and mouth gave him a kind of world-weary air that belied his age, and the way he carried himself seemed guarded. He wasn't the same guy Abby had fallen for in high school. This Wade Easton had seen and done things that had matured and jaded him. The hint of darkness in his eyes only served to make him more attractive.

"Rat bastard," Brie muttered.

Indeed.

He called up to them. "Morning, ladies!"

The voice was deeper and the drawl a little less pronounced now that he'd spent time away from Alabama. Where had he been all these years? Abby wondered.

Not that it was any of her business. Not that she really cared.

She bristled as memories betrayed her. The sight of him slipping through her open bedroom window with knowing eyes and a devastating grin. The utter thrill of their secret and forbidden liaison. Her mother hadn't approved of Wade. Yet another thing that had made him all the more attractive to Abby.

How dare you, Wade Easton! How dare you stand there on my property with that same look in your eyes as if you still know me. As if the past ten years never happened.

Oh, yes, that look…those eyes…

Some things never changed.

She drew a quick breath as she drank him in despite the sudden sting of bitterness at his betrayal. Her mother wasn't the only one who had deserted her that last summer on the lake. In her hour of greatest need, Wade Easton had turned to someone else. *How could you do that to me?* Abby had sobbed. Such melodrama. The memory made her a little uncomfortable.

Brie moved over to the edge of the terrace and planted a hand on her hip as she glared down at him. "Wade Easton, as I live and breathe."

He tipped his head. "Brianna."

"My friends call me Brie, but for you, Brianna will do just fine."

Abby's gaze remained glued to him. She saw his lips twitch and thought, *You* would *find this whole situation amusing.* She cursed him again as she once more unclenched her fists.

"You've got some nerve showing up here," Brie told him. "After everything you've done?"

He continued up the steps. "Are you referring to the past, or has something a little more immediate put you in a lather?"

"You know what I'm talking about. I shouldn't have to spell it out for you, but I will if you insist. In excruciating detail."

He cocked his head. "Is this about your brother's boat?"

"Let's get something straight right from the get-go." Her voice was like an ice cube sliding down the spine on a cold winter's morning. Abby would not want to face off against Brie Fortier in a legal battle. Or in a dark alley. "My brother's stolen boat is only one of many grievances I have against you. At least in that situation, no one was hurt, although an argument could be made for the financial hardship he's suffered. He'd like nothing more than to put the whole incident behind him and move on, but your company refuses to honor his policy. I shouldn't have to tell you how much that coverage cost him only to have his claim slow-walked by some clerk until the company can find a way to wiggle out of their obligations. Which, if I'm not mistaken, is where you come in."

Wait, what? Abby didn't have a clue what either of them were talking about. And here she'd thought Brie was outraged on her behalf. "What boat?"

They both cut her a glance as if they'd forgotten she was there. Humbling, to say the least.

"Brett's boat was stolen from the marina a couple of weeks ago," Brie explained.

"Not just any boat," Wade said. "A vessel that's worth upward of a quarter of a million dollars."

Abby's mouth dropped. "What was Brett doing with a boat like that?"

The question seemed to irritate Brie. "Why does it matter? That's his business. What matters is that the boat was fully covered by a 'reputable' company," she said with air quotes. "However, despite his account being current, they refuse to honor his claim."

"That's not exactly true," Wade said. "They haven't honored the claim yet. The company isn't obligated to cut him a check until a thorough investigation has been conducted."

"The police have already investigated," Brie said.

"No, the police wrote a report," Wade countered.

"Which should be all that is needed to process his claim."

"You're a lawyer," Wade said. "You know that's not how it works."

Brie lifted her chin. "We'll see you in court if we have to."

He shrugged. "No skin off my teeth, but you should know Global Alliance has deep pockets. If you decide to sue, they could drag this out for years. Besides all that, I'd recommend you run any legal action by your brother before you commit. I have a feeling the last thing he'll want is more scrutiny."

"Meaning?"

"Ask him," Wade said. "But this whole conversation is beside the point. I'm not here to argue about a missing boat. I came to see Abby."

"What about?" Brie demanded.

"That's between Abby and me."

The whole confrontation seemed surreal to Abby. Just a few short days ago, she'd been in Atlanta enjoying a lucrative career in commercial real estate. She had a great job, a lovely condo and a busy social life. Now here she was back in her hometown, back on the lake, listening to an argument between the two people she'd once been the closest to. Their current conflict was like the worst kind of déjà vu. The two had never gotten along.

"This is unreal," she murmured.

Brie frowned. "What is?"

"The way you two are going at it. It's like we never left high school." She fixed her gaze on Wade. "Anything you have to say to me you can say in front of Brie." She remained at the rail, keeping the wrought iron barrier between them. She didn't know why, but putting an obstacle in front of Wade Easton made her feel better.

Now who's acting like she's still in high school?

Wade gave her the strangest look, as if the same thought had crossed his mind.

"I'd prefer to speak in private," he said. "I won't take much of your time."

Brie moved to Abby's side, turning her back on Wade as she lowered her voice. "Do you believe this guy? Showing up out of the blue after all these years, insisting on being alone with you. I don't feel comfortable with that. He'll probably try to grill you about Brett."

"But I don't know anything about Brett and his boat," Abby said.

"That won't stop him. He's obviously up to something."

"You think everyone has an ulterior motive," Abby reminded her.

"Because they almost always do."

"Maybe." Abby glanced down at Wade. "It won't hurt to hear what he has to say."

"It might," Brie said with a glance over her shoulder. "It might hurt a lot."

"I'm not worried. Besides, it's a beautiful Saturday morning and you must have a million things to do on your day off. Go on. I'll be fine. I'll call you later."

"Are you sure?"

"Yes, absolutely."

Brie nodded. "If you say so. Just don't let him get to you, okay? Wade Easton has always been your kryptonite."

"When we were teenagers, maybe. Not anymore."

Brie didn't sound so certain. "Look at him. He's still—"

"I know."

"Call me as soon as he leaves. I'd like to hear what he has to say for himself these days. Plus, I want to make sure you're all right."

"Now you're just being melodramatic," Abby scolded. "It's not as if he intends to murder me in broad daylight."

"You never know." Brie gave Wade one final warning glare before exiting through the French doors and pulling them closed behind her.

A long silence ensued. Wade finally said, "That wasn't at all awkward."

Abby gave him a tight smile. "Not one bit." She tried to sound casually indifferent. "Do you want to come up or shall I come down?"

"I'll come to you."

Four loaded words if she'd ever heard any.

She took an unconscious step back as Wade bounded up the stairs. And then he was right in front of her, and she instantly regretted the invitation. She shouldn't have allowed him to come up to her private space. They were standing much too close in the intimate environment of her terrace. She could see the faint shadow of a beard on his lower face and a gleam of uncertainty in his eyes.

And behind that uncertainty was a flicker of something dark and troubling, something that sent a sharp chill straight through her heart.

Chapter Two

Disquiet settled over Abby like a dark cloud. Wade Easton obviously hadn't come to apologize for his past behavior or make amends for an old betrayal. Foolish of her to entertain such a notion. No, something more immediate had brought him to her doorstep, but she couldn't imagine what that something was.

In the split second before either of them said anything, she ran through a litany of troubling possibilities as one had a tendency to do under such circumstances. Her first thought was that something had happened to her grandmother, but they'd video-chatted earlier before Brie arrived, and everything had been fine. And, anyway, how would Wade know something about her grandmother that she didn't?

No, this wasn't about her family. Abby told herself she could relax on that front. Her stepfather was the only one with health issues at the moment, and if he'd suffered a setback or another attack, her stepsister would have called. Lydia herself appeared to be the picture of health, and Wade didn't know any of her other relatives. As for close friends, Brie was the only person she'd remained close to in Fairhope, so it didn't seem likely that Wade was here to impart bad news.

Then why the dark look in his eyes? Why that shiver of dread down her spine?

Maybe Brie was right. Maybe he'd come here hoping to uncover more information about her brother's stolen boat. That would explain why he refused to speak in front of Brie. He knew she'd run straight to Brett. But if he thought Abby could help him—or would help him—he was sorely mistaken. She had no particular affinity or allegiance to Brett Fortier, but Brie was a different matter. Abby would never do anything to hurt the one friend who had stuck by her during the hard times, who had been nothing but kind and loyal to her throughout the years. Brie had been there for her when Wade Easton had bolted. Abby strongly believed in letting bygones be bygones, but some lessons couldn't be unlearned.

All this flashed through her mind as she and Wade silently took the other's measure. She was suddenly all too aware of her bare face and windblown hair. Not exactly the look she would have chosen had she anticipated an encounter with an old boyfriend. She reminded herself that he was casual and windblown, too, but on him, it looked good.

She finally found her voice and a hint of defiance. "If this is about Brett Fortier, I'm afraid you're wasting your time. I don't know anything about a stolen boat."

"It's not about Brett. At least not directly."

She frowned. "Then why are you here?"

He seemed oddly at a loss. "At the moment, damned if I know. It seemed like a good idea at the time. I thought I owed you, but now I realize it wasn't my place to come here. I didn't stop to think that I might be the last person you'd want to see."

Well, that did nothing to clarify his intentions.

Abby shrugged. "I wouldn't go that far, but you do owe

me an explanation. It's been over ten years since we spoke, and our last conversation was hardly amicable."

"I remember."

She shivered at the unexpected note of regret in his voice. "Then you'll forgive me if I'm a little thrown by your sudden appearance."

"Yeah, I get it. I feel a little off-kilter myself."

Off-kilter? Wade Easton? She found that hard to believe. "Let's start with an easy question then. How did you even know where to find me?"

"I heard you were back in town. I took the chance you'd be here." He glanced around the sun-dappled terrace. "You always loved this cottage. So much so that you hated having strangers rent it every summer. You planned to buy it from your mother as soon as you were able so that no one but you could ever set foot in it again."

Her heart flip-flopped. "Good grief. You remember all that?"

He gave her a brief smile. "I remember a lot of things. Ten years isn't that long."

"More than ten. And it seems like a lifetime."

"Not to me." His gaze came back to her and seemed to deepen, making her even more curious about the reason for his visit. Curious and wary. Yet for some strange reason, she hesitated to press him on his motive. Call it a premonition, call it being a coward, but she wanted to hide for as long as she could behind the banality of their reunion.

"How long have you been back?" he asked as if sensing her reluctance.

"A day or so. And you?"

"A little longer. I'm here on business."

"Yes, I gathered that. Is that why you were out on the water so early?" Something suddenly occurred to her and she said anxiously, "Wait. Does this have something to do with all the sirens we heard? Has there been an accident? Is that why you didn't want to speak in front of Brie? Has something happened to Brett?"

"He's fine as far as I know. I haven't seen him in years. As to why I went out early, I took the boat as far north as the old bridge to go diving."

She said in surprise, "Scuba diving? Why?"

He paused. "It seemed like another good idea at the time."

His equivocation only fed the awkwardness and her nervousness. Maybe he really had come here to apologize, but his pride wouldn't allow him to come right out and say so.

Buy why now? Why so mysterious?

She tried to gauge his expression as she continued to quiz him. "Why would you go all the way up there to dive? There can't be much to see. The bridge was demolished years ago after the county declared it unsafe for traffic. They tried barricades, but people just knocked them down or drove around them. I guess they thought they had no choice but to tear the whole thing down before someone got hurt. Some of the iron was salvaged, but the rest…" She shrugged, realizing she had imparted more information about the old bridge than he or anyone else would ever want to know. Nerves did that to her. "I'm told it was quite a site, all those heavy girders crashing into the water."

"There's still a lot of debris on the lakebed," he said. "Not exactly an environmentally friendly demolition. I guess no one cares about that end of the lake. The old money has always been on the southern end. New money, too, judging by all the houses going up around here."

Abby turned her back on the water, leaning against one of the posts as she faced him. "What were you diving for?"

He gave her a look. "I would have thought that obvious. I was hoping to find Brett Fortier's missing speedboat."

"So this *is* about his boat." Abby didn't know whether to be relieved or aggravated. It wasn't that she wanted or expected an apology after all this time, but an acknowledgement of his past bad behavior might have been nice. That earlier flicker of regret was likely all she'd get. "Well? What is it you think I know?"

"I told you, I'm not here about the boat."

"But you just said—"

"I said I was hoping to find it at the bottom of the lake. One of my aerial photographs indicated a shadow about forty feet down that didn't appear to be bridge debris. I thought it worth a closer look."

"I don't get it. Why would someone steal an expensive boat just to sink it?"

"Maybe they were after something onboard," he said.

"Such as?"

"Something illegal would be my guess."

She gave him a knowing scrutiny. "You think Brett sunk his own boat, don't you?"

Wade stared back without flinching. "We both know he's capable."

"People can change."

"Some can. Most don't."

"Including you?" She immediately regretted the question. Not because she wanted to spare his feelings but because it revealed a little too much of hers.

"I'm probably not the best person to answer that question," he said.

There was that look again. The old simmering intensity. Maybe Brie had been right to warn her. Wade Easton was still a dangerous man. Abby had a feeling he'd been a lot of women's kryptonite over the years.

"Do you think Brett's changed?" he asked.

"I don't know. I try to give everyone the benefit of the doubt. I admit, though, that I was surprised to hear he owned a boat worth a quarter of a million dollars. That's a lot of money, especially considering I don't even know what he does for a living. Brie's always been a little evasive when it comes to her brother."

"Probably with good reason. My question isn't why he bought an expensive boat," Wade said. "Brett Fortier has always been attracted to glittery things. What I'd like to know is why he needed one with that kind of power and speed."

"Brie says he's an adrenaline junkie."

"That's one explanation."

"And another?"

"Maybe he needed to outrun someone down south. Gun runners, drug traffickers, the Coast Guard."

"That's wild speculation unless you know something I don't." When he merely shrugged, Abby said, "For someone who didn't come here to talk about Brett Fortier, you seem to spend a lot of time and energy on him."

"And here I thought I was just answering your questions."

The conversation still seemed surreal to Abby. It was disconcerting to discover that Wade Easton could still throw her off-balance. But she reminded herself she wasn't an infatuated teenager anymore. She knew how to protect herself. She unfolded her arms and visibly straightened from the post as if to prove that point.

"Okay. I have another question for you," she said. "There was always bad blood between you and Brett. You two couldn't stand each other in high school. Is it possible you *want* to believe the worst about him? Maybe this isn't so much about a stolen boat as it is your desire to take him down a peg or two."

He looked annoyed. "Believe it or not, I haven't given Brett Fortier more than a passing thought since high school. I'm here to do a job. Nothing more, nothing less."

"What exactly is your job?"

"In a nutshell, I'm paid to find expensive things that have gone missing."

That his smile could still make her pulse race was extremely irritating to Abby. She felt the need to take *him* down a peg or two, which was also irritating and not in the least admirable, but human. Or so she told herself.

"I gathered from your discussion with Brie that you work for an insurance company."

"Not exclusively. I'm not on any company's payroll except my own."

"Still, it's not quite what I would have expected of you."

"Just out of curiosity, what did you expect from me?"

She took a moment to answer. "I guess I thought you'd eventually go into law enforcement like your dad. You used to talk about it sometimes."

"I did consider it."

"But?"

"It wasn't the right fit. I like solving mysteries, but I also like making money." He glanced back at her. "Anything wrong with that?"

"I'm probably not the right person to answer *that* question," she said. "I've spent most of my professional life chasing the next big sale."

"And yet here you are back on Shutter Lake."

"Temporarily." The awkwardness had evaporated, and their chat had become almost congenial. Not good. She'd let her guard drop, and that was a very dangerous situation when it came to Wade Easton. She'd found that out the hard way.

"I heard about your stepfather," he said. "I assume that's why you're here. Frankly, I'm surprised you didn't come back a long time ago to run your mom's business."

"They've managed fine without me until now, but this is the busy season, and Lydia has her hands full. I'm here to help in any way I can."

"I'm sure your efforts will be appreciated."

She couldn't tell if he was being sarcastic or not. Did he remember Lydia's attitude back in the day? Maybe he thought she'd changed over the years. Abby still harbored that faint hope herself, but leopards rarely changed their spots. She would do well to remember that when it came to her stepsister and to her ex-boyfriend.

"What did your grandmother think about the move?" he asked. "As I recall, she couldn't wait to get you out of this town."

"To be perfectly honest, she wasn't thrilled," Abby said. "Not that I blame her. This place holds a lot of bad memories for her. For both of us."

"For all of us."

Something in his voice brought another shiver to her spine. His eyes had taken on a faraway look as if he'd drifted a million miles away. Was he thinking about that last summer? Was he sorry for the way things had ended between them? Doubtful. He'd moved on long before she had. Despite her insistence earlier that she didn't hold a grudge, she felt an unpleasant sting of the old resentment, chased by the burn of lingering humiliation. Everyone in town had known about his betrayal before she did. She could tell herself a million times over that what happened back then no longer mattered. Kids did foolish, regrettable things to one another in high school.

But it had taken her a long time to get over Wade Easton. Longer still to rebuild her confidence and ability to trust, his betrayal coming as it had on the heels of her mother's abandonment. Maybe under normal circumstances, she could have eventually put their breakup into perspective. Maybe even laughed about it in time. But being discarded by her mother *and* her first love was a double blow that had taken a toll. Not that she would ever let on to Wade or anyone else how much pain he'd caused her.

He moved to the rail and stared out over the lake. She wanted to ask him to leave, but she didn't. Instead, she studied his profile as he squinted into the sun. Strange how everything about him seemed so familiar, and yet she really didn't know anything about him.

If her scrutiny bothered him, he didn't let on. "The water is always like glass in this cove. You could travel anywhere in the world and be hard-pressed to beat this view."

Reluctantly, she turned her gaze to the scenery. "I never get tired of it," she said. "I enjoy my life in the city, but there's something magical about this place. The way the sunlight dances across the surface of the water...the play of shadows along the banks. Sometimes it almost seems too beautiful to be real."

"I prefer it by moonlight." His voice dropped intimately. "The water has a different vibe at night. Mysterious. Seductive. A little dangerous."

Like you.

His gaze was still on the water. "I rented this cottage for a few weeks one summer. Did Lydia tell you?"

"She never mentioned it." Abby's family had at least a dozen rental properties on the lake. The valuable real estate made up the bulk of the company's assets. She'd long ago become accustomed to strangers coming and going from those houses, but the image of Wade Easton sitting on her terrace, cooking in her kitchen, sleeping in her bed jolted her.

"My mother wasn't well," he said. "Like you, I came back home to lend a hand. The cottage happened to be available, so I signed a short-term lease."

Abby moved up beside him at the rail. "I didn't know. About your mother, I mean."

"Not many people did. Dad's very protective of her privacy. And his, too, I guess. He was still the police chief back then, and you know how people around here like to gossip. My mother has always suffered from clinical depression, but that summer, she had a complete breakdown. Her doctor recommended she be admitted to a mental health facility in Mobile. She was there for nearly two weeks."

"I had no idea." Abby resisted the urge to put her hand over his. "How is she now?"

"Good days and bad. If she takes her medication, more good than bad."

"And your dad?"

"He took early retirement to spend more time with her. Leaving the police department was a difficult decision for him. Being a cop was all he ever knew. He still consults on certain cases, but the past few years haven't been easy for him. He's not the same man he used to be."

"It's hard when they get older," Abby murmured.

He turned to stare down at her. "It's harder when they don't."

WADE REGRETTED NOT telling her the real reason for his visit as soon as they were alone. Revealing his discovery was proving more difficult with each passing second. But just blurting out the truth seemed wrong. Especially considering how they'd left things the last time they spoke. He wanted to believe that she'd forgiven if not forgotten, but that tiny glimmer of contempt in her eyes as she'd stared down at him from the terrace had quickly disabused him of that notion. Given the awkwardness of their first meeting, he'd felt the need to ease into his revelation.

At least, that's what he told himself. But maybe his reluctance wasn't quite so altruistic. Maybe he'd wanted to spend a few minutes in her company before he had to watch the horror of his discovery dawn in her eyes.

"Wade? Are you okay?"

He turned with a frown. "What?"

"You seemed a million miles away just now."

"I guess I was there for a minute." His fingers tightened around the wrought iron railing. The hint of huskiness in her voice had always had a powerful impact on him. That he still found her incredibly attractive was a little disconcerting. The pretty girl he'd known in high school had turned into a real knockout of a woman. The sprinkle of freckles across her bare face and the windblown tangles at her temples only added to her appeal.

"Are you worried about your mom? You said she's okay if she takes her medication, right?"

"It's not that. I mean, I'm always a little worried about her," he admitted. "But she was fine the last time we talked."

"Then what is it?"

He turned to meet her quizzical gaze. "I should have told you right from the start. There's no easy way to say this."

"Then just say it. Your evasiveness is making me nervous."

"I found something at the bottom of the lake."

She tucked back a strand of loose hair. "Not the boat?"

"No. Not the boat. A car." He glanced away, dreading what he still had to disclose. "I think it's been down there since before the bridge was demolished."

"Okay, you found a car. Why is this information I need to know?"

"It's not just any car." His hesitation was so slight he wondered if she noticed. "It's what's left of a Rolls Royce Wraith."

She said in confusion, "I don't understand—" Then she broke off on a gasp. "Wait. You don't think it's Mother's car."

He met her gaze with another nod.

"But...it can't be. She left town in that car years ago."

"We all thought she did. But have you ever known anyone else around here to drive a Rolls Royce? That's not a car you forget."

Her response was a little too quick, as if she desperately wanted to prove him wrong before the conversation went any further. "No, but I've been gone from the area for over ten years. So have you. Neither of us can possibly know all the cars that have come and gone during that time. And, yes, I imagine a Rolls Royce is still an uncommon sight in these parts, but I saw plenty of other expensive vehicles in town when I drove through." She gave a vague wave toward the water. "Look at all the multi-million-dollar homes that have been built on the lake in the past few years. People with that kind of money have a tendency to own expensive cars and boats. I'm telling you that's not my mother's car."

Wade hoped she was right, but deep down, he already knew that she wasn't. "If a vehicle like that had ended up in the lake by accident or otherwise, word would have gotten out. A car of that caliber doesn't go missing without someone noticing."

"Maybe someone did notice. Maybe a police report was filed. How would either of us know since we didn't live here?"

Wade tried to keep his tone even. He didn't want to upset her, but she needed to be prepared for the reality of his discovery. "My dad would have mentioned it. He was the police chief until just a few years ago. I'm willing to bet the car's been down there longer than he's been retired."

"Then ask him," she said. "Or don't. It should be easy enough to prove ownership by checking the registration."

"That might not be as easy as you think," Wade said. "Both front and rear license plates are missing. Maybe they disintegrated from pressure and corrosion or maybe they were removed before the car went into the lake. We've no way of knowing. The body of the vehicle is badly rusted. The police may be able to uncover a VIN etching once the car is brought up, but lifting a vehicle from forty feet of water is no easy feat. They'll have to bring in a special crane and possibly a barge if there's no access from the bank. It could take days to get the equipment in place."

Her expression remained a mixture of confusion, disbelief and maybe already a hint of dread as she stared at him in silence. "Why would the police go to that kind of effort and expense to raise an abandoned car? There must be dozens of them up and down the lake."

"I don't know about dozens, but likely a few," he said. "However, this particular car is a crime scene."

He saw her take a breath. "What do you mean?" When he hesitated, she said, "Just tell me. Don't drag this out any longer than necessary."

"Human remains are inside the car. Someone was handcuffed to the steering wheel before the vehicle went over the bridge."

Her hand flew to her mouth.

"I'm sorry," he said.

"Don't say that." She sounded almost angry. "Not yet. This may not be what you seem to think it is. It's possible you're mistaken about the make and model. What about the color?"

"The paint is too badly corroded to know for certain."

"Then how can you be so sure?"

"I just am."

Her eyes glittered. "That's not good enough. Did you even think to look for splotches of paint? How thoroughly could you have examined the car underwater?"

"I know what I saw."

"You personally saw—"

"Yes."

She squeezed her eyes closed as the color leeched from her face, highlighting the dusting of freckles across her nose and cheekbones. "This is horrible. Like something from a nightmare. The images I have in my head…" She shuddered and then seemed to shake herself as if once again gathering her resolve. "But it's not Mother's car down there. It's not my mother inside."

He gentled his tone. "I could be wrong, but I don't think I am. Let's just think about it for a minute. Aside from the make and model of the vehicle, the timing makes sense. The car's been in the water since before the bridge was demolished. Did you ever see or hear from your mother after she left town that night?"

Her eyes fluttered closed again as her fingers curled around the railing. "No, but that's the way she wanted it.

She told me not to come looking for her. She said she wanted a new life without family expectations. Without me."

Without me. Still so much hurt in those two words. He wondered how she'd coped with the pain of her mother's desertion all these years. Had she been able to put it into perspective without blaming herself as so many abandoned kids had a tendency to do? He liked to think she'd gotten on with her life after she left Fairhope. He wanted to believe she'd been happy in Atlanta. Without him.

He resisted the urge to brush back her hair, but such an intimate gesture wouldn't be appropriate or welcome. It might only serve to remind her of *his* betrayal. Instead, he said, "Once the car is brought up, the medical examiner can compare dental records or run a DNA analysis to determine the victim's identity. Then we'll know for sure."

She said nothing for the longest moment. Then softly, "Supposing it is her...what do you think happened?"

"I don't know."

"It just doesn't seem possible. For so long, I thought—" She broke off as she glanced out over the water. "The note she left on my dresser was handwritten. No one could have faked it. In the days leading up to her departure, she made a lot of complex business maneuvers. She shuffled money around, signed contracts and agreements so the company would run smoothly in her absence, saw to it that I would be taken care of financially. All of that took planning and coordination with lawyers and advisors. None of those arrangements could have been done overnight. Then she withdrew a bundle of cash, packed her suitcases and left town. I never heard from her again."

Wade nodded, but said nothing.

"Over the years, there have been sightings," she said. "A friend or acquaintance would swear they spotted her in

Spain or Italy or somewhere in South America, and Grand-mother would hire yet another private detective. Nothing ever panned out, but those sightings were enough to convince us that she was alive and well and living the life she wanted."

"Do you still have the note?"

"Yes, somewhere."

"What else did it say? The gist."

"'I know you won't understand what I'm about to do, and you may even despise me for it, but I hope in time you'll regard my decision in a kinder light. You're an adult now. You'll be going away to college soon and starting your own life, so I feel this is my time to be selfish. I've been unhappy for so very long. My marriage to James was a mistake. He's a good man, but he's not the right man for me. I've fallen in love with someone else. Deeply in love. The kind of love that comes around once in a lifetime if you're lucky. It's all very new and fragile, and we need time to ourselves far away from Shutter Lake, far away from work responsibilities and family obligations. Please know this is what I want. This is what I need. Don't come looking for me. Let me have my moment in the sun. When the time is right, I'll be in touch. Love, Mother.'"

Not just the gist but verbatim, he suspected. He wondered how many times she'd read that note over the years. How many times she'd wondered how her own mother could have abandoned her so easily and seemingly without an ounce of remorse.

She'd been staring out over the water as she recited the message, but now she turned to him, doubt flickering in her eyes. "Wade. You don't think that was a suicide note, do you?"

"Why would she pack her bags and withdraw a large

amount of cash just to drive her car over the side of the bridge? Not to mention that the victim was handcuffed to the steering wheel."

"Someone did that to her. That's what you're saying. My mother was murdered." The color had come back into her cheeks, but she still looked shaken. Who wouldn't be?

"We'll know more when they bring up the car," he said.

She ran a hand up and down her arm. "The day after she left, I had the strangest feeling that something was wrong. I wouldn't call it a premonition or even intuition. Eventually, I decided it was just my way of coping. I didn't want to believe she could leave me so easily. Without even saying goodbye. I even entertained the notion for a while that she'd been kidnapped. I imagined all kinds of scenarios, anything but the reality of her callous abandonment. I even took the note to the police station and refused to leave until I'd spoken with your dad."

"I didn't know that," Wade said in surprise. "He never told me."

"He probably wanted to protect my privacy. He kindly and gently explained to me that there was nothing he could do. By every indication, my mother had left town of her own accord. The note and the financial arrangements appeared to be well thought out by someone in full charge of her faculties. Under the circumstances, his hands were tied, he said. I later learned that he did make inquiries. He talked to my mother's attorney and business advisor, and he spoke with my stepfather at length. I guess he was satisfied by what he heard. I certainly never suspected anything was amiss."

"Why would you if everything in that note was true? I

think she meant every word of it. She planned to leave town and start a new life, but someone stopped her."

"But who?" Abby's voice was still hushed, her eyes haunted.

"Someone with a powerful motive."

"After all this time…after all the terrible things I've thought about her over the years…"

"You're not responsible for any of this," Wade said. "Don't get tangled up in misplaced guilt."

She nodded. "You're right. We don't know anything yet. There's a chance you could be mistaken about the car. But I still need talk to my grandmother. I can't let her hear about this from someone else."

"I don't think that's a good idea," Wade said. "This is a homicide investigation now. You need to let the police handle the notifications. I shouldn't even be here."

"But you came because you thought I should know. You said yourself it could take days to recover the car. Once they bring in heavy equipment, people are bound to talk. The operation may even make the local news. I can't let Grandmother find out that way. She'd be devastated."

He conceded her point. "You're right. You should go tell her in person so long as you both understand the need for discretion. Maybe it's for the best. You can stay in Atlanta until things get sorted out down here."

She bit her lip, deep in thought. "What about James? He's still legally her husband. Doesn't he have a right to know?"

Wade said carefully, "I wouldn't talk to James under any circumstances."

"But—"

"Abby, think. The spouse is always a prime suspect."

Her eyes widened in horror.

"I'm not saying he did anything wrong," Wade rushed to clarify. "But the police may want to observe his demeanor when they break the news to him."

She folded her arms and hugged them to her middle. "This is silly. James would never have done anything to hurt my mother. He was wildly in love with her."

"Which gives him a pretty powerful motive if he suspected she was leaving him for another man. Jealousy can make people lose all reason. Maybe he confronted her and things got out of hand. There's also the financial angle to consider. The company belonged to your mother. He stood to lose almost everything if she divorced him."

"But she left him in charge."

"For how long? Until you were old enough to take over?"

"I guess that makes me a suspect as well," she said. "Unless Mother changed her will at the last minute, I'm the one who stood to benefit the most from her death. We didn't exactly have the best relationship that summer. Our arguments got pretty heated at times. She didn't approve of my clothes, my friends. You…" She glanced at him. "She tried to break us up. Did you know that?"

"I guess that gives me a motive, too."

"I don't know about that. You did a pretty good job of ending our relationship all by yourself."

He'd wondered when they would get around to talking about that. "Things weren't always what they seemed that summer."

Her gaze was very direct. "It seemed pretty clear to me."

"Two sides to every story," he said. "But maybe now isn't the best time to get into all that."

"On that we agree."

"When will you go back to Atlanta?"

"Today. I'll spend the night with my grandmother and drive back tomorrow."

He frowned at that. "I thought we agreed you'd stay in the city for a few days."

"I never agreed to that. I want to be here when the car is recovered. The medical examiner may need a sample of my DNA."

"You don't have to be in town for that."

She frowned right back at him. "Why don't you want me here? What is it you're not telling me?"

"It's not a matter of what I want," he said. "You'll be safer in Atlanta."

"Safe from what?"

"Safe from your mother's killer," he said bluntly. "Don't you get it? Your inheritance not only makes you a suspect. It may also make you a target."

Chapter Three

After leaving Abby's place, Wade took the boat back north. The temperature had risen by midmorning, and the lake was already teeming with speedboats and Jet Skis and the occasional parasailer gliding by overhead. The weekend crowd had descended with a vengeance. Kids splashed and shrieked in the shallows as parents watched from loungers on the bank or floated nearby on inner tubes and air mattresses.

The incessant thrum of engines took Wade back to his younger days when he and his friends would hit the water as soon as they got off work from whatever job they'd managed to snag for the summer. Shutter Lake had been a great place to grow up, but the area was changing. The water toys were getting bigger and faster, and the houses perched atop the embankments more imposing. The crime that had always festered in the shadows had started to creep out into the sunlight.

He waited until he was well away from the traffic before he opened the throttle and stood behind the wheel so that he could enjoy the wind on his face. When he was within sight of the bridge ruins, he reduced his speed and lifted his binoculars. Several uniformed officers milled about on the bank waiting for the divers to surface. Two lake patrol vessels guarded the area from either direction, so he didn't try to approach.

Maneuvering toward the bank, he cut the engine and allowed the boat to drift underneath trailing willow branches. He wasn't trying to hide, but he had no wish to be seen. The last thing he wanted was to be tied up at the police station answering an endless stream of questions. He'd already given his statement to the first officer who had arrived on the scene after his call and then a little while later to a detective. If they needed to talk to him again, they had his number. Meanwhile, he had things to do, places to go, people to see. A missing speedboat to find. If he happened to flush out a murderer in the process, so much the better.

He told himself this was not his fight. He had no business getting tangled up in a homicide investigation. He'd done his due diligence by notifying the authorities and breaking the news to Abby. Anything else would just be meddling.

But finding Eva McRae's car at the bottom of the lake after all this time intrigued him. Gnawed at him. A murderer had been walking the streets of his hometown for ten long years, smug in the knowledge that he or she had committed the perfect crime and gotten away with it. Or had guilt slowly been eating away at the killer?

He listened to the water sloshing against the hull and thought about the night Eva had supposedly left town. He and Abby had taken his old boat out for a late-night cruise. They'd drifted for hours under the stars, listening to music while they talked and kissed. They were late getting back home. He half-expected to find every light in the house blazing and a furious Eva waiting for them on the veranda. Instead, the place was dark and quiet. Looking back now, the silence seemed portentous. According to Abby, she'd gone straight up to her room, but she hadn't found the note propped on her dresser until the following morning. The assumption had always been that Eva had left the house sometime later, well after midnight. But if Abby hadn't turned on her bedroom light, she wouldn't have noticed the note. Eva might have already been gone by the time he'd dropped Abby at the house. Her car might have been pushed off the bridge while the two of them had been floating under the stars.

Murdered. In cold blood.

The images forming inside his head were bone-chilling. It was entirely possible Eva had still been alive and conscious when the car had gone over the bridge. He could imagine her panic when she hit the water, the absolute terror she must have felt as the vehicle sank. The killer would have watched from the bridge until the car was out of sight.

As the son of a cop, Wade had learned a thing or two about murder investigations. The first and likeliest suspect was almost always the spouse. James McRae certainly had means, motive and opportunity, but Eva had made a lot of enemies in her day. Ruthless and savvy, she'd built a small empire by snatching up foreclosures and acquiring properties along the lake at rock bottom prices. She hadn't been shy about taking advantage of misery and misfortune. Any number of people could have wanted her dead. Vengeance as a motive was right up there with greed and jealousy.

And then there was the mystery man with whom she'd planned to leave town. No one had ever figured out his identity, though at one time Wade thought he might have known. Nothing concrete, but a very strong hunch that still bedeviled him on occasion.

Wouldn't hurt to make a few inquiries, he decided. Discreetly, of course. Nothing that would draw attention or arouse suspicion.

He continued to monitor the activity through his binoculars. One of the divers surfaced, followed by his partner a few minutes later. They were helped into a boat where they immediately began to shed their gear. Wade was too far away to hear voices, and he'd never mastered the ability to read lips. However, he could tell from their expressions and gestures that they'd witnessed the same grim tableau as he had. They would have photographed and recorded the scene as best they could with underwater equipment, but the car wouldn't have been touched and the remains inside left undisturbed. A crime scene that had been on the lakebed for over a decade would yield little in the way of trace evidence, but precautions would need to be taken nonetheless.

The divers' boat turned and headed south, back toward town and the police station. Several of the cops stationed on the bank climbed back up to their cars. As the engines faded in the distance, an unnerving silence settled over the water. Forty feet down, a murder victim waited for justice.

Wade lowered the binoculars and glanced around. Sunlight reflecting off the water was almost too bright, but he drifted in deep shade. He knew it was his imagination, but the gloom had started to seem unnatural somehow, as if Eva McRae's ghost had floated to the surface and hovered over his boat, watching and waiting and accusing. *You know, don't you? You've always known.*

He wasn't a superstitious person, but the sensation of being watched grew so strong he lifted a hand to rub at the chill bumps on his nape. Maybe he wasn't being stalked by Eva's ghost but by her flesh-and-blood killer. He scanned the trees along the bank, searching for the telltale rustle of branches. Even the birds had gone silent.

Grabbing the binoculars, he searched the opposite shoreline. One of the patrol boats remained in the area, along with a couple of cops on the bank. Wade wondered how they planned to secure the crime scene for the rest of the day and night. Maybe they were counting on secrecy until arrangements could be made to bring up the car, but discretion only lasted so long in a small town. Maybe word had already gotten out, and a few gawkers had made their way to the area to satisfy their curiosity. That would explain the uneasiness he couldn't seem to shake.

He skimmed the banks for several more minutes, then started the engine and guided the boat back into deeper water, waiting until he was out of sight from the lake patrol before he opened the throttle and headed back the way he'd come. Traffic on the water picked up as the lake widened. Veering to the right, he reduced speed as he entered a no-wake zone along a narrow canal where small houses on stilts lined both banks. He pulled up to a private dock and shut off the engine, letting the boat bounce gently off the bumpers. Lifting his hand to shade his eyes, he surveyed the small house perched atop the embankment.

His dad, Sam, sat on the deck drinking coffee and reading a newspaper. When he heard the engine, he folded the paper and set it aside as he watched Wade climb out of the boat and tie off. Neither of them waved or called out. Wade fiddled with the ropes for another long moment before he started up the wooden steps.

"Well, look what the cat dragged up," his dad teased as he picked up a napkin and scrubbed at the traces of ink left on his fingertips from the newsprint.

Wade nodded toward the fluttering pages as he moved into the shade of the covered deck and half-heartedly returned his dad's greeting. The good-natured ribbing made him uncomfortable given the nature of his visit. "You do know you can get the same information online these days. It's called the internet, old-timer. You should look into it."

His dad shrugged. "I like the feel of a real newspaper between my fingers. Besides, a few ink smudges never hurt anyone."

"Can't teach an old dog new tricks, I guess."

"That all depends."

At fifty-nine, his dad was still fit and trim, his posture ramrod straight, but his hair got a little grayer with each passing year, and the lines around his eyes and mouth had deepened since his retirement. He was still a vital guy. Passing time reading and fishing didn't suit him.

"I heard you'd been spotted in town a couple days ago," he said. "I wondered when you'd get around to stopping by."

"This isn't a pleasure trip," Wade said. "I'm here working a case."

"I heard that, too." His dad continued to scrub at his fingers, then gave up and tossed the napkin aside. "Something about a stolen boat. The insurance company must smell something fishy if they sent you down here."

His dad could play coy all he wanted, but Wade figured he'd already gotten the lowdown from his buddies at the station. He would know all about Wade's meeting with the detective in Major Crimes and his request for a copy of any supporting documents that had been added to the initial police report.

He glanced around the cozy deck. A ceiling fan rotated overhead, stirring his mother's potted ferns while her old tomcat snoozed on one of the rockers. The back door was open, but the shadows were too deep to glimpse anything or anyone through the screen.

"Is Mom around?" he asked in what he hoped was a casual tone.

"She's sleeping in this morning."

Wade frowned. "Kind of late for her, isn't it? Everything okay?"

"Everything is fine. She's painting again and you know how she gets. Loses all track of time. Barely even remembers to eat."

"I'm glad to hear she's painting," Wade said. "Art has always been therapeutic for her."

"Sometimes I worry she's a little too obsessive about it. She'll stay up until all hours when she gets going on a piece she likes. Says she enjoys the quiet. Says she's more creative when it's dark outside. Me? I'm in bed by nine, ten at the latest. But she seems happy, so I don't complain." He shuffled some things around on the table and motioned for Wade to sit. "You want some breakfast?"

"I'm good, thanks."

"Coffee?"

"Maybe in a minute." Instead of sitting at the table, he leaned against the deck railing, his back to the water.

"How long can you stay?"

"Depends on what I find out, but a few more days, at least."

"I meant right now. Should I go wake your mother?"

"No, let her sleep. If I don't catch her this morning, I'll come back in a day or two."

His dad gave him a measured look. "Easy for you to say, but it's my hide on the line if I let you leave before she sees you."

"Actually, I was hoping to have a word with you in private."

His dad squinted up at him. "About Brett Fortier's stolen boat? I doubt I can be of much help, but I'm happy to listen."

"Oh, come on," Wade said. "You're not fooling me with

that out-of-the-loop routine. I know how your pipeline works. You probably know more about the case than the detective in charge. More than me, too, for that matter." Wade decided to take a seat after all. He settled across the table from Sam and stretched out his legs. "What's the unofficial consensus?"

"As far as I know, there hasn't been a lot of progress on the case," Sam said. "Nothing substantial has turned up, no concrete evidence, no fingerprints or fibers, no eye-witness accounts. The boat was stolen from the marina a few days after Brett Fortier brought it up from the Gulf. The nearest security camera wasn't working, and the guard had started his rounds on the other side of the marina when it happened. In other words, no one saw or heard anything."

"Do you think it could have been an inside job?" Wade asked.

"Someone working at the marina, you mean?" Sam shrugged. "That's always a possibility, although the guard on duty that night is an ex-cop. I know him. Good man. I don't see him being involved. One of the other employees, who knows? The thieves were in and out quickly, and they knew the guard's rotation, knew which camera to disable. Boats with that kind of price tag come with safeguards. It's not easy to hot-wire the engine. Whoever took it knew what they were doing."

"Or they had a key," Wade said.

His dad gave him a sage nod. "You think Brett Fortier arranged the theft himself?"

"Like you said, I wouldn't be here if his claim hadn't raised a red flag."

"Lot of things about that missing boat seem a little hinky," Sam said. "Why do you suppose he brought it up here from the Gulf? A craft like that would stick out like a sore thumb among the pontoon and ski boats. Plus, you don't need that kind of speed on a lake. You buy a boat like that if you're trying to impress someone. Or if you need to outrun another vessel on the open water."

"You might bring it up from the Gulf if you were trying to hide it from someone," Wade said. "Or conceal something onboard."

"Drugs? That wouldn't surprise me. Brett Fortier has always skated a little too close to the edge," Sam said. "I've heard rumors about him for years, about the kind of criminals he associates with. If even half of what they say is true, he could be mixed up in some nasty business. You need to watch your back with that one. You may not be the only one looking for his boat."

His dad's genuine concern made Wade regret even more the main reason for his visit. "This isn't my first rodeo. I know enough to be careful."

"See that you are. If you need help, you know where to find me."

"I'll be fine. Don't worry about me. Speaking of nasty business, there's another matter I came here to discuss with you. I went for a dive early this morning at the north end of the lake, where the old bridge went down. I didn't find Brett's boat, but I discovered a car on the bottom. Judging by the corrosion, I'd guess it's been down there for several years. I was wondering if you remember anything about a vehicle going over the bridge or if anyone filed a police report to that effect."

He watched his dad's face closely in the split second before he answered. He didn't flinch or glance away, but there was something indefinable in his eyes that might have been the flicker of a memory. Or Wade's imagination.

"Nothing was ever reported that I can recall offhand,

but that spot was a hotbed of suspicious activity for years. Some of the guardrails were missing before the bridge was demolished. It would have been easy to roll a car off the side without anyone being the wiser."

"This isn't just any car," Wade said. "It's a Rolls Royce Wraith."

His dad had picked up his coffee cup, but now he set it back down with a clatter. "That's odd. You sure about that?"

Wade nodded.

Sam looked skeptical. "Water does a real number on metal. You're saying the vehicle is still in good enough shape that you could identify the make and model?"

"I recognized the body style, and the hood ornament is unmistakable," Wade said. "And I'd say *odd* is an understatement. Think about the implication. There's a Rolls Royce Wraith at the bottom of Shutter Lake. What's the probability that it's been down there ever since Eva Dallas McRae disappeared?"

His dad mopped at the spilled coffee with the same napkin he'd used to wipe ink from his fingers. "She didn't disappear, she left town."

"Never to be seen or heard from again," Wade reminded him.

Sam glanced up. "I'll admit the discovery is troubling, but nothing you've said so far convinces me the car is Eva's."

His denial reminded Wade of how hard Abby had initially resisted the truth. He presented his dad with the same rationale. "Have you ever known anyone else in the area to drive a car like that?"

"Could have been someone passing through town for all we know."

"That would be one hell of a coincidence," Wade said.

Sam's gaze narrowed as he studied Wade from across

the table. "Where are you going with this? You're push-ing for answers like you've got a personal stake somehow. Does this have something to do with Abby Dallas being back in town?"

At the mention of her name, Wade felt a prickle of unease at the back of his neck. He hoped like hell she wasn't in any danger, but he had a bad feeling she just might be. "This isn't about Abby. It's about murder. Given your previous ca-reer, I would have thought you'd be a little more curious."

Sam's expression froze for a split second before he growled, "Murder? What the hell are you talking about?"

"Word's bound to get out, so I came here as soon as I could to give you a heads-up. I didn't just find a car at the bottom of the lake, Dad. Someone was inside when the ve-hicle went over the bridge. The skeletal remains of the vic-tim are still handcuffed to the steering wheel."

A myriad of emotions flashed through Sam's eyes. He opened his mouth and then closed it again before glancing away. Finally, he said in strained voice, "You know this for certain?"

"Yes. I saw the remains through the window. Surpris-ingly, the cuffs are still intact. You would have thought the pressure would have pulled the wrist bone apart..." He trailed off with a grimace. "Anyway, the whole scene star-tled the hell out of me. I surfaced as soon as I found the remains and called the police. They've already sent divers down to verify. They'll have to bring the car up to make a positive identification, but the make and model of the car, along with the timing is suspect, to say the least."

Sam kept his gaze focused on the horizon. "I learned a long time ago not to jump to conclusions."

"We don't have to jump to conclusions. We'll know for a fact soon enough."

"The police are already on the scene, you say? Who's the lead?"

"A detective named Benson took my statement. Do you know him?"

He nodded. "Roy Benson. I know of him. He came onboard after I retired, but I hear good things. Smart, determined. A real hard-ass at times." Whatever emotion had been in Sam's voice a moment ago had given way to professional stoicism. "Maybe I should take a ride up there and see for myself what's going on."

"Why would you want to do that?" Wade said. "You're no longer on active duty."

"Why?" Sam shot him a frowning glance. "I was the police chief when we all thought Eva McRae skipped town with her lover. If it turns out she was murdered on my watch, then everything changes. I don't care how many years have gone, it's still my responsibility to find out what happened. I owe it to her family."

"I thought you might feel that way," Wade said carefully. He couldn't tear his gaze from his dad's rigid profile. "You never suspected foul play back then?"

"There was no reason to. We had Eva's intentions and wishes in her own words. She planned to leave town and she didn't want to be followed."

"Still, a woman in her position goes missing, the thought must have crossed your mind that the situation might not be as it seemed."

He appeared irritated by Wade's persistence. "Easy to find fault with the benefit of hindsight. You're looking back through the lens of what you found this morning. All we knew at the time was that Eva left notes for her husband and her daughter. She put her affairs in order and made it clear she wasn't coming back anytime soon. In the eyes of the law, that was that."

"What about in your eyes?"

He sighed. "I made some inquiries, but maybe not enough if what you think is true. I talked to her family and business associates. I even had a chat with her attorney. To a person, they said she never appeared unduly stressed or under duress in the days leading up to her disappearance. She was very clear about her wishes and very precise with her instructions. By every indication, she was calm and in control."

"The amount of cash she withdrew didn't trigger an alarm?"

"Again, hindsight," his dad all but snapped. "Eva was a smart woman. She knew if she didn't want to be found or followed, she couldn't leave a digital trail while traveling. That meant no credit cards, no ATM withdrawals or bank transfers until she arrived at her destination."

Wade tried to keep his voice even, but a note of urgency slipped in as he leaned slightly forward. "Why do you think she was so insistent on not being followed? Did you ever wonder if she might have gotten mixed up in something dangerous or illegal? Is it possible she was being blackmailed? Maybe there was a reason she needed all that cash. Maybe she felt she had no choice but to disappear."

"I wondered about a lot of things," Sam said. "But a small-town police department operates on a limited budget. Sometimes you have to pick and choose where to allocate your manpower and resources. In Eva's case, I had to follow the evidence. As far as I or anyone knew, she left town of her own accord."

"What about the man she mentioned in Abby's note? Were there any rumors of an affair?"

"None that I ever heard."

"You never knew who she planned to meet the night she left town?"

His dad was silent for a moment. "I'm getting a little tired of this third degree. I'll ask you again. Why is this so important to you?"

Wade cast a glance over his shoulder as he lowered his voice. "Because I'm afraid that man was you, Dad."

Chapter Four

Wade's father looked stunned, utterly aghast. His mouth went slack, and for a moment, he seemed incapable of speech. Then his hand shot across the table to grab Wade's wrist. His physical reaction startled Wade, and he jerked away reflexively.

His dad's eyes blazed with sudden anger. "What is wrong with you, bringing an accusation like that to my doorstep? Have you lost your mind? What if your mother heard you?"

Wade sent another uneasy glance toward the door. The last thing he wanted was to find his mother listening to their conversation through the screen. He kept his voice barely above a whisper as he met his dad's hard glare. "I haven't lost my mind. I only wish the explanation were that simple. I know about your affair. I saw the two of you together that summer. You and Eva."

His dad's mouth tightened. "You didn't see a damn thing. You need to stop this nonsense before you say something you can't take back. You have no idea what you're talking about."

Wade kept his own anger in check. "I know what I saw."

His dad stood abruptly, sending his chair flying backward. Without another word, he rounded the table and went down the steep stairs toward the dock. Wade waited a few minutes, then he rose, righted the chair and followed him down the steps. He didn't turn when Wade approached the dock. He stood with legs slightly apart at the edge of the platform staring down into the water. He seemed so intent that for a moment, Wade entertained the notion that he'd conjured Eva's ghost.

"I didn't come here with the intent to upset you," Wade said.

"You could have fooled me."

"I didn't come here to accuse you, either. I came because I thought you needed to know what I found."

"You came because deep down you're wondering if I had something to do with that car going over the bridge."

"I never said that."

His dad whirled. In the mottled light that sifted down through the trees, he appeared older than his fifty-nine years, rough-hewn and weary, but still with a hint of defiance in his eyes. "What is it you think you saw that summer?"

Wade hesitated, picking his way through a particularly awkward conversation. "I saw the two of you together at one of her rental houses one afternoon. I'd gotten off work early and took the boat out to test my overhauled motor. I guess I just happened to be in the right spot at the right time."

Sam looked livid. "That's it? You saw someone you thought was me from a distance?"

"It was you. I don't want to go into too much detail about what I saw, but…" A self-conscious silence followed. "Let's just say your body language was intimate. You had your arms around each other. You kissed. I assume the rental was where you'd meet that summer. That's why the house stayed vacant for so long. I drove by a few days later, and I saw your vehicle parked down the street."

Sam turned back to the water. "Was anyone with you?"

"No. I was alone both times."

"You never told anyone what you thought you saw?"

"No."

"What about Abby? Never a word even after her mother disappeared?"

"No, Dad. Not even then."

Sam was silent again.

Wade walked over to the edge of the dock, keeping space between them. Not because he was angry or disgusted—though a part of him still was—but because his dad had become a stranger to him once more. After he'd found out about Eva that summer, he'd come up with all sorts of excuses to stay away from home as much as possible. It wasn't just the guilt he felt for keeping a secret from his mother. Where he and his dad had once been close, he barely recognized the man across from him at the dinner table. He felt that same distance now.

"Did Mom know about the affair?"

"There was no affair," Sam insisted.

"I know what I saw, Dad."

"It was…" His shrug turned into a shudder. "I don't know what the hell it was. It wasn't love—I know that much. We met a few times and then it was over."

At least he was no longer denying the relationship, but a part of Wade wished that he would. Even though he'd lived with the secret of his father's betrayal for a long time, confirmation was still a hard blow. "How did it start?"

Sam scrubbed his face as if he could wipe clean his memories. "Is this really necessary? It was a long time ago."

"Given what I found at the bottom of the lake? Yeah, Dad. I think it's necessary."

"If it turns out to be her car…" He closed his eyes briefly.

"I didn't know. If you believe nothing else, believe that. I didn't know."

Are you trying to convince me or Eva?

"Let's just take it one step at a time," Wade said. "Tell me how it started."

The contempt in his dad's voice was palpable. "The way those things usually start. With a weak man and a lonely woman."

Lonely? Eva? "She was unhappy in her marriage?"

"She and James McRae were never a good match. That's what she told me, at least. I think what she really meant was that he was no match for her. Eva could be a difficult woman. Reckless in her personal life and utterly ruthless in her business affairs."

"What about you and Mom?"

"I loved your mother then and I love her now. That will never change."

And yet...

Sam made a helpless gesture with his hand. "This isn't an excuse, but that summer was an especially rough time for her. There were days when she couldn't drag herself out of bed. I was under a lot of pressure at work and... Eva was Eva."

Sounded like an excuse to Wade.

He knew things happened in a marriage that only the two people involved could understand, but his instinct was still to come to his mother's defense. He forced himself to hold back. Until he knew the full story, he would do his best to reserve judgment. After all, he was far from perfect. He'd made mistakes. He knew only too well that things were not always the way they seemed. If he'd come clean with Abby, each of their lives might have been changed. Instead, he'd let her believe the worst about him because at the time, it had seemed the easiest way out for everyone.

"I get it, Dad. Eva was a beautiful woman and you're human."

Sam frowned. "Don't patronize me."

"I'm trying to keep an open mind," Wade said. "This isn't an easy conversation for a son to have with his father."

"We can stop right now, then. No need to go any further. You got what you came for."

"Not really. I'm still trying to make sense of it all," Wade said. "Tell me about Eva."

His dad sighed. "You don't ask for much, do you?"

"I'm trying really hard to understand. What was she like? What was she like to you?"

Sam gazed out over the lake, his eyes narrowing as he searched the distant shoreline. "She was like moonlight. Luminous. Seductive. But she had a dark side. I guess it was part of her allure. When she had you under her spell, she was like a drug. That's the best way I know to describe her effect on me. The high when we were together was like nothing I'd ever experienced before. She made you want things…need things—"

Wade put up a hand. "Okay, I get the picture."

"You wanted to know."

He only thought he had. "So how did it end?"

Sam drew a long breath and released it. "One morning I woke up stone cold sober and thought, 'What the hell am I doing?' The whole thing seemed like a bad dream. Like it happened to someone else. To this day, I can't reconcile being so foolish. I risked everything, and for what?" He shook his head as if he was still trying to puzzle it out.

"Was she upset when you broke things off?"

"Upset? She laughed and told me to lighten up. It was never meant to last."

"That must have stung."

"Not really. It was typical Eva. I was relieved, actually."

Wade wondered if that was true. Pride was a fragile thing. "You never saw her again?"

"I glimpsed her around town occasionally, but we never spoke."

"And you never told Mom," Wade said. "You didn't think she had a right to know?" Bitterness soured his tone despite his best efforts to remain neutral.

His dad's voice hardened. "I didn't think I had the right to cut her to the quick just to clear my conscience. You don't have that right, either."

"If I was going to tell her, don't you think I would have done so by now?" Wade took a moment to tamp down a burst of anger. He had to remind himself he hadn't come here to judge or condemn. He just wanted the truth. "I don't want to hurt her, either," he said in a hushed tone. "But it hasn't been easy keeping that secret from her. *Your* secret. For those first few months, every time I looked at her... every time I looked at *you...*"

His dad's stare said everything.

Wade ran a hand through his hair as he thought about what still needed to be said between them. He felt tired and guilty and disillusioned, and he just wanted to get in his boat and speed away. "I won't say anything, but she's bound to find out sooner or later. Secrets always have a way of coming out, even ten years after the fact."

"Just leave it alone." His dad's anger had vanished, and now he sounded numb.

"I wish I could, but I can't. I'm not the only one who'll have these questions. Have you even thought about that?

This is a homicide investigation now. Once the police start actively pursuing leads, it's entirely possible someone else who knew about you and Eva will come out of the woodwork. Then the cops will wonder why you didn't come forward with the information at the time of her disappearance. They'll wonder why you didn't pursue your own leads. Look at it from an impartial point of view. Maybe you and Eva planned to leave town together, but you got cold feet at the last minute. Maybe she flew into a rage and threatened to tell Mom. One thing led to another…things got out of hand…" He didn't finish the thought.

"No one will believe that because it's not what happened," Sam said in that same emotionless voice.

"The police will ask questions, anyway. You don't think it would be better to get out ahead of this thing?"

His dad sighed. "What exactly are you suggesting?"

"Go to the police and tell them about the affair," Wade said. "You may be retired, but you're still one of them. You've earned their respect and the benefit of the doubt. They'll be discreet. It's the only way to keep it contained."

But his dad wasn't listening. He stood with that same rigid posture as his gaze traveled up the steps to the house. Wade turned to find his mother on the deck staring down at them.

WADE WAVED AND she lifted a hand in response. The effort seemed almost reluctant, though Wade told himself her hesitancy was only his imagination. They were far enough away that he didn't think she could have overheard their conversation, but voices did tend to carry on a breeze. There had been a few angry moments when they may not have been as careful as they should have been.

His father muttered something under his breath.

"How long do you think she's been standing there?" Wade asked.

"She wasn't there a minute ago when I checked. Anyway, she couldn't have heard us from this distance."

"I hope not."

But even if they were out of earshot, Laura Easton was a very perceptive woman. She'd know something was wrong from their expressions and body language. Wade made an effort to shake off the lingering bad taste from the unpleasant discussion as they started up the stairs. He took the lead and his dad followed a step behind him. He tried to gauge his mother's mood as he neared the top, but as sensitive as she was to his emotions, she'd always been difficult for him to read. He wondered if she'd learned to school her expression in order to hide the darkness that seemed to hover at arms' length even during the good times.

She wore a sleeveless yellow dress with a full skirt that fluttered in the breeze. From a distance, she looked like a young woman: tall, trim and tan. But like Sam, a closer inspection revealed lines in her face and shadows beneath her eyes. She waited until Wade stepped onto the deck, and then she came over and gave him a big hug. The tightness of her embrace was reassuring, and Wade returned it wholeheartedly.

"I'm so happy to see you." She reached up and touched his cheek. "Why did no one tell me you were coming?"

"It was spur of the moment," he said. "I needed to talk to Dad about a case I'm working on." That much was true. Still, he shot his dad an accusing glance for no other reason than it made him feel momentarily better.

She searched his face. "You look tired."

"Thanks, Mom."

"It wasn't an insult. A mother notices these things. You haven't been taking care of yourself."

"I didn't get much sleep last night, but I'm fine." He gently disengaged from the embrace. "I don't want to talk about me. Look at you, all dolled up. Is that a new dress?"

"This old thing? I've had it forever." She smoothed her hands down the skirt. "The style is a little young for me, but I drag it out now and then because the color makes me feel like I'm wearing sunshine."

Sunshine was the perfect foil for moonlight, Wade decided. "Looks good on you."

His deflection didn't quell her fretting. "If I'd known you were coming, I could have planned something special for lunch. As it is, there's not much in the house—"

"I wouldn't expect you to cook for me, and anyway, I can't stay. I've got a full day ahead of me."

"The boy is in town working a case," Sam reminded her. He stood with his back against a post, arms folded, his gaze meeting Wade's without darting away in guilt.

"But you have to eat," his mom protested.

"Another day, I promise."

She looked crestfallen. "Can you at least spare a few minutes to have coffee with your mother?"

How was he supposed to turn that down? "Just a quick cup, and then I really do have to go." Wade didn't know whether this was better or worse than he'd expected. His dad acted as though nothing had gone down between them, and his mom seemed perfectly fine. So why did he feel like the lowest of the low? Why did he feel as if he were the one who'd done something wrong?

His dad was still eyeing him. "I'll put on a fresh pot. Give you two a chance to catch up."

Instead of settling down at the table, his mother went

over to the edge of the deck and stood gazing out at the scenery as people who lived on the water seemed to have a tendency to do. Wade understood. Why waste the view even for a moment?

"It's nice back here," he said. "Quiet. You don't hear all the Jet Skis like you do out on the lake."

"You don't have the expansive views, either, but I like the canal," she said dreamily. "The colors of the water are constantly shifting, and the light is so moody and reflective with all the trees. When your dad first suggested we sell our house and buy this property, I was hesitant. I thought I would be lonely back here. I was so used to having everything I needed in town. But now I love it. I can't imagine living anywhere else."

"That's good. I'm glad you're happy here. Dad said you'd started painting again. I'd like to see some of your work."

"Maybe next time," she demurred. "I'm a bit rusty."

"No pressure," Wade said. "Whenever you're ready."

She gave him a sidelong glance. "Earlier when you were down on the dock with your dad, I couldn't help noticing the tension. I haven't seen either of you like that in a very long time. It made me remember how headstrong you both can be." She turned worriedly. "Is everything okay between you two?"

"Everything is fine, Mom."

"But you don't seem fine. I know you well enough to recognize when something is wrong. You look—"

"Tired?" He smiled.

"Anxious. Distracted. What's going on, Wade?"

He took a moment to answer. "The case I'm working on is complicated. It involves someone I used to know. Someone I didn't like. I don't want to let my personal feelings get in the way of my investigation."

"Who is this person?"

"Brett Fortier. His boat was stolen from the marina a couple of weeks ago. The insurance company hired me to make sure the claim he filed is legit."

"I see. Well, if you're talking about the same Brett Fortier from high school, then you're almost guaranteed to find something shady," she said. "He was always a pill."

Wade smiled at her mild description. "You used to say the same thing about me. I know I caused you and Dad more than a few gray hairs before I decided to grow up."

"Minor indiscretions compared to what you hear about these days." She reached over and gave his arm a squeeze. "Besides, you always had a good head on your shoulders and a kind heart. I never worried too much about you back then."

"But you do now?"

She sighed. "I think your work is a lot more dangerous than either you or your dad let on."

"It's really not. People do reckless things for an insurance settlement, and they sometimes do more reckless things to try and cover up their lies. There's an occasional hitch, but never anything I can't handle. Don't forget, I learned from the best."

"I hope that's true. Your dad was a good cop for a lot of years. His badge was so much a part of the man he became. He took great pride in serving his community, and he had a lot more years to give. Early retirement was his idea, but I know he left the department for me. I don't take that sacrifice lightly, so I want to thank you."

Wade was taken aback. "Me? Why?"

"I know it makes him happy that you still come to him for help."

Wade swallowed, wishing the relationship with his dad

was still that simple. "Why wouldn't I want his help? Retirement hasn't dulled his instincts."

Her smile turned wry. "Yes, well, retirement hasn't turned out to be what either of us expected. His consulting business is starting to take up more and more of his time. The department has him working through a stack of cold cases. Did he tell you?"

"No, but I can understand why they'd want him. He always had an eye for detail. Now he can afford to take as much time as he needs to go through each file without having to split his attention between active cases." Wade paused, taking in his mother's furrowed brow. "You okay with this arrangement?"

"Yes, if it makes him happy. It's just…" Her eyes were shadowed when she turned. "Sometimes I think digging into those old cases does nothing but stir up a bunch of bad memories for people who've already suffered enough."

"Everyone deserves justice," Wade said.

"Even if the truth does more harm than good?"

"Even then."

"I wonder. Maybe some things really are best left in the past." She shrugged, but something dark flickered in the depths of her eyes, something that sent an inexplicable tingle across Wade's scalp. "Maybe some secrets are best left buried."

Chapter Five

After Wade left the cottage that morning, Abby cleaned up the terrace and then sat on the steps for the longest time, deep in thought. She needed to get on the road. A good four-hour drive lay ahead of her, and yet she lingered because she dreaded the conversation with her grandmother. And because she hadn't fully absorbed the news for herself. That was normal, she supposed. No matter how many years had gone by, the death of a loved one was hard to accept, but a cold-blooded murder was nearly impossible to process. So many conflicting emotions warred inside her. Disbelief, guilt, fear. Anger. She supposed that, too, was normal.

Below her, the cove remained quiet, but the buzz of activity out on the lake drifted up through the oleanders like the distant call of an old memory. Far from an intrusion, the noise of engines and laughter made her feel more connected and less alone. Less afraid.

She couldn't stop thinking about Wade's apprehension that she, too, could be in danger. In the space of a single morning, her whole world had changed. She told herself she should be relieved that at last she finally had an answer to her mother's disappearance, but deep down, she wished she could blink her eyes and make everything normal again. Her mother had died at the bottom of the lake, the secret of her demise hidden beneath murky waters for ten long years. There was no relief in that knowledge. No closure or acceptance, only more questions.

Abby had lived most of her adulthood in the shadow of her mother's abandonment. The seemingly callous desertion had colored every aspect of her life and relationships. She'd become guarded and timid, reluctant to trust. How could she not be? After so many years of protecting herself, what was she to do now with this new information, this profound revelation? Her mother hadn't left town of her own accord. She'd been handcuffed to the steering wheel of her beloved car before it had been pushed over the edge of the bridge.

The image of a woman struggling against time and rising water was a vision too terrible to contemplate, and yet Abby couldn't get the disturbing scene out of her head. She could almost feel the abject terror as the cold lake water closed in on her, the utter shock of betrayal and the panic of being trapped. That her mother's nightmare would have ended quickly did nothing to alleviate the horror of what had been done to her, possibly by someone she knew and trusted, someone she may even have loved.

But if one drilled down deep enough, certain facts remained the same. Her mother had likely meant every word she'd written in the note she'd left on Abby's dresser. She'd wanted to start a new life far away from her home and family, far away from her daughter, and she'd justified her action by reminding Abby that she'd be leaving for college soon. As if her age made everything all right. As if her coming adulthood meant Abby would no longer need a relationship with her mother.

A relationship she would never have now. Whatever faint hope she'd harbored in the deepest part of her heart for a mother-daughter reunion had been dashed by the cold, harsh reality of Wade Easton's discovery.

Wade Easton. She drew a long breath and released it. She couldn't afford to get distracted by dwelling on an old boyfriend. Time enough later to dissect and brood about *their* reunion. Time enough later to remind herself of *his* betrayal. At the moment, she needed to stay focused on the more immediate task at hand, namely, finding her mother's killer. Before she could even contemplate the seemingly impossible mission of solving a ten-year-old murder, she first had to break the news to her grandmother. The knowledge that her only daughter had been murdered would devastate the poor woman, which was why Abby had sat on the terrace steps procrastinating all morning. But it had to be done, sooner rather than later.

Hardening her resolve, she finally got up and went inside to pack an overnight bag before locking up the cottage. The long drive to Atlanta gave her plenty of time to worry and reflect. So much so that by the time she hit Saturday afternoon traffic in the city, she'd already worked herself into quite a state. She stopped by the condo to check the mail and water the plants even though a neighbor had agreed to take care of those chores while she was away.

She found a dozen more ways to kill time until the late afternoon sunshine streaming in through her front windows reminded her that twilight would soon fall, and the news of Wade's discovery was best delivered in daylight.

Maybe the revelation would come as something of a relief to her grandmother after the initial shock. She was getting on in years. She deserved to know what happened. For far too long, she'd been stuck in a hellish limbo, clinging to the notion that her daughter had done a selfish, reckless deed because the alternative was even harder to accept.

But ten years was a long time. A decade of dwindling hope took a toll.

Her grandmother lived in the Inman Park area of Atlanta, a historic district of grand old homes surrounded by wrought iron fences and meticulously clipped hedges. Abby parked in the circular drive at the front of the house rather than pulling around to the back as she normally did. She rang the bell and waited, a part of her hoping that no one was home. A few seconds later, Lillian glanced out one of the long sidelights before pulling back the door. She was immaculately turned out as she always was in wide-leg linen trousers and a matching cream tunic intricately embroidered in shades of her signature blue at the neckline and sleeves. She'd pulled her silvery gold hair back into a sleek French twist, and her fingers and lobes were bejeweled in diamonds, platinum and her favorite sapphire ring.

"Abigail?" Her hand fluttered to her heart as she glanced over Abby's shoulder to the veranda as if checking to see if her granddaughter had come alone.

"Hi, Grandmother. Did I catch you at a bad time? You look as if you were on your way out."

"I had friends over earlier, but I'm alone now. This is a lovely surprise. I thought you'd already left for the lake." Her accent was pure Southern aristocracy, the drawled syllables softened by a slight tremor of age.

"I did leave, but I came back," Abby explained.

Her grandmother lifted a thin brow. "That was a quick trip. Did you change your mind?"

"No, I'm driving back tomorrow." She ran a nervous hand down the side of her jeans. "I'm sorry for just showing up without calling first. Do you have a minute? Can we talk?"

"You never need to call. You know that. This is still your

home. But you're certainly being mysterious." Her grandmother moved aside so that Abby could step into the foyer.

"I don't mean to be." She leaned in and bussed the older
woman's cheek, catching a whiff of her perfume before she
drew away to close the door. The scent was fresh yet time-
less, like a drop of vanilla splashed on crisp laundry. Abby
drank in the comforting fragrance as her senses wallowed
in the familiar appointments of vintage rugs, polished ma-
hogany and sparkling chandeliers. "I'll tell you everything.
It's just…maybe we should sit down first."

Diamonds flashed as her grandmother's hand once again
crept to her throat. "Now you're starting to frighten me.
Are you ill?"

"No, I'm perfectly fine as you can see. There's no reason
to be afraid. Let's just sit."

Her grandmother led her down the long hallway to the
informal den at the back of the house. Informal by her stan-
dards, anyway. She motioned Abby to a well-worn leather
chesterfield sofa while she took a seat on a mohair armchair. Perched on the edge, she remained silent and stoic
as she waited for Abby to explain the reason for the impromptu visit.

The French doors were open, and Abby could smell jasmine from the garden. The scent conjured gauzy images of
floral dresses and afternoon soirees from a forgotten era.
She closed her eyes and drew in the bouquet of those roman-
tic visions before she began to reveal to her grandmother
the hard, ugly truth of her mother's demise. She started reluctantly and built momentum until everything came pouring out. Her grandmother sat quietly through it all, posture
rigid, hands folded in her lap. But her blue eyes glittered
as brilliantly as her diamonds as the news began to sink in.

Abby finished with a helpless shrug. "That's it. That's

all I know at the moment. I'm so sorry to break it to you before we have a positive identification, but I didn't want you to hear the news from someone else."

Her grandmother got up and went over to the French doors, her back to Abby as she gathered her thoughts and poise. Neither of them spoke. Abby remained seated, giving her grandmother however much time and space she needed to digest the news.

"We can't make any arrangements until we know for certain," her grandmother finally said.

The practicality of the statement was a bit jarring to Abby. "No, I suppose not."

Her grandmother spoke softly, the drawl even more pronounced, but now there was steel around the edges. "Is it possible you could be mistaken?"

Abby cleared her throat and slid her splayed fingers over the tops of her thighs for lack of anything better to do with her hands. "As I said, we won't know conclusively until the medical examiner has a chance to compare dental and medical records. He may even need to run a DNA analysis. These things take time. But the make and model of the car, along with the location and timing…" She drew a breath. "There's also the fact that we haven't seen or heard from Mother in over a decade. I have to believe if she was still out there… still alive…one of the private detectives you hired would have found her by now."

"Not if she doesn't want to be found. Eva is a very resourceful woman."

But why wouldn't she want to be found?

"Either way, we'll know soon enough." Abby gentled her tone. "You should try to prepare yourself for the results."

"I suppose a part of me has been preparing for the past decade," her grandmother said in a resolved tone. "Still, it comes as a blow, doesn't it?" She placed her hand on the door frame for support. Abby wanted to go to her, but she didn't. Lillian Jamison was a very proud, very strong woman. She would come to Abby when she was ready.

"You say the Easton boy found the car?"

"Wade Easton, yes." Abby's heart thumped at the mention of his name. The sound of it came as another jolt in the quiet of her grandmother's den. "He's an investigator these days. People hire him to find lost things. He was looking for a stolen boat when he came upon the car."

"I remember him." Her grandmother remained at the open doorway, staring out into the fading light as if she couldn't yet bring herself to turn and meet Abby's gaze. As if she wasn't quite ready to face the undeniable truth in her granddaughter's eyes. "I met him once when I came to Fairhope for a visit. Very polite young man. Good-looking, like his father, but trouble."

Abby said in surprise, "You knew his dad?"

"Only in passing. Your grandfather and I kept our house on the lake for years after we moved to Atlanta. He made a point of getting to know the local authorities so they would keep an eye on the place while we were away."

"Did you know Sam Easton became the police chief? I understand he's retired now," Abby said.

"Retired?" Lillian's voice turned wistful. "I remember him as a young officer. Time does fly, doesn't it?"

Abby hesitated, not quite sure what to do or say next. She cleared her throat again and smoothed another imaginary crease from her jeans. "I suppose Wade Easton is one of the few things on which you and Mother were in agreement. She didn't approve of our relationship. She thought he'd hold me back, whatever that meant. I never really understood why she disliked him so much."

Her grandmother turned at that. "She saw the way he looked at you. And the way you looked at him. As much as Eva seemed to thrive in Fairhope, she wanted something more for you. As did I. And just look at you now. All grown up. Poised, confident. Successful in your own right. Eva would be so proud. I certainly am."

Abby wasn't so sure about any of that. Most days she felt like an imposter, as if she'd left the real Abigail Dallas behind when she'd fled to Atlanta ten years ago. She wasn't a born entrepreneur like her mother. She wasn't savvy or gutsy or intuitive. She didn't like taking risks. Yes, she'd carved out a successful career for herself in commercial real estate, but sometimes she wondered if it was even what she wanted. Maybe a part of her had still been trying to please and impress her mother. Maybe she felt the need to prove herself before she went back to Fairhope and took the reins of Eva's business.

Her grandmother closed the French doors against the falling twilight and came back over to sit beside Abby on the sofa. She looked composed and determined as she took her granddaughter's hand. "I needed a moment to wallow, but that's over now. I want to focus on you. You've been remarkably calm and steadfast. I can't imagine how difficult it was for you to even come here. None of this has been easy for either of us."

"To be honest, I think I'm still in shock, too," Abby said. "We spent so many years wondering and searching and hoping—"

"And all that time, she was at the bottom of Shutter Lake."

The bluntness startled Abby. "Yes."

Her grandmother squeezed her fingers. "I always wanted to believe she was out there in the world, happy and healthy despite the misery and turmoil she left behind. I didn't want to accept the possibility that she might actually be dead. Not without proof. But it never really made sense that she wouldn't eventually get in touch with us. That she could so easily leave her business and her only child behind forever." Her mouth tightened as her voice hardened. "God knows, Eva could be callous and selfish, and if I'm brutally honest, she was never cut out to be a wife and mother. But she did love you in her own way. She was very proud of the young woman you were becoming."

"Grandmother..." Abby clasped her hand in both of hers. "Who do you think could have done something like that to her?"

"I don't know, child."

"Do you know of any enemies she had? Someone with a grudge who'd want to hurt her?"

She lifted a thin shoulder. "Eva could be single-minded, even cruel, when she went after something she wanted, whether in her personal life or business. I'm certain there were any number of people with axes to grind. I don't pretend to understand what drives a person to murder, but I suppose one would have to start with the most obvious suspect."

"You mean James."

She nodded. "I always believed him to be a good man. Forgiving to a fault and in some ways, far too sensitive for Eva. She needed someone who could give back as good as she gave, and James wasn't that man. He was too besotted. Too much of a pleaser. She had that effect."

"What about my dad? Were he and my mother a good match? I'm sorry to say, I don't even remember what he looked like, let alone how he and Mother interacted."

Lillian patted her arm absently. "They were so young when they married. Still in that first blush of love when he was killed. It's impossible to know if they would have lasted. All I can say for certain is that they were very much in love at the time."

"She had no other serious relationships until James? She was still a young woman. Fifteen years is a long time to be alone."

"She certainly had her chances. Eva never lacked for admirers, but she was too busy building her empire to settle down. She didn't take any of the suitors seriously, but she loved the attention."

"Then how did she end up with James, if they were so ill-suited?"

"I've asked myself that very question," she admitted. "My only answer is that for your mother, the grass was always greener."

Abby thought about that for a moment. "I keep going back to what she said in the note. She'd fallen deeply in love. The kind of love that happens once in a lifetime. If her feelings for this man were so strong and so consuming that she was willing to leave her family and business for him, how did she manage to keep the relationship secret? Someone must have seen them together. Surely over time she would have let something slip to James. Did you know that she was seeing someone behind his back?"

"No, but it didn't surprise me," her grandmother said. "After all, James was married when they first met. He left his first wife for Eva. Although according to her, the marriage was already over. She just provided an easy way out for both of them."

Abby winced at her mother's justification for breaking up a marriage. It seemed she could rationalize almost anything so long as she ended up with what she wanted. "That divorce goes a long way in explaining Lydia's attitude," Abby said. "She could be rude, even savage at times. I often wondered why she left her mother to come live with us when she seemed to resent everything about her father's new marriage."

Her grandmother made a look of disdain. "One could sympathize if she hadn't been such a wretched young woman."

"Maybe she had reason to be."

Her grandmother bristled at the suggestion. "No one has a right to be that unpleasant. I really don't think James would have hurt Eva, no matter what he found out about her. He was that much in love with her. But I can't say the same for his daughter. You asked why Lydia left her mother. Maybe she had no choice. Maybe her mother was as exhausted and disgusted by her attitude as the rest of us."

"Grandmother." The rebuke was only half-hearted.

Her chin lifted. "It's true and you know it. A very odd duck, that one. If you ask me, she was far too involved in her father's personal life. Protective and possessive to an unhealthy degree. And such deplorable manners." She tsk-tsked with an exaggerated shudder. "You're right about her feelings for Eva. She made no bones about how deeply she despised my daughter."

"Resented, yes, but *despised* might be a bit strong," Abby said.

"Not strong enough if some of the things Eva claimed were true. I don't know why she put up with her. I would have sent her packing, but Eva thrived on chaos. I sometimes think she egged it on."

"Lydia didn't need much encouragement," Abby murmured.

"She had a huge chip on her shoulder," her grandmother agreed. "But despite all that, I notice she's had no problem living in Eva's house all these years, and she's burrowed herself like a tick in the business. When you think about it, she's basically taken over Eva's life. Now doesn't that just make you wonder?"

Abby had started to wonder about a lot of things since Wade's visit to her that morning. So many questions churned in her head. A part of her wanted to crawl in bed and pull the covers over her head while another side wanted to drive back to Shutter Lake that very night so that she could start digging for the truth.

"You don't seriously think Lydia would have hurt Mother, do you?"

"Someone did."

"I know but—"

"People do all sorts of despicable things for all kinds of reasons," Lillian insisted. "I'm telling you, there was something seriously wrong with that woman. The more I think about it, the more convinced I am that she was somehow involved in Eva's death."

Abby glanced at her grandmother in alarm. Her jaw was rigid, her cheeks bright pink with anger. "We don't know anything yet. It's best not to jump to conclusions. In fact, maybe we shouldn't talk about this anymore. You're upset, and the last thing I want to do is make things harder for you."

"I disagree. I think it's important that we get everything out in the open. We both have questions. We both want to know what happened. It's normal to speculate. How can we not, knowing what we now know?"

"As long as the speculation doesn't leave this room," Abby cautioned.

"Oh, don't worry. I'm not about to confront Lydia McRae, no matter how much I'd like to shake the truth out of her.

I'll leave her to the police if that's where the evidence takes them. This conversation is just for you and me."

Abby nodded. "That's the way it has to stay for now. At the very least, we need to give the police time to make the notifications."

Her grandmother gave her a sidelong look. "And yet here you are telling me everything. Am I supposed to feign ignorance when they call?"

"I trust you'll know how to handle the situation," Abby said. "But as long as we're playing armchair detectives..."

She leaned forward, seemingly keen to continue. "Yes, go on."

Abby hesitated. "Are you sure you want to talk about this? I don't want to upset you any more than I already have."

"Of course, I'm sure," she said in an irritated tone. "I know you mean well, Abigail, but I'm not some fragile old woman you need to protect. My mind is as sharp as ever. Besides, talking things through is far better than brooding alone in my room for the rest of the evening."

"For me, too," Abby agreed. "The thing I keep coming back to is the money. Why do you suppose she withdrew all that cash before she left? She'd already transferred enough funds into her private accounts to live on indefinitely. Why did she need the cash? Blackmail? Bribery? Was she in some kind of trouble? I find myself coming up with all these disturbing scenarios. I can't help wondering if she had a lover at all. Maybe she needed to disappear and concocted a story that she knew would keep us from coming after her."

"Anything's possible, I suppose." Her grandmother fingered the intricate embroidery at her neckline. "Other than her clashes with Lydia, she never said anything to me about trouble at work or in her personal life, but then she wouldn't. I was never her confidante. Not about serious matters."

"I don't think anyone was. For as long as I can remember, Mother was secretive and distant. In some ways cold. She kept things close to her chest."

"All by design," her grandmother fretted. "From a very early age, she purposely cultivated an air of mystery. She never wanted anyone to know the real Eva. Not even me."

"Or me. But I do know one thing. Neither of us will have any peace until we find out who killed her."

Her grandmother's voice sharpened. "I don't like the sound of that, Abigail. Remember what you told me about keeping the speculation to ourselves. You need to heed your own advice. I don't want you getting involved in anything dangerous. Let the police do their job while you keep a safe distance. The more I think about it, the more prudent I believe it would be for you to stay here with me until everything is resolved. I couldn't bear it if anything were to happen to you. Promise me you won't do anything rash."

Abby mustered a wry smile. "Grandmother, when have you ever known me to do anything rash? I always think through everything to death before I act. Please don't worry. I won't do anything risky or foolish, but someone needs to be there to keep the police on their toes. A case this old has a tendency to get pushed to the wayside. I won't let that happen."

Lillian sighed. "I know that look. You've already made up your mind."

"I have to go back. It's not just a matter of keeping the police honest. Someone needs to be there when…" *They bring her up.* Abby suppressed a shiver at the image. "In case they need a DNA sample."

"I can see we're not going to agree on this, but I'll let the matter rest for the night. We can talk more in the morning. Sunshine always brings a clearer perspective."

Not about murder, Abby thought.

FOR THE REST of the evening, they talked about other things—Abby's job, her grandmother's charity work, the garden club, how downtown traffic had become an absolute nightmare. Mindless topics to take their minds off what lay beneath Shutter Lake. When they got hungry, Abby ordered dinner and her grandmother opened a bottle of wine. They sat at the big dining room table and ate takeout by candle-light. Afterward, her grandmother went off for a soak in the tub while Abby cleared the table and locked up.

When she finally crawled into bed and dozed off, she had the strangest nightmare. She could see herself swim-ming underwater among tall steel girders and mountains of broken concrete only to discover her mother sitting on the hood of her Rolls Royce, smiling in that enigmatic way she had as she beckoned Abby to join her. But Abby couldn't move. All of a sudden, she found herself trapped inside the car and running out of air as she pounded on the window, desperate to get her mother's attention.

She woke up gasping for breath and clutching the covers, her frantic gaze darting about in the dark for a landmark. Then everything came back to her. She was in her old bed-room in her grandmother's house in Atlanta. She'd come here to tell her about Wade's discovery.

The familiarity of her surroundings did little to calm her racing heart. Panic had set in, and she couldn't seem to talk herself down. For the first time since Wade had shown up at the cottage, she felt truly afraid. Not just an uneasy prickle, but the kind of paralyzing terror that made her want to cower under the covers until daylight.

Someone had murdered her mother in a cruel and deliberate way. The method and timing took planning. No crime of passion, no momentary loss of control. Eva had been lured out to the old bridge and caught unaware by someone she knew and trusted. Someone for whom she had no fear.

Maybe Wade was right. Maybe Abby's inheritance had already made her a target, too.

The longer she lay in the dark with that creeping fear, the more convinced she became that something was amiss in the house.

As quietly as she could, she threw off the covers and swung her legs over the side of the bed, sitting on the edge for a moment as she searched every shadowy corner of that moonlit room. The balcony doors were closed to the night. She'd double-checked the lock before getting into bed, but she'd left the curtains open so that she didn't feel quite so claustrophobic.

Unlocking the doors, she stepped onto the balcony, her gaze lifting to the night sky before dropping to the garden below. The night was warm and balmy with only a mild breeze to stir the leaves. Nothing moved that she could detect. No barking dogs to alert the neighborhood of a prowler, no stealthy shadows slipping through the lush foliage. And yet she couldn't shake the feeling that something was very wrong.

She went back inside, locked the doors behind her and then padded across the thick rug to the hallway door. Poking her head out, she glanced both ways before leaving the safety of her room. Moonlight streamed in through the large window over the stairwell. She could see her way well enough without turning on any lights, which was good. She didn't want to alarm or disturb her grandmother in the middle of the night.

Easing down the curving stairway, she winced as the risers creaked beneath her bare feet. She cut through the foyer to the hallway, bypassing the formal living and dining rooms until she stood in the doorway of the den where she and her grandmother had sat earlier. The room lay in shadows except for a puddle of moonlight that streamed across the flagstone terrace and leeched through the French doors. A silhouette stood at those doors peering into the house.

Abby reacted instinctively. In the split second before the figure moved, she grabbed a poker from the fireplace hearth. Then she realized the person was on the inside looking out. "Grandmother? It's after midnight. What are you doing up?"

"Shush."

Abby lowered her voice. "What's wrong?"

"Someone's out there."

Her grandmother sounded strangely calm, almost detached. Abby's fingers tightened around the brass handle of the poker. "You saw someone in the garden just now?"

She said in a harsh whisper, "Don't turn on the lights!"

Abby kept the poker at her side as she hurried across the room to join her grandmother. She put her other hand on her grandmother's arm. "Are you okay? Should I call the police?"

She didn't turn or react to Abby's touch. Her gaze remained fixed on the garden. "Don't do anything. Just be still and watch."

Abby wanted to know who or what she was watching for, but she did as she was told, staring out into the darkness as her heart pounded and her hand around the metal handle grew clammy. In the dead of night, her elegant grandmother seemed somehow diminished, a frail and frightened old woman. Abby wanted to put a protective arm around her shoulders, but she was afraid to make a move, let alone to touch her again. What if she was sleepwalking? That would account for her strange behavior. Abby had always heard it could be dangerous to awaken a sleepwalker abruptly.

"Shush."

The sharp rebuke startled Abby. She hadn't said anything. She'd hardly dared to even breathe.

"Can you see her?" her grandmother whispered.

"I don't see anyone," Abby whispered back. "If someone's in the garden, shouldn't we call the police?"

"The police would only frighten her away. Just be quiet. She'll come back. I know she will."

"Who?"

"My Eva."

A chill shot down Abby's backbone. "Grandmother, she's not out there. She can't be. You know that, right?"

"But I saw her."

"You only thought you did. Don't you remember what we talked about earlier?" Abby chose her words carefully and kept her voice tender. "Someone found Mother's car at the bottom of Shutter Lake yesterday morning."

Her grandmother turned, eyes glittering in the moonlight. "The sapphire Wraith?"

"Yes."

"She loved that car."

"I know she did."

"She would never have left it behind."

Her family, yes, but not her car.

Abby grew even more uneasy. Had her grandmother blocked their previous conversation from her mind? Would she have to break the news to her all over again?

"Grandmother, what do you remember about the discussion we had before dinner?"

She sighed. "I remember every word of it. Don't worry, child. I haven't lost my mind. I know it can't really be Eva. Not after all these years." She swayed and Abby gripped her arm to steady her.

"It's okay, Grandmother. I'm here. Everything will be okay," she soothed, although they both knew nothing would be okay for a very long time.

"I had a dream about her before I woke up," her grandmother told her. "I suppose I became confused because she seemed so vivid to me. As if she were right there in the room with me."

"I dreamed about her, too, Grandmother."

"She called me Mommy the way she did when she was a little girl. I wanted so badly for that dream to be real."

"I know."

She drew a shuddering breath. "She was such a precocious child. She knew how to wrap me around her little finger even back then. I would forgive her anything, even when she misbehaved." Her voice cracked with emotion. "Do you think she was trying to tell me something?"

"I think it was just a dream," Abby said.

"She's really dead, isn't she? My Eva is gone."

"I think so. I'm sorry, Grandmother."

She turned back to the window, pulling her robe even more tightly around her as she shivered. "Then who is out there in my garden?"

Chapter Six

Abby edged closer to the door to probe the terrace and the darkness beyond as she reached a hand to check the dead bolt. The doors were locked. She'd made sure all the exits were secure and had activated the security system before going up to bed. No one could get inside without their knowing. As for the intruder in the garden, her grandmother had probably glimpsed a bush or a tree branch swaying in the breeze. She'd already been upset from the dream and was still half dazed with grief. Her imagination had played tricks on her in the moonlight. She'd seen what she wanted to see.

But even as Abby moved away from the French doors, the sound of shattering glass stopped her dead in her tracks. She was almost afraid to turn around, but then she realized the breach had come from the front of the house, not behind her. A second later, the overwhelming blare of the security alarm threatened to wake the dead.

She and her grandmother stood frozen until Abby finally collected herself and said over the alarm, "Stay here and call 911."

"The security company will send the police."

"Call anyway, just to be certain."

Her grandmother grabbed her arm. "Where are you going?"

Abby clutched the poker. "Please, just make the call, Grandmother. And don't leave this room until I come back."

"Abigail, be careful."

The frightened missive followed her through the door and out into the hallway. Hugging the wall, she made her way past all the open rooms and into the foyer. Shards of glass lay glistening on the floor where one of the sidelights had shattered. She stepped gingerly through the sharp fragments to check the dead bolt. Still engaged, though she wouldn't have been surprised at that point to see an arm snake through the broken window to turn the lock. She waited, heart pounding, with her weapon at the ready. When no further assault was forthcoming, she entered the code to turn off the alarm and then turned to scan the foyer. Something rested on the floor just beneath the console table.

She bent and rolled the rock toward her with the end of the poker. A piece of paper had been folded into a neat square and taped to the side. A blunt way to get someone's attention, Abby thought. The delivery method almost seemed to be a statement, as if the brashness of the vandalism was a clue.

Abby knew better than to handle the evidence. Common sense told her to remain calm and wait for the police. *Don't do anything hasty.* The rock and the note would need to be dusted for prints, but she ignored her better instincts. She picked up the stone, testing the weight in her palm before carefully removing the paper. Inside the folds, someone had scrawled two words in angry red marker: STAY AWAY.

"What's that?"

She jumped at the sound of her grandmother's voice from the doorway. Slipping the note in the pocket of her robe, she turned with the rock still in her hand. "Someone threw this through the side window." When her grandmother started toward her, she cried, "Stop! Stay where you are, Grandmother. There's broken glass all over the floor. The pieces are sharp enough to cut right through your slippers."

"What about you?"

"I had to check the door to make sure it was still locked, but I'm trying to be careful."

Her grandmother pointed to the rock. "Should you have picked that up?"

"I...wasn't thinking clearly." She bent and placed the stone on the floor where she'd found it. "The police should still be able to pull prints if any were there to begin with."

"Abigail!"

She started guiltily. "Yes, Grandmother?"

"Why would someone throw a rock through my window? I've always felt perfectly safe here."

"No place is perfectly safe," Abby said.

Her grandmother hugged her arms around her body. "Did you phone the police?"

"Yes."

Abby picked her way through the glass and put an arm around her grandmother's shoulders. "Go back to the den while I check the rest of the house. I want to make sure there's no other damage."

"Can't the police do that?"

"Yes, but it'll give me something to do while we wait. I won't be long, I promise."

When she'd seen her grandmother safely back to the den, Abby made the rounds through all the rooms. By the time she returned to the foyer, she barely had time to glance at the note a second time before a patrol car pulled to the curb, flashing blue lights reflecting ominously off the jagged fragments scattered across the floor.

She spent the next several minutes giving her statement

to the two young officers who had responded to the 911 call. She didn't mention the note, let alone remove it from her pocket and hand it over to them. She wasn't sure why. At that point, she hadn't had a chance to think it through yet. She told herself she wanted to protect her grandmother. The shock of the broken window coming as it had on the heels of Abby's terrible news had shaken her to the core. It was one thing to believe her house had been randomly violated by malicious vandals, quite another to discover her sanctuary had been deliberately targeted, perhaps by her daughter's killer. She was already anxious about Abby's return to the lake. Why distress her further by revealing the note?

The rationalization came a little too easy. Maybe she was her mother's daughter after all, Abby thought. And now she took her justification a step farther. What would happen to the note if she turned it over to the police? They would log it into evidence and then toss it into a secure locker never to be seen again. Wouldn't it be more useful to take the note back to Fairhope and compare the scrawl to handwriting samples she could pull from the files at her mother's company? She didn't know much about handwriting analysis, but luckily, she knew an investigator who could probably point her in the right direction.

The notion of working alongside Wade Easton to solve her mother's murder was as disconcerting as it was stimulating. She had no wish to revisit an old romance, but like it or not, she and Wade had unfinished business. Even after all these years, the way their relationship had ended still stung. What better way to put those old feelings to rest once and for all than a daily reminder of his dishonesty?

She wasn't at all sure he would agree to such an arrangement, but he owed her. And if he resisted, well, she could be persuasive in her own right.

AFTER THE POLICE LEFT, Abby found a board in the basement and hammered up a makeshift barricade until she could call her grandmother's handyman first thing in the morning and have the glass replaced. Once again, she and Lillian said good-night, but Abby doubted either of them would get a wink of sleep after all the havoc. She tossed and turned as doubts and suspicions plagued her. Maybe her grandmother was right. Maybe she should stay in Atlanta until the police found her mother's killer.

But resolve returned with the sunrise. She saw to the window repair and even managed to persuade her grandmother to spend a few days in Savannah with her sister, Abby's great aunt. Abby purchased the ticket, drove her to the airport and arranged for a cousin to pick her grandmother up on the other end.

Satisfied that she'd done everything she could to keep her grandmother safe, she headed back to the lake, arriving in Fairhope at four in the afternoon. Instead of driving straight out to the cottage, she stopped by the house in town. The police had had plenty of time to alert her stepfather about her mother, but Wade seemed to think notifications might be delayed until the medical examiner could make a positive identification. Sooner or later, word would get out, but if James and Lydia remained in the dark, then this might be Abby's only opportunity to ask a few subtle questions before their guards went up.

She parked at the curb rather than pulling into the driveway so that she could sit for a moment and contemplate how to go about a covert interview. She worried that her expression or a slip of the tongue might give her away, but she had one thing going for her. If neither James nor Lydia knew about Eva, then they had no reason to suspect Abby's motives.

Again, the justification for her duplicity came a little too easy. Everything that had transpired since her arrival in Fairhope had led her to this point. She now knew her mother had been murdered. Handcuffed to the wheel of the car she'd loved so much before the vehicle had been pushed off the bridge. The scene unfolded in her head, and she found herself gripping the wheel of her own car as her mind drifted back to the final conversation with her mother. And even farther back to their last argument over her relationship with Wade.

I have nothing against the young man, but he's not the right sort for you.

Not the right sort? Do you have any idea how offensive that sounds?

You know what I mean. He's small-town. Conventional. From what I can tell, he lacks ambition.

We're small-town, Mother.

It's not the same thing and you know it. If you tie yourself to someone like Wade Easton, you'll never realize your full potential. In time you'll grow bored of him. You'll come to resent him for holding you back.

Is that the voice of experience?

Her mother had left the room without answering.

A few days later, Abby had awakened to find a note on her dresser with her name scrawled across the envelope in her mother's handwriting.

Abby shook off the memory as she became aware of a dark gray sedan facing toward her on the opposite side of the street. The vehicle was nondescript with no markers or adornments, and the windows were lightly tinted. Even so, she could have sworn the person behind the wheel was staring straight at her. A tingle of alarm shot through her. Was someone watching the house, or had she been followed all the way back from Atlanta?

She lifted her phone and snapped a photo of the car before she got out and crossed the street. Pausing on the sidewalk, she gave the sedan a hard scrutiny before she walked through the brick pillars on either side of the walkway. She could barely see the driver through the glare of sunlight on the windshield, but she made a mental note of her initial impression. Short hair, glasses, slender build. And he seemed to be watching the house or her or both.

Probably nothing. Just someone visiting next door.

Abby tried to put him out of her head as she started up the steps to the veranda, but too much had happened for her to completely dismiss a stranger. She glanced over her shoulder. He was still there. Still watching.

For a moment, she thought about going back out to the street and confronting him. Rap on the glass until he lowered his window and then demand that he state his name and business. She didn't, of course. Discretion was not only advised but also necessary.

She turned back to the house, the scent of jasmine nearly overpowering in the late-afternoon heat. Closing her eyes, she took a deep breath as memories once again assailed her. She and her mother had moved into this house when Abby was ten. It had been just the two of them until one weekend after her fifteenth birthday when her mother had come back from a business trip. She'd sat Abby down and told her that she and James McRae had eloped. He and his nineteen-year-old daughter, Lydia, would be living with them from now on.

James had moved in first, and Abby still remembered her first impression of him—a tall handsome man with vivid blue eyes and an easy smile. She'd liked him from the start.

Her own dad had died when she was a baby, so she had no lingering feelings of resentment, no comparisons or a secret hope that her parents would someday get back together.

The few months that the three of them had lived together had been congenial and surprisingly fun. Abby had enjoyed James's quiet sense of humor. He was like a soothing balm to her mother's sometimes frenetic energy. When Lydia came, it was as if someone had thrown a live grenade into the house.

The day she moved in, she brought two suitcases and a boatload of drama and resentment. She didn't like her room or anything about the house, the street, the neighbors. She especially didn't like her new family and never wasted a chance to let Abby know just how galling she found the fifteen-year-old. Everyone had breathed a sigh of relief when she returned to college in the fall, though no one would admit it. The house once again became quiet and peaceful except on the occasional weekend when Lydia came for a visit. Abby could put up with her stepsister's surliness in small doses. She just learned to avoid her. Everything changed after Eva disappeared. Lydia transferred to a local school, moved back into the house and took charge. No one tried to stop her, least of all Abby. Maybe in time, she would have mustered enough gumption to push back, but once Wade was no longer in the picture, she found it easier to live with her grandmother and let Lydia have free rein over the house and later the business.

Hardening her resolve, Abby started up the steps. Her stepfather was seated on one of the cushioned chairs, eyes closed, head reclined against the back. She could see the hint of a five-o'clock shadow on his lower face, and his hair was a bit unkempt, but he was fully dressed in khakis and a white pullover shirt. Not the same dapper man from the early days, but that was understandable given the circumstances. Overall, he looked much better than Abby had expected.

He appeared to be sleeping, but his eyes flew open when a floorboard creaked beneath her feet.

Squinting into the sun behind her, he said hesitantly, "Abby?"

She winced. "I'm so sorry. I didn't realize you were napping until I'd already started up the steps."

He sat up straighter and motioned for her to join him. "I wasn't asleep. Just enjoying a little fresh air. It's actually quite pleasant underneath the ceiling fans. Come sit with me."

"I don't want to intrude. You need your rest."

"Nonsense. All I've been doing is resting. Please, sit with me. I'd love the company. I've been holed up in the hospital and now this house for far too long."

She tried to analyze his expression and tone as he shuffled aside a book on the round table next to his chair. He seemed calm and genuinely happy to see her. She could only take that to mean the police had yet to pay him a visit. He didn't know about Eva.

He smiled as she took a chair on the other side of the table. "I never got the chance to thank you for the lovely flowers you had sent to my room. I'm not much of a gardener, but I've always been partial to freesias."

"I know. You told me once your mother grew them outside your bedroom window when you were a boy."

His brows shot up. "You remember that?" He looked pleased.

"I'm sorry I didn't come see you in the hospital. I was told you weren't allowed visitors."

"Yes, they're very strict about that sort of thing these days. No matter. You're here now."

Keeping the secret of her mother's death was harder than she thought it would be. James had doted on Eva. By every indication, he'd been deeply in love with her. She didn't feel right withholding information of that magnitude. But then she reminded herself that the spouse was always a suspect. Maybe James had known all along her mother was dead, and he'd had ten long years to learn how to hide his guilt.

She tried to imagine him in a life-and-death struggle with her mother, watching stone-faced from the bridge as her car sank to the bottom of the lake.

"Abby? Are you okay?"

She jumped slightly at the sound of his voice and then looked around uneasily. "I was hoping to find Lydia at home. I wanted to talk to her about a couple of the reports she emailed to me."

He seemed to observe her as carefully as she studied him. "She's inside somewhere. Should I go look for her?"

"No, never mind. The questions can wait until tomorrow. Let's just have a nice visit." She settled back in her chair. "I must say, you're looking even better than I'd hoped."

"You're lucky you didn't see me a few days ago." His smile turned into a grimace. "I'm told I looked only slightly less dead than a corpse."

"You've had a rough time of it," she said. "But your color is coming back now, and you look rested. Lydia said the doctors are pleased with your progress."

"So they tell me. I should be back to work in a matter of weeks. In the meantime, I appreciate you coming down here to lend a hand. Lydia would never admit it, but she's overwhelmed. Summers are always busy, but this year has been especially chaotic, what with all the renovations we've undertaken. We put off what we could until the end of the busy season, but some things like plumbing and roof repairs just can't wait until fall. Your willingness to pitch in is a lifesaver."

"I'm happy to do whatever I can to ease the pressure."

He nodded. "You've always been a hard worker, and you've done well for yourself. That you'd take a leave from your own career to help us out means the world to me."

Well, it's still technically my mother's company. Why wouldn't I help? She merely nodded. "It's not a big deal. I have a lot of vacation time coming." She tucked back her hair and lifted her face to the breeze. "You're right. It's pleasant out here under the fans."

"How about a glass of lemonade? There's a pitcher in the kitchen, freshly squeezed. Hard to beat on a hot summer day."

He started to get up, but Abby said, "Sit tight. I'll get it. That is, if you don't mind me wandering around the house."

"It's your house, too," he said.

"In that case, two lemonades, coming up."

Abby got up and let herself in through the front door. She stood in the foyer for a moment, casting a curious gaze over the interior. Her first thought was that she might be able to find samples of handwriting that she could compare to the warning note. Her second impression was that the house had undergone a number of changes since she moved out ten years ago. She'd been back for a few brief visits but had never noticed until now just how extensive the transformation was. Different flooring, different paint, different furniture. Even the artwork had been swapped out, including a portrait of her that had once hung at the top of the stairs. Nothing of her mother's taste remained. Every trace had been relegated to a storage unit or the trash bin. Fair enough. She supposed it was only natural that James and Lydia would want to make the place their own.

For a moment, she was tempted to go up and have a look inside her old room. Not that she expected to find any of her mementos. Lydia had always coveted the front bedroom. She probably hadn't waited a full day after Abby left to move her stuff down the hallway.

Sunlight glistening off the edge of a gold frame drew her attention to a marble console table. She moved across the foyer and picked up the photograph. Apparently, not everything from the past had been banished. That a picture of her mother had been allowed to remain on display in such a prominent location shocked Abby. She stared down at her mother's face, remembering events and conversations that had taken place in the house, remembering the good times as well as the bad. Eva had been a complicated, secretive woman. Sometimes kind, rarely affectionate and always calculating.

"He won't allow me to put that one away," a voice said from the top of the stairs.

Abby glanced up as her stepsister came down a few steps and paused. She wore jeans, sandals and a simple cotton shirt, but even in her casual attire, she projected an air of formality and aloofness that seemed deliberately off-putting. Her dark hair was cut and styled in the same precision bob she'd worn for years, and her makeup was subtle and expertly applied. At thirty-three, she'd matured into a very attractive woman, but the hardness in her expression and a hint of cruelty in her eyes dampened features that might otherwise have been considered beautiful.

"I'm surprised to see it here," Abby admitted.

"Dad's sentimental that way. Despite what she did to him."

Abby ignored the goading remark. "Maybe he just views it as a piece of art. It's an incredible shot. Glamorous yet candid. When I was little, I thought Mother looked like a movie star in this picture."

Her stepsister's smile was cool and contemptuous. "I'm sure she thought so, too." She noted Abby's disapproving scowl and shrugged. "Eva was a vain woman. I don't have to tell you that."

Abby pounced before she could stop herself. "Was?"

Something dark and unpleasant glimmered in Lydia's eyes. "Wherever she is, she's older now. Age has a harsh way of crushing a person's vanity." Her gaze dropped to the photo on the console table. "I have no idea why he insists on keeping a shrine to her after all these years. What she did to him was unforgivable."

"Maybe we don't know the whole story," Abby said. "And I'd hardly call one photograph a shrine."

"Take a closer look. The matchbook in the bowl is from the restaurant where he proposed. The candle is her favorite scent. Need I go on? He adored that awful woman, though for the life of me, I've never understood why."

Her scorn rankled, particularly considering the circumstances. "That woman was my mother," Abby felt compelled to remind her.

"Was?"

Too late, Abby realized she'd fallen into a trap. She shrugged and muttered, "You know what I mean."

"I'm surprised you still feel the need to defend her, considering she discarded you as easily as she would last year's wardrobe."

No, she didn't. She was murdered. She may have planned to run away with her secret lover, but in time, she would have come back for me.

At least, it was comforting to think so.

"My mother is a topic you and I should probably avoid," Abby said.

"I would happily do so, but you're coming back here has not only stirred up a lot of bad memories, it's also raised questions. If we're going to work together for the next few weeks, we should clear the air once and for all. Stepsister to stepsister." As Lydia descended slowly, her derisive expression reminded Abby of the warning note thrown through her grandmother's window just the night before. *STAY AWAY.*

"What is it you think we need to clear up?" Abby asked.

Lydia paused at the bottom of the stairs, hand resting on the banister. "For one thing, you should know none of this was my idea."

"You mean my coming here? I would have been shocked to learn otherwise."

"My father is loyal to a fault. I'm not as forgiving. When you moved to Atlanta to live with your grandmother, you left him to salvage the business. It wasn't as easy as he made it look. There were a lot of challenges to overcome. Sacrifices had to be made. You were oblivious to all of it."

"I was seventeen years old," Abby said. "I was hardly in a position to run my own life, let alone a business. Besides, my mother left explicit instructions. She wanted James to have a place in the company for as long as he wanted one."

"Yes, and in catering to her wishes, he made sure you were well taken care of, sometimes at the expense of everyone else. The company would have gone under years ago if not for his hard work. His and mine." Her eyes flashed. "All you've had to do is collect a check at the end of every year."

"I didn't make the arrangements, and no one has forced you to stay. But—" Abby took a breath and managed a conciliatory tone "—you and James have done a wonderful job. I do appreciate everything you've done to keep the business afloat. The very least I can do is help out while he recuperates."

Her stepsister moved into the foyer, brushing her fingers across the top of the console as if checking for dust. Or was she asserting her position in the household? "We're clearing the air, remember? All of this would go a lot easier if you'd just admit the real reason you're here."

"I thought I just did."

Lydia turned with a frown. "We both know what's really going on here. You're using Dad's illness as an excuse to insinuate yourself into the company. I'm not as trusting as he is. I knew it was only a matter of time once the company started to flourish that you'd decide to take advantage of our hard work."

"I don't need to insinuate myself anywhere," Abby said. "It's still my mother's company. But you must know by now that I have no interesting in taking over her business. I have a career. I'm happy in Atlanta."

"Would you be willing to put that in writing?"

"It already is. You have a contract, don't you?"

Lydia's mouth thinned. "Yes, and thank you for reminding me that I'm the hired help."

Abby suppressed an eye roll. "That's not how I meant it, and you know it."

"Perhaps not intentionally, but subconsciously, I think that's exactly how you meant it." Lydia picked up the photograph of Abby's mother and placed it face down on the table. "I remember the first time I stepped foot in this house. You and Eva let me know in a million subtle and not so subtle ways that I didn't belong here."

"That's not true."

"It is true." She walked her fingers across the back of Eva's photo.

Abby suppressed a shiver. She wasn't exactly afraid, but she was so unnerved by the look on Lydia's face that she found herself taking an involuntary step back. "It wasn't all one-sided," she said. "You never failed to let us know how much you hated it here. How much you hated us."

"How was I supposed to react? Just meekly accept whatever crumbs of civility you and Eva decided to toss my way? I had no choice but to defend myself. My dad was so enamored with you both that he didn't even notice his only daughter was being treated like an unwelcome guest in this house. It was three against one. Then Eva left and everything changed." An inscrutable smile played at the corners of her lips. "Dad and I still had each other, but you, the pampered princess, suddenly became the odd man out."

Chapter Seven

Abby was still a little shaken by the conversation, but she managed a smile and what she hoped was a pleasant demeanor as she carried the lemonade out to the veranda.

"I thought I heard voices inside," James remarked as he picked up his drink. "Did you find Lydia?"

"Yes, I saw her briefly in the foyer. She went back upstairs to make some phone calls."

"Was she able to answer your questions?"

"Uh, yeah. More or less." *She may even have revealed more than she meant to, in fact.*

James smiled. "You can also come to me if you have questions. I know Lydia can be a little prickly at times, but she's an invaluable asset to the company."

"I'm sure she is."

He leaned across the table and said in a low voice, "Can I make a confession?"

Abby nodded. "Of course."

"You've always resembled your mother, but earlier when I saw you at the top of the steps with the sun shining behind you, I thought at first I was seeing a ghost."

"I didn't mean to startle you."

"It was a fleeting impression," he said. "And I meant

what I just said as a compliment. Your mother was a very beautiful woman."

Abby was silent for a moment. "I can't help noticing how fondly you still speak of her. You don't seem to have the slightest trace of resentment or regret about what happened. How do you do that? You must feel at least a little bitterness for what she did." She watched him closely as she anticipated his answer.

He sat back in his chair with a sigh. "I did at first. I won't lie and say it was easy. It wasn't. But life is short. I made peace with the past a long time ago."

"Then you're a bigger person than I," Abby said candidly. "Her abandonment still affects some of my choices to this day. I don't know that I'll ever fully make peace with what happened." She picked up her glass but didn't sip. "You never considered divorcing her? You certainly had grounds."

"Divorce by default isn't always as easy as filling out paperwork or running a notice of intent in the local paper. There are a lot of steps to be taken and consequences to be considered. Besides, a part of me hoped for the longest time that she'd tire of her adventure and come back home. After a while, it ceased to be an issue."

"You never wanted to remarry?"

"Twice is enough for me, and anyway, Eva would be a hard act to follow."

"In more ways than one," Abby muttered. She glanced up. "I'm sorry. This is probably an upsetting conversation for you. Being back here has stirred up a lot of memories for me, but that's no excuse to invade your privacy."

"You're not upsetting me. I don't mind talking about Eva. In many ways, she was a remarkable woman. I understand your curiosity about her. You can ask me anything."

"Did you know she was seeing someone else?"

"I knew things weren't right between us." He shrugged. "The signs were there, I guess, but I didn't want to believe it."

"Did you ever find out who he was?"

"At one time, I thought I knew, but my assumption has been proven wrong."

She wanted to ask him to elaborate, but Lydia came out on the porch just then, and they both fell silent. Abby had a feeling she'd been listening in at the door and decided the conversation had gone on long enough.

"It's time for your medication, Dad."

"I'll come inside in a minute," he said. "Abby and I are having a nice visit."

Abby rose. "No, that's okay. You go do what you need to do. I'll come back another day."

He smiled. "Is that a promise?"

"Yes." To Lydia she said, "I'll see you at the office in the morning."

"Not tomorrow you won't. I'll be out of town for a couple of days." Her earlier animosity had either evaporated or—a more likely explanation—she'd put on a mask for her dad's benefit. She turned to him. "Remember, I told you that I have to be in Mobile first thing in the morning. Unfortunately, I'm also scheduled to meet our general contractor at the Moon Bay property on Tuesday. I hate to cancel, considering how overbooked he is and how much time has already been wasted, but I'm worried I won't make it back in time."

"That's an easy fix," James said. "Let Abby meet with the general contractor— Oh, for heaven's sake, Liddie," he said in exasperation when she balked. "You said it yourself. We need to get moving on those repairs. The season is almost over."

"I'm happy to help out in any way I can," Abby put in.

Lydia still wasn't convinced. "Are you familiar with the Moon Bay property?"

"I haven't been out there in years, but I know where it is."

James rose. "Lydia can tell you exactly what needs to be done."

She pursed her lips as she turned to Abby. "I'll need a guarantee that you won't let him talk you into unnecessary repairs or add-ons. And for God's sake, don't sign anything until I get back."

Abby nodded. "Got it. Do you have a list already drawn up?"

"I'll finalize the details tonight. I'm getting on the road early, so I won't be going into the office. I'll leave the paperwork and a key to the property here at the house. You can drop by tomorrow and pick it up. But don't come by too early. Dad needs his rest."

Abby glanced at James. "What time is good for you?"

"Any time after nine is perfect." To his daughter he said, "Stop fretting. Abby knows what she's doing."

"Just don't—"

"Sign anything," Abby said. "Got it." She smiled at James. "I guess I'll see you in the morning."

When she reached the end of the walkway, two things stopped her. She could feel a gaze on her back and turned to find both Lydia and James watching her from the veranda. Out on the street, the mystery man also tracked her from the gray sedan. Abby hurried to her vehicle, wondering again about his identity and intent.

TWENTY MINUTES LATER, she was back at the cottage. She'd called Wade from the road and asked him to meet her there. Letting herself in the front door, she dropped her bag on the floor and then crossed the room to glance out the back windows. She'd suggested he wait for her on the terrace, but he was nowhere to be seen. Was he running late, or had he decided to stand her up?

Annoyed and disappointed, she went outside and glanced down at the water. He was stretched out on the dock, an arm slung across his face, legs dangling over the side. For a moment, Abby was taken straight back to their high school years, back to those lazy summer days when she and Wade would spend hours on the water or lying in the sun, fingers entwined as they soaked up the heat.

She allowed herself the indulgence of those memories for only a moment before she started down the steps toward him. Halfway down, she paused to call out to him. He sat up and stretched, then threw her a lazy wave as he grabbed his shirt and got to his feet.

Their gazes met and held for the briefest moment before he pulled on the shirt, but the brief interlude was enough to flutter her stomach and stand her nerves on end. She took a breath and then another as he left the dock and started up the steps toward her. She waited for him to emerge from the oleanders and banana leaves before she spoke again.

"Thanks for coming."

He halted a few steps down and gazed up at her. He wore shorts and flip-flops, and his faded T-shirt had seen better days. If Abby didn't know better, she'd think he was one of the thirtysomething partiers who hit the lake every weekend, but she did know better. She'd done an internet search before leaving Atlanta. Wade Easton had grown himself quite a successful business.

"You sounded anxious on the phone." He moved up another few steps, his dark gaze raking over her. "Everything okay?"

Her hand curled around the guardrail. "I'm not sure.

There was an incident at my grandmother's house last night. I don't know what to make of it."

"What happened?"

She swept her gaze over the lake. "Let's go up to the terrace first. We can sit in the shade while we talk."

Without another word, she turned and headed up the steps, glancing over her shoulder as she moved onto the flagstones. "Can I get you anything to drink? Water, tea… I think there may be a couple of beers in the fridge."

"Ice water sounds good if it's not too much trouble. It was pretty hot down on that dock."

Well, you were lying shirtless in the sun. "No trouble at all." She went back inside and filled two glasses from the ice and water dispensers in the refrigerator door. When she came back out, Wade had taken a seat at the wrought iron table. She placed a glass in front of him and took a seat opposite him.

Instead of taking a thirsty drink, he wrapped both hands around the glass and ran his thumbs up and down the sides. "So, what happened last night?"

"Someone threw a rock through one of Grandmother's windows. It set off the alarm and the police came."

His thumbs stilled. "Was anyone hurt?"

"No, we're both fine, but my grandmother was pretty shaken up. We both were, to be honest. I'll get back to the broken window in a minute, but something odd happened earlier, just before the alarm went off. I woke up with a very strong sense that something was wrong in the house." She paused trying to figure out how to describe the sensation. "You know how it is when you return from a trip, and you get a strange feeling that someone has been in your place? Like the air has been disturbed or something? It was that kind of impression. Nothing tangible, just an inexplicable uneasiness. When I got up to check the house, I found my grandmother standing in front of the French doors that lead out to the back terrace. She said someone was in the garden."

"Could she tell who it was?"

"She said it was Mother." She waited for his reaction, but his expression never wavered. "Did you hear what I said?"

"I'm processing. Could she have been sleepwalking?"

"I wondered the same thing. She was acting very weird, but she seemed lucid. She said she had a dream about my mother before she woke up, and I'm sure she was still upset from our earlier conversation. I think she saw what she wanted to see. The thing is, she probably did spot someone in the garden. It was only a few minutes later when the rock came crashing through the front window."

He frowned, but his tone remained impassive. "You think this person was watching the house?"

"Why else would someone be in the garden in the middle of the night? It would certainly explain my uneasiness."

"What did the police say?"

"They seemed to think it was bored kids getting the same kind of kick they get out of smashing mailboxes. You know how those things go. They asked a few questions, wrote up a report and had a look around the house. They bagged the rock, but I doubt they'll find any prints. To be fair, at that point there wasn't anything more they could do. The perpetrator was long gone by the time they arrived. I didn't think it a good idea for my grandmother to be alone in the house, so I put her on a plane to Savannah before I left the city."

"That's probably for the best," he agreed. "Have there been similar incidents in the neighborhood?"

"None that we know of, but I should probably tell you that the officers came to their conclusion without having all the facts."

"Meaning?"

She removed a baggie containing the note from her pocket and slid it across the table to him. "This was folded and taped to the rock."

He scanned the warning through the plastic protector. "Why didn't you give this to the police?"

"I had my reasons."

He glanced up in surprise, undoubtedly remembering her as the stickler for rules she'd once been. "I'd be very interested in hearing those reasons."

"I didn't want to frighten my grandmother. It seemed kinder to let her believe the act was random rather than targeted. Once I gave my abbreviated account to the police, I couldn't change my story without having to answer a lot of questions. I couldn't explain the note without telling them about my mother."

He scowled down at the paper. "A warning like this isn't something you'd normally want to keep from the police."

"I know, but the circumstances are extenuating." She reached over to retrieve the bagged note. "What could they actually do about it anyway, except check for prints and fibers? The likelihood of finding anything is pretty slim. Besides, we can do that ourselves."

That got his attention. "We?"

She hadn't meant to broach the subject of a partnership so flippantly. Better to find the right moment and then ease into the suggestion. Suddenly she wished for a good stiff drink rather than the ice water in her glass. She could be persuasive, but a little liquid courage sometimes helped. "I have something I'd like to run by you, but I'm not quite ready to discuss it yet."

"Now I think we have to discuss it."

"In due time."

He looked curious but didn't press. "Speaking of fingerprints, I don't need to point out that yours are likely all over the evidence."

"I took precautions. I put the note in a plastic bag as soon as I could, and I tried to handle only the edges of the paper. I know you think it was a mistake to conceal it from the police, but at least now I can compare it to handwriting samples at work."

"For a spur-of-the-moment decision, your rationalization seems pretty cogent." She couldn't tell from his tone if he was irritated or impressed. Maybe a little of both. "By handwriting samples at work, I assume you're referring to James and Lydia."

She nodded. "I can easily pull documents from the files without anyone knowing, but I may not have to. Lydia is giving me a list of things to go over with a general contractor tomorrow at one of the properties. If I'm lucky, she'll include a signed work order."

He stared across the table at her. "You're completely serious about this, aren't you?"

"Why wouldn't I be?"

"The police haven't even had a chance to launch an investigation yet, and here you are going full throttle."

"It's a ten-year-old cold case, Wade. That's the reality. After the novelty of your discovery wears off, the file will get shoved into the archives."

"You don't know that."

She felt a flicker of anger at his stubbornness. "Maybe I don't want to take that chance. I'm not suggesting I interrogate witnesses or search private property. All I need at the moment is a handwriting expert. Can you hook me up or not?"

"I know a guy."

"Thank you." Abby sat back in her chair and tried to relax.

Wade waited a beat before he continued. "What if one of the samples turns out to be a match? What will you do then?"

"I'll take it to the police. And contrary to what you're probably thinking, I'm not completely naive. I know a match is a long shot. At most, it's a process of elimination. James is on the mend, but I doubt he has the strength to drive all the way to Atlanta and throw a rock through my grandmother's window. As for Lydia—" Abby thought about the possibility for a moment "—she's certainly capable, and she's made it crystal clear she doesn't want me around, but throwing rocks isn't exactly her style. She's always been a bit more cunning."

Wade slid his glass aside and leaned an arm on the table. "Long shot or not, let's play this out for a minute. Say it was Lydia or James behind the warning. How would they know you'd be at your grandmother's house? How would anyone know for that matter?"

"I've wondered about that, too," Abby said. "You were the only one I talked to about my trip. I didn't even let Grandmother know I was coming. And I assume you didn't tell anyone, either."

He looked almost startled by the suggestion. His posture remained relaxed with an elbow propped on the table and his long legs sprawled in front of him, but Abby sensed tension where none had been there a moment ago. The shift made her wonder.

"I didn't mention to anyone you were going to Atlanta," he said. "But I did tell my dad about the car at the bottom of the lake." He glanced at her. "I know we agreed not to say anything until the notifications had been made, but he was the police chief back then. I thought he might have some useful insights."

"Did he?"

"Not so far, but something may come back to him." He fixed his brooding gaze on the water. Abby took a long moment to study his profile, reacquainting herself with features that were once as familiar to her as her own. She'd been obsessed with Wade Easton back in the day. The kind of intense infatuation that seemed exaggerated and ridiculous to her now, but back then, she'd been...what was the word her grandmother had used? *Besotted*.

She was a little embarrassed to remember some of those cringey moments and even more uncomfortable with the knowledge that she still found him extremely attractive.

He turned and caught her staring at him. Her face colored as she glanced away.

If he noticed her discomfort, he chose to ignore it. He continued as if their conversation had never been paused. "There is the possibility that the warning doesn't have anything to do with your mother's death. Maybe James or Lydia wants to scare you away from the business. Either or both could have hired someone to follow you. That's how they knew you were in Atlanta."

She pulled out her phone and scrolled to the image she'd snapped earlier. "This guy was parked at the curb when I went by to see James a little while ago. I had the distinct feeling he was watching me or the house or both."

Wade picked up the phone and enlarged the image. "Pretty sure that's Detective Benson. I spoke to him at the lake yesterday."

"A cop? Do you think he was there to tell James about Mother?"

"It's possible. It's more likely he had the house under surveillance."

"If that's the case, he was being pretty obvious about it."

Wade shrugged. "Maybe he wanted to rattle some cages."

"He certainly rattled mine," Abby said.

He handed her back the phone. "Did James or Lydia see him?"

"I don't think so."

"Did they behave as if they already knew about Eva?"

"No, I'm certain they didn't know. James was in a good mood, and he seemed genuinely pleased to see me."

"Maybe that's what he wants you to believe. What about Lydia?"

Abby winced. "Not so pleased. But I'd be even more suspicious if she welcomed me with open arms." She twirled her ponytail into a bun and tucked the ends into the elastic band. "Investigations are a lot harder than I would have imagined," she said. "So many possibilities with so little to go on."

He gave her a quick grin. "Yeah, but my work wouldn't be nearly as much fun if everyone could do it."

"This is fun for you?"

His amusement vanished. "Not this particular case. Especially not this particular victim."

"I keep coming back to what you said about the spouse being the most likely suspect. Grandmother said the same thing, but neither of us could actually picture James as a killer. Lydia, on the other hand, had the added incentive of hating my mother. She hated me, too, for that matter."

"All the more reason why you need to be careful how you get those handwriting samples. You think the investigation is hard now, just wait. Once you start taking files out of the office or asking too many questions of the wrong people, alarms are going to get tripped. You need to remember that at the heart of this case is a cold-blooded killer."

She ran a hand up and down her arm where goose bumps

suddenly prickled. "I know that. I'm not so naive as to think I can do this on my own. I work in real estate, for God's sake. Which is why I'd like to hire you to help me investigate."

"You want to hire me?" He looked at her as if she'd taken leave of her senses. Then he expelled a long breath. "Wow. That was unexpected."

She said awkwardly, "I know there's history between us. We didn't exactly part on the best of terms, but that was a long time ago. Who cares what happened in high school? Nothing matters to me more than bringing my mother's killer to justice. You're the one who found her car. You found her. Don't you have a vested interest in seeing this through?"

"It's a really bad idea," he said.

His resistance heaped humiliation on top of her embarrassment, but she pressed on. "Why?"

He sat up straighter as if preparing to flee. "I'm already working a case, and even if I weren't, I'm not that kind of investigator."

"Sometimes you are."

He lifted a brow. "How do you know that?"

"I went to your website," she said. "I even spoke with your assistant. She said you sometimes do private detective-type work for individuals if the money is right and the case or the client interests you."

"Did she also inform you of my rates?"

"She gave me a general idea. It's not a problem." Abby met his gaze without flinching. "I don't expect you to give me an answer on the spot. Take the night and think it over. We can talk again in the morning."

"I'm not saying I will, but if I did decide to take you on as a client, we'd need to establish some ground rules," he said. "No going rogue. No spur-of-the-moment decisions.

No putting yourself in dangerous situations. You'd need to run everything by me before you acted. We'd do it my way or not at all. Could you live with those conditions?"

She answered without hesitation. "Yes."

"You say that now, but it may not be as easy as you think. I can be bossy and not always very tactful. I'd advise you to take some time to think about what you may be getting yourself into."

"I have thought about it. I came to you because you're the expert," Abby said. "I have no problem deferring to your knowledge and experience. But you're right, we should both take the night to think it over." When he started to get up, she said quickly, "Before you go... I need to ask a favor."

He sat back down. "Should I be worried?"

"I guess it depends on your perspective. I want to see the spot where you found the car."

"Why?" He looked slightly disconcerted by the request. "You won't be able to see anything unless you dive forty feet down, and I really don't think you want to do that."

She sat quietly with hands folded in her lap. "It won't make any sense to anyone but me, but I feel compelled to see where her car went down. I think it's a little like visiting a grave. The physical space is all you have left, and you cling to the hope that somehow there's still a connection. It probably sounds silly and maybe a little macabre, but if you don't take me, I'll just go out there alone."

He sighed and rubbed the back of his neck. "It's not silly. I get why you want to go, but we're running out of daylight. The sun will be going down by the time we get out there. Wouldn't it be better to wait and see how you feel in the morning?"

"Tomorrow is Monday. The police will have had all week-end to arrange for the necessary equipment to bring up the car. By morning, it could be too late. She might not still be there."

He searched her face. "This is really what you want?"

"Yes. And contrary to how it may seem, I'm in full control of my faculties."

He thought about that for a minute. "You impulsively withheld evidence from the Atlanta police, and now for whatever reason, you seem to think the two of us can solve a ten-year-old murder on our own. Sure. Sounds perfectly logical to me."

Chapter Eight

Abby cast off the lines and hopped down into the boat as Wade started the engine and reversed from the dock. He turned the prow toward the lake, puttering along until they were out of the no-wake zone before he pushed the throttle forward and trimmed the prop for maximum acceleration. Abby had been sitting in the back, but she moved up beside him as they zoomed across the choppy water, putting her hand on top of the windshield to steady her balance.

He glanced over, taking note of her profile as she stared straight ahead, her expression hidden behind oversized sunglasses. Her hair had come loose from the bun and flew about her face like strands of bronze and gold silk. She wore no makeup, and she didn't need any, though he doubted she would believe him if he told her so. It seemed to Wade that she'd always compared herself to her mother and came up lacking. Eva Dallas McRae had been a beautiful woman, but Abby was Abby. No comparison in his book.

She turned her head at that exact moment and caught him staring. Instead of glancing away, he met her gaze straight on, letting his attraction flare in his eyes and in a slow, easy smile. "Just like old times," he said over the engine.

An answering smile flashed before she turned to face forward. In that brief interlude, something changed between them. She'd let down her guard if only for a moment, but Wade wasn't so sure that was a good thing. Maybe his mother was right. Digging up the past did nothing but hurt the ones who had already been wounded.

He forced his attention back to the lake. With the setting sun, the weekend had officially come to a close. Most of the locals had already called it a day in order to rest up for Monday morning. The summer vacationers were still going strong on their Jet Skis and party boats, but the farther north they traveled, the lighter the traffic. The sun had dipped below the treetops as they approached the bridge ruins. Wade pulled back the throttle and put the boat in neutral as they rocked back and forth on the wake.

Unlike the last time he'd been there, the place looked deserted. No lake patrol, no dive boat, no police officers milling about on the bank. At the very least, a perimeter of ropes and buoys should have been set, but he knew only too well the limitations of a small-town police department. The current police chief probably thought it best not to call attention to the area until the car could be brought up.

After the wake settled, the boat sloshed gently in the water. Wade stood braced with feet slightly apart as he scanned the area with his binoculars. About five hundred yards upstream, something metallic sparked near the bank. His gaze had darted ahead, but he jerked his focus back to the spot, waiting another long moment before moving on again. Probably just a can floating in the shallow water near the bank, he decided.

He turned off the engine and allowed the silence to envelope them. The breeze brought the barest hint of smoke, the woodsy aroma stirring memories of campfires and cookouts. Beside him, Abby stood gazing around, too.

"It's so quiet," she said in a hushed voice. "Where are the police?"

"Not enough manpower, not enough resources. Take your pick," he said. "This isn't Atlanta. Small-town police departments are always spread too thin and this is the busy season."

She turned with a scowl. "Still, it seems strange they'd leave the area unguarded."

"Maybe it's for the best," he said. "A police presence would bring out the gawkers. Too many boats in the area could compromise the recovery operation."

"When do you think they'll bring her up?"

The significance of the pronoun wasn't lost on Wade. "Depends on how quickly they can locate the right equipment. The car is forty feet down and the bank isn't easily accessible. It's a tricky operation. They won't bring the remains up without the car," he added gently. "You'd risk losing whatever evidence might be trapped inside the vehicle."

"So we wait," she said.

"We wait," he agreed.

She took off her sunglasses and tossed them onto one of the rear seats as she lifted her gaze to the deepening sky. "It's spooky out here. Even the birds have gone silent. Did you notice?"

Her uneasiness matched his own. He rubbed the back of his neck as he scanned the water. He was reminded again of the meticulous research that had brought him to this spot in the first place. If someone wanted to get rid of a stolen boat, this would be a good location to sink it.

"Is this the spot?" she asked.

He pointed to the crumbling concrete braces on either side of the lake. "The car must have gone over several feet right of center. My dad said some of the guardrails were missing before the bridge was demolished. A car could have gone over the side without anyone ever noticing. Without safety barricades, that bridge was a tragedy waiting to happen."

He saw a shiver go through her as she hugged her arms to herself. "I can't stop thinking about what she must have experienced in those last few moments. The shock and panic as the car hit the water—the absolute terror as it sank and the water inside started to rise. She must have tried so hard to free herself from those handcuffs."

He took one look at her face and said, "I shouldn't have brought you out here."

Her arms tightened around her middle. "Do you think I wouldn't have those same thoughts back at the cottage? Or anywhere else, for that matter. It's all I see when I close my eyes. I keep asking myself, who could have done something that cruel to another human being? Mother was no angel, but she didn't deserve that. No one does."

He was careful how he responded. "It's possible she was unconscious before the car hit the water."

"Then why handcuff her to the steering wheel?"

"Maybe whoever trapped her wanted to make sure she couldn't get out of the car and swim to safety if she came to. Who knows what really happened? Ten years is a long time for a murderer to cover his or her tracks. You may never get all the answers you need."

"I refuse to believe that," she said. "My mother's killer was human, and humans make mistakes. All it takes is one clue, one lead, one witness to come forward to unravel the whole mystery."

Wade wasn't so optimistic. Or maybe a part of him was still afraid that his dad knew more about that night than he'd let on. Maybe he wasn't ready for the whole truth to be revealed. "We'll see what happens when word gets out."

Abby put a knee on the seat as she peered over the side into the water. He didn't need to be clairvoyant to know what she was thinking. Forty feet down, her mother's remains called out for justice.

While she stared down into the water, he once again lifted the binoculars. He scanned the bank where he'd seen the earlier flash. Maybe it was his imagination but he could have sworn he saw someone in the water. The person looked to be wearing a black wetsuit that rendered him virtually invisible among the shadows. As Wade continued to watch, the diver vanished underwater.

He swore and tossed the binoculars aside as he moved to the back of the boat and started pulling his dive gear from one of the compartments.

Abby followed him. "What are you doing?" she asked in alarm.

He was already checking his gauges. "Something isn't right. I'm going down to take a look."

"What do you mean something isn't right?"

He hauled on his harness and tank. "I just want to make sure everything below is the same as I left it."

She put her hand on his arm. "Stop for a minute. Tell me what you saw."

"I'm not sure," he admitted. "Could be nothing. I thought I saw someone with dive gear go underwater several hundred yards upstream."

She turned to glance past the bridge ruins. "I don't see another boat around. I didn't hear a motor, either."

"They wouldn't necessarily need a boat. They could have parked on the road and walked in from the bank. But like I said, it could be nothing."

Her hand was still on his arm. "What aren't you telling me?"

He didn't really want to spell it out, but he didn't want to leave her hanging, either. "Think about it for a minute. Supposing someone decided to compromise the remains before the police have a chance to bring up the car. A ten-year-old murder case will be hard enough to solve. Without a body, a conviction might be damn near impossible."

Her hand dropped from his arm as she stared at him aghast. "What do you mean by compromise the remains? *Steal?*"

He kept his tone impassive. "It's not likely. I'm erring on the side of caution. I've still got plenty of air in one of my tanks. It can't hurt to go down and take a quick look to put our minds at ease."

She gazed past him into the water. "What if someone *is* down there?"

"Then I'll chase them off."

She took another glance over the side of the boat. "I don't like this."

"It'll be fine. I'm an experienced diver."

"It's not your expertise that worries me. Whoever is down there may already have killed once before. Shouldn't we call the police?"

"How long do you think it would take for them to get out here? The damage could be done by then. I'll be fine." He nodded toward the bank. "See that stand of willow trees? Pull the boat underneath the branches while I'm down. The water is plenty deep even that close to the bank. Just raise the prop, and you shouldn't have any problems."

She still looked worried. "What then?"

"You wait. If you see another boat or a diver in the water, don't do anything. If they see you, get the hell out of here and call the cops. Otherwise, stay hidden until I surface. I'll give you a signal so you'll know it's me. Three waves over my head like this." He demonstrated. "I'll repeat in intervals until you see me. Got that?"

She nodded. "I still think we should call 911 and wait for backup."

"Says the woman who withheld evidence from the cops." He gave her a quick grin, trying to lighten the atmosphere. "I'll go down, have a look and then we'll know for sure that everything is okay."

He spent the next few minutes gearing up. Then he gave her a nod and a smile as he stepped over the back of the boat and balanced on the narrow platform to pull on his mask and fins. "Be back before you know it."

Fitting his regulator into his mouth, he gave her a thumbs-up and entered the water with a wide stride. As soon as he was under, he deflated his BCD and equalized the pressure in his ears. His light sparked off iridescent scales and bulging eyes as he descended into that strange, weightless world beneath the surface. Without the benefit of sunbeams filtering down through the water, his visibility was limited to a narrow path of illumination. His descent stirred up a cloud of sediment. He hovered for a moment until the particles settled before he began maneuvering through the bridge ruins.

Once more, he swam through gateways of rusted iron girders and around mountains of concrete and rebar until his light picked out the Rolls Royce Wraith sitting apparently undisturbed on the murky lakebed. He felt a momentary relief before the tomb-like silence engulfed him. He wasn't a superstitious person, and he didn't believe in ghosts or the paranormal, but as he swam toward the vehicle, he had the strangest feeling of being watched, of being tracked. He did a 360-degree turn in the water. Nothing amiss in any direction. Nothing out of place above or below him. Yet he couldn't shake off the same disquiet he'd experienced on the surface. Something was wrong.

He kept his light focused on the car as he swam up to the driver's side door and shined the beam inside the vehicle. The skeleton of Eva Dallas McRae floated behind the wheel, her empty eye sockets still searching for a destination that had eluded her for ten long years.

Observing the remains through the window seemed oddly intrusive and Wade started to move away when something whizzed past him in the water. He caught the movement out of the corner of his mask and thought at first a fish had darted by his cheek. In the next instant, he realized someone had launched a tiny missile from a speargun and the razor-sharp point was embedded in the corroded car door only inches from where he'd been a second earlier.

He was so startled, and he whirled so quickly that the light slipped from his hands. The beam hung eerily suspended in the water. He left it floating as he propelled himself toward the back of the car and hunkered on the lakebed. When no other assault was forthcoming, he swam up to grab the light and then circled the car, widening his search with each orbit.

At that point, he had no idea how long he'd been in the water. He checked his watch. Only twenty minutes had gone by, but he felt like he'd been under for a lot longer. Abby was probably getting concerned by now and may even have called the police. He searched for another few minutes, and then he inflated his BCD and surfaced.

The light was fading rapidly over the water. He wasn't sure Abby would be able to see him even with the binoculars, but he didn't want to call out to her. Sound carried over water. The last thing he needed was to alert his would-be assailant of his location. Or even worse, of Abby's.

Before he could signal a second time, he heard the boat engine start up. A few minutes later, she pulled alongside him, putting the shifter in neutral so that she could lend a hand as he hoisted himself over the side. Then she helped him shed his equipment as the boat rocked gently beneath their feet.

"What happened down there? You were gone for so long I started to panic. Another minute and I would have called 911."

He pushed his mask to the top of his head and sat down on the cushioned bench to remove his fins. "Someone shot at me. The spear missed me by inches."

"What?" She looked horrified as she crouched in front of him, her gaze darting over him. "Are you okay?"

"Yeah, I'm fine." He removed the mask and tossed it aside. "The line was cut. Which means it wasn't someone down there shooting at fish. They never intended to retrieve that spear."

She bit her lip in consternation. "How did they know you were down there? How could they even see you?"

Her hands were resting on his knees. He wondered if she even noticed. "They probably shot at my light." He finished with his gear and then, taking her hands, drew her up with him. "Did you see or hear anything? A boat, a car, anything?" He surveyed their surroundings as he cut the engine and listened to the silence.

"No, but my visibility was pretty limited behind those willow branches." She peered over the side of the boat as if she could spot someone still in the water. "Do you think they were trying to sabotage the car? I keep thinking about what you said earlier. That a conviction would be nearly impossible without a body. Is that really true?"

Before he could answer, a low rumble, like muffled thunder, rolled across the lake a split second before a geyser of water shot skyward several hundred yards north of them, just past the bridge ruins where he'd seen the diver. The shockwave that followed rocked the boat so violently they were almost tossed overboard. Abby clung to the rail, looking confused and terrified. Wade grabbed her and held on tight.

When the water finally calmed and the boat stopped pitching, she said in a dazed voice, "What just happened?"

He grabbed the binoculars and searched upstream. The light was nearly gone by that time. He could barely make out what looked to be bits of debris floating on the surface of the lake. "Someone detonated an underwater explosive," he said. "You okay?"

She still looked stunned by the impact. "You think someone blew up the car?"

"No, the blast site is too far away. I'm going to go out on a limb and say someone just blew up Brett Fortier's stolen boat."

"Why?"

"My guess is, they already unloaded what they came for."

"By *they*, do you mean Brett?"

"Yes, but it's also possible someone else came looking for that boat. They probably got spooked by all the cops out here yesterday. They moved the cargo and then got rid of the evidence." He assessed her expression in the near dusk. "Are you sure you're okay?"

She stared back at him. "I'm fine. Are you? You're the one who was shot at underwater."

"Shot at, not shot. I'm good."

She drew a shaky breath and released it. "We seem to be dealing with some dangerous and desperate people, Wade. What do we do now?"

He scanned the area uneasily. "We get the hell out of here."

"Shouldn't we check the water to see if anyone is hurt?"

His response was blunt. "Do you really want to get that close? Your description of 'dangerous and desperate' seems pretty apt. If they have spearguns, they probably have other weapons, as well. We're unarmed, and right now, we're sitting ducks."

She nodded. "You're right. We shouldn't intervene, but we have to call the police. They should be out here, anyway. The area should never have been left unguarded."

Despite what he'd just said, Wade's first inclination was to get to the blast site before the cops arrived. The chance to explore the debris before the pieces were picked over and logged into evidence could have been helpful to his investigation. If he'd been alone, he would have done exactly that. But he wasn't about to take any chances with Abby's safety. If his suspicions were right, then whatever contraband had been hidden onboard had been moved ashore before the explosion. He remembered what his dad had said about the kind of people who might come looking for that boat.

He moved up behind the wheel and started the engine. "We'll call the police when we've put distance between us and whoever set those charges."

She came up beside him, but instead of balancing behind the windshield, she sat down and clutched the side of the boat. He wondered if she'd changed her mind about investigating her mother's murder. That first taste of real danger could be sobering.

Whipping the prow around, he pushed the shifter forward, and they shot across the water toward lights and safety.

A LITTLE WHILE LATER, Wade eased the boat alongside the bumpers on Abby's dock and turned off the motor. They both jumped out to tie off, and then she turned, her expression tense as she smoothed back her tangled hair. "What a mess."

"You look fine," Wade told her.

"You know that's not what I mean," she said in frustration. "I couldn't care less how I look. I'm talking about what just happened out there on the water. You could have been killed or seriously injured, and it would have been my fault."

"Your fault?" He frowned down at her. "How do you figure that?"

"I should never have asked you to take me out there in the first place. You didn't want to go, but I wouldn't listen. I all but badgered you into it." The night was warm and balmy, but she was still shivering.

He resisted the urge to put his arms around her and pull her into him. Hold her close until the adrenaline settled, and the shakes subsided. Instead, he tried to alleviate her guilt with a dismissive response. "First of all, nobody badgers me into doing anything I don't want to do. I can dig in my heels with the best of them. And second, I'm the one who found the car, remember? I'm the one who brought all this to your doorstep. So if anyone's to blame, it's me."

"I'm glad you came to me," she said. "I wouldn't have wanted to hear about Mother from a stranger."

"Regardless, I should have been more aware of the situation and our surroundings tonight. I knew the kind of people that would be out looking for Brett Fortier's boat. I also know Brett Fortier. Dangerous and desperate people do dangerous and desperate things. You didn't want me to dive, but I went down, anyway. So, no, none of this is your fault. Put that right out of your head."

They stood facing each other on the dock. Wade had the strongest urge to tuck back those tangled strands of hair and then take her face in his hands. Stare deeply into her eyes and promise her that everything would be okay. He'd make sure of it. But he continued to rein in his impulses because they were nowhere near comfortable enough with one another for that kind of intimacy. And because any promise from him would likely be meaningless to her.

"Wade?"

He shook himself out of his reverie and refocused his attention. "I'm sorry, what?"

"I asked what the police said when you called. I could hear a little of your side over the engine, but I think I was still too stunned to absorb it."

"I was patched through to Detective Benson. He's the one who took my statement yesterday after I found your mother's car, and I suspect he's the guy you saw earlier. He'll be lead investigator on both cases from here on out. I'm to meet him back at the blast site after I drop you off."

She said in alarm, "You're going back out there tonight? Isn't that risky? Whoever set those charges could still be lurking around."

"I doubt it. I'm sure they're long gone by now. But on the slim chance they're still in the vicinity covering their tracks, then a police presence is just what we need to safeguard the whole area. Not just the blast site but anything underwater that's evidence of a crime."

"The remains, you mean."

"And the car. It's a crime scene and needs to be protected. Forget what I said about gawkers. They're the least of our worries now. Hopefully, the necessary precautions will be put in place, but if not, I'll stand guard on my own if I have to."

"Not alone, you won't. If you stay, I stay."

The resolve in her voice impressed him. She'd been shaken earlier by the blast, but now she was ready to go back out there if and when he said the word. "Let's hope it doesn't come to that. We should both try to get some rest tonight. Benson wants both of us at the station tomorrow to give our official statements."

"What time?"

"I'll give you his number. You can call and set up an appointment before you go in. He'll probably want to talk to us separately."

"Why? He doesn't think we had anything to do with the explosion, does he?"

"It's routine. Nothing to worry about. Just tell him everything you saw and heard."

Her nod seemed absent, as if her mind had already strayed to other things. "What would have happened if you'd still been underwater when the charges were detonated?"

He told her the grim truth without the graphic details. "It wouldn't have been good. An underwater explosion transmits pressure with greater intensity over a longer distance. A shockwave that seems relatively mild on the surface can be deadly below."

Her voice turned solemn. "Do you think whoever shot at you with the speargun was trying to frighten you out of the water?"

"I guess that's one possibility."

She shook her head in disbelief. "I'm finding it hard to process all the things that have happened in such a short amount of time. You find my mother's car on the lakebed and discover that she was murdered. A day later, someone blows up a boat a few hundred yards away. You don't think the two things could be related?"

"Only in proximity. Like I said earlier, the police presence on the lake yesterday probably spooked someone into action. Any other connection is extremely slim in my book. But it's too early, and there are too many unanswered questions to rule anything out at this point."

She sighed. "We could stand here all night trying to figure things out, but you have a police detective waiting for you. Unless you want me to go back out there with you tonight?"

"No, get some rest. Tomorrow will be a long day for both of us."

"Tomorrow, I have to face Lydia," she said with an exaggerated shudder.

He smiled at her mild attempt to lighten the mood. "She won't stand a chance." He touched her arm briefly. "Come on. I'll walk you up."

"You don't have to. I'm fine now that my nerves have finally settled."

She didn't look fine. She still seemed jittery, and no wonder, after what she'd been through. Wade was still on edge himself, and the annoying ringing in his ears from the explosion was only now starting to subside. However, that was a mild irritation compared to what could have happened if he hadn't gotten out of the water in time. He'd likely be lying on the bottom of the lake with ruptured lungs and a bleeding brain.

"Humor me," he said. "I'd like to check things out for my own peace of mind before I leave."

She looked as if she wanted to argue his point but instead nodded and turned toward the cottage.

He followed her up the steps, and while she went through the inside of the house, he scoured the outside for breaches. They met back on the terrace.

"All clear," he said.

"Inside too."

He nodded toward the French doors. "Who has keys to this place besides you?"

"I assume there are spares at the office for the cleaning staff, painters, handymen and the like."

"You might want to think about changing the locks for the duration of your stay," he said.

"Oh, Lydia will love that added expense. But you're right. Better safe than sorry after everything that's happened. I'll pay for a locksmith out of my own pocket if she makes a fuss."

"Lydia never has to know. I can change out the locks myself. That is, if you trust me enough to loan me your key."

She went back inside, returning seconds later to drop a key in his hand. He didn't want to make too much of the gesture. Earning back her trust was never going to be this easy.

"Thank you," she said. "I feel like you're going above and beyond, and you haven't even agreed to take me on as a client."

"About that." He closed his fingers around the key. "I'm in."

She looked slightly startled and maybe a little apprehensive. "You don't have to say that because you feel responsible. What happened on the lake wasn't your fault. Don't let guilt or adrenaline make you agree to something you might end up regretting. Take the night and think it through."

He slid the key in his pocket. "I don't need to think. I've made up my mind."

"Well, then…" She sounded breathless. "What do we do first?"

"We'll strategize tomorrow after we've both given our statements to the police. Speaking of… I should get going before Detective Benson comes looking for me."

"Okay." When he would have turned away, she put her hand on his arm to stop him. "Wade?"

He waited.

She still looked tense, but there was a glimmer of something in her blue eyes that made his heart skip a beat as he stared down at her in the moonlight. He told himself to calm down, take it slow. *Don't do anything to scare her away.* "You wanted to say something?"

"Maybe now isn't the right time."

"Just tell me."

"I think if we're going to work together, we need to talk about how things ended ten years ago. Otherwise, it'll be hanging over everything we say and do."

Sooner or later, this conversation was bound to happen. He was a little surprised she'd brought it up so early, though. "You really want to open that can of worms tonight?"

"No, but I think we have to. I meant what I said earlier. It shouldn't matter what happened in the past. We're adults now. We've both lived our lives, and there are more important things to worry about than a high school breakup. But if I'm being honest, a part of me still resents you for what you did. I was pretty crushed by the betrayal, and I still don't understand how it even happened. Or why it happened. One day we were together, and the next thing I knew, you were with someone else. You said it yourself yesterday. Some people change but most don't. A part of me still wonders if I can trust you."

"You just gave me a key to your house."

"Because I *want* to trust you."

He took a moment before he responded. "I also said that things back then weren't always what they seemed."

"You did say that, but I don't know what it means."

"People made assumptions and I didn't correct them. I let them believe what they wanted to."

"Including me?"

"Especially you."

"Why?"

He scrubbed a hand down the side of his face in frustration, not knowing how to give a satisfactory answer while still holding back. "It sounds silly now," he said with no small amount of self-deprecation. "Silly and naive and probably a testament to how full of myself I was back then. I let you believe I was with someone else, because I thought it would be easier for you to leave town—leave me—and go live with your grandmother if we weren't together."

And because he'd been worried sick that his father had been planning to leave town with Abby's mother. Once he'd seen his dad with Eva, he couldn't look Abby in the eyes without wanting to blurt out the truth. He hated keeping things from her, but he had to think of his mother. Her mental health had declined significantly that summer. The gloom was so deep that some days, she couldn't even get out of bed. How far she might sink into the depression had been a constant worry for Wade. He would have done anything to spare her more pain. Even if it meant hurting Abby. He told himself it was best for everyone that she go live with her grandmother in Atlanta. He needed her gone and over him, because her absence made it easier for him to keep his dad's secret.

She searched his face. "Is that the truth?"

His hesitation was so infinitesimal, he didn't think she would have noticed. "Yes." But not the complete truth.

"That doesn't explain why you didn't come see me in Atlanta."

"Do you think your grandmother would have allowed it?"

"Once I turned eighteen, she had no say in the matter."

"By then, we'd both moved on. We were at different schools in different states. After a while, it seemed like high school was a million years ago."

She released a long breath. "Well, thank you for finally telling me."

Ten years too late.

"Wade?"

"I should go, Abby."

"I know." But instead of saying goodbye, she took his hand and tugged lightly.

Their gazes held for the longest moment before he bent and kissed her. She stood on tiptoes, placing her hands on his cheeks and kissed him back. He hadn't expected this. A part of him had hoped for it since the moment he'd spotted her on the terrace yesterday morning. But never in a million years would he have imagined she could feel the same.

They broke apart. Without a word, he turned and went down the steps to the dock, a decade's old secret still hanging between them.

Chapter Nine

Night had fallen by the time Wade returned to the blast site. Searchlights from the patrol boats raked over the dark waters while officers with flashlights combed the woods. He cut his engine and running lights and let the boat drift toward the shallows. Then he jumped down and sloshed through ankle-deep water to where Roy Benson waited for him on the bank.

The lanky police detective rocked a crew cut and an affable demeanor that belied his hardcore reputation. The spotlights from the lake reflected off his glasses, giving him an eerie, almost sightless appearance as he stood with hands in his pockets surveying the debris that had washed ashore.

"Seems like you have a nose for trouble, my friend."

"Just a run of bad luck," Wade replied.

Benson angled his head. "Let's talk over there."

They moved to a quieter area and spoke in low tones, mostly a repeat of what Wade had reported earlier on the phone. Benson didn't take notes. His questions were routine, but Wade had a feeling the detective listened intently to his answers so that he could pounce on any discrepancies. Wade knew how to play that game. He had a memory for minutia, and when he'd finished his second account nearly verbatim to the first, they both turned as one toward the water.

"I've seen a lot of out-there stuff on this lake, but underwater demolition is a new one," the detective said. "Boats usually explode on the surface when some fool sets off fireworks too close to the gas tank."

"Have you found anything in the debris to identify the boat?" Wade asked.

"The pieces that have floated up so far are pretty small. We don't even know for sure that it was a boat."

"What else would leave chunks of fiberglass in the water?"

"You've got me there." The detective skimmed his gaze over the lake. "Most likely you're right. We'll gather up what we can tonight and then send divers down in the morning to take a closer look. At least we haven't found any fresh bodies yet."

"I don't think you'll find bodies," Wade said. "Whoever set off those charges knew what they were doing."

"They?" Benson's voice sharpened as he gave Wade a sidelong glance in the cast-off glow from the spotlights. Suddenly, he didn't seem so genial anymore, but the hard-nosed cop his dad had warned him about the day before. The same detective who had apparently been watching Abby outside her childhood home. "Why do I get the feeling you know more about this explosion than you're letting on?"

Wade braced himself, but he kept his tone even and his expression benign as they continued their awkward little dance. "I've told you everything I know."

"But you have to admit, the timing is pretty coincidental. You just happened to be in the exact area at the exact time when someone detonated underwater charges. You seem to have a knack for stumbling across unusual circumstances and events."

"Like I said, just a run of bad luck. Besides, I wouldn't

call it that much of a coincidence. I've been looking for a stolen boat for days now. A boat your department didn't seem all that interested in until now," Wade added. "I had reason to believe it went down somewhere in this area. But you know that. I already explained everything to you yesterday when I reported the car with human remains inside."

Benson nodded. "You did say that, but I'm still a little unclear as to why you picked this particular spot to search."

"Sonar, aerial photography, common sense. Just take a look around, Detective. This part of the lake is remote. Hardly anyone comes back here anymore since they built the new bridge on the other side of town. You run out of gas or bend a propeller, you'd have to swim ashore and walk for miles. Perfect place to hide contraband on a sunken boat."

"Contraband?" Again, that sharp note in his voice. "You mean drugs?"

"Would that surprise you?"

"Nothing surprises me anymore. Superficially, we may seem like any other small town, but a place like this where strangers can come and go without being noticed attracts a certain element. You mix that with the casinos a few miles down the road, and you've got the makings of an underground criminal enterprise that could operate under the radar for years." He bent to retrieve a piece of debris from the water and examined it in the moonlight. "How well do you know Brett Fortier?"

Wade's reply was frank. "Not well. We went to high school together years ago. I can tell you that I wasn't a fan of his even back then."

"I heard you two used to get into it regularly. Over a girl, was it?"

Wade frowned. "Who told you that?"

"I asked around after we talked yesterday. An independent investigator hits town, we like to know what he's up to. Make sure he's not meddling where he has no business." Benson gave a low whistle to attract the attention of a nearby officer, and then he tossed over the chunk of fiberglass to be bagged and logged. "You had any run-ins with Fortier lately?"

"I haven't seen him since our high school graduation."

Benson feigned surprise. "I find that hard believe. His insurance company sent you down here to investigate what they believe to be a fraudulent claim. I'd have thought the first thing you'd want to do is get his statement on the record."

"I already have the signed police report and his insurance claim. I was hoping to keep a low profile for a few days while I searched for the boat."

"Didn't want to spook him?"

"Something like that."

"Too late for that now, looks like." The detective nodded toward the floating pieces of wreckage in the shallow water. "Can't keep something like this under wraps for long. The police activity out here for the past two days won't have gone unnoticed. As soon as we start moving in the heavy equipment to bring up that car, this area will be crawling with sightseers."

"Which is probably why someone blew up the boat."

"By someone, you mean Brett Fortier."

Wade nodded. "That's my guess. He salvaged whatever he'd hidden onboard and then got rid of the evidence."

"Any idea where he's staying?"

"He's pretty elusive," Wade said. "If I were him, I'd try to stay somewhere close enough to keep an eye on things."

Benson scanned the darkness. "Plenty of rentals up and

down the lake. Unless he checked in using an assumed name, we should be able to track him down."

"His sister still lives in town, but I wouldn't count on her being much help," Wade said. "She's pretty protective of her brother."

Benson scratched the back of his neck. "Let me ask you this. Do you think the explosion is somehow connected to the car you found?"

"I don't see how. Eva McRae disappeared ten years ago. The likelihood of a connection seems pretty slim to me."

"Maybe not as slim as you think. It's my understanding Brett Fortier used to work for her."

Wade shrugged. "He might have. She hired a lot of high school kids in the summer."

"How well did you know *her*?"

"I dated her daughter and she didn't approve. Beyond that, I didn't know much about her."

"You never heard her name connected to anything illegal? Rumor has it, she crossed paths with some pretty unsavory people in the early days of her business."

The detective's question jolted Wade even though the same thought had already crossed his mind. "I wouldn't know anything about that."

"Your dad was the police chief back then, right?" Benson's gaze narrowed as if he were trying to call up a forgotten detail. "He held the office for...what? Fifteen, sixteen years? He never mentioned anything about a money laundering operation? Some people think that's where Eva got the cash to buy up so much lakefront property."

"Her family is well off," Wade said. "I doubt she'd need to resort to a life of crime to finance a new business."

"But it's not just about the money for some people, is it?" Benson toed a can from the sandy bank. "They do it for the excitement. For the thrill of walking on the dark side. Does that sound like Eva McRae to you?"

"I was all of seventeen when she left town. I didn't do much analyzing back then."

"No, I guess you had other things on your mind." The detective's grin was quick and knowing. "I'll admit my theory is a long shot, but her involvement in the drug trade could explain why she made detailed plans to disappear without being followed. It could also explain how she ended up at the bottom of the lake."

"I don't know anything about that, either," Wade said. "As for my dad, he thought like everyone else in town that she left of her own accord. He had no reason at the time to suspect foul play. As you said, she made a lot of plans. Her husband and daughter found notes the next morning explaining her decision in her own handwriting."

"Yeah, but there's still something about her disappearance that I can't quite wrap my head around. Does it make sense that a law enforcement officer with Sam Easton's experience would buy a story like that so easily? Eva was a well-to-do woman with a thriving business and a devoted family, and she decides one day to throw it all away for a new boyfriend? And she leaves her husband and stepdaughter in charge of the company she built from the ground up? That's odd behavior any way you slice it."

"Hindsight is always twenty-twenty." Wasn't that what his dad had said the day before? "You have human remains inside a car. That's irrefutable evidence of foul play that my dad didn't have ten years ago."

"True enough. Let's focus on the daughter for a minute. The one you dated. Abigail, is it?"

"Abby."

"How did she get on with her mother? You said Eva didn't

approve of your relationship. That must have caused a lot of friction, especially if she tried to break the two of you up."

"I never said she tried to break us up."

"That usually follows with parent disapproval. What was the deal, anyway? She didn't think a cop's son was good enough for her daughter?"

Wade hesitated. "That was part of it, I guess. Mostly, she thought Abby was too young to be in a serious relationship."

"How serious were you?"

"We were in high school. Those relationships rarely make it past the first semester of college."

"But they can be pretty intense while they last."

Wade gave him a long stare. "Where is this going, Detective?"

"I'm just trying to get the full picture. Ten years is a long time. Details get forgotten. Disagreements get swept under the rug. I can't help wondering...did Abby have a temper back then?"

"What?"

"We've already established that a guy like Brett Fortier could push your buttons. What about Abby? Was she the type to lash out when someone angered her?"

"No. The opposite, in fact."

"She was the quiet type?"

Wade didn't need to be clairvoyant to intuit where this conversation was headed. They were entering dangerous territory, and he needed to watch what he said and how he said it. He'd come out here ostensibly to talk about the explosion. Roy Benson's attention had already reverted back to Eva McRae's murder.

"You're barking up the wrong tree if you think Abby had anything to do with her mother's death. She was devastated when Eva disappeared."

"I'm sure she was, but there are any number of reasons why a teenage girl might be distraught in a situation like that. In my experience, guilt can be a debilitating emotion."

Wade stifled the four-letter response that sprang to his tongue even as he recognized Benson's tactic. He was trying to goad Wade into an unfiltered retort. "If Abby had been responsible, would she have gone to the police station and demanded an investigation?"

"She might if she wanted to throw off suspicion."

"You've got this all wrong," Wade insisted.

"Maybe, but it's early days in the investigation. I've barely scratched the surface. Plenty of time for new evidence to surface or eyewitnesses to come forward. Maybe we'll hear from the same witness who reported a dispute between Abby and her mother a few days before Eva disappeared."

Wade rose to the bait before he could stop himself. "What are you talking about?"

"You didn't know about the argument? I understand it got pretty loud and heated. The upshot was Eva threatened to send Abby to live with her grandmother if she didn't stop seeing you. That's a pretty powerful motive, wouldn't you agree? Especially if you factor in the potential of an inheritance that would allow her to go where she wanted with whomever she wanted." The detective seemed pretty satisfied with his conclusion.

"Who is this witness?" Wade demanded.

"An anonymous caller, apparently. We usually take those kinds of tips with a grain of salt, but Chief Easton thought it important enough to note in the file."

"What file?" The detective's fishing expedition had taken a turn that completely caught Wade off guard. He felt as if he were trying to pedal a bike with a broken chain.

"We'll get back to that in a minute," Benson assured him. "I still have a few questions about Abby."

"You're forgetting something pretty important about her mother's disappearance," Wade said. "If you really think Abby had something to do with Eva's death, then how do you explain away the handwritten notes that were left for her and her stepfather?"

"Yes, those notes are a puzzle," Benson agreed. "I'd be interested to know if a handwriting expert was brought in."

"All I know is that Abby had nothing to do with Eva's disappearance. She would never hurt anyone, least of all her own mother."

"So you keep saying." The detective tilted his head to study him. "You're pretty defensive of someone you dated back in high school. How close are you two these days?"

"Yesterday was the first time I'd seen her in years."

"When you went to tell her about her mother's car at the bottom of the lake?"

Wade figured it was pointless to deny it. "I didn't want her to hear about it on the news."

"Or maybe you wanted to make sure you two still had your stories straight after all this time."

"That's ridiculous." For the first time, Wade allowed a hint of outrage to creep into his tone. "Why would I report the car if I was involved in putting it down there?"

Benson commiserated. "Hey, I understand your frustration, but I'm just trying to do my job with what we have to go on so far. Even if you weren't involved back then, maybe Abby confessed to you after you went ahead and told her what you found. She spins her versions of events, and now you're protecting her."

"That didn't happen."

He shrugged. "Other theories will develop, and the suspect list will undoubtedly grow over the course of the investigation. One thing remains static, however. Someone killed that poor woman. Handcuffed her to the steering wheel and pushed her car into the lake. That's a rough way to go. Of course, we don't even know for sure the body is Eva's. If it turns out to be someone else in her car, then that's a whole new ball game. I was hoping to keep a lid on the investigation until we have the ME's report, but I guess that's out now that you've told Abby. You talk to anyone else?"

Wade had a feeling the detective already knew the answer to that question, or at least he suspected. Now was not the time to withhold information. "I talked to my dad. I thought he might have some insight into what happened. He didn't. He was as shocked as I was by the discovery of Eva's car."

"You sure about that?"

"Yes, I'm sure." Why did he feel as though he'd pedaled that chainless bike right into a minefield?

"Did you know he kept a file on Eva?"

"You keep talking about a file. *What* file?"

"Goes back to the time when she was still Eva Dallas. I've been reading through some of his notes. Pretty illuminating stuff. Do you think Sam would agree to consult on the case?"

His dad had kept a file on Eva? Why? "You'd have to ask him."

Benson nodded. "He could be a valuable resource given his history. I have to say, though, I'm surprised he never mentioned his interest in Eva. Seemed almost like an obsession. We all have cases like that in our careers. We know in our gut someone is guilty, but we can't find the evidence to prove it. We keep digging and digging until a single investigation becomes all-consuming."

Or until the obsession turns personal. "I'm not surprised

he didn't talk about it," Wade said. "He rarely brought home his work. He didn't want to worry my mother."

"Or maybe he thought you'd run straight to Abby if you knew. He put a tail on her after her mother disappeared. I'm guessing you didn't know about that, either. Or did you? Maybe you had your own doubts about that girl. Maybe that's why the two of you broke up."

Wade had kept control of his emotions pretty well until that point, but he was finding it harder and harder to conceal his anger. Benson was like a dog with a bone. He wouldn't let up, and Wade was starting to feel the pressure. He reminded himself that was exactly what the detective wanted.

"Why we broke up is irrelevant and none of your business," he said.

Benson goaded him with a coy smile. "You know better than that. You're a cop's son. Ever since you found that Rolls Royce Wraith at the bottom of the lake with a corpse inside, everything about Eva McRae is my business. As far as I'm concerned, anyone she ever crossed paths with is a suspect. That includes family, friends, business associates. You. It most definitely includes Abigail Dallas."

ABBY HAD JUST climbed out of the shower when the doorbell rang. She wanted to ignore the summons. Just turn out the light and pretend she wasn't home. The day had left her exhausted, and she was still on edge from the explosion and Wade's underwater brush with death. And maybe still a little unnerved at how quickly things had escalated between them. She needed some quiet to think about that kiss and to analyze her emotions. Mostly, she just wanted to be left alone. The last thing she needed tonight was another visitor. But what if the police had come to question her about the events of the past two days? What if Wade had returned from the blast site with some new information? She drew on a robe and hurried down the hallway to answer the door.

Brie Fortier gave an exaggerated sigh of relief when Abby opened the door. Her blond hair was pulled back into a tight ponytail, highlighting her tense features as she breezed past Abby into the foyer. "You're home. Thank God." She took in Abby's robe and then craned her neck to see into other parts of the house. "I hope I'm not catching you at a bad time. You are alone, aren't you?"

"Yes." Abby combed fingers through her wet tangles, buying herself a moment to figure out what to say to her friend as she closed the door.

Her immediate worry was that Brie had heard about the car at the bottom of the lake. She had to be careful not to confirm or deny any of her friend's suspicions in order to allow the police time to make their notifications. Even though she didn't trust the local authorities to solve her mother's murder, she wanted to give the appearance of co-operation while she and Wade conducted their own investigation. This was the second time today she'd had to pretend not to know things, and she wondered if she'd be up to the task. Brie was nobody's fool, and Abby had never been any good at keeping secrets from her friend. She had a bad feeling the attorney in Brie would see right through her.

The doubts flashed through her head in a mere split-second as she assumed an expression of concern and mild curiosity. "You look upset. What's wrong?"

"It's Brett. I still haven't been able to reach him."

"You haven't heard from him all weekend? Is that unusual?"

"Not really. It's just... I can't get those sirens we heard yesterday out of my head. There's nothing in the local news about an accident, so where were all those police cars headed? I've been imagining all sorts of dire scenarios. I realize I'm overreacting, but..." She sighed. "You know me. That's what I do."

Abby took care with her response. "If those sirens had been about Brett, you would have heard something by now."

"That's what I keep telling myself." She gave Abby a worried look. "You haven't heard anything, have you?"

"I haven't checked the news," she evaded. "I've been pretty busy all weekend."

"It's not like he hasn't done this to me before. He's always disappearing, and I sometimes don't hear from him for days or even weeks at a time. But that still doesn't stop me from worrying."

"No, of course not. When was the last time you heard from him?"

Brie furrowed her brow as she thought back. "He came by the house on Friday just as I was getting home from work. We talked for a bit and then he left."

"Did he say where he was going?"

"To meet some people for drinks."

"You don't know who he saw?"

"He was pretty vague. And before you ask, I don't know where he's staying. It's pretty sad, isn't it? I don't even know who my brother's friends are anymore, let alone any of his business associates. I don't have a single contact I can call to check up on him."

If Brett had the kind of business associates that Wade suspected, then keeping Brie in the dark was probably for her own protection. Her brother may well have been out on the lake earlier in the evening blowing up his own boat. He may even have been the one who shot at Wade with a speargun. All speculation at this point, but Brie had every right to worry. Her brother could be involved in a very dangerous business.

She said none of this to Brie, of course. Why upset her even more than she already was? "Doesn't he have a place on the beach? Maybe he invited his friends down to the Gulf for the weekend."

Brie was still frowning. "I suppose that's possible, but it still doesn't explain why he isn't taking my calls."

"Have you been to the police?"

"That's not an option," she blurted.

Her vehemence only stoked Abby's suspicions. "Why not?"

Brie tempered her answer with another shrug. "He hasn't even been gone that long. And like I said, he does this all the time. I should be used to it by now."

Abby didn't buy that excuse. Brie either knew or had a strong inkling as to what her brother was up to, hence her reluctance to involve the police. "What can I do?"

"Nothing. He'll turn up. He always does. I guess I just needed to let off a little steam." Brie paused, then said, "If I'm being honest, he's not even the reason I'm here. Not the only reason."

Abby tried to keep her tone and expression impassive. "Has something else happened?"

"I was hoping you could tell me." Something subtle shifted in Brie's tone.

Abby frowned. "What do you mean?"

"You said you'd call yesterday after Wade left, but you didn't. I've been on pins and needles all weekend trying to figure out what he wanted."

That was the reason she'd driven all the way out to the lake at nine thirty on a Sunday night? Abby tried not to sound impatient as she brushed off her lack of a follow-up phone call. "I guess it slipped my mind. I've had a lot going on this weekend, too. I'm trying to prepare for my first week in the office with Lydia. She'll be scrutinizing my every move, so I want to be ready."

Brie gave her a pointed look. "I thought you weren't worried about Lydia. You said you could handle her."

"I can, but putting in the extra effort never hurts. I've been going back through the quarterly financial records. Rental revenue is down this season and I've been trying to figure out why. But we don't need to get into all that right now." Abby tucked back her damp hair. "You really came all the way out here to talk about Wade Easton? You weren't seriously concerned for my safety, were you?"

"Not for your physical safety, but when you didn't call after you said you would, I started thinking something might have happened that you didn't want to talk about."

"Like what?"

She lifted a shoulder, but Abby had the impression she wasn't nearly as blasé as her mannerisms would indicate. "Maybe he brought up a bunch of bad memories or maybe he's trying to worm his way back into your life. I just hope you have the good sense to steer clear of him. Remember what I said yesterday. Once a cheater, always a cheater." When Abby would have protested, she hurried to add, "You can pretend all you want that a high school romance doesn't mean anything ten years down the road, but I was there. I know how badly he hurt you, and I know how long it took for you to get over him."

Abby thought again about the kiss on the terrace. She hadn't yet come to terms with the fact that she'd been the instigator or that the kiss had happened at all. The next logical step to resolving their unfinished business was suddenly an anvil hanging over her head.

"Well?" Brie demanded. "Am I right?"

"Give me some credit. Do you really think I'm that easily manipulated?"

"When it comes to Wade Easton? One word. *Kryptonite.*"

"You're relentless," Abby grumbled.

"That's because I'm very protective when it comes to my friends and family. I just don't want to see you get hurt."

Abby suppressed an impatient sigh. She didn't want to talk about Wade Easton or Brett Fortier or anyone else, for that matter. She just wanted to go to bed and get some sleep so that she would be fresh for her meeting with Detective Benson the next day. Apparently, she was already on his radar. The last thing she needed was to be so tired that she let something slip about the warning note she'd kept from the police in Atlanta.

"I appreciate your concern," she said. "But you're making a mountain out of a molehill. Wade and I barely know each other these days."

"Then put my mind at ease and tell me why he came to see you so early on a Saturday morning."

What exactly are you fishing for? Abby wondered. She hated having so many doubts about Brie, but the conversation was as troubling as it was bizarre. They'd managed to maintain a long-distance friendship since high school, but they hadn't been close enough in years to warrant this kind of overprotectiveness. What was the real concern here? What underlying motive had brought her all the way out to the lake when she could have easily called to get her answers?

They were still standing in the narrow foyer. The overhead light was on, and Abby used the opportunity to study Brie's features. Nothing gave her away on the surface. She always looked a bit stressed. Abby supposed it came from years of cleaning up her twin brother's messes. But something was different about her tonight. She wasn't just concerned. Abby could have sworn she'd spotted a flicker of fear when her friend's guard was down.

She leaned a shoulder against the door and folded her arms. "I have a question for you."

Brie's frown deepened. "What?"

"If you were really so worried about my meeting with Wade, why didn't you just call yesterday? Why did you wait the whole weekend to drive out here?"

"You've always valued your privacy, and I didn't want you to think I was being pushy or nosy. And, yes, I'm well aware of the irony of my barging in like this." She flashed a self-deprecating smile. "I was already brooding about Brett, and I got myself all worked up thinking I needed to come out here in person and check up on you." She glanced once more into the family room as if expecting to find Wade lurking in one of the corners.

"At least you realize when you're overreacting," Abby said.

"Yes, but it never seems to stop me. That's what happens when you go through life waiting for the next shoe to drop." She was starting to sound like the old Brie, a prickly combination of pragmatism, fatalism and anxiety topped with a large dollop of self-awareness. "My doctor says I may be getting an ulcer. An *ulcer* and I'm not even thirty yet. Ouch." She flattened her hands on her stomach and winced.

"Are you okay?"

She closed her eyes on a deep breath. "I will be." Another breath. "You're being awfully patient with me. I can't imagine what you really think about me showing up at your door so late and babbling on about things that are none of my business."

"I think this is all camouflage," Abby said. "You've got something else on your mind. You don't know how to bring it up, so you keep dancing around the real issue."

Brie instantly sobered. "Anyone ever tell you that you missed your true calling? As a matter of fact, there is something else I'd like to talk to you about. I'm not sure how you'll take it, though."

"Then maybe we should go inside and sit down." Abby waved her into the family room.

Brie stalled for a bit. "Are you sure? I know it's getting late, and we both have work tomorrow. Luckily, I only have to deal with an irate client and a possible lawsuit. You have to face Lydia."

"She's not as bad as we make her out to be."

"Yes, she is." Brie was still clutching her stomach. "She's worse, in fact."

As soon as they moved into the family room, Brie dropped the subject of Abby's stepsister and went straight to the windows to peer out into the darkness. For the longest moment, she seemed lost in thought as a strange sort of energy crept into the room. Something was definitely going on with her. Despite those flashes of the old, fretful Brie, a deeper moodiness hung over her tonight, along with an air of uneasiness that seemed almost tangible. Earlier, Abby had attributed the flickers of darkness in her friend's eyes to an inexplicable fear, but now the emotion permeating the room seemed more like dread.

What do you know that you're not telling me?

Abby suppressed another shiver as she thought back to some of their conversations over the years and how Brie would so often bring up Wade's name as a subtle, repetitive reminder of his betrayal. Was it possible she had unrequited feelings for Wade? That would certainly explain her unusual behavior tonight and her near obsession with what had transpired between Abby and Wade. Maybe she really did need to get something off her chest.

"Brie?"

Without turning, she said, "I've always loved this cottage. I tried to buy it once. Lydia said it couldn't be done without your signature, and I knew you'd never part with it."

"You tried to buy my cottage? Why?"

"The view, the location. It's the perfect place. I didn't think you'd ever come back to the lake, and it seemed a shame to waste all this charm on renters." She turned. "But here you are."

Of all the properties her mother had ever owned, the cottage was the only place to which Abby had ever felt a real connection. She didn't know how she felt about Brie's revelation. There were dozens of houses up and down the lake. Why this place specifically?

Abby tried to shake off her disquiet as she motioned to the sofa. "Why don't we sit? Tell me what's going on with you tonight."

"That's a long story." Brie perched on the edge of the sofa like a bird waiting to take flight.

"You wanted to talk, so let's talk." Abby sat down in a chair facing the sofa and curled up her legs.

Brie clasped her hands in her lap and met Abby's gaze with a hint of defiance. "It's about Wade."

Abby said in disbelief, "*Still?* Haven't we exhausted that subject?"

"Not quite. Please, just hear me out. It's not only about yesterday morning, though his showing up out of the blue was certainly the catalyst. I feel I haven't properly expressed the depth of my concern. I know this is none of my business, but you're my best friend and there are things you need to know. Things I've heard over the years."

"About Wade? What things?"

"He's very ambitious. Driven, one might say."

"That's not a crime," Abby said. "Some might consider it an attribute."

"And others like me might consider it a pitfall. I saw the way he looked at you yesterday and the way you looked at him. It was like high school all over again, except the stakes are much higher now. Besides your trust fund and your future inheritances, you've become successful in your own right. I'm willing to bet he has a pretty good idea of how much you're currently worth."

Abby sat stunned. She hadn't expected that. "You think Wade is after my money?"

"I think he's always been after your money," Brie replied bluntly.

"Well, thanks. It's not like anyone could want me for myself."

"You know that's not what I mean. He's attracted to you. Anyone can see that, but I can't help wondering why he made a beeline to the cottage the moment he learned you were back in town."

"You're wrong about him." Since when did she feel the need to leap to Wade Easton's defense? He was a grown man. He didn't need her or anyone else protecting his honor. And, anyway, he'd probably find the whole conversation more amusing than offensive.

"If I'm wrong, then why are you so evasive about what went down between you two yesterday morning?"

Abby said coolly, "Maybe your instincts were right. Maybe it's not something I want to talk about."

"Or maybe you just don't want to talk to *me* about it. Is

that it?" She pursed her lips in disapproval. "The only other reason your evasiveness makes sense is Brett. Wade wanted information about my brother." She leaned forward. "What did you tell him?"

"I didn't tell him anything because I don't know anything." Abby was still trying to get a handle on Brie's peculiar behavior, the way she kept slipping from one subject to another but always coming back to Wade.

Maybe Abby was the one overreacting, but her mother's murder was starting to color her every conversation and interaction. She couldn't help questioning motives or searching for flickers of guilt. Fairhope was a small town. It wasn't a stretch to think the killer might have been someone both she and her mother had known. But Brie? They were the same age. Abby found it hard to imagine a seventeen-year-old luring Eva out to the bridge and then getting the jump on her.

"I don't understand why you think that he'd think that I'd know anything about Brett," she said. "I just arrived a couple of days ago. I didn't even know his boat had been stolen."

"You and I were best friends in high school. Inseparable until Wade came along. Why wouldn't he assume that I'd confide in you?"

"But you didn't."

"Because there's nothing *to* confide, but he doesn't know that. You know how he's always felt about Brett. Ever since you went out with my brother—"

"We didn't go out. We had one date," Abby hastened to clarify.

"One or a dozen, what does it matter? Wade never forgot and he sure as hell never forgave."

"There was nothing to forgive. He and I weren't even a couple then."

"Tell that to Wade."

Now it was Abby who leaned forward. "Tell me the truth, Brie. Is Brett in some kind of trouble?"

A mask immediately dropped. "Why would you ask that? What did Wade tell you?"

"I just don't think an insurance company would go to the expense of hiring a fraud investigator if they believed Brett's claim was on the up-and-up."

"Has Wade gone to the cops?"

Abby blinked in confusion. "About the boat?"

"What did he tell them?"

"You'd have to ask him." Were they even still talking about a stolen boat? "You never answered my question."

Brie dismissed the query with a wave of her hand. "Insurance companies are notorious for denying claims. They don't need to prove fraud to renege on a policy. But if they're looking to make an example out of my brother, they certainly picked the right investigator to dig up dirt. If Wade can't find anything, he'll just make something up."

"He wouldn't do that," Abby said. "He takes his job seriously. And I doubt he's been holding a grudge against Brett since high school."

Brie stared at her in silence. "Well, that didn't take long."

"What?"

"All these years in the cutthroat business of commercial real estate, and you're still as naive as you were at seventeen when it comes to Wade Easton."

"I may not be as naive as you think," Abby said. "And I notice you *still* haven't given me a straight answer."

Anger flared in Brie's eyes before she glanced away. "Brett is no angel. I'll be the first to admit he's had his troubles over the years, but his past in this matter is irrelevant."

"If that were true, you wouldn't feel the need to cover for

him. I think you came here to find out if Wade has managed to connect all the dots."

Brie went absolutely still. For a moment, she seemed to hold her breath. "What dots?"

"Why did Brett bring that boat up here in the first place? Was he running from someone? Hiding from someone? What's he involved in?"

It didn't make any sense, but the look that flashed across Brie's face almost seemed like one of relief. She hid the fleeting emotion behind a guise of hurt feelings. "That's not my friend talking. That's Wade Easton talking."

"No, it's me," Abby assured her. "You came over here looking for answers. You must have known your questions would make me curious."

Brie stood abruptly. "This was a bad idea. I can see he's already started to turn you against me. Just like he tried to do in high school."

"Wade has never said a bad word against you to me."

"No, he's a little more subtle than that. He uses my brother to come between us."

"You're the one who keeps bringing Brett into the conversation." Abby untucked her legs and slowly rose. "Your brother's stolen boat doesn't concern me. What I can't figure out is why you keep trying to involve me."

"That's not what I'm doing."

"Why did you really come here tonight? What aren't you telling me?"

Brie started for the door. "Maybe you should ask Wade that same question."

Abby followed her into the foyer. "If you've got something to say, just spit it out."

She whirled. "Did you know your grandmother paid him to stop seeing you?"

Abby was taken aback. "What?"

"That's what I heard. He took money from your grand-mother, and then he started seeing someone else. He was paid to break up with you."

Abby didn't believe a word of the accusation, and yet... "That's not true."

"Ask him. He's good at keeping secrets. Before you get too involved, maybe you should find out what else he's been keeping from you all these years."

The look in Brie's eyes sent a chill straight through Abby's heart. Then she opened the door and disappeared into the night.

Abby stood staring after her, wondering what on earth had just happened. Brie had always been protective of her brother, but this was different. Something had changed in the short time since Abby had last seen her. Yesterday morning, Brie's warning about Wade had seemed almost rote. Tonight, her attack had turned vicious.

She glanced out the sidelight, then moved to one of the front windows that had a view of the street. Brie was already backing out of the driveway, but then she braked, and a split second later, someone emerged from the bushes and got into the car. The dome light flashed on, illuminating a man's profile. The headlights were turned off and the security lights around the cottage didn't penetrate the tinted windows. Brie and her companion sat in the dark for a few minutes before the dome light flashed again.

The man turned to stare at the house as he emerged from the vehicle. For a split second, his gaze seemed to connect with Abby's through the glass. She gasped and jerked back from the window. When she chanced another glance, Brett Fortier had already vanished into the shadows.

Chapter Ten

Abby tossed and turned for the longest time, unable to get that strange conversation with Brie out of her head. She didn't want to believe the accusations about Wade, but like it or not, a nerve had been touched. How much did she even know about him these days? Or about Brie, for that matter. They'd kept in contact after Abby had moved to Atlanta and had seen each other on occasion, but they were no longer close. Tonight, she'd seemed almost like a stranger.

On and on Abby's thoughts churned until she finally fell asleep only to startle awake sometime later with the terrifying notion that she was no longer alone in the house. Heart pounding, she peered into the dark and listened to the quiet.

A soft rustling sound came to her, followed by a faint breeze. She told herself it was just the air conditioner. She'd checked all the locks after Brie left. Knowing that Brett Fortier might be lurking outside had made her especially cautious. She thought about calling Wade, but Brie had successfully planted a seed of doubt. Come morning, she might be able to see things more clearly, but tonight she was on her own. If someone was in the house, she'd have to deal with the intruder without any help from Wade Easton.

The sound of stealthy footsteps in the hallway froze her. Her gaze darted about the room, searching frantically for a weapon even as the sound faded, leaving her to wonder if she'd imagined the footfalls. Maybe she was still half asleep, experiencing something she'd read about called a waking dream.

She lay perfectly still for a moment longer before throwing off the covers and swinging her legs over the side of the bed. Then she opened the nightstand drawer and removed the heavy flashlight that had been placed there by a previous guest. Gripping the metal in one hand and her phone in the other, she rose and tiptoed to the doorway, glancing both ways down the hallway before venturing out of the bedroom.

It was a cloudy night. No moonlight to guide her, but she didn't dare turn on the flashlight. Not yet. Not until she could convince herself she was alone with only her imagination. Her waking dream.

Down the hallway she crept, past the other bedroom and a bathroom and into the family room. Nothing seemed amiss at first. No lurking shadows. No more stealthy footfalls. Yet the very air seemed charged as if negative energy lingered from a prowler.

Her fingers tightened around the flashlight as she inched into the room, her gaze roaming ahead of her, searching every darkened corner until the rustling sound came to her again, follow by a wispy breeze that stirred her hair.

A gauzy curtain floated ghostlike in the draft. She stared at the movement in bewilderment until she realized one of the French doors had been left open. Her initial reaction was one of relief. That explained the rustling sound. Then she reminded herself she'd checked the doors before retiring. Someone had come into her house while she slept and left by way of the terrace. Or were they still inside?

Her instinct was to make a dash for the bedroom and lock herself inside, then call the police. She did none of those things. As she stood searching the darkness, anger momentarily nudged aside her fear. First her grandmother's home in Atlanta had been vandalized, and now someone had invaded her private space at the lake.

Holding up her lit phone, she said into the darkness, "If you're still here, I've already called 911. The police will be here at any moment now."

As if on cue, a siren sounded in the distance, unrelated to her circumstances, but the intruder wouldn't know that. She held her breath and waited. Nothing stirred save for the curtain. After several long moments, she decided she really was alone. Keeping her phone at the ready, she hurried over to the French door and stepped out on the terrace. The stairs to the dock lay in deep shadow, and the water below looked dark and menacing, with only a faint shimmer on the surface.

Somewhere out on the lake, an engine fired up. She listened to the putter until the driver hit the throttle and the sound hit a crescendo, then faded. As she turned back to the door, part of the conversation she'd had earlier with Wade came back to her.

Who has keys to this place besides you?

You might want to think about changing the locks for the duration of your stay.

Lydia never has to know. I can change out the locks myself. That is, if you trust me enough to loan me your key.

Now Abby really was letting her imagination get the better of her, she decided. She straightened her shoulders and gave herself a pep talk as she went back into the house and locked the door. Then she turned on all the overhead lights as she made the rounds through the rooms.

The envelope with her name scrawled across the face went unnoticed until she returned from the back of the

house. Someone had left a note for her on the kitchen island. She reached for the envelope and then jerked back her
hand, realizing she needed to be more careful about prints.

Rummaging underneath the sink, she found a pair of
cleaning gloves and slipped them on before removing the
note and scanning the brief message: *YOU WERE WARNED.*

FROM HIS STAKEOUT spot on the bank, Wade shifted his position to alleviate a cramp in his calf. He'd been hunkered in
the bushes for hours, it seemed. He glanced at the clock on
his phone. Just after one in the morning. Already Monday.
Going on two days since he'd found the car at the bottom
of the lake, and Eva McRae's murderer still roamed free.
He could picture her down there now, trapped and waiting
restlessly for justice.

Detective Benson had said arrangements were underway to bring up the vehicle, though he'd been vague on a
time line. Possibly in a matter of hours, the skeletal remains
would be on the way to the morgue, where the ME would
compare the teeth and bones to Eva's dental and medical
records.

If the results were inclusive, then Abby would be asked
to submit a DNA swab. Either way, they'd soon know if her
mother was the murder victim or if someone else had ended
up in her car at the bottom of the lake. That would certainly
complicate an already multifaceted investigation. Once the
remains were identified, the question on everyone's mind
would be the same as it had been ten years ago. Where was
Eva Dallas McRae?

Wade's boat was well hidden by the willow branches, and
the moonless night helped conceal him from prying eyes
on either side of the lake. Earlier, he'd pretended to head
back to town when the police left, but once out of sight, he'd

doubled back. Detective Benson had agreed the area needed protecting, but the best he could promise was a drive-by patrol for the rest of the night. A squad car up on the road could too easily be eluded by someone with malicious intent. A diver could either hide a boat in the shadows near the shoreline as Wade had done or enter the water from the bank. The same kind of demolition used earlier to destroy a sunken boat could also obliterate Eva McRae's car and the evidence that remained inside.

Rummaging in his backpack for his night-vision scope, he scanned the trees on the opposite shore. He could just make out the trail that led up to the old highway. A similar trail remained on his side of the lake. The original road had been bisected by the demolished bridge, and each section was now a dead end. Without water or ground traffic, the isolated area was the perfect place to conduct nefarious business.

Time dragged as he listened to the sounds of the lake and the surrounding woods. The cicadas were loud tonight and almost as incessant as the mosquitos that buzzed around his face. He lifted a hand to swat them away as the sound of a car engine came to him through the trees. The roar grew louder as high beams swept over the empty space where the bridge used to be. The engine died and the headlights went out. A moment later, a car door closed with a soft thud. In the ensuing silence, Wade adjusted his position so that he had a better view as he followed the path up the embankment with his scope. He could see someone at the top facing the water.

He returned the scope to his backpack and then slipped from his hiding place to inch up the embankment, inwardly cursing at the soft crunch his footfalls made in the underbrush. He hoped the person at the top would attribute the sound to a night creature stirring. He also hoped they were unarmed.

The moon peeked briefly from behind a cloud, the sudden illumination both a blessing and a curse. He stayed crouched, using the shadows for cover as he crept closer. If the moonlight would just hold for a few seconds longer, he'd be able to see who was at the top of the bank and what they were up to.

Whether alerted by a sound or instinct, she turned. Wade could have sworn his mother's gaze met his in the split second before a cloud drifted back over the moon and the shadows once again veiled her features.

He held his position, stunned and unwilling to believe his own eyes. For a moment, he thought about calling out to her. What was she doing out here alone at this time of night? Terrible thoughts raced through his head. A parade of unbearable visions. He had to remind himself that she was better now and had been for a long time. She was painting again and seemed happy. She wouldn't hurt herself. She would never bring that kind of pain to a husband who loved her and to a son who had dedicated himself, even at the age of seventeen, to her protection.

Shaking off his own gloom, he edged closer until he could make out her silhouette even without the benefit of moonlight. She stood perfectly still as if listening to the night. Or as if the shock of their brief encounter had rendered her motionless.

Had she really seen him? Should he approach and make sure she really was okay? Or would she prefer that he vanish back into the woods and forget he'd seen her out here?

Something came to him as he watched her. She wasn't so much frozen in shock as she was mesmerized by the water.

Another thought followed. *She knows.*

Maybe his father had told her about Wade's discovery at the bottom of the lake, or maybe she'd overheard them on the deck before they'd relocated to the dock. Why else would she drive out here in the middle of the night to stare at the water? Of all the places on the lake, why *here*?

Yes, she knew.

About the car. The affair. All of it.

She knew…but for how long?

He followed her gaze to the water as a deeper dread descended. He couldn't allow those dark thoughts to morph into images. He wouldn't let his questions turn into suspicion. His mother was a gentle soul. She wouldn't hurt a fly, let alone a human being. There must be a reason she'd driven out to this particular spot in the middle of the night, and Wade told himself he should make his presence known and ask her. He didn't. He couldn't. *Maybe some secrets are best left buried.*

When he returned his gaze to the top of the embankment, she was gone. He'd lost her in the darkness. Crouching in the bushes, he listened for sounds of her departure. Nothing came to him. He could only assume she was still up there somewhere, but he could no longer see her. He felt weighed down by that heavy trepidation even as the whole scene struck him as surreal. Dreamlike. He could never have imagined in a million years that his search for a stolen boat would lead him here. That he would find himself hiding in the dark from his own mother.

He felt almost relieved when he finally heard the soft bump of the car door, and a moment later, the engine fired up. The headlights beamed out over the water and then arced through the trees as she turned her vehicle and headed back the way she'd come.

Now a new question niggled. Should he call his dad and

let him know she'd left the house? Was his dad already pacing the floor, worried where she'd gone, and if and when she'd come home?

Wade decided he'd call as soon as he made it back to the boat. He was so focused on what he would say to his dad and what his mother's trip to the lake meant that he failed to take note of the sound of a stealthy tracker. A twig snapped behind him, but his senses and reflexes were still dulled by shock.

Before he could turn or deflect, he was struck at the back of his head with a blunt instrument. The pain barely registered before he hit the ground facedown, and everything faded to black.

WADE OPENED HIS eyes to darkness and a loud ringing in his ears. He had no sense of where he was or what had happened. For a moment, he didn't even know his own name. But he was acutely aware of two things: a sharp pain at the back of his head and a rocking motion that made his stomach churn. He lay on his back staring up at the ceiling. He blinked and saw a light above him. He blinked again and willed away the cobwebs. Not a ceiling but the sky. Not a light, but the moon cloaked in wispy clouds.

Swallowing back the nausea, he tried to sit up, groaned and collapsed, putting a hand behind his head to cushion the blow. Taking several deep breaths, he tried again, grabbing onto the first thing he could find and heaving himself up to a sitting position. He looked around and saw nothing but water. Slowly, his predicament penetrated his fuzzy brain. He was adrift in the middle of the lake.

He glanced around for his backpack. His boat key was inside, along with his cell phone and the night-vision scope and—

What was that noise?

As his head cleared and his senses sharpened, he realized the resonance in his ears was, in fact, the muffled ringtone of a cell phone. He followed the sound to the back of the boat and lifted one of the bench seats. He fumbled in the dark with the unfamiliar phone before he managed to accept the call.

A male voice instantly responded. "Get off the boat."

"Wha—"

"An explosive device with a remote detonator has been placed underneath one of the seats. Don't bother looking for it. You've got less than two minutes to make it to shore."

Wade didn't waste time with questions or a search. He dove over the side of the boat and swam for all he was worth. Once he could feel the sandy bottom beneath his feet, he rose and sprinted through the shallow water to collapse on the bank. A split second later, a plume of sparks shot skyward, exploding into a shower of colorful stars that rained down upon the water.

Not a bomb but fireworks. Set off by a remote firing system.

Cruel joke. Somebody having a little fun at his expense.

Wade was relieved and ticked off at the same time.

He watched as the last sparks sizzled out on the surface, and then he scrambled up the embankment and made his way back to where he'd been ambushed. His backpack lay on the ground where he'd dropped it. His phone was still inside, the ringtone already pealing.

The same voice said, "It could have been a bomb."

Wade glanced at the caller ID: Number Unavailable. Then he searched the darkness all around him. Someone was obviously watching him, possibly using his own night-vision scope to track him.

"Who is this?"

"The guy you've been trying to shaft out of a quarter of a million dollars."

"Brett Fortier."

The caller gave a low laugh. "Sorry about the bump on your head, but I needed to get your attention."

"Well, you have it," Wade said. "What do you want?"

"You need to back off, buddy. You're bringing a lot of scrutiny to the area—to *me*—and that's bad for business. Not to mention my health."

"What business would that be?"

"The kind that doesn't concern you."

"I disagree," Wade said. "You made it my concern when you tried to kill me."

"Actually, I probably saved your life."

"You'll understand if I have a hard time mustering my gratitude." Wade continued to skim the area, looking for a telltale flash of light at the top of the embankment or a sudden movement in the trees. "What was on the boat before you blew it up?"

"See, questions like that are just going to get you in trouble. But for old time's sake, I'm willing to cut you some slack if you agree to keep your mouth shut. It'll all be over in a couple of days, anyway."

"What will?"

"Walk away, Wade."

"You know I can't do that."

The affable tone vanished. "Then consider yourself warned."

Chapter Eleven

Abby rose early the next morning, exhausted from stress, fear and lack of sleep. Wade texted while she was having coffee on the terrace. He wanted to know when he could come by and change the locks. Securing the cottage had become a top priority since last night's intruder, but her instincts warned that she should proceed with caution. Had her grandmother really paid Wade to stop seeing her? She wanted to dismiss Brie's accusation as nonsense, but the fact that he'd dumped her so abruptly had always niggled.

He said he'd let the rumors of his cheating stand back then so that she would have an easier time moving to Atlanta. In hindsight, maybe she'd accepted that explanation a little too easily. If he really was still keeping things from her, then Brie's claim was a good reminder that she needed to take things slow. Easier said than done, though, since he'd occupied her thoughts so thoroughly these past two days. She wanted to brush off the attraction as a lingering memory of first love, but she needed to be honest with herself. She would have been drawn to Wade Easton had she met him ten years ago or two days ago.

It was still early, but already sunlight blazed across the surface of the lake. The movement of light on water had a calming effect and Abby took her time before calling Wade back. She told him about the break-in and the second warning note, and when she finished, he said simply, "I'm coming over."

She put him off. "No, don't. I have to leave for work soon. We'll meet up later and I'll bring the note. Hopefully, I can get handwriting samples at the office. That is, if you're still willing to take them to your analyst."

"Bring both notes," he said. "And be careful how you go about getting those samples. The situation is starting to heat up. I have some things to tell you, too."

She gripped the phone in alarm. "What things? What's happened?"

"I'd rather we talk in person. Text me a time and place. I'll make sure I'm available."

"Wade—"

"Text me. I'll tell you everything when I see you. And Abby? Be careful."

She had no choice but to leave it at that. A little while later, she stood on the veranda of her mother's house and knocked for a second time to try and rouse her stepfather. When he still didn't answer, she thought about calling Lydia. Maybe he'd had a setback and wasn't well enough to answer the door. Or worse, he might even be back in the hospital.

Standing on tiptoes, she felt along the top of the door frame until her fingers closed around the spare key. Something else had occurred to her while she'd waited for him to answer. If no one was home, this might be the perfect opportunity to search for handwritten notes or letters and anything else that might be incriminating.

She unlocked the door and stuck her head inside. "Hello? Anybody home? It's Abby." She stepped into the foyer and glanced upstairs. "James? Are you awake? I'm here to pick up the paperwork for the Moon Bay Property."

Closing the door softly, she stood for a moment listening to the silence. "Lydia? James? Hello?"

A manila envelope lay on the console table beside her mother's photograph. She hurried over to check the contents. Rather than a scrawled name on the face, Lydia had taken the time to type and print a label. So much for a handwriting sample.

Abby picked up the envelope to scan the contents, but just then a floorboard creaked somewhere above her. Lifting her gaze to the ceiling, she listened intently. Someone was moving down the hall toward the stairs. In a matter of seconds, whoever was up there would be on the landing staring down at her. Common sense told her it was James. She'd called out loudly enough to wake him if he'd been asleep. Maybe he'd forgotten to set the alarm or maybe he'd been in the shower when she first arrived. Whatever the case, Abby had no wish to be caught lurking in the foyer. How would he feel about her using the spare key to let herself in?

She didn't try to analyze her trepidation, but instead, she left the envelope on the table and slipped into the coat closet at the bottom of the stairwell. Her mother had used the narrow space to store seasonal clothing that was rarely used and often forgotten. Stifling a sneeze, Abby pressed herself into the cramped space and tried to ignore the faint scent of lavender sachet that tickled her nostrils.

A few seconds later, she heard someone whistling as they bounded down the stairs. Peering through a crack in the door, she watched as her stepfather paused in the foyer to check himself out in the mirror that hung over the console table.

Gone was the five-o'clock shadow and mussed hair from the day before. In the place of a man recuperating from a serious heart attack was someone who had taken care with his appearance. He continued to whistle as he straightened his collar. Then he smiled at his reflection before he picked up her mother's photo and kissed the image.

Abby stood motionless, heart pounding as she watched him. She tried not to make a sound—the last thing she wanted was to be caught hiding in the coat closet—but his actions disturbed her on so many levels. First of all, she was amazed by his apparent vigor. Observing him now, she could easily imagine he'd had enough strength to drive to Atlanta and throw a rock through her grandmother's window. Or to let himself into the cottage while she slept.

She clamped her lips together as she studied his reflection in the mirror. It was like looking at the image of a stranger. A tall, handsome stranger who looked a good ten years younger than the man who'd sipped lemonade on the veranda less than twenty-four hours ago.

He returned the photograph to the table and then moved from the foyer into the living room, finally disappearing through the cased opening into the dining room and the kitchen beyond. All the while, he continued to whistle as if he didn't have a care in the world.

Abby left her hiding place and slipped across the foyer to exit through the front door, easing it closed behind her. Then she stood on the veranda and took a few deep breaths before she rang the bell.

When James drew back the door, his demeanor instantly shifted. The change was subtle. A furrowed brow. A slight droop to his shoulders. Gone was the vitality she'd witnessed only a few minutes ago. Or was the transformation only her imagination?

"Abby!" He looked past her to the street. "I hope you haven't been waiting long. Sometimes I don't hear the bell if I'm out in the kitchen listening to music."

"I just got here," she fibbed.

He opened the door wider and stepped back. "Would you like to come in? Lydia left some time ago. I was just putting on the coffee. Decaf for me these days, but I'm happy to make a second pot."

"That's a kind offer but I can't stay." Abby tried to act normal, but she couldn't help noting the flicker of puzzlement in his eyes and a slight twitch at the corner of his lips. Maybe he wasn't as composed as he seemed, she thought. "I just came by to pick up the paperwork she left for me."

"Oh, right. For the Moon Bay property. Should be around here somewhere." His gaze lit on the envelope. "Ah, here it is. Let me check…yes, the key is inside." He handed the package to Abby with a flourish. "Are you sure you don't have time for coffee?"

"Thanks, but I should get going. I'm still reading through some of the financial reports Lydia sent over. It'll take me a couple of days to get up to speed."

"I see. Well, my only advice about your meeting with the general contractor is to document everything with notes and photographs. And if you have questions, don't hesitate to call."

"I will."

She turned to leave but he stopped her with a tentative query. "Is everything okay?"

She managed a smile. "Yes, of course. Why?"

"You seem different this morning. Subdued. Are you sure Lydia didn't say something to upset you yesterday while the two of you were alone in the house?"

"We had a very brief conversation," Abby said. "It was nothing. I've already forgotten it."

He didn't look convinced. "I'm well aware of how abrasive she can be. She never warmed up to Eva and I'm afraid she often took her resentment out on you."

"That was in the past. You were right yesterday," Abby said. "Life is too short for bitterness and regrets."

"A word to the wise?"

"Of course."

"Don't let her bully you. She's accustomed to doing things her way so you may have to push back now and then. She'll resist but she'll also respect you for standing up to her."

"I'll remember that."

They said their goodbyes and Abby hurried down the walkway to the street, glancing back once to see if her step-father watched from the veranda. He didn't. The door to the house was closed and she saw no sign of him at any of the windows. She still didn't know why that earlier glimpse of him at the mirror had left her so unsettled. She already knew that he was on the mend. The doctors were so pleased with his progress he'd been released from the hospital in record time. That he now felt well enough to care about his appearance was a good thing.

She tried to shake off the lingering doubts as she headed out to the street only to halt in her tracks when she saw who waited for her.

BRETT FORTIER LEANED against her car, arms folded, feet crossed, a casual stance that belied everything that had gone down last night on the lake. Despite the sunglasses and the passage of time, he didn't appear to have changed much since high school. A little harder around the edges perhaps, but the smile he flashed was the same lopsided grin that seemed to suggest he knew her deepest, darkest secrets.

He was dressed to blend in with the lake crowd—board shorts, T-shirt and flip-flops—but Abby had a feeling there was nothing spontaneous about his attire or his visit. She hovered on the sidewalk, unsure if she actually wanted to approach him. His reputation preceded him and then some. A part of her wanted to turn and head back to the house while another part—the curious part—stood on the sidewalk staring back at him.

When she was directly across the street from the car, he called over to her. "Heard a rumor you were back in town so I decided to come see for myself."

She crossed the street slowly. "You did more than hear I was back. You were at my house last night. And now here you are again. Should I be worried?"

"Worried? About me?" He chuckled. "I happened to be passing by, saw your car and decided to stop. A complete coincidence, I assure you."

"Right." She drew out the syllable as she gave him a cool appraisal.

"You've gotten cynical." He dipped his head and observed her over the rim of his sunglasses. "You wear it well."

She ignored the comment and kept a safe distance between them. "What were you doing lurking in the bushes outside the cottage last night?"

He grinned in the disarming way he had that made people forget not to trust him. "Lurking is such a loaded word, especially when there's an innocent explanation. I was waiting for my sister."

"How did you know she was there? Did she tell you she was coming to see me?" Abby didn't wait for his answer. "Brie said she hadn't seen you in days and yet there you were waiting for her in my driveway."

He sighed. "Why do I get the feeling this is some kind of interrogation?"

"You would know about interrogations," Abby shot back.

He mocked her with an exaggerated frown. "That hurt."

"But it's true, isn't it?" She placed her hand on the warm car fender. "Brie's visit was extremely odd. I'd never seen her like that. She was tense, secretive. At times even combative. Her attitude only makes sense if you filled her head with nonsense and then sent her to pump me for information."

He feigned innocence. "No one sends my sister anywhere she doesn't want to go. Besides, why would she need a reason to come and see you? You're still her best friend, aren't you?"

"We're friends," Abby said. "But her loyalty will always lie with you."

The teasing faded as he straightened. "Just as yours seems to always lie with Wade Easton."

His tone sent a shiver down her spine. "Why are you here, Brett? What do you want?"

He shrugged. "I just wanted to see you. We used to be friends, too, back in the day. But sure. I'll admit, it would be helpful to know what Wade's up to."

She gazed back at him without reaction. "What makes you think I know anything?"

"I hear you've been spending an awful lot of time with him lately."

"Who told you that?"

"It's not a secret, is it?"

She started to retort that who she saw and what she did was none of his business. Best thing she could do was send Brett Fortier on his way. He was big time trouble and had been since their high school days. But another part of her was curious to find out what *he* knew. Even as a teenager, he was always on the lake. He had a boat before he could drive a car. Maybe he'd seen something ten years ago. A chance meeting or an overheard conversation that would have meant nothing to him then, but could change everything in the context of her mother's murder.

"I can't speak for Wade, but here's what I think," she said. "You sunk your own boat to hide whatever you brought up with you from the Gulf. Probably drugs, probably stolen. Something spooked you so you had to move the product before you were ready. Then you blew up the boat to cover your tracks. Does that sound about right?"

"I admire your imagination," he said. "You always did live in a fantasy world."

"In the past maybe. But I've been grounded in reality for a long time. I see things—and people—for the way they really are."

"Even Wade Easton?"

"Never mind Wade Easton. Are you denying any of what I just said is true?"

The grin flashed again. "Denying nothing, admitting to nothing."

"Then I think we've exhausted the conversation. If you'll just—" She tried to wave him aside. "Do you mind?"

He took his time moving away from the car. "Where's all this hostility coming from? You were never like this before. Is it Wade's influence or have you really changed that much?"

She turned to face him. "You want to know why I'm hostile? You could have killed someone when you blew up that boat last night. Wade was in the water just minutes before you detonated the explosives. Given your history and the current circumstances, I can't help wondering if he was as much a target as your boat."

"You know what they say. If I'd wanted him dead…" He trailed off as he folded his sunglasses and slipped them in his pocket. His eyes were the same icy blue as his sister's. The color was beautiful, but the glittery hardness was not. "He might not be so lucky next time."

Abby narrowed her gaze. "Is that a threat?"

"Just a friendly piece of advice. For his own good—and yours—he needs to lay low for a few days. I'll withdraw my insurance claim if it'll get him off my back. Forget about the explosion and what may or may not have been onboard my boat. Nothing can be proven, anyway. Convince him to walk away before someone gets hurt."

"Wade doesn't walk away."

"He will if you persuade him to. He'll listen to you."

"Since when?"

His gaze dropped almost imperceptibly as he cocked his head. "You really don't give yourself enough credit."

"And you seem intent on giving me too much."

He checked the street behind her. "Maybe you'll be more inclined to see things my way if I tell you what I know."

"I very much doubt it."

He paused, eyes still glittering. "I know what was found at the bottom of the lake."

Her heart started to knock. "What are you talking about?"

"You know exactly what I'm talking about." His tone shifted. "There was a big police presence on the lake early Saturday morning near the old bridge ruins. They brought in divers and at least one salvage boat. If someone got curious about all the excitement, they might have asked around. It's possible they did a little more than ask."

"By *they*, I assume you mean you." Even as Abby told herself not to fall for his ploy, she found herself asking, "What is it you think you know?"

"Ten years ago, your mother planned to leave town with

her lover. For a price, I'll tell you the name of her mystery man."

Abby stared at him in shock. Was he telling the truth?

"Do we have a deal?" he prompted.

"How can I agree to something I can't deliver," she said in frustration. "Contrary to what you seem to think, I don't have any pull with Wade Easton. Not anymore. I'm not sure I ever did. I can ask him to back off, but if he's anything like he used to be, he'll just dig his heels in that much deeper."

"In that case, I guess we really don't have anything more to discuss." He started to walk away but she stopped him.

"Wait. You can't just drop a bombshell like that and leave me hanging. If you have information regarding my mother, then please, just tell me what you know."

"Even if it circles back to Wade Easton? He's not the man you think he is, Abby."

"How do you know what I think?"

He pinned her with a penetrating stare. "You really want to know what happened ten years ago?"

"Of course, I do. But I want to talk about my mother's disappearance, not Wade Easton."

"What if I told you they're connected?"

She tried to ignore the tug of fear that threatened her composure. "I'd say you're lying."

"But I'm not and I think a part of you already suspects that he hasn't been honest with you." He leaned in. "Wade has always been real good at keeping secrets."

Like accepting money from her grandmother to break up with her? She moistened her suddenly dry lips. "What secrets?"

His gaze darted past her to the house. "This isn't the

place for a heavy discussion. We've been standing out in the open for too long."

"Are you worried about being a target?"

"Always," he said with a careless shrug. "But besides that, your stepfather has been watching you like a hawk ever since you left the house."

Abby turned, lifting her gaze to the upstairs window where James stared down at them. She felt a sudden chill though she couldn't say why exactly. Maybe her disquiet had something to do with his earlier behavior or maybe it was because the man with whom she stood talking to had nearly killed Wade the night before and had all but confessed to blowing up his own boat. It was an unnerving moment to stay the least. She wasn't sure who she could trust anymore. Certainly not Brett Fortier. But even knowing what she knew about Brie's brother, his provocation worked. She wasn't about to walk away yet.

"Where do you suggest we talk?" she asked.

"I know a place. Quiet but not too remote. Or, if you prefer, you pick the spot."

"There's a small cafe on Front Street that overlooks the lake. We can get coffee and sit out under the trees." Private but within shouting distance of help if she needed it.

He grinned as if reading her mind. "My car or yours?"

"Both. I'll meet you there."

He winked. "Lead the way."

He opened her car door and waited for her to climb inside. Abby tracked him from the rearview mirror. He headed toward a luxury SUV parked at the curb. Black, heavily tinted windows. Expensive. A vehicle that made a statement. What that statement was, she wasn't quite sure. In the split second before she started the engine, she thought, *Am I really doing this?* She could only imagine what her stepfather must think. Or what Wade would say. However, this was her decision.

She glanced at the upstairs window again, but James was nowhere to be seen.

ABBY DROVE THROUGH TOWN, still with one eye on the rearview mirror. Brett was still back there. Not exactly riding her bumper, but close enough to make her anxious. The thought crossed her mind more than once that she should just lose him. Make a quick turn and put some distance between them. Then she shrugged off her foreboding with a reminder that if he'd wanted to hurt her, he could have easily done so the night before. He had an agenda. Of that she felt certain. But they were meeting in a public place in broad daylight. What would be the harm in hearing what he had to say? Maybe he knew something about her mother and maybe he didn't. Maybe he knew something about Wade and maybe he didn't. Either way, she wasn't about to turn back now.

The Oleander Café was one of several shops and restaurants situated along a narrow one-way street bordering a wooded park that swooped down toward the lake. A few blocks to the south, the new bridge—a metal monstrosity of girders and cables—loomed over the low-rise skyline. Traffic was heavy on the main thoroughfares, and she could see a steady stream of boats puttering to and from the marina. Good. She'd counted on having plenty of people around.

She quickly found a parking space, but Brett had to circle a few times to locate a spot wide enough to accommodate the SUV. Abby didn't wait for him. She went inside and ordered two black coffees, then carried both drinks outside. When he finally caught up with her, she handed him a cup. He accepted with a cheery thanks and then followed her down the wooded embankment toward the picnic tables that overlooked the water.

Only a handful of people were seated at the scattered tables. She indicated her choice with a wave of her coffee cup.

Once they were settled, he said, "Nice spot. I'm surprised your mother's company hasn't bulldozed this block to build condos." When she didn't respond, he folded his arms on the table and leaned in. "Maybe you could build them yourself if you manage to wrest control of the business from the evil Lydia."

Did he really expect her to talk business after the shock he'd created earlier? "I'm only here to help out until my stepfather is back on his feet. But I have a feeling you already know that."

"You still live in Atlanta?"

She frowned. "What is the point of these questions?"

He shrugged. "No point. Just catching up. There was a time when you and I were a bit more than friendly."

Her reply was blunt. "You remember things differently than I do."

He grinned. "The way *I* remember it, we were a good match until Wade came along."

"Now who's living in a fantasy world?" She lifted her chin. "I do remember how much you liked to cause trouble. Brie had to bail you out of one scrape after another. I have a feeling nothing much has changed since then."

"You might be surprised."

"I doubt it." She gazed across the lake at the marina wondering from which slot his boat had been stolen. Allegedly stolen. "Can we just get on with this? You made a provocative statement earlier about Wade and my mother's disappearance. I'm still waiting to see if you can follow through on what I consider an outrageous claim."

He pried off the plastic lid to sip his coffee from the cup. "Did you know I used to work for your mother?"

Abby nodded. "I have a vague recollection. She employed a lot of high school kids during the summer. What was your job?"

"You name it, I did it. I started out part-time and then she gradually increased my workload until I was putting in ten to twelve hours a day. I did everything from filing paperwork at the courthouse to ferrying clients up and down the lake in one of the company's boats."

"What kind of clients?"

"Investors, prospective buyers and the like. She had a lot of property she was looking to unload. I'd heard rumors about a condo project, and I got curious about some of the big money she was courting from the Gulf Coast. I decided to pay attention to who came and went from her rentals. I figured it wouldn't hurt to make a few contacts. Maybe some of those high rollers could be useful to me in the future. But the more I saw, the more I saw. If you get my drift."

"I'm not sure that I do."

"Put it this way. I started to observe not only her business associates, but also Eva herself. Where she went and who she spent time with."

"In other words, you spied on her."

"If you want to be blunt. That's how I found out she was having an affair. I saw them together. And I'd be willing to bet she met this person on the bridge the night she supposedly left town."

Abby didn't want to appear too eager, but she couldn't help herself. "Who was he? Give me a name."

Brett let the mystery play out for a moment. "Are you sure you want to know? There's no going back once you find out his identity."

Her heart pounded even harder. "Just tell me."

His smile turned smug. "Sam Easton. The chief of police. Your boyfriend's father. *That* Sam Easton."

Abby sucked in a sharp breath. "I don't believe you."

He lifted his coffee cup. She couldn't help noticing that his hand was steady. "You can believe me or not. I'm telling you what I know to be a fact."

"How can you be so sure?"

"I told you. I saw them together."

"Where?"

"They met several afternoons a week in one of her rental houses."

Abby sat quietly for a moment. "Did anyone else know?"

"Besides Wade, you mean?"

Her gaze shot back to Brett. "What makes you think he knew?"

"I've always been good at reading people. I let a few things slip and watched his expression. He didn't have much of a poker face back then."

"If he knew, he would have told me," Abby said without much conviction.

"You understand why he didn't, right? He was afraid his old man had something to do with your mother's disappearance."

"I don't believe that."

"Poor Abby, All these years, Wade Easton has been protecting his family at the expense of yours."

Chapter Twelve

By midafternoon, Wade was headed back out to the lake. Detective Benson had called to inform him the equipment was on-site, and the salvage operation would soon be underway. With any luck, the car would be lifted and transported to a protected lot and the remains to the morgue within the hour.

He tried to call Abby, but she didn't answer, so he left a voicemail and then a text message. He hated to deliver the news in such an impersonal manner, and a part of him wondered if he should have told her at all. Her mother's car swinging over the water was a sight she wouldn't easily forget. If he could have spared her that memory, he would have, but he'd kept too many things from her as it was.

By the time he arrived on the scene, the divers were all geared up and waiting in a boat while a few uniformed officers milled about on the bank. The crane operator climbed into the cab, and after a few false starts, extended the boom out over the water and lowered the jib. The divers rolled backward off the side of the boat and went down to secure the hooks to the vehicle.

Detective Benson stood at the edge of the water to observe the operation. Wade didn't call out to him or try to approach. Instead, he took a position at the top of the embankment, where he hoped to keep a low profile.

He'd been waiting in the shade for only a few minutes when a shout from one of the crew members drew his gaze back down to the bank. The hustle of activity around the equipment caught his attention first. Something had obviously malfunctioned. As he scanned the area, he spotted a solitary figure standing apart from the other spectators. Recognition jolted him. He studied his dad's profile for a moment before he scrambled down the embankment to join him.

Sam Easton appeared deep in contemplation as he stared out at the dive boat. When Wade touched his shoulder, he visibly jumped before he turned.

Wade took a step back. "Sorry. I didn't mean to startle you."

"Then don't sneak up on me," his dad grumbled.

"I wasn't trying to sneak up on you. I thought you heard me coming."

"Well, I didn't. Lost in thought, I guess." He turned back to the water.

Yes, Wade thought. There was a lot to consider. He wondered what was going through his dad's head at that moment. A woman he'd had an affair with had been murdered, her body hidden beneath the lake for a decade. He claimed the relationship had been over by the time Eva left town, yet here he was.

"What's going on?" Wade asked.

"Cable snapped. That'll cause a delay."

"How long do you think?"

His dad shrugged. "Minutes, hours, a day. Depends on whether they can repair it on-site."

"That's not good," Wade said. "I don't like the idea of that car being underwater for another night."

His dad shot him a glance. "You think someone might try to destroy evidence?"

"That thought crossed my mind." Wade paused. "What are you doing out here, anyway? How did you know they were bringing the car up today?"

"Roy Benson called. He thought I'd want to be here."

"Why?"

The question seemed to annoy him. He sounded impatient when he tried to explain his rationale. "I already told you. The car went over the bridge while I was still the chief. Someone was apparently murdered on my watch. I feel responsible."

"Is that the only reason you're here?"

His dad's mouth tightened in anger, but he didn't respond.

"Well, is it?" Wade pressed.

Despite his dad's anger, he seemed to measure his words carefully. "I'm not going to let you goad me into saying something we both might later regret. You've got a problem with what happened in the past. I get it. But I can't go back and change what I did, and I'm not going to keep apologizing for it. Where that leaves us is up to you."

Wade's own temper flared, but he tamped it back down. The past couldn't be changed no matter what either of them said. Provoking his dad was at best a petty satisfaction.

"I'm sorry. I was out of line."

He sighed. "You don't owe me an apology. I let you down. I let your mother down. You've a right to your resentment. But I'd like to set all that aside for a moment and talk about what happened out here on the lake last night. Detective Benson said someone set charges beneath the surface and blew up a boat. I assume that's why you're worried about sabotage, but I'm more concerned about your safety. He said you were in the water just minutes before the explosion. You could have been badly injured or killed."

Wade tried to downplay the close call. "But I wasn't."

His dad frowned. "You don't seem to be taking this seriously. I warned you about the kind of people that would come looking for that boat."

"And I told you I know how to take care of myself. Besides, I'm reasonably certain Brett Fortier blew up his own boat."

"Is that supposed to make me feel better? Don't underestimate him," his dad warned.

"I don't underestimate anyone when enough money is involved."

"Good." He stared at the activity on the water in silent contemplation for a moment. "Benson said Abby Dallas was with you last night. Are you sure you want to start that up again?"

Wade's temper stirred yet again as he scowled in response. "Start what up again?"

"You know damn well what I mean. You were way too serious about that girl in high school. Teenagers do foolish things when their hormones are raging."

"Adults too," Wade muttered.

His dad ignored the insinuation. "Have you ever stopped to consider who stood to benefit the most from Eva's death?"

Wade didn't like where the conversation appeared to be heading. "What are you getting at, Dad?"

"Abby was her mother's sole heir. She stands to inherit Eva's estate once the dust settles."

"How do you know anything about Eva McRae's will?"

"She told me."

Wade wanted to believe the conversation was nothing

more than idle speculation, but something seemed to be brewing beneath the surface. A subtle machination that he hadn't expected from his dad. He wanted to blurt out an irate retort, but instead he took his time to reply. "You're surely not suggesting Abby had anything to do with her mother's death."

"It's not as far-fetched as you make it out to be."

"Yes, it is. Think about what you're saying. A seventeen-year-old with no history of violence lured her mother to the lake, pushed her car off the bridge and then waited ten years for someone to discover the wreckage so that she could collect an inheritance."

"Not someone. You."

Wade felt baffled. He stared at his dad in disbelief. "Are you implying I had something to do with Eva's death?"

"No, of course not. But you told me yesterday to look at the situation through the eyes of an outsider. You should do the same. Don't think for a minute Detective Benson isn't already compiling a list of suspects. Be careful how you deal with him," his dad advised. "And make damn sure you don't let yourself become a patsy."

"A patsy?"

"Remember what you said earlier. Never underestimate anyone when enough money is involved."

Wade let the implication sink in for a moment. "You couldn't be more wrong about Abby. But I'll return the favor and give you the same advice. Be careful how you deal with Detective Benson. He has a lot of questions about the way you handled Eva's disappearance."

His dad frowned. "Why would he have questions? We had no reason to suspect foul play at the time. How could we? Everyone assumed she left town of her own accord."

"He thinks you accepted that story a little too easily."

There was a note of something that might have been fear in his dad's voice. "He said that?"

Wade nodded. "He also said you kept a file on Eva going back years. But you told me you never suspected she was involved in anything illegal."

"I never had anything concrete to go on," he said. "Just a few rumors that cropped up now and then. It was my job to check them out. Nothing ever came of them. As far as I know, she was a straight arrow when it came to her business."

"Did you plan on leaving town with her?"

A shout from the dive boat caught his dad's attention. He watched the commotion without answering.

"Dad?"

"I loved your mother. I was never going to leave her for another woman."

That didn't precisely answer his question, but Wade didn't press. Maybe he was afraid of the answer.

"You were right about Benson," he said. "He's a dog with a bone. The longer and deeper he digs, the more likely Mom is to find out about the affair. If she doesn't already know."

"She doesn't."

"How can you be so sure? You didn't think I knew, either."

"I'm telling you, she doesn't know," his dad insisted.

Wade lowered his voice. "Then why did she come out here last night? To this very spot? Why was she staring at the water in the exact place where the car went over the bridge?"

His dad looked taken aback. "What are you talking about? She never left the house last night."

"She did. I saw her."

His dad's tone turned icy. "I don't know what you think

you saw, but I'm telling you your mother was in her studio all night."

"Dad, I saw her."

"Let it go. Do you hear me? *Let it go.*"

His rigid denial shook Wade. He had the resolved demeanor of a man trying to hide something. Or protect someone.

Before Wade could react, something drew his focus back up the embankment to the place where he'd seen his mother the night before. For a moment, he thought she might have returned, but then he realized the person who stood staring down at him was Abby.

Their gazes held for the longest moment before she turned and walked away. By the time Wade climbed to the top of the embankment, she was nowhere to be found.

Chapter Thirteen

Wade was waiting for Abby on the dock steps when she got home late that afternoon. He sat with his arms folded over his knees watching a small sailboat glide across the cove. Hovering at the top of the stairs, Abby stared down at him for the longest time. She didn't want to believe him capable of accepting money to break up with her, let alone withholding information about her mother's death, but neither could she dismiss the claims out of hand. She didn't really know him anymore. Maybe she never had, she thought morosely as she started down the stairs.

He turned at the sound of her footsteps. "There you are."

"I hope you haven't been waiting too long. There's so much to catch up on at the office. More files and records than I'll ever be able to wade through. Time got away from me."

"No problem. I never get tired of this view." He moved over so she could sit beside him and then handed her a set of keys. "You left earlier before I had a chance to give you these."

"Thank you for taking care of the locks," she said. "I'll sleep a lot better tonight."

"So will I."

She toyed with the keys for a moment. "Were they able

to lift the car?" She sounded stilted and reluctant even to her ears.

He gave her a sidelong glance, as if trying to figure out her mood. "Yes. The Wraith is in a locked compound at the police station. Everything is where it's supposed to be."

Meaning the remains had been transported to the morgue. Abby gave a brief nod as she hugged her knees to her chest. "I'm sorry I left so abruptly. Turns out, the salvage operation was a lot more emotional than I thought it would be."

His gaze was still on her. "You don't need to apologize for anything. I'm the one who owes you an apology."

"For what?"

"There's something I need to tell you about that last summer." His voice turned solemn, remorseful. "I should have told you a long time ago. Now I don't even know where to start."

She braced herself for his confession. "I think I know what you're about to say. My mother had an affair with your father. And you kept it from me."

He stared back at her in astonishment. "How long have you known?"

"Brett Fortier told me this morning."

His expression darkened. "Brett Fortier? How did that happen?"

"He tracked me down at my stepfather's house. He wanted to make a deal."

Wade's voice turned cynical. "Oh, I can't wait to hear about this," he muttered. "What kind of deal?"

"He would tell me what he knew about my mother's disappearance if I persuaded you to drop your investigation. He said you needed to lay low for a few days."

"At least he's consistent. He told me the same thing last night."

Now she was the one taken aback. "You saw Brett last night? Where?"

"At the bridge ruins." He shifted his gaze to the sailboat, lifting his hand briefly when the young sailors waved at them. "After I met with Detective Benson, I stayed in the area to keep an eye out."

"Why didn't you tell me? I would have gone with you."

"There was no need for both of us to stand guard."

"I disagree. We're supposed to be in this together." She studied his profile. "So Brett was at the ruins?"

"Yes, but we didn't meet face-to-face. Well, not exactly face-to-face." He massaged the back of his head. "He had a few tricks up his sleeve to get my attention."

"What kind of tricks?" she asked in alarm.

"We'll get into that later. The intent of the interaction was to warn me to back off. He said none of it would matter in a few days, anyway."

"What do you think he meant?"

"I'm guessing it had something to do with whatever he salvaged from the boat."

"Drugs?"

"I'd bet money on it. That's why he expects everything to be resolved soon. He's probably found a buyer. A quick payday will allow him to disappear without the insurance settlement."

"You still think someone's after him?"

He glanced her way. "Would that surprise you?"

"No. In fact, it would explain why he didn't want to be out in the open. He said he always worries about being a target."

"Even more reason to steer clear of him," Wade said. "A hunted man on a time line is a dangerous man. He'll consider anyone who gets in his way a threat. Last night, we both witnessed how far he's willing to go to cover his tracks."

"I'm well aware of the danger," Abby said. "But I didn't seek him out. He came to me. And I'm glad he did. He told me something about my mother that I needed to know. He said the reason you kept it from me was because you were protecting your dad." She paused on a shiver. "Is that true?"

"He got in your head," Wade said. "He's good at that."

"You didn't answer my question."

He continued to evade. "Is that the reason you left the salvage area earlier without speaking to me earlier? You weren't just emotional about the operation. Seeing me with my dad confirmed what Brett had told you earlier."

She started to deny his charge, then shrugged. "Okay. He did plant doubts. But that doesn't make what he said any less true. You kept something important from me, Wade. Even after I hired you to help me investigate my mother's murder, you withheld vital information. I'm only human. A part of me has to wonder if you agreed to take the case so that you'd have control of the evidence."

He didn't look pleased with her assessment. "I took the case because I wanted to help you find the truth. Brett is very convincing. It's why he's such a good con man. But not everything he told you is true. I wasn't protecting my dad," he said. "I was protecting my mother."

"Why?"

He squinted at the water. "That was the summer her doctor diagnosed her with clinical depression. The medication she was given didn't help much back then. Some days she could barely muster the will to get out of bed. She was sad, lonely, distant. She seemed to be wasting away before our eyes, and my dad and I were powerless to help her. There were times during the worst of it when I was afraid to go home. Afraid of what I might find when I opened the door."

Abby swallowed back a sudden lump. "I didn't know."

"When I saw them together—my dad and your mother—all I could think was how the affair would hurt my mother. She was already in so much pain. I wanted to tell you, but I couldn't take the chance it would somehow get back to her."

"I wouldn't have told anyone."

His smile was sad. "Not on purpose, but you might have let something slip. I wasn't willing to take that chance. For my mother's sake, I couldn't. Then Eva left, and I thought keeping that secret from you would get easier, but it didn't. Her disappearance just made me worry that I might come home one day to find that my dad had packed his bags and left, too. How would I take care of my mother on my own?"

"That's a heavy burden for a seventeen-year-old," she said in a soft voice.

He dismissed her acknowledgment. "It was selfish, actually. Worrying about how everything would affect me. I wasn't mature enough to consider all the angles. The only way I knew to help my mom was to keep my mouth shut."

"You weren't selfish," she said almost fiercely. "Your protectiveness is admirable. Noble, even."

"I wasn't noble. I was scared. And I hurt you because of it. When Brie started the rumor that I'd been with someone else, I didn't deny it because in some ways, it was easier to let you hate me."

She stared at him for the longest moment. "What makes you think Brie started the rumor?"

"I was told by a friend it came from her. Made sense. She and I never got along. It was no secret how much she disliked me." He glanced her way. "I think she wanted you to be with Brett."

Abby thought back to her conversation with Brie the night before. "I don't think Brett had anything to do with it. I've been going back over some of the conversations Brie and I had over the years. Certain things she let slip from time to time. I think she was in love with you."

He looked taken aback. "What? No. I never got that vibe from her."

"She hid her emotions well, but it's so clear to me now," Abby said. "It explains so much about her attitude since you've been back. She told me that my grandmother paid you to break up with me."

"That never happened."

"I know. But after Brett told me about the affair, you can see why I jumped to conclusions. You were right. I let both of them get in my head. That is why I avoided you at the lake earlier. That's why I didn't return your calls and texts. I needed time to sort through their accusations. They played me. They've both done everything they could to discredit you in my eyes, and I let them. I'm sorry."

He reached over and brushed back a strand of hair from her face. "Like I said. You don't owe me an apology. You don't owe me anything. If I'd been straight with you from the start, they wouldn't have been able to manipulate either of us. I'm sorry for my part in all this. I'm deeply sorry for the pain I caused you. I wish I could go back and change things, but I can't. The past is past."

She nodded. "I know."

"It does make you wonder about their motive, though, doesn't it? How do you suppose Brett found out about the affair?"

"He worked for my mother that summer. He started fol-lowing her around to see if he could make inroads with some of the money people she brought to the lake, and apparently, he saw them together."

"He never told anyone until now?"

She shrugged. "I guess not."

Wade looked skeptical. "That doesn't sound like Brett. It's not like him to pass up an opportunity. Even back then, he was always looking for an angle. If he tried to blackmail your mother, that could explain the large amount of cash she withdrew. It could also explain why he seems hell-bent on pinning her murder on my dad."

"And Brie?"

"She's always covered for him. You know that better than anyone."

"Yes, but to think she's pretended to be my friend when she's known all along what happened to my mother...that's a bitter pill to swallow," Abby said.

"It's speculation at this point."

"I know. But it makes sense."

"We don't know anything yet. Try to keep an open mind."

"Can you?"

He let out a breath. "I'm trying."

In the brief silence that followed, she felt something shift between them. The air had been cleared, leaving an intimacy that was at once comforting and unsettling. They talked for a long time, until the sun dipped below the horizon and twilight settled in with a breeze. The fireflies came out and then the mosquitoes. Abby rose and brushed her hand across his shoulder before she started up the steps. Their gazes connected, and then he rose slowly and came up the steps behind her. She used one of the new keys to let them in through the patio door. Inside, he drew her to him, and they kissed.

When they finally parted, she said in a near whisper, "Is this a mistake?"

He rested his forehead against hers. "Time will tell, I guess. It doesn't feel like a mistake."

"To me, either." She took his hand and led him down the hallway. The bedroom was cool and dim. She sat on the edge of the bed while he went over to the window to glance out.

"It'll be dark soon," he said.

"You like the water by moonlight."

He smiled. "Yes, I do." He came over and sat down beside her. "You seem nervous."

"I guess I am a little."

"There's no need to be." He took her hand and entwined their fingers. "Today was hard. Lots of bad things going on out there." He nodded to the window. "In here, it's just you and me."

She lay back on the bed and he joined her. "Do you know what I find strange? How difficult it's been to adjust my perception. For so many years, I thought my mother abandoned me. It shaped my life in ways I probably still don't understand. I don't trust easily. I don't make friends easily. But the strangest part of all is that her murder doesn't really change anything. Because she actually did plan to leave me."

"Yes, but given the opportunity, she might have had a change of heart." He rolled to his side to gaze at her profile. "Or she might have come back for you."

"I'll never know." She turned to face him. "About that trust thing...before we go any farther, I need to ask you something. Is there anything else you haven't told me?"

His hesitation made her heart skip a beat. Then he brushed his knuckles down the side of her face and said, "There's something you should know about me."

She tried to brace herself. "What is it?"

"I think I'm still in love with you."

ABBY WAS UTTERLY stunned by his confession. She remained speechless for so long that the silence became awkward. "I…never expected that."

"Neither did I, if I'm honest. It's not like I've been pining all these years."

"Thanks."

He smiled. "All I'm saying is that I've lived a full life since I left this place. I've traveled the world and had my fill of adventures. It's been a good life and I've been happy. But Saturday morning, my first sight of you on the terrace hit me like a ton of bricks. It sounds like a bad piece of melodrama, but that's the best way I know to describe how I felt."

"If we're being honest…it hit me like that, too," she admitted. "I've also lived a life. Maybe I wasn't as adventurous as you. Maybe not as happy as you. But I carved out a nice place for myself in Atlanta. Seeing you after so many years has disrupted everything. I never expected to still care. To still want you. I haven't been able to stop thinking about you. I don't know if that's love, but I do know it's something powerful." She rose and started taking off her clothes.

When only her underwear remained, he stood, too, and tugged his shirt over his head. He ran a hand down her arm, drawing a shiver. Then he kissed her as he unsnapped her bra and tossed it aside. They fell back on the bed once more, lips crushed together, hips moving in unison until a shuddering release left them spent, panting and laughing softly in wonder.

Chapter Fourteen

Abby awakened the next morning to the smell of fresh coffee. She drew on her robe and followed the scent out to the kitchen. Wade sat barefoot and shirtless on the terrace with his phone. She poured a cup, retrieved an envelope from her bag and went outside to join him.

He looked up with a smile that quickened her breath. "Good morning. Hope the coffee's not too strong for you."

"I like strong coffee."

He put away his phone and leaned his arms on the table. "How did you sleep last night?"

"Better than I have in a long time." She eyed him over the rim of her cup. "Except for when you kept me up."

He sat back and folded his hands behind his head. "I remember it differently. You were the one who kept me up."

"Let's not quibble over petty details." She took a tentative sip of her coffee. "Wow. That is strong."

"Don't say I didn't warn you. What's in the envelope?"

She handed him the packet. "Handwriting samples from work. Signatures mostly, but I did find handwritten notations on some old work orders. I labeled them so you would know who they belonged to. The warning notes are also inside for comparison."

He removed the contents and thumbed through the pages. "No one saw you take these?"

"I was careful. Lydia is out of town, so that made things a little easier. How long do you think the analysis will take?"

"I'll scan and email this morning. But the analyst will probably want the originals to make an informed decision. I'll have to overnight them, so be prepared to wait at least a couple of days." He spread the pages on the table and scrutinized the signatures.

Abby said anxiously, "What do you think?"

He shrugged. "I'm no expert. Take what I say with a grain of salt. Could be nothing more than the power of suggestion, but I do see a similarity with the notes."

"Show me." She got up and came around the table to stand behind him.

"Compare Lydia's signature on some of the work orders with the warning notes. The loop through the lowercase *a* is similar. See what I mean?"

Abby squinted. "Not really. That seems a common way to write a lowercase *a* to me. And, anyway, now that I think about it, why wouldn't the person who wrote those notes disguise their handwriting?"

"Maybe they were in a hurry." He gathered up the pages and returned them to the envelope. "In any case, we'll see what a real expert has to say." He slid the envelope aside and picked up his coffee. "What else is on the day's agenda?"

"I'm sure Detective Benson has been to see James by now, and he'll have informed Lydia about Mother's murder. She won't be back until late this afternoon, so I should probably stop by and make sure he's okay. At least I won't have to pretend not to know things."

"Just be careful. Remember, no one has been ruled out as a suspect."

"I'll be fine." But she sounded far more confident than she felt. Her stepfather's odd behavior the day before had left her uncomfortable. "Before that, I'm meeting with a general contractor at one of our properties in the Moon Bay neighborhood."

"Moon Bay?" He frowned.

"It's just a few miles north of here."

"I remember the area as being fairly isolated," he said.

"Not anymore. Hardly any place on the lake is isolated these days."

"Moon Bay." He repeated the name, then glanced away as if something had occurred to him.

"What?" she prompted.

"With everything going on, I don't think it's a good idea for you to be alone with a stranger. Give me the address. I'll clear my schedule and meet you there."

She complied, then said, "Why did you get that look on your face when I mentioned Moon Bay?"

"What look?"

"Like you remembered something. What's going on?"

"I've been out there before," he said.

She didn't make the connection at first, but then the significance of the place dawned on her. "Wait. Is that where you saw them together?" She winced. "Now I won't be able to get that picture out of my head."

"It may not even be the same house," he said. "They probably used whatever place was empty at the time."

BUT THE IMAGE wouldn't go away, and a little while later when Abby let herself in the front door of the rental, she could almost hear the echoes of their passion . She'd made sure to arrive early so that she could walk the property before the general contractor arrived. Wade wasn't around, either. She thumbed a message to let him know she'd arrived and then put her phone away as she stepped from the foyer into the large family room. A wall of windows provided an amazing view of the lake.

She started forward only to halt with a gasp. For a moment she stood frozen, her gaze pinned to the body on the floor. To Brett Fortier's ashen face. Blood puddled beneath his head. He didn't appear to be breathing.

Heart pounding, she fished for her phone as she hurried across the room to offer assistance even though instinct and the pallor of his skin told her that he was dead. How could anyone survive a wound that produced so much blood?

Her first thought was that he'd been murdered by whoever had come looking for his boat. The killer might still be in the house—

"Put away the phone," a familiar voice said behind her. She whirled in shock.

Her stepfather gestured with the barrel of his gun. "Put the phone on the floor and back away from the body."

"James?" She stared at him in horror. "What have you done?" she asked in a near whisper.

His features hardened into someone she barely recognized. "Do as I say. The phone. Now!"

She put the phone on the floor and slowly rose. "What are you doing?"

"Isn't it obvious? I'm protecting myself." His gaze dropped to the body. "He was a drug dealer. Think of how many lives he ruined. I wouldn't waste my time mourning the lies of Brett Fortier if I were you."

"He was a human being!" she cried, still unable to put the pieces together. "How did killing him protect you?"

"Do I really have to spell it out? Anyone who knew Brett Fortier could have predicted his demise years ago. The police will conclude that you walked in on a drug deal gone bad. His buyers panicked and took you both out."

Abby swallowed. He was right. The police would come to the same conclusion she had, but not Wade. He would never buy such an easy explanation. He would keep digging even if it meant putting himself in danger.

Wade. She drew a breath and tried to slow her racing heart. He would be here soon and he had no idea what he would be walking into. She had to stay calm while she searched for a way out. She had to remain alive so that she could warn him. "Wade Easton will never let you get away with this. You know that, don't you?"

He smiled, showing a hint of the old charming James. "I doubt he'll have much credibility once the local authorities realize he and his father have been lying to them for years." He feigned surprise. "Oh, wait. You didn't think I knew about the affair?"

"What affair?"

He gave a low chuckle. "You never were a good liar. Unlike your mother." He took a step into the room. "Oh, I knew all right. She never bothered to hide it. The covert phone calls in the middle of the night. The new hairstyle, the new underwear. All the working late excuses. And to think, I left my first wife for that…woman. One could almost appreciate the irony."

"That was a long time ago," Abby said. "Surely, you're not still holding a grudge. You can't blame me for what happened."

"Blame you? No. I've always been fond of you."

"Then what do you want?" she asked in desperation. "Money? The company? You don't have to do this. We can make a deal."

"A deal that will expire as soon as I let you walk out that

door." His shook his head. "Give me more credit than that. I've poured my life into that company, *your* company, and for what? So that you can waltz in and take what should rightfully be mine?"

"That was never my intention," Abby said. "I don't want the company. I never wanted it."

"Maybe not now, but you would eventually. Big things are in the works. I've put together the kind of deals that Eva could only dream about. All that money. You wouldn't be able to resist."

Abby shifted her position imperceptibly, putting her weight on her back foot so that she could try and make a run for it if and when the opportunity arose. "What did Brett have to do with any of this?"

"His arrival in town was serendipitous. When I heard about his stolen boat, I figured he was up to his neck in something dangerous. Drugs, most likely. We'd crossed paths before, he and I. In fact, we had an arrangement. I'd let him hole up in a rental now and then when he needed a place to lay low."

"Why would you do that?"

Another quick smile. "In addition to dealing drugs, Brett dabbled in blackmail."

"What did he have on you?"

"Can't you guess?"

Abby's hands tightened into fists at her sides. "He saw you on the bridge the night my mother was murdered."

"Now are you starting to put it all together?"

A wave of red-hot hanger washed over her. "You're a monster. You couldn't just kill her outright. You wanted to watch her suffer."

"You don't think she deserved it?"

"No one deserves what you did to her. All these years, you let everyone believe she ran off with another man."

He waved the gun in her direction. "You want the cold, hard truth about that night? Your mother was a heartless bitch. She would have left her only child without a backward glance if not for Sam Easton's conscience. He got cold feet at the last minute. He called it off, but she couldn't accept his rejection."

"How do you know that?"

"Because I heard her on the phone. She pleaded with him to meet her at the bridge, to give her one last chance. That must have killed her, having to beg for a man's affection." He smirked.

"So you went instead," Abby said. "And Brett saw what you did."

"We came to an agreement that worked out well over the years, but people like him always get greedy. They always start clawing for more. I knew it was only a matter of time before I'd have to find a permanent solution to his blackmail. It may sound strange, but my heart attack turned out to be fortuitous. I had days and days in the hospital to plan. All I had to do was get you back here. Then make it look as though you were simply in the wrong place at the wrong time."

"But you didn't count on Mother's body being found, did you?"

"An interesting confluence of events," he said. "But it doesn't change anything. With you out of the way, the business is mine."

"What about Lydia?"

"What about her?"

Abby inched toward the patio door. "Does she know about your plan?"

"She's a wonderful daughter, but a little thick sometimes. I could never trust her with something this important. Why do you think I arranged for her to be out of town? It'll be over by the time she returns."

"She may not be as clueless as you think," Abby said. "She's been trying to warn me."

He scoffed at the notion of his daughter's betrayal. "Don't be ridiculous. She doesn't know anything."

"Maybe she does. Maybe she knows everything. What if she decides the business should be hers? You've got a bad heart. It wouldn't take much—"

"Stop," he said. "I see what you're trying to do. Take another step toward the door and I'll drop you where you stand."

"Why haven't you already pulled the trigger?" Abby taunted. "Why take the time to tell me all about your plan? Maybe you want me to appreciate how clever you are. Or maybe it's proving harder than you thought it would be."

"What are you talking about?"

"Killing me in cold blood. You can't quite bring yourself to do it, can you? That's why it's taking so long."

She worried that she'd goaded him too far, but then her ringtone sounded, and they both jumped. Her gaze shot to the phone. "That'll be Wade. He's on his way here. He may be outside already. If you shoot me now, he'll hear the gunshots. You won't be able to get away from him."

James looked momentarily panicked. His gaze darted around the room before coming back to her. "You're lying."

"I'm not. He didn't want me to come out here alone. He said he would meet me here. He'll be at the door any minute."

"You better hope that's not true."

He took a step back into the foyer so that he could glance out the window. Abby reacted instinctively. She lunged for the patio door, fumbling with the lock and then ducking as a shot rang out. Then she was out the door and flying down the dock steps. She screamed and waved her arms at a passing boat. The passengers waved back and were gone by the time James came after her.

Desperate now, he fired from the top of the steps. She dove off the dock and swam to the bottom, holding her breath until her lungs forced her to surface. Keeping to the side of the dock, she pressed up against the bumpers as she eased through the water to the bank.

James stood at the end of the platform gazing down into the water where she'd gone in. For a moment, Abby considered hoisting herself on the dock and catching him by surprise. She had to make a move soon. She couldn't hide in the water forever.

As she vacillated, she saw movement out of the corner of her eye. Before she had time to catch her breath, Wade rushed down the steps and flew past her at a dead run. James whirled at the sound of his footsteps. He fired as Wade slammed into him. The momentum toppled them into the lake.

Abby scrambled up on the dock and ran to the end, dropping to her knees as she tried to peer through the murk. She didn't know whether Wade had been hit or not. They were underwater for what seemed an eternity. Then James bobbled to the surface. She stared at him in horror, bracing herself until she realized something was wrong with him. Wade came up then, grabbed James and heaved him onto the platform.

"We need a phone," he said on a breath. "I think he's having a heart attack."

For a moment, Abby just stood staring down at her stepfather as the image of another struggle played out in her head. James handcuffing her mother to the steering wheel and then watching from the bridge as the car sank to the bottom.

"Abby, move!"

She snapped back to the present. Wade was already starting CPR.

Turning without a word, she dashed up the steps to the house.

"HE'LL LIVE," Wade said a few hours later as he sat down beside her on the cottage steps. She'd been deep in thought before he arrived. Her life had drastically changed in the blink of an eye, and she hardly knew how or where to start processing.

"That's good to know, I guess." She felt numb to the news.

"He'll likely spend the rest of his life in prison, if that's any consolation."

"A small one." She hugged her knees to her chest. "What about Lydia?"

"She claims she didn't know anything, though she must have suspected. Why else would she have left those notes if not to scare you away?"

"She admitted to writing the notes?" Abby shook her head in disbelief. "Of all the people in my life, I would never have guessed in a million years that my evil stepsister would be the one to try and save me."

"People are complicated," Wade said. "At least you now know what happened to your mother."

She nodded. "I need to go see my grandmother. I have to be the one to tell her about James."

"When will you leave?"

"In the morning." Abby sighed. "She'll want to plan a service. I can't even bear to think about that right now, but if it helps her get through this, then I'll go along with whatever she wants." She turned reluctantly from the water. "Can I ask you something?"

"Anything."

"Do you think your dad meant to leave town with my mother?"

Wade answered slowly. "I think he considered it but changed his mind at the last minute, just like James said."

"The affair is bound to come out at the trial," Abby said. "Have you thought about that?"

He nodded. "I won't be able to protect my mother from the truth. I think deep down she knows. She's probably always known."

Abby said softly, "So what comes next?"

He turned at that. "You tell me. You're leaving for Atlanta tomorrow. Is this goodbye?"

She couldn't bear the thought of never seeing him again. "I'll be coming back here in a few days. There are so many things to settle. The business, the properties. It'll take months to sort everything out. But what about you? Your business is done here."

"Not all of it. I think I'll stick around for a while, too."

"For your mom?"

"For a lot of reasons." He turned from the water to gaze down at her. "Not the least of which is this view."

Her heart started to thud. "Wade—"

"It's our time, Abby."

She sighed. "I've waited a long time to hear you say that."

"I've waited a long time to say it."

They exchanged a smile, and then he took her hand and entwined their fingers as they turned in unison to watch the sunset.

* * * * *

POINT OF DISAPPEARANCE

CAROL ERICSON

Chapter One

The smoke unfurled like a suffocating blanket, obscuring Tate's view of the green pines in the distance. Despite the damp weather, sweat ran down his back beneath his fire shirt, which clung to him like a second skin. He hoisted his ax and buried it into a smoldering log.

The fire had already rushed through this area, but his hand crew wanted to make sure nothing reignited as the helicopters dumped flame retardant on the blaze, shifting to the right with the wind. He kicked at some blackened logs with the toe of his boot, and a flurry of sparks scattered in the air.

Turning around, he pulled the N95 mask away from his face. "I think we're almost finished with this area. The rain should be helping us out soon."

As if on cue, the skies opened, and a torrent of water pummeled the December forest fire, sending plumes of dark gray smoke billowing upward to meet the clouds. The sudden onslaught of rain turned the ashy ground beneath Tate's feet to mush.

His teammates whooped and hollered behind him, the wait for the storm break finally over, making their job easier.

Tate yelled over his shoulder. "We're not done yet, boys.

Let's break up a few more of these fallen logs. Plenty are still live."

To emphasize his point, Tate hoisted his pick ax over his head and brought it down on a smoldering stump. It hissed at him, as the rain soaked the wood, dampening the embers.

As Tate kicked at a few more logs with the toe of his heavy boot, the ground gave way beneath his other foot. He slid down an incline to the amusement of his crew.

Rivulets of water rushed past him, pooling into a muddy dip in the land. He grunted and propped himself up on his elbows, surveying the scorched trees before him.

As he scrambled to his knees they sunk in the soft earth, and he pitched forward. He thrust out a hand. It landed on a smooth rock, and he pushed against the solid object to gain some purchase.

The rock moved beneath his palm, shifting to the side. The eye sockets of a skull stared back at him. Choking, he snatched his hand back.

Like a faint echo, his teammates' voices swirled through the roaring in his ears. He licked his lips, his tongue sweeping through the wet ash clinging to his mouth.

"How long are you gonna stay down there wallowing in the mud, Tate? C'mon, man. It's almost quittin' time."

A twig cracked behind him, and Tate twisted around. "Stay where you are. We have a crime scene here."

James Clugston, his second-in-command, snorted. "What the hell are you talking about? The crime scene is where this firebug lit this blaze. We'll find it, but this ain't it."

Tate struggled to his feet, his legs rubbery. One arm windmilled for balance, as he planted his boots in the muck.

"I found a skeleton down here, so I guess we have two crime scenes."

The whooping and hollering stopped, and James coughed and spit. "Are you kidding me? How old is it?"

Turning his back on the bones, Tate faced his teammates and took a deep breath, tasting the smoke from the fire on the back of his tongue. "What the hell do I look like, a medical examiner?"

"You look like a tired, overworked US Forest Service agent. Like I'm looking in the mirror." Aaron Huang stepped aside as Tate slogged up the incline.

James stood on a fallen, blackened log and peered down the gully. "Who are we calling for this? Dead Falls Sheriff's Department? I'm sure they'll be able to crack the case in about fifty years."

Despite Tate's agreement that the Dead Falls Sheriff's Department was useless, his crew's laughter rubbed him the wrong way. He snapped. "Have some respect. That's someone's kid."

Aaron choked. "Kid? That's a kid's skeleton down there? I thought you didn't know crap about forensics."

Tate gulped. Was it a kid's skeleton? Did the skull seem small? "I—I just mean, that's someone's family member. I don't know the age or the sex or anything else, but we'd better call someone who can figure that out before we trample all over everything."

Cocking his head, James said, "Haven't we already done that? We just put out a major fire on top of this crime scene."

"As incompetent as he is, we need to start with Sheriff Hopkins." Tate unzipped his vest and dug in his pocket for his cell phone.

His thumb quivered as it hovered over the numbers on

the display. Was Hopkins too inept to handle the discovery of these bones? One part of Tate hoped so. He wasn't sure he wanted to know the identity of the person in that shallow grave.

BLANCA LOPEZ STEPPED off the ferry from Seattle to Dead Falls Island, rolling her suitcase beside her and clamping her laptop bag between her arm and her body. Her heels clicked authoritatively on the concrete dock, even though she hadn't a clue where she was going.

The words of her mentor, Manny Rodriguez, pinged in her brain. *Always act like you know what you're doing and where you're going.* Even though she now despised Manny, he had gotten a few things right.

She mumbled, "Got it, Manny."

"Ah, miss, er, ma'am?"

She spun around so quickly her heel caught in a crack in the concrete and she stumbled. The young deputy caught her arm, a sea of red suffusing his baby face. "Yeah, sorry."

She flicked her ponytail over her shoulder and straightened her shoulders. "No need to apologize, Deputy. You saved me from an embarrassing start to my assignment."

Dropping her arm, he said, "I'm Deputy Fletcher."

Blanca thrust out her hand. "Good to meet you, Deputy Fletcher. I'm FBI Special Agent Blanca Lopez."

When he took her hand, she squeezed hard to make up for her earlier klutziness. Had Manny ever fallen on his face when meeting the local law?

When she ended the handshake, Fletcher flexed his fingers and said, "Do you want me to take you to your hotel or straight to the station? We have a car for you at the station."

"I think station." She jiggled the handle of her suitcase. "I can dump my stuff in the car, maybe have a quick meeting with Sheriff Hopkins and pick up any files he has for me."

"Sounds good, ma'am. Can I take your bags for you?"

Blanca wrinkled her nose. "You can call me Agent Lopez, Deputy, and I can handle my own bags."

"Sure, ma— Agent Lopez." He strode ahead of her, his back stiff. "This way to the car."

Blanca bit her lip. Manny always told her to command respect, but she didn't want to get off on the wrong foot with the locals. Manny never seemed to care about local law enforcement, but Blanca had come to realize it helped the investigation if they didn't hate you. Manny wasn't always right.

She cleared her throat. "The island looked beautiful coming in on the ferry. So green. Are the falls dead? Is that the reason for the name?"

"Dead?" Fletcher cranked his gaze over his shoulder and raised his eyebrows. "Not sure what a dead waterfall would look like, but no. It's called Dead Falls because the angle on that water is a dead drop. Get it?"

"Makes sense." A lot more sense than a dead waterfall. What was a dead waterfall?

Her high heels wobbled on a pebble in the parking lot, and she took a little hopping step to avoid further embarrassment.

She eyed the suitcase trundling beside her over the rough asphalt. She'd filled it with similar work clothes—skirts, slacks, jackets, blouses and heels. She just hoped her new hiking boots would work out here and that she'd packed enough jeans and sweaters to last for the duration of her stay, and that depended on how much information the Dead Falls Sheriff's Department had on her cold case.

Maybe that fire a few days ago had already done her work

for her. Case closed if the bones exposed by that blaze belonged to Jeremy Ruesler...or at least that part of the case solved. They could put Jeremy down as a murder instead of a missing child, but most law enforcement agencies and probably the poor boy's family already knew that.

If that skeleton did belong to Jeremy, they still needed to figure out who killed him—and she had a perfect starting point for that.

Fletcher pointed out a few landmarks on their drive from the dock to the station. The rugged terrain of the island that she'd spied from the ferry spread inland, covered by dense forest and rushing bodies of water, including those falls. She'd never been much of an outdoorsy girl, but the sight of that deep green and the smell of pine mingling with the salt of the ocean had caused prickles to rush across her skin. The atmosphere of the island charged her with a sense of awakening, a new start, and she sat on the edge of the passenger seat, drinking in Fletcher's impromptu guided tour. God knew she needed a new start.

By the time the deputy pulled into the parking lot of the Dead Falls Sheriff's Station, Blanca's newfound appreciation of the world hit reality. The beige, one-story stucco building looked like police stations all across the country. She had a hard time believing the course of her future resided within those prosaic walls, but she *had* turned a corner this past year, and this assignment was going to be the culmination of her reset.

She could almost hear Manny's low laugh in her ear. *Follow me, kid, and I'll steer you right.*

She curled her fingers around the strap of her purse. Manny had steered her straight to hell. Maybe the fresh air of Dead Falls Island could blow his memory right out of her mind.

"Agent Lopez?" Fletcher sat beside her, his door open, one foot already planted on the parking lot. "This is it."

"That didn't take long. Thanks for the guided tour." She flashed him a quick smile before releasing her seat belt and pulling the handle of the door.

The deputy waited for her at the entrance of the station and held open the door for her. "Would you like me to transfer your suitcase to the trunk of your car, Agent Lopez?"

"Whatever's most convenient for you, Deputy Fletcher."

"That way, when you're done talking to Sheriff Hopkins, I can just hand you the keys to the car and you can be on your way. There's a GPS in the car, so you can follow that to your hotel."

"That works for me. Thanks." She walked through the swinging door he held open for her and followed him down a short hallway. Her heel taps echoed in the mostly empty station. All patrol cars must be out on duty. These small stations definitely didn't have the same buzz as their big-city counterparts. The fact that they couldn't handle homicide investigations didn't surprise her. It had been a PI and a forensic psychologist who had solved the latest murder in Dead Falls. No wonder they'd had this cold case on the books for the past nineteen years.

The clicking of fingers on a keyboard intensified as they drew closer to the end of the hallway. Deputy Fletcher tapped on an open door, and the clicking stopped.

"Sheriff Hopkins, I have FBI Special Agent Blanca Lopez with me."

Blanca peeked around the corner of the office door, and a balding man with crumbs on the chest of his uniform stood up behind the desk. "Thanks, Fletch. Agent Lopez, welcome to Dead Falls Island. C'mon in. Car ready, Fletch?"

"Yes, sir. I'm just going to move Agent Lopez's suit-

case from the squad car to the sedan…and the other stuff."
Fletcher backed out of the sheriff's office awkwardly, his
long legs almost not up to the intricate maneuver.

Blanca thanked the deputy again and stepped into Hopkins's office. Family pictures populated the bookshelf behind his desk, and plaques and awards dotted the wall. Her
gaze tracked across his messy workspace, noting the absence of anything that looked like cold-case files.

Clearing her throat, she reached over the desk to shake
hands. She didn't give this one the death squeeze, as his
hand lay limp and damp in her own. When they broke apart,
she resisted the urge to wipe her palm on her slacks.

She shuffled back, and when the back of her knees
touched the edge of the chair, she sat. "Thanks for having
me here, Sheriff Hopkins."

Smiling, he folded hands. "When the FBI calls and tells
you they want to look into one of your cold cases, you jump."

"We appreciate the response." She settled her laptop case
on the floor. "I'm assuming you haven't gotten any DNA
results back from the bones, yet?"

"Nope." He transferred a batch of papers from one side
of his desk to the other. "We don't have the familial DNA
yet for comparison."

She widened her eyes. Were the locals just waiting for
the FBI to do all the work? "Is the Ruesler family still on
the island?"

"The mother is. She's not being particularly cooperative.
Never was, after the initial investigation failed to locate her
boy." Hopkins finally folded his hands as if to keep them
from fidgeting among the mess on his desk.

"I would think…" Blanca rubbed her chin. "No, I take
that back. Maybe she doesn't want to know. Some people

would prefer to have that closure, and some would rather keep believing."

Hopkins lifted his rounded shoulders, spreading his hands, as if he'd never even considered the matter. "Maybe as an outsider, you can get her DNA."

"I'll try." She bent forward to retrieve a notebook and pen from the side of her bag, her ponytail slipping over her shoulder. "Is there anything you can tell me about the site where the skeleton was found? Any items there beside the bones?"

His rather dull eyes, a muddy gray, stared at her. He blinked once. "I wasn't there. US Forest Service Agent Tate Mitchell found the remains while wrapping up a forest fire."

Blanca gripped the arms of her chair, as a zing shot up her spine. Tate Mitchell found the remains? How had she missed that all-important detail?

"Tate Mitchell? You mean the one…?"

Hopkins nodded. "Yep. Strange, isn't it?"

Strange and fortuitous at the same time. Anxious to end her pointless interview with Hopkins and start the real investigation, she shoved the notebook back in her bag, her hand hovering over the strap. "The files. Do you have the cold-case files?"

Hopkins sat back in his chair, his hands folded over his paunch, a satisfied smile on his lips. "I asked Fletcher earlier to put them in the trunk of the car we're loaning you for your stay. You'll find them next to your luggage, most likely."

"Perfect." She sprang up from the chair, hauling her bag with her. "Thanks for your time."

Hopkins nodded, a look of relief spreading across his face as he eyed the half-eaten sandwich on his desk. "Anything we can do for you, just ask."

Blanca hoisted her bag over her shoulder and stopped at the door. "One more thing."

Hopkins's hand paused, halfway to his sandwich. "Yes?"

"Do you know where I can find Tate Mitchell?"

After Hopkins scribbled down directions to Mitchell's cabin, Blanca clutched the piece of paper in her hand and strode from the station. As she pushed through the glass door, a fat drop of rain plonked on the back of her hand.

She glanced at the darkening skies. Something had to keep this island green.

Deputy Fletcher emerged from a dark sedan and waved. "I got your car, Agent Lopez. Suitcase in the trunk."

Taking a zigzag path as if she could avoid the scattered rain, she navigated to the open driver's-side door. "Thanks, Deputy. Ruesler case files?"

"In the trunk with your suitcase." He dropped the key fob in her hand. "Ma'am, you can call me Fletch. Everyone does."

"Okay, Fletch, and you can call me Blanca. Just anything besides *ma'am*." She curled her fist around the fob and ducked into the car. To hell with Manny's rules of conduct. Where had they ever got her?

She tucked the key fob into her purse on the passenger seat and punched the ignition button with her knuckle. The sedan's engine purred to life. At least they hadn't saddled her with a junker.

She smoothed the crumpled piece of paper with Mitchell's address on the console and tapped in the name of the road on the GPS. The cabin didn't have an actual house number to enter, but the GPS should get her to the general location, and then she could rely on Hopkins's directions.

Hunching over the steering wheel, she peered at the sky through the windshield. As far as she could tell, no forest fires were currently consuming the island, so Mitchell should be around and available. What were the odds that Tate Mitchell had been the one to find those bones? He must have something buried in his memory—and she was going to find out what it was.

The journey from the station took her on a windy road that ended in the town, but she took the bypass. After a few miles, the coastline and Discovery Bay disappeared as she wound her way inland, getting sucked into the emerald landscape. She'd figured it would be gray and dull out here at this time of year, but the vibrant blue of the bay and lush green of the forest dazzled her vision.

The rain had stopped by the time she made her way to Mitchell's cabin. She rolled up behind a Jeep, the tires of the sedan crunching over dirt and gravel. The *cabin* label hardly gave this abode justice.

The log exterior and Alpine roof screamed cabin, but the deck running the length of the house and the massive windows that had to afford views of the forest and bay beyond gave off luxury-resort vibes. Once again, she got the feeling of her chest expanding and her pores opening.

As she cut the engine, a tall blonde woman exited the structure, dragging a suitcase, a boy trailing behind her, a backpack slung over one shoulder. Uh-oh, had she stumbled on the Mitchell family leaving for a vacation? Maybe a Christmas vacation?

Blanca shoved open the car door, her high heel landing on the uneven ground. She should've changed before coming out here, but then maybe she would've missed the Mitchells completely.

The woman parked the suitcase on the driveway and called over her shoulder. "It's okay. The car's already here."

Blanca opened her mouth to protest when the woman's

head whipped around, her long, blond hair cascading over one shoulder. Tate Mitchell's luck must've changed somewhere along the line: he had a beautiful wife, cute son, gorgeous home and exciting job. Jeremy Ruesler was just dead.

"Go on, Olly. You can put our bags in the trunk yourself. Don't make the driver do it." The woman nudged the boy while flashing her pearly whites at Blanca.

A man clumped down the steps of the house behind the woman and child. "I told you I'd drive you, Astrid."

Blanca kept her jaw firmly in place as she eyed the tall Nordic-looking man dressed like a lumberjack in jeans, boots and a blue-plaid flannel shirt. Tate Mitchell had lucked out in the looks department, too. He resembled a modern-day Thor. All he needed was a giant square hammer over his shoulder.

So, Thor wasn't going with his wife and child. She'd lucked out, too.

The boy, Olly, grabbed his mother's suitcase and dragged it behind him as he trundled toward Blanca. "C-can I put this in the back, please?"

Blanca waved her hands. "I'm so sorry for the confusion. I'm not your driver."

"I didn't think so." Mitchell drew up beside his statuesque wife and hung his arm around her shoulders, but his gaze flicked from Blanca's ponytail, which was now frizzing in the moisture, to the tips of her high heels. Her toes curled in the very shoes under his scrutiny, and a little ball of fury formed in her gut at his assessing stare. Men shouldn't eye other women like that in the presence of their families.

The rattle of an engine behind her took away Mitchell's focus as he leveled a finger at the small car. "That must be your ride. Is the car even big enough for your bag?"

"Stop worrying." Astrid placed two hands on his broad

chest and shoved. Then she gave Blanca another smile that made her skin glow even more. "My apologies for the mistake."

"No worries." Blanca held up her hands. "I'm actually here to see Tate Mitchell."

"That would be him." Astrid jerked her thumb toward her husband. "Olly, put the bags in the car."

Both she and her husband followed the boy to the car. A young man jumped out and took the suitcase from him. "I got this, my man."

With Olly settled in the back seat, Astrid turned to Tate and gave him a kiss on the cheek. "Don't forget to join us for the holiday. I'll text you from Mom's."

If her husband seemed disappointed in the chaste farewell, he didn't show it. Hunching his shoulder, Tate shoved his hands in his pockets and watched the car turn in the driveway.

Then he faced her and raised his eyebrows over a pair of eyes so blue they could've been drops from Discovery Bay. "I suppose you're here about the bones. Hopkins call you in from Seattle?"

Blanca squared her shoulders. "I'm FBI Special Agent Blanca Lopez, Mr. Mitchell. I'm here to investigate the cold case of Jeremy Ruesler. And I want to start my investigation by asking you what you remember about the day you two were playing in the forest and authorities found you tied to a tree with blood in your shoes…and no sign of Jeremy."

Chapter Two

Tate swallowed hard, the hands in his pockets curling into fists. He knew this day would come. He should've known it would as soon as he discovered those bones in the ash of the forest fire. What he didn't expect was the accusatory tone of the FBI agent in charge of the investigation...at least not right out of the box. She seemed angry with him.

He cleared his throat and glanced at the morose sky, his gaze meandering to the agent's olive-green pantsuit, her pale-yellow blouse, open to reveal the tan, slim column of her neck and settling on her high heels rapidly sinking into the dirt. "It's probably going to start raining in earnest. Let's take this inside."

He shifted to the right to allow her to walk ahead of him. Her heels wobbled on the driveway, and he resisted the urge to place a hand on her hip to steady her. She managed to make it to the porch without stumbling and climbed the two steps to the wooden deck.

As he reached past her to open the front door, her heel must've caught in a groove in the wood, and she tripped. This time he grabbed her arm. "If you're planning to stick around, you need to get yourself a different pair of shoes."

She glanced at his hand still on her sleeve and ran her tongue along her pillowy bottom lip. "I figured that out already. I'm still in my work clothes from the office, but I brought more appropriate attire."

He released his grip and patted the wrinkled material of her suit jacket. "Sorry about that. C'mon in."

He beckoned to her as he took a few steps down to the great room, one glass wall facing the forest, the stone fireplace cold for now.

Her dark eyes widened. "This is a beautiful room. It's like you're in the middle of the forest."

Cocking his head, he said, "I guess so. Would you like something to drink? Coffee? Tea? Water?"

"Tea would be nice, thanks."

He moved toward the kitchen, and she parked herself on one of the stools at the island. She dragged a notebook from her expensive-looking leather satchel and plopped it on the granite countertop. She lined up her cell phone next to the notepad. "Do you mind if I record our conversation?"

He jerked his hand, and the water filling the teapot splashed his fingers. "I guess not, but I'm afraid you're in for a disappointment. I don't remember what occurred that day. I've been to hypnotists and therapists, and whatever happened is buried deep."

She tapped the display on her phone and adjusted its position on the swirling green granite. "I had read that, but maybe with the discovery of those bones—*your* discovery of the bones—something might click in your brain."

He set the kettle on the burner and turned toward her, folding his arms. "Forensics isn't back, yet. We don't even know if those bones belong to Jeremy."

"Did you find them near where he went missing nineteen years ago?"

"No." He rubbed his eye. He and Jeremy had never

played on that side of the island. Too dangerous, their parents had said.

He grabbed a mug from the cupboard and a stash of several different tea bags Astrid liked. He held them up to Lopez. "Anything catch your fancy?"

"Anything herbal is fine."

Holding the selection up to his face, he squinted at the print and selected one with orange and cinnamon. A few minutes later, the kettle started whistling, and he ripped open the packet and hung the string of the tea bag over the edge of the cup while he poured the hot water over it. Steam rose from the cup, the smell of the cinnamon with it.

He placed the cup in front of Lopez. "My sister drinks this one a lot. I recognize the smell."

"Your sister?" She dredged the bag in the water, raising her eyes to his face.

"That stubborn blonde you met earlier. That's my sister, Astrid, and her son, Olly. They've been staying with me temporarily since my sister...uh, had some problems." He shrugged. "I told her I'd take her to the ferry to Seattle where she was catching a flight to Florida to visit our mother, but she didn't want to put me out."

"Oh, your sister." Lopez's shoulders rounded and she released a long breath. "I thought that was your wife."

"God, no." He laughed and smacked his forehead.

"And your wife doesn't mind sharing her home with your sister?" She cranked her head back and forth as if expecting this wife to pop out of the woodwork at any time. Why was she so insistent on him having a wife?

"She might mind if I had one. A wife, I mean." He held up his left hand as if he felt he needed to show her proof of his marital status. "Single."

Lopez's gaze slid to her phone, still recording their every

word, and a blush tinted her cheeks beneath her tanned skin. She picked up the phone by its edges, and her thumb grazed the screen.

Had she thought better of exposing their conversation to other ears? It's not like asking about his marital status was unprofessional, but she must've felt the underlying tension to their dialogue, too.

He pointed a finger at the tea bag still swirling in her cup. "I'll get you a plate for that."

When he turned back around, small plate in hand, Lopez had regained her composure. Her pen moved across the notebook in a fluid script, as her short, polished nails gleamed under the pendant lights hanging above the island.

She thanked him for the plate and then said, "Tell me everything you remember about that day with Jeremy Ruesler. Did you notice anyone following you? Anyone suspicious? Strangers in the area?"

Spreading his hands, he said, "I'm sure this is all in the case files, and my statements back then would've been fresher than anything I can give you today. Have you read the case files, yet?"

"I read what the special agent in charge gave me when he assigned this case to me." She jerked a thumb over her shoulder. "The case files from the Dead Falls Sheriff's Department are in the trunk of my car. I haven't gone through them yet."

"Maybe you should do that first and then follow up with me." Despite his words, a knot formed in his gut at the thought of this woman peering at him as a child through the lens of the present. Not that he'd done anything wrong. He hadn't done anything wrong.

"I thought it would be more helpful to question you now, as an adult. Find out if any of those memories have surfaced.

You were a boy then, traumatized, in shock." She peered at him over the rim of her cup as she took a sip of tea.

Her brown eyes skewered him, as if she could read his mind. As if she knew on some level that the event still traumatized him. His parents had sent him to a therapist after Jeremy's disappearance, but he hadn't talked to her much. Law enforcement at the time had even tried hypnosis, but he hadn't been susceptible. He'd never been able to go back to that time and remember. Why did Agent Lopez believe he could do it now?

She asked in a soft voice. "Can we try?"

"Why not?" He circled the island and dragged a stool from beneath the counter overhang. He sat down, facing her, his knees almost touching the side of her stool.

He remembered his first interview after the deputies found him tied to a tree. He'd spoken to Sheriff Maddox at the time, and even though a female deputy had sat in on the interview, Tate had been scared to death.

As he watched Agent Lopez scoot her stool around so that she faced him, her knees inches from his, her curvy figure visible as her jacket gaped open, he figured she could probably get a lot more out of him than gruff Maddox and the dour-faced female deputy.

She cleared her throat and tugged her jacket closed. "What kind of day was it? Did you and Jeremy always play together in the woods?"

"It was after Christmas. We were still on winter break from school, so probably about three weeks from today's date. Jeremy had a new bike, so of course we were going to go out riding in the forest. He was my best friend." Tate's nose tingled, but he didn't dare sniff. "Harry van Pelt also hung out with us, but he was sick that week."

"You always rode your bikes in the forest? People would know that?"

"Sure, yeah. A lot of the kids did. We were twelve at the time, so, uh, we were kind of coming to the end of our childhood. Boys a year ahead of us were already hanging out by the falls, teasing the girls." A smile tugged at his lips as he remembered how conflicted he, Jeremy and Harry were about girls.

"What time of day was it?"

"Late afternoon, but not dark yet. Our parents always gave us the directive to be home before dark. We took it seriously because our parents would ground us if we broke curfew." He rubbed his chin as he stared over her shoulder. "This island can be a dangerous place, Agent Lopez."

"Call me Blanca, please." She flicked her slim fingers in the air. "Was there a particular game you played, or did you just ride your bikes through the woods?"

"We'd ride and do some stunts like hop over logs or skid sideways down an incline. Honestly, we were pretending to be motocross riders." He put a finger to his lips. "But don't tell anyone that. We never did."

"You never told the police that?" She tilted her head and her ponytail, which had curled at the ends, danced on her shoulder.

"That's not a big deal, is it? Kids' make-believe?" He drummed his fingers on the table. Did Blanca think she'd just coaxed him into a breakthrough?

"Probably not, but it means you didn't tell the deputies everything. You held back. Makes me wonder what else you didn't disclose." She wrapped her ponytail around her hand before tossing it over her shoulder. "So you and Jeremy were playing motocross in the forest in the late afternoon. What's the last thing you remember before coming to, tied to the tree?"

"I just remember the playing. Nothing happened. Nobody approached us. Neither of us got hurt or..." He stopped and chewed on his bottom lip.

"Or what?" She shimmied up to the edge of the stool, her knee bumping his. "Did one of you crash, fall, get hurt?"

He nodded. "I did hit a log and crash, and there was blood in my shoes. The bottoms of my feet and my socks were ripped up, like I'd been running without my shoes. But that makes no sense to me. I don't have any recollection of taking off my shoes or running without them."

"It was your blood, not Jeremy's."

"That's correct." He clenched the edges of the stool with both hands. "I didn't have any of Jeremy's blood on me."

He released the chair and flexed his fingers. Had Blanca noticed the defensive hysteria in his voice?

Her luminous eyes studied his face, and the look she gave him caused a lump to form in his throat and made him feel like crying, something he'd never done as a shell-shocked twelve-year-old.

Her hand grazed his leg as she resettled herself in her seat. "In fact, Jeremy's blood wasn't found at the scene, was it?"

"They didn't find anything of Jeremy's, except his new bike and his Linkin Park hat. There was nothing in the hat. No other DNA except Jeremy's, no blood, no sign of trauma to the hat."

She asked, "Was the hat found near the bike?"

"It was."

"But not near where you were located." She crossed one leg over the other and clasped her hands over her knee.

"What did you remember when you woke up against that tree? Had you come to before the deputies found you?"

"I didn't remember a thing. I was out until the deputies discovered me. They called my name and started untying me. I panicked." He scooped in a deep breath. "I thought maybe Jeremy and I had been playing some other sort of game and he tied me up. I didn't even know Jeremy was missing until they all started asking me where he was. His mother. Everybody. *Where's Jeremy?*"

He must've drifted off because Blanca touched his leg, on purpose this time.

"That must've been terrifying. And you could never remember what happened out there." She clicked her nails on the granite. "You said they tried hypnosis?"

"I'm not a good subject." He drew back his shoulders as if that fact made him proud. Did it? If he were a good subject, he could've helped solve Jeremy's disappearance. Could've given Mrs. Ruesler some answers.

"Have you tried lately?"

Tate's jaw dropped. "Now? How would that even be reliable after nineteen years?"

"That's the point of hypnosis. It's revealing memories that occurred in the past, undiluted by time and other impressions." Blanca scribbled some words in the notebook and flipped it shut.

"Is it, though? Can't hypnosis plant memories?" He pushed back from the stool and stood up. If she was done with him, he didn't want to encourage her to continue. He'd had enough.

"I suppose it can, but we've used it before to good effect."

"I think it's a certain personality type that's not responsive to hypnosis." He thumped his chest with a fist. "Not then, not now."

She raised her perfectly sculpted eyebrows. "I think it's more of a cognitive style than a personality type, but if you already strongly believe it won't work on you, then it probably won't."

"More tea?" He pinged her cup with his fingernail, and then held his breath. He was supposed to be getting rid of her.

"I'll finish what I have." She curled her fingers around the handle of the mug and swirled the remaining liquid. "How did you feel when you found those bones last week?"

Her words hit him like a punch to the gut. Just when he thought she'd finished with him, she had to dig deeper.

Crossing his arms, he wedged his hip against the counter. "Surprised. Distressed. I was putting out a forest fire. I didn't expect to find a shallow grave."

"It must have occurred to you that the bones could be Jeremy's." She narrowed her eyes, ready to disbelieve any lie that sprang to his lips.

With his arms still folded, he hunched his shoulders, closing her out. "I found bones. I didn't immediately think of Jeremy. Like I said... Blanca, Dead Falls Island is a dangerous place."

She scooted off the stool, giving a little hop to reach the floor. "I'm sure I'll have more questions after I go through the case file, Mr. Mitchell."

His lips quirked at her formality. "It's Tate. This ain't Washington, DC, Blanca."

"I gathered that." She turned to place her cup in the sink and tripped to a stop at the view outside the windows in the great room. "It's dark already."

"Well, it is winter. Or almost." He took the cup from her grasp, his fingers brushing the soft skin on the back of her hand. He didn't see a ring on her finger, either. He hadn't had a girlfriend in the longest time and enjoyed playing the field, but he drew the line at married women. He hoped he didn't have to draw any lines with Blanca Lopez.

She smoothed her slacks over her rounded hips and tugged at the hem of her jacket. "Are you going to be joining your sister soon at your mother's place, or will you be around for a while?"

"I'll be here for a while. You?"

"Until I solve this cold case." She flattened her lush lips against her teeth and still managed to look sexy as hell.

"You may be here a long time, Blanca." He rubbed his hands together. "Do you want a jacket to go over your suit for your walk to the car? If you thought it was cold this afternoon, wait until you feel it when the sun goes down. I'm sure Astrid has something you can borrow."

"I have a raincoat in my car, thanks." As she reached for her purse on the counter, Tate's phone rang.

His pulse ticked up a few notches when he saw the incoming number of the Dead Falls Sheriff's Department. Had they IDed the bones?

He held up a finger to Blanca. "Let me get this, and then I'll walk you to the car."

He tapped the phone. "Tate Mitchell."

"Tate, it's Amanda at the station."

Frowning, he asked, "Why are you whispering, Amanda?"

"I'm not sure if I'm allowed to release this info yet, but I thought you should know."

"The bones?" He glanced at Blanca, who'd stopped digging around in her purse. "Did you get the DNA results back on the bones?"

"No, it's not that, Tate." Amanda sighed over the phone. "It's another boy. Another boy has gone missing from the island."

Chapter Three

Blanca watched Tate's handsome face lose all color, and her heart tripped. Was it the DNA? Had the medical examiner determined the bones belonged to an adolescent male? They couldn't have a match yet for Jeremy without the familial DNA to compare.

She clutched her purse to her chest as she listened to Tate on the phone.

"When?" He ran a hand through his spiky blond hair. "So he could've just wandered off. Is there a search underway?"

Blanca curled her fingers into the leather of her purse and swallowed, her throat suddenly dry. Search for whom?

Tate continued. "Okay, let me know when it starts. I'll be there. Thanks, Amanda."

When he ended the call, Tate stood frozen, the phone pressed against his chin.

Blanca took a tentative step toward him. "What was that about? Who's missing?"

Tate shook his head. "A boy. A tourist. His family was camping near Prescott River. He wandered off this morning and didn't come back for breakfast. The family reported him missing after a few hours of searching for him."

"Just this morning?" Blanca hissed out a little breath she didn't know she'd been holding. "Maybe he's lost. Maybe he had a fight with his parents and took off to make a point. That's something I probably would've done if my parents had dragged me on a camping trip in the middle of December."

"Fishing trip for Christmas break. Not too unusual, but not the height of the season by any stretch, which is why nobody saw Noah."

"Are the deputies searching for him now?" Blanca drew her bottom lip between her teeth. Would the DFSD call in the FBI if they couldn't find him? Probably not, if they believed his disappearance was an accident.

Tate answered. "They're just starting to organize a night search for him. If he's not found by tomorrow morning, the deputies will most likely launch a search from the air."

"And you're going to join the night search."

"I am." His forehead crinkled. "It's odd, isn't it?"

She knew exactly what he meant. She'd felt it, too, despite her attempt to make light of the boy's disappearance. "You mean that one week after you find those bones, another boy goes missing."

He jerked his head up, his eyes widening, as if her take surprised him. "Yeah."

"People have gone missing on the island since Jeremy, right? Kids?"

"Sure, sure. A few have even died, victims of the rough terrain." He glanced at his phone as it buzzed in his hand. "The news is going public. The sheriff's department just invited interested people to meet at the parents' campsite."

"The family isn't still there, are they?" She put a hand to her throat. She couldn't imagine their terror.

"They've been moved to a motel in town." Tate clasped the back of his neck. "I'm going to get ready now. I'll walk you out to your car first."

"I'm joining the search, too."

He dipped his head, taking in her high heels. "Uh, that foot wear ain't gonna cut it."

She silently cursed Manny's bad advice about dressing to impress. Had he purposely led her astray? "I told you I had different clothes in my suitcase. I'll change and join the search. You and I both know this might be connected to the bones."

"You just got here. You don't even know the layout of the island."

She shrugged. "I can head to the sheriff's department and present myself as a volunteer. I'm sure someone, maybe Fletch, will take me to the search."

"Tell you what." He smacked the countertop. "I'll get ready and then follow you to your hotel. You can change there, and we'll go over to the search together."

"Why waste time?" She dragged out the key fob to the sheriff's sedan. "My suitcase is in my trunk. I'll change here, and we can head out directly without any detours."

His mouth opened a closed a few times.

Did he find her presumptuous? They'd just met, and she was proposing she change clothes in his house. Was she overstepping?

He held out his hand. "I'll bring it in."

She placed the key fob in his palm, and he strode outside. As she watched him from the window, he popped the trunk and hoisted her hard-sided suitcase to the ground.

He stared into the trunk. He must be looking at those boxes. Had he ever read the case files as an adult? She should suggest he peruse them. If he did, he might actually remember something from that day.

As he slammed the trunk and dragged the case to the

house, she jumped back from the window and pulled out her phone.

"Reporting to the home office?" He parked the suitcase at the foot of the stairs.

"Not yet." She dropped her phone in her pocket. She had no intention of telling her supervisor about this new case—not yet, anyway.

Tate aimed a toe at the suitcase. "I'll carry this upstairs. There are four bedrooms. The two on the right belong to Astrid and Olly. The main one's at the end, and there's a spare on the left. A friend of mine was staying there until recently, but I've cleaned up everything. You're welcome to change there."

"Got it."

She followed him up the stairs, noting the way his flannel shirt tightened across his back muscles as he carried her heavy suitcase. Too bad the cold weather had him all covered up.

He placed the suitcase on the floor and wheeled it into a bedroom, complete with queen-size bed, nightstands and a dresser with a mirror. "Let me know if you need any additional clothes. Astrid wouldn't mind."

Blanca smirked. "Except Astrid's about six feet tall."

"Not quite, and she's skinny." As soon as the words left his mouth, he pursed his lips.

Drawing back her shoulders, Blanca wedged a hand on her hip. "And I'm…?"

"Thin, but not as skinny as Astrid. She's a bean pole."

"Your sister looks like a supermodel. Don't insult her to save yourself." She wanted to put the poor guy out of his misery, so she laughed. "Don't worry. I'm not that sensitive about my appearance."

"And why would you be? You look—" He cleared his throat. "I'll meet you downstairs in a few."

When he shut the door behind him, she turned to the mirror. Whatever he was going to say, it wasn't that she looked ready to search the wilderness for a lost child.

She kicked off her high heels, shrugged out of her jacket and unzipped her slacks. When she finished undressing, she folded her clothes on the bed. Who'd been his recent guest? The room didn't look particularly masculine or feminine.

She pulled a pair of jeans, socks and a fuzzy red sweater from her bag. She dressed quickly in front of the mirror and then sat on the edge of the bed to step into her new hiking boots. She hadn't had much time to wear them, but the reviews had said they didn't need much breaking in.

She clumped down the stairs, calling Tate's name. "I'm ready to go." She jumped when Tate came through the front door.

Holding up a backpack, he said, "I put some supplies together. First-aid kit, rope, extra flashlights, headlamp. That boy could in the water, stuck on a cliff or stranded in the forest."

"I hope it is one of those." She turned around in front of him. "Will this do?"

He screwed up one side of his mouth, as he inspected her outfit. "Jacket?"

She pointed to her dark green puffy coat with a fur-lined hood.

He nodded. "What do you have on underneath that sweater?"

She cocked an eyebrow at him. Was he really going there? "Umm, a bra."

"I know *that*." His gaze seemed to caress her breasts, and an excited tingle raced across her skin. "I mean, you should probably have a thermal beneath the sweater. You know, like a long underwear top."

"You think it'll get that cold?"

"It can. I'll run upstairs and get something from Astrid's room. You need a pair of gloves, too."

"I have those." Did he think she was totally unprepared? She pulled a pair of fuzzy gloves from the pocket of her jacket and dangled them in the air.

"Those will work." He turned toward the stairs. "Be right back."

She watched his backside as he took the stairs two at a time with excitement fizzing through her veins. She didn't know if the thrill came from her attraction to Tate or the thought of joining in on a search that might be related to her cold case, but she'd take either one.

Two minutes later, he came charging back down the stairs with a thin white long-sleeved shirt bunched in his hand. He tossed it toward her. "Put that on under your sweater. I'll start the Jeep. Just pull the door closed behind you when you leave. I can arm the security system from my phone."

As soon as the front door shut, she pulled her arms from the sleeves of her sweater and lifted it from her head, careful not to disturb the bun that would keep her hair from going wild in this moist air. She ducked her head into the hole of the thermal and tugged it over her body, tucking the hem into her jeans. She put her sweater back on, grabbed her jacket and clicked the front door behind her, checking that it was locked.

Her new boots crunched over the gravel of the driveway, and she marched to the passenger side of the Jeep with confidence. She hopped in beside Tate and yanked on the seat belt. "How far?"

"About twenty minutes. Gets a little rugged and slow as we near the campsites. That's why people like them. They're always booked in the summer."

She shivered in the heated car. "I can't imagine camping in the cold like this."

He circled around the driveway, a smile quirking his lips. "Have you ever been camping before?"

"A few times." She waved her hand in the air. "There was a school trip to some cabins in Malibu."

A muffled noise came from Tate's side of the car, and Blanca decided to quit while she was ahead. "Did the deputy send you any more information?"

"Nope. Just verified that the search was still on. Sheriff Hopkins should be there. You met him, right?"

"That was my first stop when the ferry docked. Deputy Fletcher picked me up and took me to the station. Wasn't impressed."

"With the station or with Sheriff Hopkins?"

"Both. Neither." She placed two fingers against her lips. "Am I speaking out of turn here? Is he some beloved sheriff who makes everyone feel safe and cozy on the island?"

"Absolutely not. He's not elected, and the council members who appointed him already know the majority of the island wants to see a change next year. I suppose it might depend on how he handles Noah's case, maybe even Jeremy's cold case."

"Great." She smacked her knees. "You're telling me if I solve that cold case, it could keep Hopkins in his position?"

"It'll make him look good." He turned his head and studied her face in the darkness of the car. "It'll make you look good."

"It's my job." She tapped her fingers on the glass, hoping to change the subject from her job and why the agent in charge sent her out here. "That waterfall is amazing."

"The Dead Falls from which the island gets its name. Powerful."

"Beautiful." She took a deep breath. Even the air in the car smelled better than car air in DC. "We're crossing the bridge?"

"The area across the bridge is called Misty Hollow due to the spray from the falls. A Samish Indian reservation is on this side, also, and then the campsites. The Indian nation owns the campsite, but the Dead Falls Sheriff's Department provides the law enforcement."

Blanca placed a palm on the cold glass as they crossed the bridge, the rushing water of the falls to her right. "I hope Noah is okay. Could he have come this far to the falls?"

"It's possible." He tipped his head toward her window. "There are caves behind the falls, and Dead Falls teens have been creeping back there for years. I'm sure Noah would've known about the falls if his parents had any tourist brochures about the area lying around, but maybe not about those caves."

Blanca turned away from the pounding water, the images in her head making her nauseous. "Will they search the falls?"

"Someone probably already searched the caves. The water below will have to wait until tomorrow and daylight."

Blanca pinned her hands between her bouncing knees. "It might be too late by then."

"There's only so much searching we can do at night." Tate made a sharp left turn off the bridge and flicked on the windshield wipers to take care of the fine mist that gathered on the glass.

She sat forward in her seat, the seat belt rustling against

the slick material of her jacket. "This side of the island is definitely wilder than the other side."

"And more dangerous."

Tate took his vehicle down a road, and Blanca felt as if the trees had swallowed them whole. Slivers of silver sparkling streams peeked through the forest like some fairy wonderland. Maybe Noah was just enjoying his freedom. They had no idea if he were the type of boy who'd be concerned about worrying his parents.

A sign announced their entrance to the Samish Nation's area, but the reservation wasn't visible from the road. Blanca could see some taillights ahead, and she pointed. "Looks like we're not the only ones out for the search."

"There's usually a good turnout, especially for children." Tate's jaw tightened, and a small muscle ticked at the corner of his mouth. This had to be bringing back memories for him.

"Did they find you at night?"

"What?" He jerked his head to the side, a scowl marring his face. "Yeah, they found me at night. Do you think this is going to bring it all back to me?"

Her back stiffened at the ferocity of his tone. Just because she found the man insanely attractive was no reason to back down. "It could."

"Sorry to disappoint you, Agent Lopez, but this isn't my first rodeo. I've joined searches before without any bells going off."

"I'm not excited that another child might have been snatched, if that's what you mean." She stuffed her hands in her pockets. "But you found the bones, now this. You could open your mind."

Tate slammed his hands on the steering wheel. "Is that what you think? I just haven't *opened my mind*?"

She'd blinked when his hands hit the wheel, and she decided to keep her mouth shut. Of course he'd tried to remember what had happened. Why wouldn't he want to know? Unless he felt he'd done something wrong at the time.

A glow of light appeared over the next ridge, and they soon drew close to a clutch of cars and some emergency vehicles. Her heart jumped. "Do you think they found him?"

"The ambulances are probably there for insurance, in case he's found and needs treatment or transport to the hospital. I have an app on my phone. I would've been alerted if he'd been found."

When Tate pulled to the side of the road, Blanca closed her eyes and said a silent prayer for Noah's safety.

When she opened her eyes, Tate nodded at her. "You ready?"

In answer, she shoved open the door and hopped to the ground, her boots making a satisfying crunch.

Tate led the way, and she followed him toward the crowd, a deputy calling out instructions to them.

"We're putting you in groups of six. If you have a flashlight of your own, raise it in the air. We don't have enough for everyone." The deputy pointed to Tate. "Tate, you can lead one group. Stand by the sign."

The deputy called out a few more groups leaders, but Blanca clung to Tate's sleeve. "I'm on your team."

A big burly redhead had a group of teens around him, as he gave them instructions. A mom, a worried expression on her face, gathered her family around her and handed out flashlights.

About ten minutes later, nine groups had been formed, and four people had joined her on Tate's team—a total of two women and four men. One couple introduced themselves. The man, Steven, was a fisherman and his wife,

Jeanie, a nurse. One of the single men stuck his hand out to Blanca.

"Dr. Scotty Summers. Happy to work with you."

Blanca shook his hand and introduced herself by name only. "We have a doctor and a nurse. Seems like we have a good group."

He nodded toward Tate returning from a discussion with the deputies. "And Tate there knows this forest like the back of his hand."

As Tate approached the group, he scanned them with his light and reiterated the search instructions the deputy had given them. Then their group moved into the darkness, flashlights scanning the ground beneath them.

Tate turned and walked backward a few steps. "Noah was wearing blue jeans, high-top sneakers, a blue windbreaker and a black beanie with a smiley face on it. His parents don't recall what shirt he had on, but he favored black shirts with band names. Remember, if you do come across something suspicious, don't touch it. I have some gloves if you need them, but we'll call Deputy Cheswick if we do find something."

Following close on Tate's heels, Blanca aimed her flashlight at the ground, skimming over dead leaves, twigs, rocks and dirt. Tate provided a running commentary about signs that indicated a human had moved through the area.

Blanca again got the feeling that the forest was engulfing her. The pine trees on the island didn't lose their needles in winter. If anything, they created a lush landscape that looked almost impenetrable...but here they were.

In this terrain, they couldn't space out and move as one. Everyone tried to stay in a straight horizontal line, but they were separated by boulders and trees. Blanca could keep track of her teammates by the bobbing lights that would suddenly appear to her left and right.

She clambered over a log, grateful for Astrid's thermal beneath her sweater as the wind picked up and tried to blow through her.

After what seemed like hours but was most likely minutes, Blanca stopped to take a deep breath. She'd been panting as her legs cranked up and down over the uneven terrain. She could use some water and knew Tate had some in his pack.

She aimed her flashlight in front of her and saw Tate ahead, still churning through the landscape. Figuring she could backtrack over the ground between her and Tate, she picked up her pace and made a beeline for him.

When she was almost upon him, he disappeared from her view. She swept the beam of her light back and forth, and it picked him up crouched on the ground.

"Tate?" She tripped on a root and righted herself, coming up behind him, still bent forward. "Did you find something?"

He turned his head over his shoulder, squinting into her light. With a gloved hand, he picked up a dark object. "It's his. It's Noah's hat."

"His hat? That's great. Maybe he dropped it here. Is there anything else?" Her light skimmed across the dark beanie in Tate's unsteady hand, and his eyes glistened. Her heart pounded. "Tate?"

"It has blood on it."

Chapter Four

Tate held the black beanie between two gloved fingertips where it dangled in the path of Blanca's light. A dark red substance stained the smiley face on the front of the cap. The knots in his gut twisted until he couldn't breathe.

The blood could be from a fall, getting whacked in the face with a tree branch, even a wild animal. It didn't mean a predator of the human kind had gotten to Noah.

What was the name of the band on Noah's shirt? He glanced at his boots. Did he have blood in his shoes? He expanded his chest against the ropes that bound him to the tree. Had the whistling stopped?

"Tate!"

Blanca's voice pulled him back from some dark abyss where his mind was teetering. He jerked his head up to find her standing next to him, her hand on his shoulder.

"Tate, are you all right? Should I call Deputy Cheswick?"

He gulped in a deep breath and dropped the hat where he'd found it. "Yeah, call him. They can bag it. I'm going to blow the whistle for our team. We can fan out from this spot to see if there's anything else. It doesn't look good."

Her wide-eyed gaze dropped to the hat. "It *is* good. It's a start. Noah might have fallen and cut himself. It's just a hat and a little blood."

He rose to his feet beside her. Was she trying to convince him or herself? "You call Cheswick. I'll get the rest of our team over here."

He lifted the whistle that hung around his neck to his mouth and put it between his lips. He barely had enough air in his lungs to blow. He scooped in a deep breath, and the sound of the whistle pierced the night air just as it had almost twenty years ago.

AN HOUR LATER, Tate cranked on the heat in the Jeep and leaned back against the headrest, his hands on the steering wheel. He finally felt back in control of his senses after being out in the forest in the dark with that bloody cap.

"I'll bring you back to my place, so you can pick up your bags and head to your hotel."

"If they'll still have me." Blanca rubbed her hands together in front of the vent spewing warm air. "I think it's way past check-in time."

"The island is small-town. The folks at the hotel will know exactly who you are, why you're on the island and why you haven't checked in yet." He started the car and followed a few other cars leaving the search site.

"That's kind of scary."

"Scary?" He sent a sideways glance toward Blanca, still flexing her fingers in front of the heat. "Most people find it comforting."

"*Anonymity* is comfort. I don't want people to know my business." Her lips flattened into a thin line.

"Big-city girl?"

"Born and raised in LA, attended a big state school. Kept things private. Once people know your business, they can use it against you." She tapped the window as they passed the falls again. "Are they going to search the water and rocks below the falls tomorrow?"

"As far as I know. I suppose he could've lost that hat on the way to the falls." He tightened his fingers on the steering wheel. He'd discovered the only clue tonight, the hat. They'd test the blood to see if it matched Noah's or if it was animal blood…or someone else's. Could they get that lucky?

Nineteen years ago, the blood in his shoes when they'd found him had been his own. Law enforcement hadn't discovered any other DNA on him.

"What led you to that spot tonight?" Blanca traced a seam on her jacket with the tip of her finger. "You're the only one who found anything, and you're the one who found the bones earlier in the week."

He took the turn off the bridge a little sharply, and Blanca had to grab the edge of her seat to keep from pitching to the side. "Are you implying that my subconscious led me to the bones and that cap? I hate to poke a hole in your theory, but I was fighting a forest fire when I found those bones. Any one of my crew could've discovered them. And tonight? That's where Cheswick sent our team, remember?"

"But nobody else on your team found them. And as I recall, you thrashed through the forest ahead of the rest of us like a homing beacon."

"You're kidding." He hit the steering wheel with one hand. "You're grasping at straws, Agent Lopez. Nothing led me to the location of that hat except common sense and searching techniques."

He felt her attention on his face, and he tried to keep it impassive as he remembered those flashes that had bombarded him when he'd held the cap between his fingers. The unease had started early in the search when the deputy had mentioned Noah's clothing. Jeremy favored those black band T-shirts, too—not that he believed for a minute some crazed pedophile was hell-bent on finding boys wearing band T-shirts.

He wiped a trickle of sweat from the side of his face with the heel of his hand and turned down the heat. "You warm enough now?"

"Finally. I'm glad you suggested your sister's thermal top. I think I needed that extra layer." She unzipped her jacket and flapped it over her body. "I need to ask you a favor."

"Ask away." His heart skipped a beat in his chest. Was she going to ask him to stay at his place? Maybe share his bed for warmth?

"I need you to come with me to talk to Mrs. Ruesler."

Her words socked him in the gut, and he gulped. "Talk to Mrs. Ruesler about what?"

"I need to get a DNA sample from her, and I gather up until this point she's refused." She formed her fingers into a gun and pointed it at him. "I'm thinking you can help persuade her."

Blanca had thought wrong. "Wait, why do you need her DNA? If it's just to find out if the bones I discovered belong to Jeremy, why not use the DNA you have on Jeremy?"

"Funny thing happened on the way to the lab." She rolled her eyes in an exaggerated manner. "The DNA sample we had for Jeremy is corrupted. Apparently, some genius stored it when it was still damp and bacteria has grown in the container and destroyed the DNA."

Thunking his forehead with his fist, Tate said, "Unbelievable."

"I know, right? But it's okay. Mrs. Ruesler is still in the area, and we can see if there's a match between the DNA extracted from the bones and hers. We can get enough of a relational match to verify the bones belong to Jeremy." Blanca twisted in her seat. "She is the only family still here, right?"

"She and Mr. Ruesler divorced about a year after Jeremy's disappearance, and when Jeremy's sister Celine graduated from high school a few years later, she left. I think she's married and living in Idaho. I don't know why Mrs. Ruesler stays here." Tate blinked and swallowed a lump in his throat.

Blanca said, "I know why she stays here."

Tate flicked on his high beams as he turned down the road to his cabin. "Because she's waiting for Jeremy to return."

"Exactly." Blanca sniffed and patted the end of her nose. "Sad, isn't it? Maybe if we can ID Jeremy, it might give her permission to leave."

Tate pulled in beside Blanca's sedan. "I'll load your suitcase back in your car. Do you want me to follow you to the hotel?"

Her head swiveled toward him as she fumbled with the door handle. "That's okay. I have the address...and my weapon."

"I didn't mean... I wasn't implying..." He ran a hand over his mouth. What had he been implying? Ever since he'd found those bones, something had felt off about the island. Some creeping menace had invaded the forest, the bay, the rivers and creeks. But he knew that menace had always been here.

She flashed her phone at him. "I'll follow the GPS. I'll be fine, but I wouldn't mind your cell phone number...just in case."

Had he ever *not* given his number to a pretty woman? Especially a knockout like Blanca Lopez. He was beginning to feel like his old self again.

"Sure, of course." He entered his number in her phone

and when the call rang through to his phone, he saved her in his contacts.

As they got to his front door, he opened it and ushered her in ahead of him. "I'll get your suitcase from upstairs."

He bounded up the stairs and veered into the guest room. He tripped to a stop as the scent of Blanca's perfume engulfed him—sweet with a hint of spice. He'd seen both sides of her already.

The sleek pantsuit she'd worn earlier sat at the edge of the bed in a neatly folded stack, her high heels on the floor, one shoe on its side. Her suitcase gaped open on the floor.

He opened his mouth to call her upstairs to pack away her clothes and then mentally shrugged. He wouldn't be handling any of her personal items by putting her suit and shoes on top of the other clothes in the bag.

He lifted the clothes and put them in the suitcase. Then he shoved her heels into the edges of the bag. As he reached for the lid to close the suitcase, he noticed an array of pastel-colored panties and lacy bras zipped into the top. He slammed the lid and zipped it.

Feeling like a perv, he wheeled the bag out of the room and hit the lights behind him. He grabbed the handle to carry it downstairs and almost tumbled to the bottom when he noticed Blanca, puffer jacket off, her arms inside her sweater as the empty sleeves dangled on either side of her body.

"Uh, excuse me?"

She looked up, her dark hair falling into her face as it came loose from her bun. "Oh, I'm just taking off your sister's thermal."

She turned her back on him and continued to wriggle inside the sweater. With a flourish, she pulled the white shirt from inside her sweater and dangled it in the air. "Ta-da!"

"Impressive." He did a slow clap.

She stuffed her arms into the sleeves and folded the thermal. "Thank you so much for this."

"You could've kept it. It's only going to get colder on the island."

"I'll do a little shopping while I'm here." She placed the shirt on the arm of a chair and patted it. "Tomorrow, then?"

He raised his eyebrows as he wheeled her suitcase to the door. "Tomorrow?"

"Mrs. Ruesler. I have her address, although I suppose you already know where she lives. I'll swing by and pick you up around ten o'clock, if that's okay."

"Right. Sure." He dragged her bag over the uneven surface of his driveway and listened for the pop of the trunk before nudging it open. He was hoping Blanca would've forgotten about asking him to accompany her to Birdie Ruesler's place. He'd rather sit on the edge of Dead Falls than return to that house, but he didn't want to give Blanca the wrong impression. Saying no would seem strange.

He hoisted her bag into the trunk, eyeing the boxes that contained Jeremy's case.

Blanca touched his arm. "Have you ever read the case files?"

"Nope." He slammed the trunk, and Blanca's hand fell from his arm.

"Would you like to?"

"Maybe." He stepped around her and opened the driver's-side door. "Drive carefully."

"Thanks." She slid behind the wheel and turned her head toward him. "I'm sure the sheriff's department and Noah's parents were glad you were on the search tonight."

She still thought some subconscious memory had led him to that spot.

"I'm glad I was there, too. Good night, Blanca."

She swung her door shut and started the engine. He watched her car until the taillights disappeared over the first ridge. Then he headed back inside.

When he secured the house, he swept up his sister's thermal and pressed it to his face. The warmth of Blanca's body still clung to the light material, and the scent of her skin invaded his senses.

He didn't believe the answers to Jeremy's disappearance lay in his subconscious, but if Blanca Lopez thought so, he'd humor her just to explore this attraction between them.

BLANCA TOOK THE hotel clerk's recommendation and had breakfast at the café down the street. As she bit into a second piece of crisp bacon and savored the smoky flavor, she was glad she had.

She glanced at her phone. The Dead Falls Sheriff's Department had promised to keep her posted on the Noah Fielding case, but so far they didn't have the results of the DNA test on the hat. She had her own buccal swab kit in her briefcase, ready for Mrs. Ruesler.

Mrs. Ruesler had been notified about the discovery of the bones. Maybe she'd see the sense in giving her DNA now, especially as they didn't have Jeremy's anymore. DNA only worked for cold cases if it hadn't been corrupted.

Her phone buzzed on the table, and she lunged for it. She paused and caught her breath when she saw the number. She couldn't avoid him forever.

She tapped the display to answer. "Hello, Manny."

"There's my girl."

Her breakfast churned in her stomach. "I'm not your *girl*, Manny. What do you want?"

"That's what I admire about you, Blanca, always right

to the point." He coughed. "Of course, that's not the only thing I admire about you."

"Get to it, Manny. I'm busy." She took a sip of water and swished it in her mouth.

He sucked in a sharp breath. "I heard you're out in the middle of nowhere investigating a cold case. Ouch."

"It's a missing boy. I'd say that's important."

"Yeah, but a nineteen-year-old cold case. One kid, not even a serial." He clucked his tongue. "You could've had it all, babe. You hear about the freeway shootings in Atlanta? That's my case."

"Congratulations, Manny. Is that what you called to tell me?"

"No. Hey, just wanted to let you know if you need any help or advice out there on that island, let me know. I'd be happy to lend my expertise. I've worked a couple of cold—"

Not needing nor wanting to hear another litany of his cases, she interrupted Manny. "Gotta go. Say hello to your wife for me."

She ended the call with a smile and stuffed the last forkful of eggs into her mouth. She had an appointment with a real man.

Getting close to Tate Mitchell would be invaluable for her. The way his blue eyes burned with intensity didn't hurt, either.

She left a hefty tip for the waitress and plugged in Tate's location again. She could probably get back there without directions, but a lot of these little roads off the main highway looked the same.

Twenty minutes later, she pulled behind his Jeep and honked the horn. He must've been waiting for her because he stepped out onto the porch immediately. He waved and turned to lock the door.

That gave her an opportunity to drink in his masculine form, the down vest he wore over a blue fleece Henley that had to match his eyes, enhancing his broad shoulders. She whistled softly between her teeth.

She powered down the window as he approached. "Is it okay if I drive? If not, we can switch cars."

"No, I prefer it. I can navigate." He circled the car and dropped into the passenger seat beside her.

He even smelled like the outdoors—in a good way— smoky, piney and fresh. He must bathe in it, or it was in his pores. That should've been her first clue about Manny. He smelled like expensive men's cologne, which he splashed on to hide his deceit.

"You ready?"

She started at the sound of his voice. "Yeah, I have the address in my phone."

"No need. I know how to get there. I'll guide you." He jerked his thumb to the left. "Go toward the falls, but you're not going to cross the bridge. Birdie—Mrs. Ruesler lives on this side."

"Her name's Birdie?"

"Yeah, but I've always called her Mrs. Ruesler, and Birdie doesn't fit her much anymore."

Blanca's bottom lip quivered. "I don't know how anyone lives through the loss of a child, especially one that age."

"If you wanna call it living." Tate slouched in his seat and barked out the next set of directions.

She slid a glance at him. Had he gotten up on the wrong side of the bed?

She cleared her throat. "I haven't heard from Deputy Cheswick yet about the beanie you found."

"He's in charge of the investigation? I thought he was just in charge of the search parties last night."

"He's the one who told me he'd contact me. Where was Sheriff Hopkins last night? I didn't see him. Shouldn't he be in charge of a case like this?"

"You'll come to find out Sheriff Hopkins is lazy. He likes the position, not the job."

"Yeah, I know a few people like that in the FBI." She gripped the steering wheel and took the next turn a little faster than she'd intended.

Minutes later, Tate directed her into a small subdivision of houses with neatly manicured lawns and spiffy paint jobs. He pointed ahead. "Mrs. Ruesler's house is on the left, second to the end."

Blanca's gaze tracked to the only house on the block with an overgrown yard, a broken fence and paint peeling from the clapboard. She sucked in a breath. "Can't someone help her out?"

"I—I didn't realize she'd let the house go like this. Haven't been out this way for a while." Tate rubbed his eyes. "She's expecting you?"

"Not exactly." Blanca made a U-turn at the end of the block and pulled up to the curb in front of the neglected house. She opened her door and paused, as Tate seemed frozen in his seat. "You coming?"

"Right behind you."

Blanca's low-heeled boots scuffed against the leaves carpeting the walkway up to the porch. She took a big step over a piece of rotting wood and knocked on the door, glancing over her shoulder at Tate waiting at the bottom of the steps, his hands shoved in his pockets.

Shuffling noises answered Blanca's knock, and she felt, rather than saw, an eye peering at her from the peephole. "Mrs. Ruesler? I'm FBI Special Agent Blanca Lopez. I've been assigned to your son's cold case. Tate Mitchell is with me."

The door creaked open, and a woman with white, fluffy hair stared at her from the crack. "FBI? Is it about those bones?"

Blanca eased out a breath. At least she wouldn't be coming in cold here. "Yes, it is, Mrs. Ruesler. Can we come in?"

Mrs. Ruesler widened the door, her gaze traveling over Blanca's shoulder to take in Tate behind her. The woman's thin lips tightened, and her nostrils flared.

For a second, Blanca feared Mrs. Ruesler would deny Tate entry to her home. She'd thought having Tate as her wingman would help her out, but the animosity pouring from Mrs. Ruesler threatened to bowl them both over.

Then Mrs. Ruesler backed up into the house and said, "Suit yourselves."

Blanca followed Mrs. Ruesler, and Tate came in behind her. He had to slam the warped door to get it to shut properly, and Blanca jumped. It didn't bother Mrs. Ruesler, though.

She turned to face Blanca, folding her scrawny arms over her sunken chest, covered in a baggy, checked blouse with the sleeves rolled up to her elbows. "What do you want?"

"Can we sit down?" Blanca gestured to the threadbare sofa as Tate stood awkwardly near the door, as if ready to give flight at any moment. He and Mrs. Ruesler hadn't exchanged one word.

"Go ahead." Mrs. Ruesler sank into the chair across from the sofa, her backside dropping into a well in the flattened cushion.

Blanca noticed that the chair Mrs. Ruesler had probably occupied for the past twenty years faced the front window. How long had she sat there waiting for Jeremy?

Placing the bag containing the DNA test kit at her feet,

Blanca cleared her throat. "As you know, Mrs. Ruesler, a set of bones was discovered last week during a forest fire."

"By him." Mrs. Ruesler pointed a crooked finger at Tate, who stiffened beside Blanca on the sofa.

"That's right. I stumbled upon a set of bones. Forensics is ready to analyze them, but Agent Lopez told me the DNA they had from Jeremy has been corrupted. They don't have anything they can compare with the genetic material from the bones to find out if they belong to Jeremy."

Mrs. Ruesler's dull eyes shifted from Tate to Blanca. "Is that true?"

"Yes, unfortunately. These things can happen with cold cases."

"So you're here for my DNA. Is that right? You think my boy is dead and someone dumped his body in the forest." She looked past them through the window.

"If it's okay with you, we'd like to get a sample from you, Mrs. Ruesler." Blanca patted the bag on the floor. "We can do it right here. You don't need to come into the station. I'm trained to take the sample. It would…help to know, wouldn't it?"

Blanca held her breath, as the woman slowly dragged her gaze from the window and settled it on the bag. "I don't know if it would help."

"Listen, Birdie." Tate sat forward on the edge of the sofa, bracing his elbows on his knees. "If the FBI can positively identify Jeremy's…remains, Agent Lopez can start working on the case. Maybe we can find out who did this. Find out what happened."

Mrs. Ruesler ignored Tate and spoke directly to Blanca. "I'll let you take a sample. I know if I refuse, you'll just go to my daughter Celine in Boise and get it from her. She'd do it, but I don't want you bothering her. She has her own life—away from this place."

Blanca gave her a small smile. "It's the right decision. Can we sit at the kitchen table?"

Mrs. Ruesler nodded and made a move to rise from the chair. She struggled against the soft cushion, and Tate jumped up to take her arm. She put a clawlike hand on his forearm and then when she got to her feet dropped it as if it burned.

Blanca kept her face impassive at this exchange. Tate had seemed reluctant when she'd suggested he accompany her here, and now she knew why.

When she sat at the kitchen table with Mrs. Ruesler, Tate stood apart, looking out the kitchen window to the backyard. Blanca swabbed the inside of Mrs. Ruesler's mouth and bagged the swab, sealing it and dropping it into an envelope.

"That's it. We'll keep you posted."

Tate had already moved to the front door and hovered there as Blanca packed up the bag.

She said, "I promise you, Mrs. Ruesler. I'll do everything in my power to solve this case, even if those bones don't belong to Jeremy."

The older woman shoved her chair back so hard it hit the wall. "Everything? Then, ask him."

Tate closed his eyes as Jeremy's distraught mother jabbed a finger at him. "Ask him what he knows. Ask him why he came home to his parents and Jeremy didn't. Ask him about the Whistler."

Chapter Five

Tate could feel the blood drain from his face. He grabbed the door handle to steady himself, as his rubbery knees threatened to fail him.

The Whistler. How did she know about the Whistler?

He licked his lips. He wanted to turn and run out of the house, just as he and Jeremy used to when Mrs. Ruesler caught them stealing cookies tagged for the bake sale or when they'd let Jeremy's dog on the bed with them in her immaculate home. But he wasn't a kid anymore, and Birdie no longer treated him like a son. She hated him.

"Birdie." He reached out a hand but snatched it back when she screamed at him.

"It's your fault! It's your fault he's gone. He wanted to be just like you. He followed you. He did everything you told him to do." She clawed at her white hair. "What did you tell him to do that day? Why did you come home without him?"

Tate took a step forward, but Blanca shook her head at him and tipped her head at the door.

As he turned to leave, he saw Blanca take Birdie's arm and lead her back to the living room.

After he jogged through the broken gate, he paced outside Blanca's car along the sidewalk he'd once known as well as the one that fronted his parents' house. The cold air hit his hot cheeks, and he could almost hear the sizzle of contact.

He'd heard the whistle last night when he found the bloody cap. What was the tune? What did it mean, and how was it connected to Jeremy's disappearance?

Blanca exited the house and strode down the walkway. When she aimed the remote at the car, he circled around and opened the back door for her.

"I'll take that." He grabbed her bag with the precious DNA sample and put it on the seat. By the time he backed out of the car, Blanca was seated behind the wheel. He slid into the passenger seat.

"That went well." A muscle ticked in his jaw, and he pressed a thumb against it.

She took a deep breath. "Are you all right?"

Jerking his head to the side, he said, "Me? You should be asking if Mrs. Ruesler is all right."

"I know she's fine. I settled her down in her favorite chair and brought her a cup of tea. She'll be okay." She placed a hand on his arm. "Will you?"

With a creeping dread, Tate felt tears pricking behind his eyes. He was a grown man. He was not a twelve-year-old boy. He ran a hand beneath his nose. "I'm fine. I sort of expected that. I haven't seen Birdie for a while, but it always ends the same way, her blaming me for Jeremy's disappearance. I thought it might go differently this time—I mean, with the discovery of the bones and you being here."

"That must be hard for you to hear. Of course it wasn't your fault, Tate."

"Wasn't it?" He covered his eyes with his hand. He'd always gotten the girl by being carefree, happy-go-lucky, charming. He'd never tried crying before.

Blanca squeezed his shoulder. "Is that how you feel?"

"I suppose." It had been a long time since someone had offered him any sympathy. Most people had moved on. Even his sister didn't bring up Jeremy anymore. "It's survivor's guilt, isn't it? Someone took Jeremy that night and left me. Why? Why didn't he take both of us?"

"I think the most logical answer to that is there was only one perpetrator and two preteen boys. He couldn't handle both of you at the same time. Were you bigger, stronger than Jeremy?"

"Not really." He rubbed his chin. "We were about the same height. I was a skinny kid but always athletic. Jeremy still had some baby fat on him. I think he was getting ready for a growth spurt. His dad is tall, like really tall, and I think Jeremy was going to catch up to his old man."

"So Jeremy was slower than you?"

Tate caught a glimpse of shifting curtains at the window. "Can we get out of here?"

Blanca started the engine and pulled away from the Ruesler house. "Slower? Maybe that's why it was Jeremy instead of you."

"I don't know. We were on bikes. He could pedal just as fast as I could."

"But you didn't stay on the bikes, did you?" Blanca took a careful turn out of the subdivision. "That blood in your shoes was your own. Your socks were tattered, and your feet were bleeding. You lost your shoes at some point."

"I can't remember." He pinched the bridge of his nose.

Blanca remained silent as she navigated her way to the main highway. Then she gave a little cough. "What did Mrs. Ruesler mean about the Whistler? Who's the Whistler?"

Tate scooped a hand through his hair, digging his nails into his scalp. "I—I don't know. I don't know why she said that."

"Yeah, you do." Blanca glanced at him with narrowed eyes. "The look on your face when she mentioned the Whistler said it all."

Tate's head snapped back. What happened to the comforting words? "It did?"

Tapping her fingers on the steering wheel, she said, "I don't recall anything about a Whistler in the summary I read, but I haven't gotten to the file notes yet. Will I find anything there?"

"I told you. I never read them."

"Something about her words triggered you. What was it?" She smacked the dashboard with her hand. "C'mon, Tate. This isn't a date where you're trying to impress the girl. If I have any hope of solving this case, I'm going to need the only witness to Jeremy's disappearance to come clean with me. What do you know about the Whistler?"

Tate squeezed his eyes closed and willed himself back in the forest when he found Noah's beanie. He'd heard whistling then—in his head. Why? How had Birdie known about it?

"Okay." He gripped his knees and hunched forward. "Last night when I found Noah's cap, I lost it for a few minutes. Felt disconnected from my body. I heard...whistling."

"Whistling? Like wind whistling through the trees or a human whistling?"

"Human. Someone whistling a tune." He whipped his head around. "How did Mrs. Ruesler know that I heard something last night? I must've said something about whistling at the time of Jeremy's disappearance, but I don't remember now."

"Do you remember the tune?"

"I don't." He rolled his eyes upward, as if he could find the answer on the ceiling of the car. "It was maybe a kids' song or something like that. I mean, that's what I heard last night."

"Could you duplicate it now?" She lifted her eyebrows. "If you whistle it, maybe I could recognize it."

"Do you have kids?" He eyed her left hand on the steering wheel, devoid of jewelry. Lots of married women didn't wear wedding ring, so he'd try the direct approach here.

"I don't have kids, but I have several siblings with kids, and when I'm in LA, Auntie Blanca is the go-to babysitter. I've watched my fair share of cartoons." She nudged his arm with her elbow. "So go ahead, put your lips together and blow."

He watched her pucker her own plump lips and decided she couldn't possibly be married, not the way she was flirting with him.

Spreading his hands, he said, "I wouldn't know where to start. I can't remember the tune—last night or before. I just know it wasn't random whistling."

"Then, we have a date tonight."

"We do?"

"I haven't had a minute to dig into the files yet, and you've never looked at them at all. Sounds like we have some work ahead of us."

From sympathetic cop to hard-hitting interrogator to flirtatious siren, this woman gave him whiplash. "Where does the date part come in?"

"I will order pizza and buy a six-pack for sustenance before we dig into the files in my hotel room. Deal?"

"Only if we order from Luigi's and you let me pick it up on the way."

"Does Luigi's deliver to my hotel?"

"I'm sure they do, but it's on my way."

"Tell you what." She swung into his driveway, the gravel

and dirt crunching beneath the tires. "I'll spring for the pizza because the agency will pay for food. You grab the beer, which doesn't fall into my reimbursement category."

"What time?"

"Let's make it seven o'clock." She leveled a finger at him, as he got out of the car. "But don't for one second think just because we're eating pizza and throwing back a few beers that I'm gonna go easy on you, Tate."

He saluted and said, "Yes, ma'am," before slamming the car door and stepping back.

As she drove away with a wave out the window, he whispered. "Oh, please, please don't go easy on me."

AFTER SENDING MRS. RUESLER'S DNA sample to the FBI lab, Blanca spent the rest of the day with the Dead Falls sheriff's deputies on the Noah Fielding case. She met Mr. and Mrs. Fielding and saw the same lost look she'd seen in Mrs. Ruesler's eyes. Only, Mrs. Ruesler's had hardened into hopelessness. She'd do everything in her power to keep that from happening to the Fieldings.

She'd grabbed a quick sandwich for lunch while poring over the pithy witness statements they'd received on Noah's case. A few people had seen him leave the campsite, and a few more noticed him walking along the river, but nobody reported seeing anyone else in his vicinity—and nobody mentioned any whistling.

Her stomach rumbled as she packed it in for the day, so when she noticed Luigi's Pizza on her way back to her hotel, she pulled into the parking lot. As she sat in her car, she called Tate.

He picked up after the first ring. "Are we still on?"

"I'm sitting in front of Luigi's as we speak. Just wanted to check if you're a kitchen-sink guy, a minimalist or a weird pineapple type."

"Kitchen sink." He cleared his throat. "And are you a standard Bud girl, foreign imports or craft beer?"

"All of the above. Surprise me."

She couldn't wipe the smile from her face as she practically skipped into Luigi's. She hadn't been on a date since that fiasco with Manny—not that this was a date. Pizza, beer and work did not equal a date.

The warmth of the restaurant engulfed her when she walked in, the smell of garlic and oregano permeating the air. Few empty tables verified Tate's assertion that Luigi's ruled. Blanca joined the line for takeout orders, her head tilted back as she studied the menu above the counter.

When she reached the front, she ordered an extra-large supreme and a Diet Coke. After paying with her government credit card, she skirted the counter, paper cup in hand and joined another line for the soda machine.

She filled her cup with ice and soda, snapped on a lid, grabbed a straw and headed for the wooden bench that lined the wall in the front of the restaurant. Perching on the edge of the bench, she sucked down the icy drink.

A man sat heavily beside her, holding his own drink, his shoulder jostling hers. She scooted to the side to create some separation.

The man turned his head. "I'm sorry. Am I crowding you?"

"It's a crowded place." She uncrossed her legs and put her knees together.

His eyes popped open. "I know you. You're the FBI agent the sheriff's brought in for the Jeremy Ruesler case."

Her gaze darted among the people waiting for their food,

but although the man's voice sounded like a shout to her, nobody seemed to notice.

Dipping her head, she said, "That's right."

"Terrible business. And the new case? This tourist boy? Do you think it's related? Kind of suspicious Tate finds those bones and another boy goes missing." He shook his finger. "There have been others, too, but nobody wants to talk about those."

"Others?" He had her full attention now. "Other missing boys here on Dead Falls?"

"Let's just say Dead Falls isn't the only island in Discovery Bay." He jumped to his feet. "That's me."

"Wait." She stood up beside him and grabbed his jacket. "Who are these other boys? Can you give me a name?"

He squinted, the light freckles on his face bunching around his nose. "Andrew. Andrew Finnigan for starters."

She typed the name into her phone, as the red-haired stranger grabbed a stack of pizzas and barreled out of the restaurant without giving her any more names.

Was this guy serious, or was he just trying to insert himself into the case? How had he recognized her? Had to be a serious follower of the case to know her identity.

When she heard her number, she scurried to the soda machine for a refill before picking up the gigantic pizza and balancing her cup on top of the box, a plastic bag with paper plates, napkins and utensils swinging from her wrist. A kind soul opened the door for her, and she whisked the pizza back to the car and put it on the front seat.

By the time she got to her hotel, she had about twenty minutes to make herself decent. She slid the pizza box onto the credenza next to the microwave and hit the shower.

She'd scaled down her work clothes today, ditching the high heels for a pair of low-heeled boots and replacing the blouse and jacket with a sweater, but she still couldn't bring herself to adopt jeans for work attire, even out here in the wilderness, and that didn't have to mark her as Manny's protegee. She'd been forging her own work style lately, forcing Manny's voice from her head.

She took a quick shower, releasing her hair from its ponytail and scrunching up her waves with wet hands. She slipped into a pair of jeans and ducked into a fresh sweater. She checked her pedicure before leaving her feet bare and spritzed on a little perfume.

The knock on the door came before she could freshen her makeup. She checked herself in the full-length mirror before opening the door.

Tate held up two six-packs of bottled beer—a mixture of IPAs in one and a Mexican beer in the other.

"Ooh, you're my new best friend." She took the pack of IPAs from his hand. "And they're cold."

Lifting his nose in the air, he sniffed. "And you're mine. How was Luigi's?"

"Crowded…and weird." She plucked a bottle from the carrier and held it up. As he nodded, she used an opener from the hotel to snap off the lid.

"Weird how?" He thanked her for the beer and took a gulp.

"Some guy there recognized me and asked me about the cases. Said there were other missing boys in Discovery Bay that the sheriffs haven't looked at."

"He might be talking about a few runaways. A few accidental deaths."

"Andrew Finnigan ring any bells?"

"Yeah, one of the accidentals." He tapped the box. "I'm starving."

"Do you want me to put a couple of slices in the microwave? I picked it up over a half hour ago."

"I don't like what the microwave does to the crust. I'm good. You?"

"Lukewarm pizza is fine by me." She opened the plastic bag from Luigi's and peeled off a couple paper plates from the stack they'd given her. She placed them on the credenza and dropped some napkins beside them.

Tate had flipped open the pizza box, and the aroma of Italian spices filled the hotel room. He nudged the box toward her. "You first."

Blanca used her fingers and a plastic knife to separate a large piece of pizza from the whole and plopped it onto her plate. A clump of cheese stuck to the knife, and she licked it off. Then she lowered herself to the sofa, placing her plate on the coffee table in front of it.

Kicking a box on the floor, she said, "I have the files right here. Sustenance first and then we'll do a deep dive... into the case."

Tate settled next to her. "I think I'm going to need a lot of sustenance to get through those boxes."

"I can't believe you never looked through the files before." She took a dainty sip of beer before tearing into her first piece of pizza.

"Nobody ever offered when I was an adult. I just didn't think it was worth it." He tapped his bottle with his finger. "You like the beer? It's from a microbrewery in Seattle."

She smacked her lips. "It's citrusy and piney all at once. It tastes like this island."

Tasted like she imagined Tate would taste. She stuffed more pizza in her mouth before she blurted out something inappropriate.

"And the pizza?"

With her mouth full, she gave him a thumbs-up sign.

They scarfed down more than half the pizza and drank two beers each before Blanca pushed up from the sofa and made a beeline toward the bathroom. "I'm going to wash my hands first. I don't want to leave pizza grease on the files."

"Good point. Jeremy's DNA was already disqualified. We don't need to add any more corruption."

Blanca turned from the sink with her hands dripping and ran into Tate, hovering behind her. The small space practically smooshed her nose into his chest. "Sorry. Just grabbing a towel."

Tate whipped it off the rack and handed it to her.

She took it from him and stepped to the side to dry her hands, as he slid into her place at the sink. She wanted to use it to cover her heated cheeks instead.

She hung the towel back on the rack when she finished and then hurried back to the other room, fanning herself. If she planned to work with this guy closely, she'd better get a grip. She didn't need to get caught in the trap of falling for every man she worked with. Her rep had already taken a hit once.

She cleared the plates from the coffee table, leaving their beers, and scooped out a handful of file folders from the first box. She plopped them on the table just as Tate joined her. "Here we go."

"What are we gonna start with here?" He downed the dregs of his beer, as if he needed the liquid courage to continue.

Tapping the file on top, she said, "These are the witness statements, including your own, which the deputies conducted in the hospital. Do you remember that?"

"I remember." His blue eyes stared past her shoulder, their glassiness giving them an otherworldly appearance.

Was he seeing into the past now? Would that help him re-call what happened that night?

Blanca scooted close to him, until her thigh pressed against his, and slipped open the folder on the table, so they could both see the contents. She ran the tip of her fin-ger down a short list of names. "These are the people who were in the general area that night, or I guess late afternoon. That's when it happened, right? Late afternoon? They found you at night, but that's not when Jeremy disappeared. You'd mentioned something about your parents not allowing you in the forest at night."

"Did I?" He tugged on an earlobe, the gesture seeming to bring him back to the present. "That's right. No way our parents would've allowed us out after dark, but it was sum-mertime and the sun set late. We left Jeremy's house around three o'clock in the afternoon that day."

She shuffled through some papers. "They found you at eleven o'clock at night. You were tied to a tree, and you had a contusion on your head." She peered at a form from the hospital. "The doc thinks that's why you couldn't remem-ber anything."

"Probably." Tate rubbed the back of his head, as if touch-ing the phantom wound. "But how would the kidnapper know that? He couldn't have known that a blow to the back of my head would cause amnesia."

"What's your point?" She peered at him over the top of the paper.

"After the abduction, my parents were terrified that the man would come for me to shut me up…but he never did. He wasn't worried that I'd be able to identify him because I probably never saw him." He shifted on the sofa, and Blanca tipped toward him, bumping his shoulder with hers. "Look, Jeremy and I didn't always ride bikes side by side. We'd take different paths sometimes. He was on the wrong path at the wrong time, and someone took him. The kidnapper realized too late that Jeremy wasn't alone, so he hit me on the head and tied me up to that tree to give him some time to get away with Jeremy. I never saw him, and he knew that. I was no threat to him. I'm still not a threat to him."

"But you heard a whistle."

Tate lifted the box by the corner and dropped it. "Is that in there? Nobody ever asked me about whistling before... before Mrs. Ruesler brought it up."

"You heard it last night when you found Noah's cap. You heard it *before* we talked to Mrs. Ruesler." Blanca plunged her hands in the box. "You must've told somebody."

Tate eyed the pages she'd fanned out on the table. Blanca picked out all the pieces of paper that contained witness statements and interviews. "If I could get the online files, we could just do a search for whistling, but we'll have to sift through the old-fashioned way. You take half, and I'll take half."

Sliding half the pages to his side of the table, Tate said, "We can try."

They worked in silence for several minutes, or almost silence. Tate would catch his breath or sigh or click his tongue as he shuffled through the pages.

As Blanca stood up to stretch, he jabbed a piece of paper with his finger. "Here it is."

Blanca stopped midstretch and plopped on the sofa next to him. "You found something?"

He picked up the page and waved it in the air. "It's an interview with Birdie. She said I'd told her someone had been whistling in the forest while Jeremy and I were playing. That we kept hearing it, and then it would go away."

Blanca sucked in her bottom lip. "She said you said. Secondhand. Did you ever tell the police that? Did they ever follow up with any of the other witnesses?"

"Not that I've come across yet. I don't even remember telling her that."

"What was the tune?" She snatched the paper from his hand.

Instead of an answer, Tate began to whistle the "Hokey Pokey" song, but instead of the upbeat melody designed to get you to put your various body parts in and out, he'd slowed it down so it sounded like a creepy warning.

"Really? The 'Hokey Pokey' song? We played that when we were kids." Her gaze raked the questions and answers with Mrs. Ruesler, and a chill touched the back of her neck when she read her words.

She held out the paper with an unsteady hand. "Mrs. Ruesler doesn't name the tune here, Tate. She said you told her you didn't know what it was and couldn't repeat it."

Tate lifted his icy blue gaze to her face. "I know. I just remembered it."

Chapter Six

Tate sprang to his feet and jerked open the door to the mini fridge. He grabbed a bottle of beer and pried the cap off on the edge of the credenza. He practically poured the alcohol down his throat to drown the feeling of dread gathering in his gut.

How come he'd never remembered that tune before? How many times had he heard that song when his nephew had been a toddler? How many times had it brought him no other emotion except annoyance?

He glanced at Blanca who had her arms crossed over her chest. "You're kidding. You just remembered the song now?"

"It's the tune I heard in my head last night. It hit me right here." He pounded his chest with his fist. "Like a sledge-hammer."

"You heard him whistle it like that? Slow? It's usually kind of fast and chirpy."

"I have no idea. What did Birdie say?" He took a long step over the coffee table and snatched up the piece of paper Blanca had dropped on the floor. He skimmed the words until he found the spot. *"Tate told me he didn't see any-one while the boys were playing, but he and Jeremy heard someone whistling a tune. He didn't know what song it was. They heard it more than once and in different locations in the forest. They thought someone was following them. They thought it was a joke."*

"Wow." Blanca rose to her feet and paced the length of the room. "Why do you think you didn't tell the police the same thing?"

"Not sure." Tate finished off the first beer and grabbed another, taking a long slug. "All I remember about that interrogation is people seemed to think it was my fault. My idea to go riding. My idea to go deep into the forest. My idea to stay out late. That I was saying and doing whatever I thought might get me off the hook. Maybe I thought if I'd told the deputies about the whistling, they'd get mad at me for not telling them before, or they'd tell me I should've known we were being followed. Or maybe I just told Mrs. Ruesler about a whistler because I thought she needed to hear something—anything."

"You don't believe that. You remembered the whistling before she said anything about it. The rest..." Her dark eyes shimmered as she walked toward him. She circled the coffee table and placed both hands on his shoulders. "I'm sorry they made you feel that way. They should've had a therapist talk to you."

"That's what my buddy's fiancée does. She's a forensic psychologist who specializes in children. Maybe if I'd had someone like Hannah Maddox on my side all those years ago, I would've been able to help the sheriff's department solve the case."

She squeezed his shoulders. "You were a kid. It wasn't up to you to solve the case."

"But you think it is now?" He narrowed his eyes.

Blanca dropped her hands and took a step back. "You're not a kid anymore. Maybe something can jog your memory—it just did. Thinking about the whistling that night prompted you to remember the tune."

He downed the rest of his second beer and swiped a hand across his mouth. "Now if we can just interrogate every man on the island who whistles."

"It's a start. Not many men wander around whistling the 'Hokey Pokey' tune."

Tate held up his empty bottle. "I'm going for another. Do you want the remaining IPA? I'll take the other."

Raising her eyebrows, she asked, "Are you going to be able to drive? That'll be your third."

"Two and then one more after a break and several slices of pizza?" He stopped and covered his heart with his hand. "That's what all drunk drivers say, isn't it?"

"I—I'm not implying that you're drunk."

"I know, but you're right." He walked to the recycling trash and dropped his bottle into it. "If I had another, I'd have to spend the night."

Blanca's dark eyes brightened as a rosy pink touched her cheeks. "If that's what you want, go for it. The sofa pulls out to a bed."

"I'm good." He held up his hands. "I think I've had enough tonight."

"Enough beer or enough memories?"

"Maybe both." He gathered up the rest of their trash, stuffed it in the plastic bag from Luigi's and shoved it into the small waste basket.

She perched on the edge of the sofa. "I think it's a good clue, Tate. If any of the people who were near the site of Noah's abduction heard whistling, that could link the two cases."

"Do you really think the person who kidnapped Jeremy almost twenty years ago is active again? Why? How?"

Blanca held up her hand and ticked off her fingers. "You find bones. Boy is same age. Same MO. You found his cap."

"Didn't you learn at the academy that the chances of a kidnapper, or any kind of criminal, staying dormant for twenty years is atypical?" He jabbed his thumb into his chest. "Even I know that."

"Was he really dormant? You said it yourself. Boys have gone missing from the island in the interim. What if those weren't runaways or accidents?" She snapped her fingers. "That guy at the pizza place mentioned that other islands in Discovery Bay may have had similar cases."

"I didn't pay that much attention. If the Dead Falls Sheriff's Department called the boys missing or runaways, I figured they had a reason, and the other islands in the bay are small. Dead Falls is the biggest."

"You told me yourself the sheriff's department is incompetent. How long have they been inept?"

"Wait a minute." He shook his head. "I didn't mean every deputy in the department. We have some good people. It's the current sheriff, Hopkins, and the one before him, my friend Hannah's father, Sheriff Maddox—he was more corrupt than incompetent."

"Great. If they've been running things for a while, they could've missed signs. Even I can see Hopkins is lazy. It's a lot easier to call a twelve-year-old boy a runaway than actually launch an investigation, bring in the FBI."

Tate chewed on his bottom lip. "Are you going to look into some of those cases?"

"I am." She folded her arms as if she expected an argument from him, but who was he to disagree with the FBI?

If he stayed another minute, he'd need another beer. And if he had another beer, he'd have to stay in her hotel room. And if he stayed in her hotel room...

He coughed. "I gotta go. Thanks for the pizza."

She hopped off the arm of the sofa and tapped the pizza box. "Please take this with you when you leave, or I'll be tempted to sneak out here for a midnight snack."

"You have a fridge. Put a few slices in there and have it for breakfast." Tate reached for his hoodie.

"You're assuming I have any self-control at all." One dark eyebrow arched. "I don't."

And neither did he—not where Blanca Lopez was concerned.

"I'll do you this favor." He grabbed the pizza box. "But then you owe me."

"I'll let you know as soon as I hear anything about a DNA match between Mrs. Ruesler and the bones, and I'll let you know about the results of the blood on Noah's hat." She made a cross over her heart with her finger.

With an effort, he pulled his gaze away from the gesture. "That's no fun."

"Wh-what isn't?" She tilted her head, and her wavy dark hair cascaded over her shoulder.

"I'm not going to ask you for something you already want to give me." He winked and got the hell out her hotel room before he got in any deeper.

WHEN THE HOTEL door slammed behind Tate, Blanca exhaled and collapsed on the sofa. If he'd spent the night in her hotel room, she wouldn't have needed that pizza for a midnight snack. Groaning, she touched her forehead to her knees. What was with her? Did she give off some kind of flirty vibes with the men she worked with? She knew damned well she wasn't irresistible.

She gathered up the papers strewn across the coffee table and sorted them back into order. This plan had worked, even if Tate thought the information was worthless. A man who whistled a usually happy tune while he was stalking two boys gave off strong psycho vibes. How did someone like that hide in plain sight?

She finished packing the papers and then shifted the box from the table to the floor, next to the other box. She flipped the lid off the second box and lifted a file folder filled with photos. She'd started their search with the other box for a reason. Better to ease Tate back into the case than slam him over the head with it.

She pinched the first photo between her thumb and index finger and studied the bloody shoes that had been on Tate's feet when the search team had found him. Nobody could figure out why the bottoms of Tate's feet were bloody when he had his shoes on. When had he taken them off? Had he lost them in his flight from the threat? Had the kidnapper then put Tate's shoes back on his feet when he'd tied him to that tree? Why? To reduce the amount of evidence at the scene?

Tate had been right about one thing. If he'd seen his friend's abductor, that monster never would've let him live. Even if Tate hadn't laid eyes on the man, why had he spared Tate's life? Put his shoes back on?

She picked up the next picture. The vacant stare from Tate's twelve-year-old self unnerved her. He'd been in shock. Scratches marred his face, where the hint of his strong jaw was just emerging from his chubby cheeks. A line of dried blood connected one of his nostrils to his top lip. The white edges of a bandage poked out behind his ear.

She traced a finger from the top of his messy blond hair to his chin and whispered, "What happened out there, Tate?"

Her phone buzzed, and she jumped. Had Tate remembered something else? She answered the call and said, "Did you have second thoughts about that pizza?"

A long pause on the other end sent her pulse into a flutter, and she glanced at the display, which she should've done in the first place.

Manny's voice purred in her ear. "Sharing pizza with someone at this time of night already, Blanca?"

Closing her eyes, she gripped the phone. "What do you want, Manny? If you don't stop calling and harassing me, I'm going to report you."

He clicked his tongue. "After what happened last time, nobody is going to believe you, sweetheart."

Shame burned her cheeks, and anger gave an edge to her tongue. She clamped her mouth shut before she showed him how much he still got to her. "What is it?"

"Wondering if you needed a little help with that cold case of yours, but it sounds like you may have found a source already to…work with. If you're eating pizza in your hotel room with him, you must be on the right track."

"How do you know it's a him, and how do you know I'm in my hotel room?" She scooted off the sofa and sauntered to the sliding glass doors to the small balcony. Twitching back the drapes, she stared at her reflection. Her balcony faced the hotel parking lot and a line of trees beyond—always trees hemming you in on this island. She yanked the drapes closed.

"Don't forget, B. I know you very well. *Very* well."

"I don't need your help, Manny, not now, not in the future—never. All that time you pretended to help me, and you were just helping yourself. Now you can't stand it that I might find success, standing on my own two feet, proving you wrong. Back off. Don't call me again, or I will report you. And I don't give a damn what the agency thinks about it." She ended the call with a stab of her thumb and tossed the phone onto the sofa.

She placed the rest of the photos in the box and slid the lid back on it. Then she changed into a pair of flannel pajama bottoms and a camisole and washed her face. She grabbed her toothbrush and then set it on the edge of the sink.

Tate had left her one IPA, and she needed it. She padded into the sitting room and snagged the beer from the fridge. Aiming the remote at the TV, she dropped onto the bed and adjusted the pillows behind her. After a few sips of beer and ten minutes of a reality TV show, she set her bottle on the nightstand and wriggled off the bed.

She needed a snack with the beer. That pizza would've been better than a bag of chips, but she had to pretend to Tate that she was the kind of girl who didn't like to nosh into the night, diets be damned.

She opened her purse and slipped her debit card from her wallet. She had it on good authority that the vending machines on the fourth floor took plastic.

Clutching her debit card and her room key card, she crept down the hallway on bare feet to the elevator. A door behind her closed softly, but she didn't bother to turn around. When she entered the elevator, she pressed the button for the fourth floor, hoping she wouldn't run into any other late-night snackers.

The doors opened on an empty hallway, and she followed the low buzz of the ice machine. She hung a left across from the stairwell and stole into the room that housed an ice machine, soda machine and a tempting array of chips, cookies and candy.

Balancing one foot on top of the other, she studied the display in the case. Chips with her beer would be the natural choice, but that pizza had sated her salty craving. She needed something sweet.

She inserted her card, tapped the letter-number combo

for a pack of cupcakes and bent down to retrieve them. A squeak of a shoe and a rustle behind her made her jerk her head up quickly.

Out of the corner of her eye, she saw an object flying toward her. It landed on the back of her head, and she opened her mouth to protest through her dizziness.

A hand clamped over her lips, a cloth pressing against her nose. She dragged in a breath and knew her mistake instantly, as a sweet smell invaded her nostrils and hit the back of her throat.

She dropped to the floor on her knees and saw her cupcakes in the dispenser as she keeled over.

Chapter Seven

Tate finished the last piece of pizza in his Jeep looking out at the falls—the falls where Andrew Finnigan's body had been found. He remembered the case. Andrew had gone missing after school one day. The boy had been a loner, troubled, drugs already at the age of thirteen.

Even his parents, who'd reported him missing at ten o'clock that night, had been more worried about suicide or running away than foul play. About a week later, his broken body had been discovered on the first ledge beneath the falls, and the sheriff's department had quickly ruled it an accidental death, a fall.

Some suspected suicide, but maybe the deputies were trying to spare Andrew's parents. In their haste to settle on a manner and cause of death, had law enforcement missed something? Andrew's death had occurred in the early 2000s. Tate had been away at college in Seattle during that time, but his sister had told him about it.

Tate had then read about the case and had been surprised that Andrew's body had remained intact for almost a week. Plenty of wild animals in the area could've made short work of his corpse. Sheriff Maddox was still very popular around that time. Had he wrapped up the investigation early to stoke that popularity? As corrupt as the man was, he was a lot more efficient than Hopkins.

Tate wiped his hands on a crumpled napkin and grabbed his phone. If Blanca planned to keep him updated on her side of the investigation, he owed it to her to feed her everything he remembered. She'd asked about Andrew before, and this information might give her a starting point.

He called her number, putting the phone on Speaker. It rang several times before going to voice mail. Tate ended the call and tried again. He sucked in his bottom lip. He'd heard her phone ring, and she had it on full blast. Would be hard for her to sleep through that, and that's why she had it that way. She didn't want to miss a thing.

She'd also mentioned that she was a night owl, and it wasn't even midnight yet. He tapped her contact info again. Maybe the beers had made her sleepy, although she'd seemed wired when he left her.

When he heard her voice mail pick up for a third time, he ended the call and dropped the phone on the console. She could wait until tomorrow for this information on Andrew. It wasn't going anywhere, but when he pulled away from the viewing point for the falls, he turned back toward town and her hotel instead of in the direction of his place.

A pulse throbbed at the base of his throat, and his foot pressed the accelerator. He eased off the gas pedal when he hit the main road. She was probably sleeping. She didn't have to be at his beck and call. What excuse could he possibly give for showing up at her hotel room after he'd just left?

She'd laugh in his face if he told her the uneasiness he'd been feeling ever since he remembered that tune had filtered into his thoughts of her. A kidnapper of adolescent boys didn't pose any threat to Blanca—or to him, anymore.

Still, he drove straight back to her hotel and parked in

the lot. She had a room on the second floor, and it faced the parking lot, but he couldn't tell from here which one she occupied. Lights glowed in only one window on the second floor, though, and the room, halfway down the hallway, could definitely be hers. So if she were awake with the lights on, why didn't she answer her phone?

With his pulse thrumming, Tate exited his car and strode toward the hotel entrance. He waved at the clerk, who'd been working earlier, and jogged to the stairwell. He took the stairs two at a time to the second floor and burst onto the hallway from the fire door.

He took a few deep breaths to control his panting and squared himself in front of Blanca's door. He tapped lightly, his ear to the door. When she didn't respond, he knocked louder and called her name.

"Blanca, I just thought of something." He could explain later that she hadn't answered her phone. He'd have a harder time explaining why this piece of information about Andrew couldn't wait for tomorrow.

He rested his forehead against the door, pressing his palms flat against it. "Blanca?"

Could she be sleeping? Her room was a suite with a separate bedroom. She could have that door closed and be dead to the world. A shiver ran up his spine. He pulled out his phone and called her.

Holding his breath, he cocked his head toward the door and heard the faint sound of her cell phone ringing from the interior of the room. He took a step back from the door so she would be able to see him through the peephole...but only silence came from the other side.

A door opened behind him, and he jumped.

A middle-aged woman, clutching a robe to her throat

with one hand, a half-full wineglass in the other, peered at him. "Is that your room?"

"Uh, no. It's my friend's room. I was here earlier, and I…uh, forgot something. Sorry to disturb you." He gestured toward Blanca's room. "She's either sound asleep, or she went out."

He doubted Blanca had left her room without her phone.

"Oh, she went out." The woman swirled her wine, seeming to enjoy her late-night encounter. "But that was a while ago. I thought I heard her come back, though."

"She went out?" Tate took a step toward the woman. "You saw her go out?"

"Yeah." She aimed a toe at a tray on the floor. "I was putting my room service out, and I saw her walking toward the elevator. I don't think she was planning to leave the hotel, though."

"How do you know that?"

"She was wearing what could've been pajamas, and she was barefoot. You wouldn't go outside like that, would you?" She took a sip of her wine and then waved the glass in the air unsteadily. "If you ask me, she was heading for the vending machines. I could've told her the hotel room service would deliver French fries…and even a bottle of wine."

"Vending machines? When was this? Wouldn't she be back by now?" Tate licked his dry lips. None of this made sense.

"Less than an hour ago, but probably more than thirty minutes. Maybe she got a snack and then took a midnight dip in the indoor pool." She flung her arm out. "You sure she's not in there? I could've sworn I heard a door open on the corridor."

"I don't think so." Tate eyed his phone. "Is the vending machine down the hallway toward the elevator?"

"Not on this floor. You have to go to the lobby or the fourth floor for the vending machines. I doubt she was going down to the lobby dressed like she was."

"Okay, thanks. I'll try the vending machines first."

As he marched back to the stairwell, the nosy neighbor called out. "And then try the pool, handsome. I wouldn't mind a little midnight skinny-dipping myself."

That woman didn't belong anywhere near water right now. He climbed two flights of stairs to the fourth floor. Even if Blanca had gone to the vending machines, why would she still be there? Maybe she came back to her room and then left again. Maybe that's the door the guest heard. If she weren't there, if he couldn't find her, did he have a right to ask the hotel clerk to open her door?

What if she were in her room with someone? God, he'd never be able to face her again.

He cranked down the handle of the fire door to the fourth floor and bumped it open with his hip. The hum of the ice machine drew him toward an alcove a few doors down.

He drew up to the open door, and his heart slammed against his rib cage. "Blanca!"

He crouched beside her still form, her body on its side, one arm over her head, one flung across her chest. Thank God her chest rose and fell and her flesh was warm to his touch.

As he brought his face close to her mouth to check her breathing, a sickeningly sweet scent made him gag. He'd eaten a lot of those cupcakes sitting in that vending machine tray and none ever smelled like that.

Brushing a lock of her hair from her face, he said, "Blanca? Blanca, wake up."

She moaned softly from her parted lips.

Tate sprang up and got a bottle of water from the machine. He twisted off the cap and scooped an arm beneath

Blanca to raise her to a sitting position between his legs, her back against his chest. He put the water to her lips and tipped a little of the liquid into her mouth.

"Drink this, Blanca. C'mon, wake up. You're okay." Actually, he wasn't sure if she was okay or not. He patted her head but didn't feel any bumps or sticky hair. He smoothed his hands down her bare arms and encircled her waist with his hands. No blood. No injuries.

Just the smell of ether emanating from the lower half of her face. Had someone done this to her? He knew people took strange things for a high, but he doubted an adult woman of means would use ether for a bump.

The water he poured into her mouth trickled down her chin, but she gurgled. He tried a little more and dabbed his wet fingers on her forehead. "Open your eyes, Blanca."

Her long dark lashes fluttered against her cheeks, and she began to slouch against his body. He wrapped an arm around her waist and hoisted her up, holding her against him.

"Drink the water." He tilted the bottle into her mouth, and she swallowed, even though more ran down her neck, soaking her cami top.

"Okay, we're gonna stand up. The sooner you get out of this lethargic state, the better." He maneuvered himself back into a crouch and hooked his arms beneath hers. He braced himself against the soda machine and straightened up, dragging her with him.

She wobbled and fell against his body.

"It's okay. I've got you. Just move one foot in front of the other."

She shuffled forward and then bent over at the waist, retching.

Patting her back, he said, "Attagirl. We can always clean up regurgitated pizza later."

Luckily, Blanca didn't throw up any pizza, but she had a few more dry heaves before uncurling her body. She listed to the side, and he caught her, planting one hand firmly on her hip.

"Let's go, sailor. Keep walking." As he watched her feet take a few more unsteady steps forward, Tate spotted a red credit card on the floor. With one hand tucked into the waistband of her flannel pajama bottoms, he ducked quickly to peel the card from the floor.

Blanca must've used it for the vending machines. His head swiveled as he searched the floor for any other items she might've had. His heart stuttered. Where was her room key?

Clamping Blanca's body next to his, Tate staggered down the hallway to the elevators. When they got to the lobby, he half dragged, half carried Blanca across the tiled floor to the reception desk.

The clerk's eyes widened at their approach. "Is Ms. Lopez okay? What happened?"

"I'm not sure yet—" Tate peered at the kid's name tag "—Richard, but she was by the vending machines, and she doesn't have her room key. Can you give me a card key for her room? I'll take her up and try to find out what happened."

"Sh-should I call the police?" Richard swallowed hard, his Adam's apple bobbing in his skinny neck dotted with acne.

"Not yet." Tate readjusted his hold on Blanca, fixing her top to cover her cleavage from Richard's goggling.

He didn't want the police involved yet—didn't want to get Blanca into any trouble, just in case. He really didn't know her. She could be hiding all kinds of secrets.

"Maybe you could look at the camera footage from the second and fourth floors, though, for any unusual activity."

"Sure, sure." Richard swiped a plastic card through a machine and handed it to Tate. "There you go. Room 226."

"Thanks, Richard. I'll let you know if we need to bring law enforcement into this."

Richard reached beneath the counter and shoved two bottles of water at Tate. "She might need these."

Having left the other bottle of water at the vending machine, Tate nodded, swiping up the bottles and holding them both in one hand as he navigated Blanca toward the elevator. "That's it. Keep walking. You're doing great."

When they got into the elevator car, Blanca leaned against the mirrored wall and wiped a hand across her mouth. At least she'd stopped gagging and heaving.

"How do you feel? You coming out of it?" He cracked open one of the water bottles and held it to her lips. "I think it was just chloroform. You're not gonna die."

She nodded, or maybe her chin just dropped to her chest, but when she lifted her head, she drank some of the water without spewing it down her chin. Progress.

They arrived at her room, and Tate slid the card key into the slot. As the green lights flashed, a door opened on the hallway.

"You find your friend?" The woman from earlier stepped out of her room. "Whoa. Looks like she ordered a few bottles from room service after all."

"Yeah, thanks for your help." Tate hustled Blanca into the room and let the door slam behind them.

Blanca veered toward the sofa, but Tate held her upright. "Stay upright for a while and try to walk this off. Otherwise, you'll just fall asleep—and I need to know what happened."

She blinked several times and said, "Okay, okay."

The knots in Tate's gut loosened. He strode to the sliding glass door and dragged it open. The cool air that wafted into the room ruffled the drapes, and Tate walked Blanca to the fresh air. "Breathe deeply. You must've inhaled a ton of that chloroform to knock you out like that."

Blanca raised a hand to the back of her head and patted her hair. "Here. He hit me."

"I missed that." He positioned her next to the open door and placed her hand on the edge. He used his fingers to part her thick wavy hair and ran the tips along her scalp. He didn't feel any broken skin, but he did detect a small lump. "We need to get some ice on this."

She grabbed a handful of his hoodie. "Don't."

"I'm not leaving you. The door's locked and even if your attacker took your card key, the hotel attendant reprogrammed it and gave me another key. We're safe." He pulled her close and rubbed her back.

Blanca nestled closer to him, breathing deeply, her chest rising and falling against his, their hearts hammering out the same rhythm.

"I'm cold." She shifted out of his grasp, glancing down at her top, the water that had spilled down her front making the thin material cling to her breasts.

Tate shrugged out of his hoodie, warm from his body heat, and wrapped it around her. "How about some coffee? That might help."

"Yeah." She wriggled into the hoodie, slipping her arms in the sleeves and pulling it tight around her body. She licked her lips and then reached past him to chug some water from the bottle. "H-he attacked me in the ice-machine room."

Tate eased out a breath as he popped a pod into the coffee maker. "Can you start at the beginning?"

"I…" She scooped a hand through her hair and turned

in a circle. Then she gasped and stumbled toward the coffee table.

Thinking she was going to collapse again, Tate jumped forward to grab her, but she spun around, her eyes wide, her arms flailing at her sides.

"The files. He stole the case files."

Chapter Eight

The sudden, swift movement made Blanca dizzy, and she placed a hand against Tate's broad chest to steady herself. She wouldn't mind sinking against that safe harbor again, but she had a big problem on her hands that cuddling with Tate wouldn't help.

"Whoa." He placed a hand on her hip. "Are you sure?"

Looking behind her, she stared at the empty spot on the floor next to the coffee table. "I left them right there. I never moved them. Oh God, he incapacitated me in the snack room, stole my room key and availed himself of those files."

"As long as you don't feel like you're going to pass out or go to sleep, have a seat. I'll get you some coffee and call the sheriff's department." He led her to the sofa as if she were a frail elderly person, and she sank down on the edge, not wanting to get engulfed by the soft cushions.

"Wait." She pushed the hair from her face and winced when her fingers met the sore spot on the back of her head. "You haven't called the police yet? You found me passed out and didn't immediately call 911?"

"I…um." He kept his back to her as he poured some coffee. "You probably should drink this black."

He carried the mug of steaming liquid to her and placed it on the coffee table. Then he took his cell phone from his pocket and called the DFSD. After he explained the basics, he raised his eyebrows at her. "She seems fine, but maybe you can send an EMT to check her out."

Sipping the hot brew from the cup, she watched Tate over the rim.

He ended the call and said, "They're on the way. I'm hoping Richard downstairs has some footage of your attacker."

"So why is this your first call to the police?"

"You were out. I wasn't sure what happened."

She narrowed her eyes, which hurt the back of her eyeballs. "But even if it was an accident, you didn't think I might need assistance?"

"I'm sorry, Blanca. I just wanted to make sure it wasn't a case of…"

He spread his hands, and a light bulb went on in her foggy brain. "You thought I ODed or something?"

"Look, I just didn't know. I didn't want to embarrass you in case it was some kind of something gone wrong." His face reddened up to his naturally blond roots.

"Thanks, I guess. Not sure what kind of vibes I'm giving you if that's your first instinct."

"None. No. No vibes like that. I just wanted to protect you."

A little queasiness invaded her stomach, and it didn't have anything to do with the chloroform clapped over her nose and mouth. Had Tate heard something about her? Done a little digging?

"It's fine." She waved one hand in the air. "I'm pretty sure by the time you found me, the perpetrator was long gone. Why were you here again?"

"That can wait. Tell me from the beginning what happened."

"Got ready for bed." She plucked at the flannel material

of her pajama bottoms. "Fancied a snack and made tracks for the vending machines on the fourth floor. Told you I had no self-control. Obviously, I didn't think I'd run into anything or I would've put more clothes on."

His gaze dipped to her chest, and she pulled his sweatshirt tighter.

"You didn't see or hear anyone?"

"Just a door behind me, but I didn't turn around." Her mouth dropped open. "Do you think it was someone staying on this floor?"

"I'm pretty sure that was your wine-swilling neighbor across the hall. She was putting her room-service tray outside. She's actually the one who told me you'd probably headed to the fourth-floor vending machines."

"Had I known this hotel had room service, that would've saved me a lot of trouble." She shot a look at the place where the boxes had been. "Got in the elevator, got to the fourth floor without seeing a soul and whipped out my card to get some cupcakes. While I was bending down to retrieve them, someone came at me. Thunked me on the head with something just enough to daze me and then went in for the kill with a chloroform-soaked cloth. He let me fall, and that's the last thing I remember before you poured water in my face."

"I didn't—I wasn't—that was for you to drink." He smacked a hand on the credenza and an inverted coffee cup rattled in its saucer. "He must've been watching you, waiting. If you hadn't come out of your room, maybe he would've broken in."

"Why take the boxes? How'd this person even know I had them?" She hunched her shoulders, Tate's sweatshirt not even offering enough warmth to ward off the chill snaking across her flesh.

"I told you, small town. That guy at the pizza place knew

who you were." He snapped his fingers. "Who was that guy, anyway?"

"I have no clue. He didn't give me his card or anything. Ginger, though."

"What?" He jerked his head up.

"Redhead." She tapped her own dark locks. "He was kind of beefy, freckled, middle-aged and had red hair."

"Porter Monroe?" Tate dragged his knuckles across the sexy reddish-blond stubble on his chin.

"You know him?"

"I know Porter. There are a few redheads on the island, but he works out with weights. Can't miss him."

"That could definitely be him." She slurped up more coffee. "Are you saying Porter Monroe followed me to the hotel, waited for you to leave and then looked for a way in?"

"I don't know if it was Porter, but that's exactly what someone did." Tate shoved his hands in his pockets. "I'm almost glad you did go out. What would he have done if he'd broken into your room and you caught him in the act?"

"I do sleep with my weapon under my pillow." She clapped a hand over her mouth. "Oh no. Is it still there? If someone stole my service weapon, I'm in deep trouble."

"Stay there. I'll check." A few seconds later he called from the other room. "Still here. He only wanted those boxes."

"But why?" Blanca clasped her hands between her knees.

"He doesn't want you reviewing the evidence. It could've been Jeremy's abductor." Tate massaged his neck.

"The Dead Falls Sheriff's Department is going to have the majority of those records online now, anyway." She leveled a gaze at him and gulped against her dry throat. "Aren't they?"

"Your guess is as good as mine. I'm not in law enforcement. I'm sure they're not going to tell me."

She groaned and touched her forehead to her knees. "This is gonna look so bad."

"It's not your fault, Blanca. You didn't leave your door unlocked with the files inside. You were assaulted."

A knock on the door made them both jump, and Tate made the first move to answer, and then opened it after verifying it was a deputy outside.

He swung open the door, and Blanca swallowed as two sheriff's deputies, Fletch and another guy, entered the room followed by two EMTs with a gurney.

"I don't need a ride to the emergency room. I'm fine."

Tate explained to them what happened as they swarmed her. "So check out the bump on her head and her vitals."

While the EMTs had her remove Tate's sweatshirt and recline on the sofa, Tate talked to the two deputies. The guy who wasn't Fletch pivoted and left the room.

Tate called to Blanca as the EMT wrapped the blood pressure cuff around her arm. "He's going to check the security footage."

"Take a deep breath, Blanca."

The silver cup on the stethoscope gave her a chill when he pressed it against her back, and she scooped in a large breath and released it on his command.

Fletch sauntered over. "Are you all right, Blanca? Did someone really steal Jeremy Ruesler's case files?"

"Unfortunately, yes." She made a grab for Tate's sweatshirt when the EMT stopped listening to her heart and lungs. How many times could she flash her breasts in one night?

"I'll have to report that to Sheriff Hopkins." Fletch rubbed his chin.

"I would expect you to, or I'll do it myself." She crossed

her fingers. "Please, please, please tell me the department has the case files online. You didn't provide me with any physical evidence in those boxes, just paperwork and photos."

"We do—at least for current cases, and I seem to remember a lot of scanning going on a few years ago." Fletch scratched a point over his ear. "Why would someone want to steal that stuff?"

"Because someone doesn't want the FBI looking at the cold case." Tate touched the EMT's shoulder as he packed away his instruments. "Is she going to be okay?"

"She's fine. I'll leave some ibuprofen for the bump on her head, no broken skin. The chloroform is leaving her body." He turned to Blanca. "Keep drinking water. If you experience any other symptoms tonight, head to the ER."

"The only symptom I'm experiencing is embarrassment for losing those files."

The other deputy returned to the room. "Bad news."

"Don't tell me the hotel doesn't have security cameras. I've seen them." Tate folded his arms.

"Oh, they have them, but the floor cameras aren't working. Haven't worked for several months. The camera on the lobby doesn't show any activity, except you leaving around ten thirty and then coming back about forty-five minutes later."

"Side doors?"

"Don't work there, either, and the cameras on the parking lot picked up only a few guests. The clerk IDed them." The deputy shrugged.

Blanca snorted. "Are the cameras just for show, or what?"

"Don't know what to tell you, Agent Lopez. Security cameras didn't pick up your attacker. I also questioned a few people on this floor and the fourth, and nobody noticed anything unusual."

"Unbelievable. But he wouldn't have tried this stunt if he didn't think he could get away with it."

The deputies took a few more notes, and the EMT handed Blanca an ice pack before Tate shooed them all out of the room. Then he collapsed on the sofa beside her, rubbing his temple with two fingers. "How are you feeling?"

"Looks like you're the one who needs the ibuprofen." She jerked her thumb at her purse, undisturbed on the desk chair. "I have more in my bag if you want these."

"Has he been watching you? Us?"

Blanca curled one leg beneath her. "By *he*, do you mean Jeremy's kidnapper?"

"Who else? Who else would want those files?"

"A journalist, maybe? Perhaps someone's writing a big story, and they figured they could get all the details from the files for an exclusive."

"A journalist would hit you over the head and chloroform you to get a couple of boxes?"

She repositioned the ice pack on the back of her head. "They'd do it in DC."

He rolled his baby blues at her. "Do you need anything?"

Besides your strong arms around me again?

"Damn, I could use that cupcake." She snapped her fingers. "Or the pizza. I wouldn't object if you went out to your car and grabbed that pizza."

"I ate it."

She put her hands on her hips. "You took it home, ate it and then drove back here for some reason you haven't told me about yet."

"I never made it home. I stopped at the lookout for Dead Falls and ate it in the car, thought of something and then turned around to head back here." He rubbed her calf. "I'm glad I did."

Her eyelashes fluttered at the warm gush his touch sent coursing through her body. She could almost forgive him for eating all the pizza. "I'm glad, too. Thanks for helping me out and for having my back—just in case I was a secret chloroform-snorter on my off time."

A chuckle rumbled deep in his throat. "You have to admit, you know a lot more about me than I do about you."

"That's because you—" she leveled a finger at him "—are part of my case. I'm just the agent on the case. Big difference."

"Do you want that cupcake? It was still in the tray of the machine when I hauled you out of that room."

"That's all right. I don't want you to go out of your way when you leave."

"I'm not leaving."

"Excuse me?" A thrill ran through her body making her nipples tingle, and once again, she was grateful for his sweatshirt.

He patted the sofa. "I'm staying right here. What if you have some reaction tonight? What if the guy comes back after he decides the key to his identity is in those files after you've already gone through them?"

The thrill turned to a chill, and she hugged herself. "I seriously doubt that's going to happen, and you forgot I have a weapon. I actually know how to use it."

"I don't doubt it, but I'd feel better if you let me stay. I'll have another beer if you need to give me an excuse."

"Fine. I think there's an extra blanket in the closet, but after you bring me that cupcake you need to tell me why you came back here. What did you remember?"

He held up one finger. "Deal."

When Tate left the room, Blanca shrugged out of his hoodie and hung it on the back of a chair. Then she scurried into the bedroom and pulled a baggy Georgetown T-shirt over her skimpy camisole. Having him in the next room was going to be enough of a temptation. She didn't need to be parading around half-naked to add any more fuel to this fire kindling between them.

When he came back to the room, he tossed her the package of cupcakes, and she caught it with one hand, slightly squishing the contents. As she unwrapped the package, she said, "I hope these are worth it."

She bit into the chocolate and closed her eyes. "Totally worth it."

"More coffee?"

"No, thanks. I do eventually want to get to sleep tonight." She kicked her feet up on the coffee table. "Do you want the other one?"

"I don't know. You sacrificed a lot for that snack."

Using her toe, she scooted the plastic-wrapped cupcake to the edge of the table. "Go ahead. I sure as heck don't need it."

"You look great to me." He leaned over to snag the cupcake. "But if you're sure."

"Sit down and stop stalling." She licked a piece of chocolate frosting from her fingers. "Why'd you come back?"

He eased down to the edge of the table, his knees spread open, and bit into the cupcake. A dab of the cream in the center clung to his chin. "It's about Andrew Finnigan. The kid Porter mentioned to you in Luigi's. He disappeared in the mid-2000s, maybe 2010, about seven years after the incident with Jeremy."

"Disappeared, like never found again?" She tapped her chin, but Tate didn't take the hint.

"No, disappeared as in ran away and then was found dead on a ledge beneath the falls."

She put a hand to her throat. "How awful. How old was he?"

"About thirteen, I think. With some encouragement by the sheriff's department, the medical examiner ruled it an accident. Parents accepted it because it beat suicide."

"And? Why is it in question?"

"For me, it's mostly the condition of the body. He'd been out there for about a week, and there are plenty of wild animals on that ridge. It's unusual that none...fed on his body. Sorry."

"That is odd." She waved her hand at him. "You have a little bit of cream on your chin."

"Oh." He grabbed a napkin left over from the pizza and swiped it across his face. "And I know that info about Andrew isn't urgent, but I did try to call you, and you didn't answer. I thought that was strange, and then I got worried. I admit it."

"You don't have to apologize for being concerned about me." She popped the last bite of her cupcake into her mouth and dusted her fingers together. "Thanks again. I'm definitely going to look into the Andrew Finnigan case—if I'm still working Jeremy's cold one."

"Don't see how your bosses can blame you. You left the boxes in a locked hotel room."

"Let's just say I don't have the best track record with the agents in charge." She stood up, brushing crumbs from her pajama bottoms. "I'll find you that blanket. I'm afraid I don't have a toothbrush for you, though."

"That's okay. I'll use my finger and swish some water around in my mouth."

"That'll work." She pushed up from the sofa and slid open the mirrored closet door.

"I'll get that." Tate had come up behind her and reached up to get the blanket folded on the top shelf.

She stepped back from the warm invitation of his body. "I'll brush my teeth and leave my toothpaste on the sink for you."

"Thanks." He hugged the blanket to his chest and pivoted toward the sitting room.

Blanca dipped into the bathroom, brushed her teeth and splashed some water on her face. She could probably do with another shower after napping on the floor next to the ice machine, but the night's events had hit her like a sledge-hammer and her head ached. She capped the toothpaste and left it on the counter, and then slid into the bedroom without looking at Tate.

She snapped the door behind her, dragged the T-shirt over her head and crawled into bed, feeling for the gun beneath her pillow. Too bad she hadn't taken it with her to the snack machine.

She snuggled under the covers as she heard the water running in the bathroom. What had been the real reason for Tate returning to the hotel? Had he really been worried about her?

A smile curled her lips, and she closed her eyes. It had been a long time since someone had been worried about her safety, and it felt good. Too good.

Chapter Nine

What felt like several seconds later, Blanca rolled to her side to the sound of more water in the bathroom. Was Tate in the shower now?

She rubbed her eyes and squinted at the green numbers floating beside the bed. She knew it couldn't be seven thirty at night, so it must be morning.

She didn't want Tate to catch her sleeping in, so she scooted from the bed. She yanked her phone off the charger and dropped the T-shirt over her head as she padded to the bedroom door. She peeked into the sitting room and blinked at the light pouring in from the window, laying stripes on the sofa and the blanket folded neatly on one cushion.

She crossed the room to the credenza and slid in a pod for some coffee. She rinsed out her cup from last night in case Tate wanted a cup. As the coffee dripped into the cup, Blanca took a deep breath and checked her messages.

Nothing from her boss, Crandall. Either Sheriff Hopkins hadn't heard about the missing files yet, or he hadn't had time to call Crandall. Maybe Hopkins hadn't heard about them himself. It would probably be best if she told the sheriff first. She should've mentioned that to the deputies last night.

"Anything new?"

She jumped at the sound of Tate's voice behind her and

spun around, clutching the phone in her hand. She almost dropped it when she got an eyeful of Tate sluicing wet hair back from his face, a towel hanging dangerously low on his hips.

She took a shallow breath and squeaked, "You seem to be missing some clothes."

"Sorry. I left them out here. Didn't think you'd be up this early. I probably woke you up, huh?" He whipped the towel off his body and bunched it in one hand as he sauntered past her, smelling like a juicy piece of citrus fruit.

Her heart skipped a few beats and then returned to its normal pace when she saw the boxers beneath the towel—but just barely. She somehow kept her tongue from hanging out of her mouth as he shook out his jeans, his back to her, and flashed those shifting plates of muscle. He pulled on his pants and tugged his shirt over his head before turning around, but not before she caught sight of his six-pack as it dipped into his jeans.

She nodded toward the credenza. "Coffee? I made a cup for myself, using the mug from last night, but there's another, clean one."

"Sure, I'll take a cup. How are you feeling?"

"I feel fine. No lingering effects from either the chloroform or the bump on the head." She dumped some creamer and sweetener into her cup and swirled the liquid with a stir stick.

"Any idea what he used to hit you?"

"None. It was hard and solid, and he needed only one blow to take me down so he could finish the job with the chloroform."

He chewed his lip. "Definitely a man, though."

"Definitely." She shoved another pod into the coffee

maker and put the remaining cup beneath the dispenser. "Could be a relative."

"A relative of the kidnapper?"

"Jeremy was taken almost twenty years ago. How old would his abductor have to be today?" She sipped the coffee, inhaling the scent, and cupping it on her tongue before swallowing.

"Are you kidding?" Tate spread his hands. "He could've been twenty then, forty now, like Porter. Thirty then, fifty now, and everything in between. You think he's too old to get up to his old tricks? Does someone like that ever stop? Maybe he moved away and came back."

"I don't know, Tate. How could he be hiding in plain sight?"

"You went through the FBI academy. You know better than most. If they looked like monsters and stood out to the rest of us, they wouldn't be able to act on their evil."

"I know." She let the last few drips of coffee land in the mug and asked, "Cream or sugar?"

"Black is fine. I'll gulp some down, and then I have to get going. We have some training today." He took the cup from her, his fingers brushing hers. "What are your plans for the day?"

"I have a feeling I'll be spending most of the day at the sheriff's station—explaining to Hopkins what happened to his files and hopefully going through the online version. I also plan to do a little research on Andrew Finnigan's case. His parents still here?"

"Long gone." He slurped some coffee and set the cup down. He dropped onto the sofa and pulled on his socks and boots. "I'll check in on you at the end of the day to see how you're feeling. Anything seems off, head to the hospital."

"I will." As he got up and took another sip of coffee,

she handed his sweatshirt to him. "Thanks again for everything last night—the beer and pizza, too, although that seems ages ago now."

"Yeah, it does." He held the sweatshirt to his face for a second before shaking his head and slipping into it. He paused at the open door. "Take it easy today."

"Will do." Blanca closed the door behind him with a sigh. Why did the grown-up Tate Mitchell have to be so hot?

She showered and put on one of her pantsuits. She needed all the professionalism she could muster today.

Tooling into the station, she hoped that she could reach Sheriff Hopkins before the bad news did. She nodded to a few of the deputies she saw at the search for Noah the other night and pointed down the hallway toward Hopkins's office. "Is he in?"

With permission from the deputy at the front desk, Blanca squared her shoulders and strode toward the sheriff's office. She rapped on the open door. "Sheriff Hopkins?"

"Come in, come in. I was expecting you, Agent Lopez."

Her stomach sank to her toes. "Oh? You heard about the... incident last night at my hotel?"

"I did." He waved her into his office. "Are you okay?"

"I'm fine. I'm sorry about those files, though. Totally unacceptable." She cleared her throat through his silence. "I'm hoping you have most of those online, so I can continue my research."

He steepled his fingers and peered at her over the tips. "We have most of the witness statements online. I'm not sure about the photos, though. We'll give you access to the database, so you can look."

She eked out a small breath, trying not to collapse with relief. "Good to hear that. What's not good is that I think Jeremy's kidnapper or a family member may have stolen the evidence. Who else would go through that much trouble to get the files?"

"I wouldn't jump to conclusions, Agent Lopez. It could've been anyone, really." He flicked his fingers. "Bloggers, you know, those podcast people. Some true-crime nut. Teenage troublemakers. Maybe even Ruesler family members hoping to get some inside info they think we left out."

She widened her eyes. "You think Birdie Ruesler attacked me to look at evidence regarding her son's disappearance?"

"Birdie's not Jeremy's only living relative. He has a sister. His dad isn't on the island, but he's in the vicinity."

"Maybe." She didn't want to argue with Hopkins before asking a favor. "In addition to looking at the Ruesler case online, I'd like to have a look at the files for the Andrew Finnigan case, accidental death at the falls, around 2010, I believe."

"Finnigan?" He scratched his chin. "I remember that case—runaway. May have been a suicide, but the medical examiner ruled it accidental. Why do you think that's connected to the Ruesler case?"

"Some irregularities with the body." She clasped her hands in her lap. "Is it okay?"

"Sure, sure. I'm going to send you to Deputy Amanda Robard. She's our current computer whiz, and she's two doors down." He dropped his gaze to the Danish on his desktop. "Anything else?"

Did the guy actually do anything in this office other than eat?

"That's all. Just wanted to apologize for losing the files." She stood up, hitching her purse over her shoulder. "I'll take care of notifying my supervisor, Agent Crandall."

"Sure, sure. Not your fault, Agent Lopez. I'm sorry you were attacked in our little town." He scooped up his Danish with one hand, pausing it halfway to his open mouth. "I understand you were with Tate Mitchell at the time."

She stopped at the door, pinning her purse against her side. "Not exactly. I questioned him in my hotel room about the night Jeremy disappeared. He left, forgot something and returned to find me conked out next to the ice machine."

He mumbled around chews. "Did he tell you anything?"

"No." She made a quick pivot out of his office. The FBI kept things from the local law all the time. Why should she be the exception?

She stopped two offices down from Hopkins's and barged in on a female deputy, her dark hair pulled into a tight bun to complement her crisp uniform.

"Deputy Robard? I'm FBI Special Agent Blanca Lopez. We met the other night during the search for Noah."

Robard looked up and squinted. "Oh yeah. FBI. You can call me Amanda."

"And you can call me Blanca." She jerked her thumb toward Hopkins's office. "The Sheriff told me you could get me into the database. There are a couple of cases I want to research."

"I heard about what happened last night." Amanda tapped her head. "You okay?"

Blanca slumped against the wall. "Who didn't hear about the incident last night?"

"Small town. Local kid working the front desk." Amanda shrugged. "Stuff gets around."

"Except who kidnapped Jeremy Ruesler and snatched Noah Fielding—*that* stuff doesn't get around."

"I know, right?" Amanda kicked a chair on wheels out toward her. "Have a seat, and I'll get you a log-in. You can work in here. I just finished."

Blanca wheeled the chair next to Amanda, who took her

through the log-in process to the database and showed her how to do a search.

When she finished, Amanda grabbed her coffee cup and pushed back from the desk. "You were with Tate last night?"

Uh-oh. Was she stepping on an ex's toes? Or a wannabe love interest?

"Just professional. I had a lot of questions for him regarding the Ruesler case."

Amanda laughed. "I don't care if you wanna jump his bones. I'm not into dudes. Just know that Tate's wound pretty tightly, despite his easy-breezy demeanor and success with the girlies. Don't know how much you can get out of him. He doesn't wanna remember that night, even though he pretends he does."

"Thanks for the tip." Blanca willed the hot blush rushing up her throat to back down. Was her attraction to Tate that obvious?

As she left the office, Amanda said, "Just make sure you log-out when you're done and close the door behind you. It locks automatically."

"Thanks."

As soon as Blanca heard Amanda's footsteps retreat down the hall, she jumped up and closed the door. She'd prefer privacy. Seemed like you couldn't keep anything a secret in this town.

She accessed the Ruesler file first, just to make sure she could. She released a breath, as she discovered most of the paperwork that had been stolen last night had already been entered online; even the photos had been scanned. Her attacker's actions hadn't accomplished what he'd wanted—whatever that was.

She perused the file for over an hour, taking notes, before doing a search for the Finnigan case.

That case had been more recent, and it too was all on-line. She clicked through the notes and even did a search for various forms of the word *whistle*, but nothing popped up.

She pressed her fingers to her lips as she brought up the pictures of Andrew's dead body. She hoped his parents hadn't seen these, but Tate had been right. The boy's body looked fairly pristine for being out in the wild for almost a week.

She'd seen bodies that had been in the elements for more than a day or two, and they usually displayed evidence of animal activity. No wildlife had bothered to investigate Andrew's body near a forest with actual wild animals?

What did that mean, exactly? Maybe he'd been hiding in those caves behind the falls before deciding to kill himself or before slipping from the outcropping. Just because law enforcement couldn't find Andrew, it didn't mean he wasn't alive out there while they were looking for him. Surely, it didn't mean he'd been killed elsewhere and thrown from the falls. Would it even be possible for someone to get a dead body up there? The ME had indicated that Andrew had been dead for several days. Could he have been mistaken, given the temperature?

She brought up the clearest photo of the boy's entire body and zoomed in on different parts. She enlarged his hands and leaned forward, spotting an injury on his wrist.

Her heart skipped a beat when she zoomed in on his other wrist. The same mark appeared in the same place as the other one. She snagged a still of both wrists and transferred the photo to another app where she could focus and clarify the image.

When she finished her manipulations of the photo, she sat

back in her chair and sucked in her bottom lip. The marks on Andrew's wrists were from restraints.

Someone had been holding Andrew somewhere before killing him. This was no accidental death.

Chapter Ten

Tate cranked on the warm water and stood under the spray as the soot and dirt from his body ran down the drain. Training had felt extra hard today, or maybe it was the pizza and beer from last night—or his restless sleep.

The narrow sofa in Blanca's hotel room hadn't helped, but it was Blanca's presence in the next room that had made sleep so elusive. Any other time, any other situation, any other woman and he'd have been making moves to get into her bed.

She'd been injured, woozy. No way he would've taken advantage of that with any woman, but especially not Blanca. Something about their interactions seemed…different. Every encounter with her made him feel as if he were standing on the edge of some precipice. If he made one wrong move, he could fall and be banished from her presence forever.

Aaron jabbed at the plastic shower curtain and shouted, "Dude, could you save some water for the rest of us. What are you doing in there?"

"You should know, Huang. Why are you spying on me?" Tate turned off the water and grabbed his towel hanging over the curtain rod.

He dried off quickly, wrapped the towel around his waist

and stepped into the locker room. The agency didn't have enough showers for all the crew members, although some elected to drive home in their filthy uniforms after training to shower in the privacy of their own homes. The married people tended to do that more than the singles, as they had spouses and kids waiting for them.

Tate had never been interested in that life, and the thought of having kids terrified him. He'd never forget what losing Jeremy had done to the Rueslers. Birdie had been the best mom on the island among his friends' mothers. Baked the best cookies. Told the funniest jokes. Knew all the cool music. The woman he'd seen yesterday was a shell of the one he'd known as a child.

He shoved his dirty uniform in a bag and finished dressing. When he checked his phone on the way out, the message notification from Blanca put a spring in his step. He threw his bag in the back seat of his Jeep and tapped on her message.

She'd found something and wanted him to call her. He blew out a breath. At least she hadn't been recalled from the case for the missing files. He started the engine but stayed in Park, buzzing down a window.

He placed the call, and she answered almost immediately. He said, "Got your text. What's up?"

"First of all, Hopkins didn't seem too upset that the files were stolen, and most of the paperwork and photos are online. So I lucked out there. Secondly, I got into Andrew Finnigan's case, and I saw something on his photos."

"What did you see?" He took a gulp of water from the bottle in his cup holder.

"Marks on his wrist. Tate, it looks as if Andrew had been restrained. I checked the autopsy report, and the medical examiner made a note of abrasions on the wrists but didn't make any connection to the boy being manacled."

Tate pushed up the sleeve of his jacket on his left arm and stared at his own wrist. The marks on his wrists had lasted for days where Jeremy's abductor had tied him up. His body had been lashed to the trunk of a tree, but his hands and feet had been bound, as well.

"Tate? Don't you think that's important?"

"I do, yeah. It's strange they didn't make a bigger deal out of it, but I know they were quick to settle on accidental." He rubbed his wrist.

"Settle on accidental to avoid a determination of suicide, but why rush to accidental if it was homicide?"

"I don't know, Blanca. You can question Hopkins, but he'd just started around that time. Maddox was the sheriff then, and he's dead."

"How about the medical examiner?" He heard some papers rustle over the line. "Dr. Scott Summers?"

"Summers? Yeah, I think he still lives on the island, but he's retired."

"Wait. I know that name." Blanca clicked her tongue. "He was at the search for Noah. He was in our group, so he's still active, at least. The fact that he's retired doesn't matter. I have his autopsy report. I can show it to him and see if he remembers anything about the case. I don't see on the report that he ever provided an explanation for the marks on Andrew's wrists, but maybe he remembers the reason for that."

Tate massaged his temple with his knuckle. "So what does this mean to you? Do you think Jeremy was held before he was...murdered? I don't believe there was anything near the bones to indicate that, but I'm no forensic scientist."

"I suppose we'll find out. We haven't even gotten the

DNA results back. But what this might mean?" She paused and took a sip of something. "Maybe Noah Fielding isn't dead, yet. Maybe he's being held somewhere, like Andrew was. He might still have a chance."

"Like Andrew *maybe* was. You don't know that."

"You're right, but that's what I'm here for."

"You're still here. How'd your boss back in DC react to the missing files?"

She cleared her throat. "I haven't heard from him, yet."

"Shouldn't you tell him yourself?"

"Yeah, yeah. I will. I just wanted to make sure Dead Falls had the files online. That way, I can give Crandall a good news-bad news situation." She giggled, and Tate could tell she was nervous about talking to her boss.

She'd made a couple of references about being in the doghouse with upper command but hadn't gone into any detail about it. He could imagine her going rogue now and then, but she seemed dedicated to the job...and good at it.

"No ill effects from last night?"

"No. I feel great today."

Obviously, she hadn't tossed and turned like he had. "Free for dinner? To, uh, discuss the cases."

"Sure. Takeout at my hotel again?"

"We do actually have restaurants in Dead Falls, you know."

"I know that, but maybe it's best if we're not seen out together. I don't know."

Tate furrowed his brow. "All right, but how about my place instead of your hotel? If anyone's creeping around the cabin, I'll know about it."

"Didn't you have training today? You shouldn't have to go home and cook."

He snorted. "What gave you the impression I cooked?

The most I can handle is barbecue, but Astrid left some food in the freezer. I think she has some lasagna in there. I can make a salad."

"Perfect. I'll bring the red wine and dessert."

And just like that, he had something and someone to go home to like some of the other guys.

He ended the call, and his lead foot got him home in record time. He'd already showered, so he dumped his uniform, along with some other clothes, in the washing machine and ran a critical eye over his space. Some areas were neater without his nephew around, but some decidedly needed work before Blanca got here.

By the time he heard her car in his driveway, he'd put the breakfast dishes in the dishwasher, wiped the crumbs from the counter, swept the kitchen floor and put the lasagna in the oven.

He opened the door with a flourish, and Blanca greeted him with two plastic bags swinging in her hands. "I hope you like cabernet sauvignon and ice cream."

"Together?" He took the bags from her hands and winked.

Wedging her hands on her curvy hips, she tilted her head at him.

"What?" He raised his eyebrows.

"Nothing." She sniffed the air. "Garlic two nights in a row. Nobody is going to want to get too close to me."

"I, um…" The words died on his lips, and he pivoted toward the kitchen, bringing the bags with him. She hadn't seemed to appreciate the wink, so he should probably cool the flirty act. "You'll like Astrid's lasagna. She's a good cook."

Blanca followed him into the kitchen and ran her hand along the quartz counter. "Anyone could be a good cook in this kitchen."

He glanced over his shoulder at her as he uncorked the wine to let it breathe. "Do you cook much?"

"I have my phases, especially when I'm trying to eat healthy. Then a big case comes up, and I'm grabbing fast food." She shrugged. "You said you had stuff for a salad. I *can* do that."

"Sure." He pointed to the fridge. "You can grab some veggies from the crisper. Olly doesn't like cooked vegetables, so Astrid makes him eat raw ones. A lot of those are still good."

"Has your sister always lived here with you?" She bent forward to open the crisper drawer, and he shifted his gaze away from her luscious derriere before she caught him.

"No, just since the divorce. Her ex is a jerk with violent tendencies, so she took refuge here."

"Lot of those running around." Blanca dumped several plastic bags on the countertop and slid a knife from the block. She held it up to the light and ran a finger along the blade, which glinted.

Tate held up his hands. "I swear, that's not me—at least not the violent part."

The side of her mouth lifted. "At least you're honest—with others."

He almost dropped the wineglass he'd just slid from the shelf. "What is that supposed to mean?"

"I talked to your friend Amanda today."

"Oh, Amanda. She's in the wrong line of work. She should be a therapist, and then she could actually charge for all that advice she's always handing out."

Blanca started chopping the vegetables with quick, precise strokes. "You know her theory about you?"

"I do, but she's wrong. I already helped you with the case, right? I remembered the whistling, and I told you about

Andrew." He poured the ruby-red liquid into the first glass where it shimmered.

"That's true." She held up the knife, a piece of carrot stuck to the side of the blade. "But Porter Monroe's the one who told me about Andrew Finnigan."

"Yeah." He poured another glass of wine and ran his finger along the neck of the bottle to catch a drop. He sucked it off.

She stopped dicing. "Yeah, what?"

"I mean, why did he approach you? Especially about the cold case. I could see if he had something pertinent to add to the search for Noah Fielding."

"Not sure. What are you thinking?" She used the knife to slide the veggies into the two bowls of lettuce.

"Just seems odd. Law enforcement looked into Porter when Jeremy went missing." Tate rubbed his chin. That's another thing that had come back to him out of the blue, and he couldn't remember seeing that in the files last night.

"Really?" The knife and cutting board clattered in the sink where Blanca dropped them. "Why? He hardly looks old enough."

"He was about twenty at the time. Very big youth volunteer."

Blanca narrowed her eyes. "He was? Like scouts and stuff like that?"

"Uh-huh. He knew us boys. He knew a lot of boys, still does."

"Is he married with kids of his own now?"

"He's married with one daughter, but he wasn't at the time. He played football in high school and started helping the coaches out. It began with that." The timer for the oven beeped, and he grabbed an oven mitt. "I don't know. Just forget it."

"Why would I forget that?"

He opened the oven door and a blast of heat hit his face. "I don't like the idea of accusing someone with no proof. A good friend of mine served time for a crime he didn't commit, just because of appearances."

"That's terrible, but sometimes where there's smoke, there's fire." She set the bowls on the kitchen table where he'd put out a couple of place mats and silverware. "I can take a look at him, and he won't even know it."

"Be subtle." As he placed the pan on top of the stove and cut into the layers of meat, cheese and pasta, he felt eyes boring into his back. Without even turning around, he asked, "What?"

"I didn't see anything about Porter Monroe in the files—not last night, not today when I went through them more thoroughly."

He turned toward her, the two plates loaded with food in his hands. "I didn't, either."

"You remembered, didn't you? All this poking around is jostling those memories in your brain."

"Probably." He brushed past her on his way to the table. "But like I told you before, I know I didn't see Jeremy's abductor. If I had and could ID him, he would never have left me alive. There was no way at the time when he captured me and tied me up that he would've known I'd suffer from memory loss. He knew then I wouldn't be able to pick him out."

"He must've been wearing a mask. It was winter, chilly outside. He wouldn't have looked odd to anyone for wearing a balaclava or beanie and scarf in that weather, right?" She pulled out a chair and sat at the table, pinching the stem of her wineglass between her fingers.

He clinked his glass with hers. "Or I didn't get a look at

him at all. He could've knocked me out from a distance or snuck up behind me. I was unconscious when he dragged me to the tree and tied me to it. He then slipped away."

"Where was Jeremy all this time when he was dealing with you?"

"Incapacitated, maybe...dead." Tate pinched the bridge of his nose and then took a long draw from his glass. The wine's warm trickle down his throat didn't do anything for his sudden headache, but he felt the ease in his muscles.

"I don't think he killed Jeremy there, Tate. There was no murder scene, no body. And if he was going to kill Jeremy, he would've killed you, too." She swirled her wine in the glass. "No, he took him. Just like he took Andrew Finnigan and now Noah Fielding."

"You're making some leaps here." He cut into his lasagna, the cheese that oozed from the side making his stomach feel queasy. Or was it the thought that someone had imprisoned these boys before killing them that had turned his stomach? "Why didn't the sheriff's department investigate the marks on Andrew's wrists?"

"I have no clue, but you can bet I'm going to track down Dr. Scott Summers, the medical examiner, to find out." She chewed and patted her lips with a napkin. "This lasagna is so good. Give my compliments to Astrid."

"I will." He ran the tines of his fork through the tomato sauce on his plate. "Is this cold case a plum job for you or busywork to get you out of the way?"

She stopped midchew and clenched her fork as if ready to kill her dinner. "You get right to the point, huh?"

"It just feels as if there's an imbalance here—you know so much about me, and I know nothing about you."

"There's supposed to be an imbalance, Tate. I'm the investigator, and you're the witness." She dropped her fork and grabbed her wineglass, draining it.

Pointing his fork at the glass, he asked, "Do you want another?"

"Our positions are reversed tonight." She pinged her empty glass with her fingernail. "I'd love another glass, but I have to drive back to my hotel on dark, unfamiliar roads. The last thing I need here on Dead Falls is a DUI."

"Same solution as last night. You can stay the night here—in the guest room if you choose to...indulge."

Blanca's eyes burned with a dark intensity that made him feel drunker than if he'd downed the rest of the bottle himself. Was he really suggesting that she spend the night? He needed to be careful here. If he got involved with Blanca, he didn't think he'd be able to extricate himself as easily as he'd done from other relationships.

She lodged the tip of her tongue in the corner of her mouth, and Tate's heart pounded with expectation and excitement.

When her cell phone rang, he blinked. He almost told her to forget it, but she glanced at the display and held up her finger.

"It's my contact at the FBI lab." She wiped her hands and tapped the phone once to answer and then again, as she showed him she was putting the caller on Speaker.

"Hi, Gwen. Do you have the results on the bones?"

"I do, Blanca."

Tate tensed his muscles, his mouth suddenly dry.

"I'm afraid it's not good news...or maybe it is." Gwen coughed. "The bones we found are not a match for Jeremy Ruesler."

The roaring in Tate's ears subsided, and he gripped the edge of the table.

Blanca widened her eyes at him. "I can't believe it. Birdie Ruesler's DNA isn't a match for the bones?"

"Nope, but there's more."

Tate shifted his aching jaw from side to side.

"The bones do belong to a young male—not a child but not an adult."

"Older than Jeremy?" Blanca put her wineglass to her lips, obviously forgetting she'd finished it.

"A little older. This boy was about fifteen years old and, based on certain characteristics of the skull, Native American. Further, we can date the bones from about 2012 to 2018."

Blanca blew out a breath. "Okay, thanks, Gwen. You'll send me the full report?"

Tate had stopped listening to Blanca's conversation, as the roaring had returned to his ears.

Blanca ended the call and cocked her head. "Are you okay?"

Tate muttered through dry lips, "It's Gabe Whitecotton."

Chapter Eleven

Blanca's disappointment surged into confusion and renewed excitement as her heart pounded so hard it made the buttons on her sweater quiver. "Who is Gabe Whitecotton? I haven't heard that name before."

Tate tossed off the rest of his wine and jumped from his chair to take a turn around the kitchen, clasping the back of his neck in a gesture becoming familiar to her. "That's because he was listed as a runaway. He's from the Samish nation. Lived on the reservation across the river."

Folding her arms, she dug her fingernails into her biceps. "Why were the authorities so sure he was a runaway? Because of the age?"

"It had nothing to do with his age, Blanca. He disappeared when he was thirteen around 2017."

"But Gwen just told me the bones belong to a fifteen-year-old." She stopped and placed her hands over her mouth.

"Exactly." Tate punched a fist into his palm. "Where was he for those two years?"

"Maybe—" she planted her hands on either side of her plate, fingers spread "—Gwen's estimate is off. Maybe the bones are from a twelve-year-old."

"She sounded confident to me. I'm pretty sure there are measurements and other tests they perform to pinpoint the age." He grabbed the wine bottle by the neck. "Why are you trying to talk yourself out of your own theory? This would match with the marks on Andrew's wrists. It would explain why Jeremy's body has never been found—to this day."

With an unsteady hand, she held out her glass for a pour. "Jeremy in 2003, Andrew in 2010, Gabe you think in 2017, and now Noah. Are there more? Does every missing boy from the Discovery Bay islands in the past twenty, thirty years have to be reinvestigated?"

Tate shook his head as he added a steady stream of red liquid to her glass. So much for staying sober.

"Why were the authorities so quick to call Gabe a runaway?"

Rubbing his eyes, Tate slumped back in his chair. "He'd done it before. I had just finished my training around that time and had moved back to the island, so I remember the case."

She studied his face, his jaw a straight, hard line despite his relaxed position in the chair. She'd bet that he remembered that case…and every other case of boys gone missing. He'd pulled Gabe's name and date missing right out of his brain as soon as Gwen had provided the details.

"Gabe had a troubled home life, had skipped out a few times…and he lived on the reservation." Tate rolled his shoulders. "Hate to say it, but Sheriff Maddox was more likely to gloss over a case when it involved the Samish."

"Sounds to me like he glossed over a lot of cases."

Tate hung his head and covered his face with his hands. "I was dreading the news but needed the closure. I can't imagine how Birdie's going to feel when she finds out the bones don't match Jeremy's."

"I'll tell her myself. No point in putting yourself through that again." Blanca pushed back from her chair and crossed to Tate's side of the table. She squeezed his shoulder. "I'm sorry. I really thought you had found Jeremy."

He glanced up, dropping his hands to his lap. "What now? Are you going to be pulled from the case? The FBI sent you out here to investigate the cold case of Jeremy Ruesler's disappearance and the discovery of his bones. Those aren't Jeremy's bones. Now what?"

"I'll present the rest of this information to my boss. It really looks like we have a serial killer here. And there's Noah Fielding." She took a gulp of wine. She couldn't leave now, even if she wanted to—and she really didn't want to.

Tate scratched his chin. "Whatever we *believe*, there's no clear evidence that any of these boys are linked. Noah could've gotten lost on a walk. That blood on his hat could've been from anything."

"I think once I tell my boss about all the cases, he'll see it my way."

"It's important to you, isn't it?" Tate crossed his arms and tipped back in his chair. "Why does this case mean so much to you?"

Besides giving her more time to explore all the sides of Tate Mitchell? She cleared her throat and took another swig of wine. "I need a win here. I have to prove myself to the agency, to my boss."

"I figured that, Blanca, but why? Did you accidentally shoot someone? Seriously get on the wrong side of someone important?"

"Worse. I slept with someone." She downed the rest of her wine and grabbed the bottle. Might as well go all in.

Tate's head jerked up, and a slow smile spread across his face. "If that were all, a lot of us would be in a lot of trouble."

Her lips twitched. "It wasn't some random person. He was my mentor at the agency, Manny Rodriguez."

"Ah, so he sexually harassed you in the workplace, and *you're* the one in trouble." He clicked his tongue. "Sounds about right."

"Ugh." She ran her fingers through her hair. "It's more complicated than that. He was married and didn't tell me. He also tried to control my career. Everyone knew I was Manny's protégée. When he found out we were about to be discovered, he went to the brass first and confessed, but he put his own twist on it. He said I offered him sex in exchange for promoting my career, even though I knew he was married."

"Jerk." He clasped his hands together. "End of the day, he was having an extramarital relationship with someone he was supervising."

"Yeah, well, he got reprimanded, but my reputation took the hit. In some circles, the situation only served to embellish his." She sighed, propped her elbow on the table and sunk her chin into her hand. "I blame myself. He had me starry-eyed, and I did have definite perks being in his orbit. But that's *not* why I slept with him."

"Why did you? Because he was such a great guy?" Tate snorted, but she could tell he'd aimed his derision at Manny, not her.

"It's hard to explain. Manny was—*is* a superstar in the agency. When he took an interest in me—purely professional at first—I was flattered. I don't know how I fell into his trap. He's a smooth talker."

"I know the type." He wiggled his eyebrows at her. "You don't have to explain. My sister fell for the same kind of guy, and that ended badly."

"Anyway—" she ran a finger along the rim of her glass "—me out here is kind of my exile and my redemptive moment at the same time. I have to prove that my meteoric rise in the agency was not the result of Manny's favoritism."

"And you do that by solving Jeremy's case."

"All of them, Tate. I'm going to solve every damned one of them. Someone is taking boys here on Dead Falls, and I'm going to catch him."

"You're not going to do it tonight. You're not even getting back on the road tonight." He pinged the almost empty bottle of wine with his fingernail. "You've almost polished off that whole bottle yourself."

She sucked in her bottom lip, which had all the fruity hints of the wine. After what she'd just told him, would he think she'd done this on purpose? "I—I can leave my car here and call for a cab."

"Out here? You'd be lucky to find one in the radius in the next hour." He pointed to the ceiling. "You've already been in the spare room. It's all set up."

She stretched her arms over her head. Could she manage to spend the night in the room next to this man again without making a move? Maybe if she stuck to business.

She cleared her throat. "Is there any way we can prove those bones belong to Gabe? Does he still have family here?"

"His parents are gone, but he still has relatives living. You shouldn't have any problem getting DNA samples from them." He rose from the table and picked up their plates. "I can go with you, and nobody is going to run me off their property this time."

"Mrs. Ruesler doesn't really blame you. You were a child then. There's nothing you could've done."

"I know that, but I always did wonder, and she probably does too, why the guy grabbed Jeremy and not me."

"Like we said before—convenience. He probably spotted Jeremy first. He didn't want both of you, so he left you there unable to identify him." She scooped up the salad bowls and followed him to the sink. "Let me rinse the dishes and put them in the dishwasher. You can take care of the rest."

While she scraped the remains of their meal down the garbage disposal and loaded the dishwasher, Tate wrapped up the rest of the lasagna and put it in the fridge.

He bumped her hip as he put the pan under the water and added some soap. "I do actually have an extra toothbrush you can use, courtesy of my dentist."

"I'm set. Don't worry about me. I'll crash in the spare room. With all that food and adrenaline, though, I barely feel buzzed."

"Don't even think about driving back to your hotel."

"Oh, don't worry."

"When are you going to give Mrs. Ruesler the news?" Tate finished wiping the lasagna pan and flicked the dish towel over his shoulder.

"Tomorrow, first thing, before she hears from another source." She held up her hand to tick off her fingers. "Then I'm going to contact Dr. Summers and head to the Samish reservation to track down Gabe Whitecotton's relatives. I'll be too busy to think about getting pulled from this case— these cases."

"I'll skip your meeting with Birdie, but I can help with the Whitecottons. I know who some of Gabe's relatives are, and my friend Jed can give me an intro. He's currently on the mainland, going through the Forest Service academy, but he's half-Samish. His mom is from the reservation, and he can grease the wheels for you."

"Perfect. Thanks for helping." She put her hand to her throbbing head, as she recalled throwing out all her personal details. "As for that other stuff I told you…"

He put a soapy finger against her lips. "Don't worry about it. I believe your side of the story."

Against her will and better judgment, she puckered her lips against his finger. Then she shook her head. "Thank you. I'm not proud of it."

"You don't have to be ashamed of it, either." He whipped the towel from his shoulder and dried his hands. "Do I need to show you the guest room?"

"I think I can find it on my own."

"I'll put a new toothbrush and some toothpaste in the bathroom. Will you need anything else? The sheets on the bed are clean." He held up two fingers Boy Scout-style. "I promise."

"At this point, I'd sleep in my car. I can handle some used sheets." Especially if Tate were the one who'd used them. She could inhale his fresh scent all night like a drug.

Stepping back from his intoxicating presence, she said, "All right, then. I'll see you in the morning. I'm sorry those bones didn't belong to your friend—and I'm sorry they belonged to another boy."

"Me, too."

She escaped upstairs, practically taking the steps two at a time. She ducked into the extra bedroom and kicked off her shoes. Sitting on the edge of the bed, she dug into her purse and found a ponytail holder. She scooped back her hair from her face and took shallow breaths as she listened to Tate come upstairs and open some cupboards. She didn't want to take a chance of running into him in the bathroom.

Finally, she heard the water running, so she crept to the bathroom across the hall. She unwrapped the toothbrush Tate had left for her and brushed her teeth. She washed her face with the liquid hand soap and used a tissue to wipe off the smudge of makeup beneath her eyes.

Blanca tiptoed back to the bedroom and peeled off her clothes. She slid between the sheets and curled on her side, burying her face in the pillow. The clean scent of laundry detergent engulfed her. Tate hadn't been kidding—not that she expected to smell him on these sheets. He was probably fast asleep in the room down the hall.

She rolled onto her back and stared at the ceiling. She'd been nervous about telling him about her past with Manny and the FBI, but he hadn't judged her. She'd been afraid to get too close to him, not wanting to reveal her past to him. But now? Did she have an excuse now? Was she going to allow one mistake to dictate future relationships? That would be giving Manny too much control, and she'd had enough of his dominance in her life.

She flipped back the covers and planted her bare feet on the cold floor. Hugging her naked body, she padded down the hallway to Tate's closed bedroom door. She rested her forehead against the wood, her breath shallow in her chest. She placed her hand on the doorknob and turned.

What the hell was she doing? She stepped back and released the doorknob. Hadn't she learned her lesson about mixing business and pleasure?

She needed to put Tate Mitchell, the traumatized survivor, ahead of Tate Mitchell, the man she wanted to bed. Or she'd end up with another black mark against her…and her heart broken again.

TATE WOKE UP with a dry mouth, an uncomfortable reminder for why he never drank wine. He hoisted himself up on his elbows and eyed his bedroom door. Had he been dreaming last night when he saw the handle turn?

He'd willed Blanca to enter his room, but his mind games must be on the fritz. Just as he'd been ready to turn back the covers in invitation, she'd fled down the hallway. Probably for the best. She'd had a lot to drink last night, and he liked his women stone-cold sober.

He rolled out of bed and poked his head outside his door. Light from the guest room streamed into the hallway. He cocked his head, on the alert for sounds from downstairs. He thought he'd be up before Blanca, even though it seemed she'd had a hard time getting to sleep, too.

He pulled on a pair of sweats and veered into the spare room. He ran a hand along the fully made-up bed where Blanca's perfume lingered. He then crossed the hall to the bathroom. Droplets of water sparkled in the sink basin, and the toothbrush he'd left for her hung over the edge.

He jogged downstairs, calling her name. A pink sticky note on the front door caught his attention. She'd ditched him.

He ripped the note from the door and read aloud. "Thanks for the dinner. Wanted to get an early start today. Keep you posted."

With the note stuck to the tip of his finger, he tapped his chin. Blanca had taken a giant leap from almost hitting him up for a booty call last night to hightailing it out of here this morning. Had she heard him snoring?

On his way to the kitchen, he texted her to make sure she'd gotten back to the hotel okay and nobody had broken into her room again.

He stared at his phone's display for a minute and then tossed it on the counter. While he made some eggs and bacon, he kept an eye on his phone. Blanca must've gone straight to work.

Straddling a stool at the counter with his breakfast in front of him, Tate grabbed his phone and left a text for his friend, Jed Swain. In the Forest Service academy, Jed wouldn't have access to his phone until lunch, but Tate laid out why he needed to contact Gabe Whitecotton's people.

He could at least help Blanca with that, even if he couldn't hand her Jeremy's kidnapper.

When Tate got out of the shower, he checked his phone and saw a text from Jed. He'd sent it between classes, but he'd managed to contact Isaiah Whitecotton, Gabe's cousin, and he was okay with meeting with him and Blanca this afternoon.

Blanca still hadn't responded to him, so he called her—harder to ignore that.

She picked up on the third ring, her voice breathy. "Hi, Tate. I was going to text you back from the station. I just came from Mrs. Ruesler's house."

His heart lurched painfully in his chest. "How'd she take it?"

"I guess how you'd think she would. Relieved but tortured at the same time. That's how I'd characterize it." Blanca sniffled. "I obviously did get home okay, and I apologize for sneaking out of there this morning."

Had she snuck out? She must have, as he didn't hear her leave. "No worries. You have a lot on your plate today, and I'm adding more. Made contact with my friend Jed, and he set things up with Gabe's cousin for this afternoon. Does that still work for you?"

"That's great. Thank you." He heard a car door slam and the rev of an engine. "I'm heading for the station right now. Sheriff Hopkins is going to officially reopen Gabe White-cotton's case. The bones show no cause of death yet, so who knows? Hopkins might try to frame this as another accident, but there's no denying Gabe disappeared as a thirteen-year-old and his fifteen-year-old bones resurfaced."

"The FBI is going to have to send more agents out here, Blanca. Our sheriff's department can't handle this."

"I'm aware of that. Text me a time and location for Gabe's cousin. I also contacted Dr. Summers and left him a message, reminding him we'd met on the search. So I'll need to set something up with him, as well."

"I'll let you know when Isaiah wants to meet."

They ended the call on an awkward note. At least Tate felt the awkwardness. Should he have told her he would've welcomed her into his room and his bed if she'd had the courage to open that door?

He whipped off the towel around his waist and tossed it into the corner. Now, *that* would've been awkward.

LATER THAT AFTERNOON after going through a few reports for work, confirming a meeting time with Isaiah Whitecotton and communicating that time to Blanca, Tate grabbed a jacket from the closet and headed out to his Jeep. He wanted to make a stop before meeting with Blanca and Isaiah.

He drove across the bridge at the falls and made a left turn. Blanca had made a comment the night of the search for Noah Fielding that Tate seemed to make a beeline for that area. He had because it was the same area where he and Jeremy had played, an area not far from the Samish reservation where Gabe had been living at the time of his disappearance.

He parked at the side of the road where small, indistinct trails led into the forest. Taking these trails wouldn't necessarily get you lost. If you knew to follow the river, you could always make it back to the bridge. The same types of trails fanned out from the campsite where the Fieldings had pitched their tent—and lost their son.

Twigs snapped and leaves crackled beneath his hiking

boots as he tromped into the woods. Even with winter approaching, the trees closed around him quickly, blocking the weak sunlight. He pumped his legs, one foot after the other, before he could think too clearly about what he intended to do.

He pushed through the underbrush, the bare branches scratching his hands and slapping against his thighs. When he reached the small clearing, he blinked. His gaze locked onto the tree.

With one hand in front of him, he walked toward it as if in a trance. He'd never been back to the tree where his attacker had left him. Closing his eyes, he ran his hand along the bark. What had happened that day?

He and Jeremy were riding their bikes. They'd gotten separated because he'd charged ahead without his friend, but he'd done that many times before. Jeremy was resilient. He never got lost in the woods.

They'd heard the whistling before but had laughed it off. Someone whistling some baby song in the forest didn't scare them.

It should have.

He remembered heading down an incline and then flying through the air as his bike hit something. Is that how he'd gotten the lump on his skull? The doctors didn't seem to think so. The next thing he remembered was someone calling his name and flashlights shining all around him. Jeremy was gone.

He crouched down and scrabbled through the dirt and leaves with his fingers, searching for clues that he'd missed almost twenty years ago. He leaned forward and rested his head against the rough bark of the trunk. It wasn't his fault. He'd been a kid.

The whistling came to him again. This time he knew

the tune. The words rasped in his throat. "Put your right foot in…"

His head jerked up, and he choked. He heard the whistle pierce through the trees…and it wasn't his imagination this time. Before he had time to think, his body reacted, fueled by adrenaline and fury.

"Come out, come out, wherever you are. I'm not a kid anymore."

Chapter Twelve

Blanca spied Tate's Jeep on the side of the road, and she hunched over the steering wheel to get a better look. Had his car broken down? Maybe he'd decided to wait for her, so they could enter the reservation together.

She pulled up behind him but couldn't see anyone in the car. She exited the sedan and called his name, cupping her hand around her mouth.

She took a tentative step to the edge of a trail. Even during the day, the forest presented a dark and menacing force. Shaking her head, she barreled ahead on the trail. She was dressed for it today. "Tate?"

A man's shouting seemed to bounce off the trees, coming from everywhere, all at once. She pressed a hand to her galloping heart. "Tate? Is that you?"

More yelling met her question, so she plunged into the forest toward the initial sound. She dropped her gaze to the ground and could tell someone had recently taken this path. Tate had taught her to recognize the signs of flattened grasses and broken twigs on their first search through these woods.

When she got to a small clearing, she caught sight of a blur of blue amid the brown leaves and evergreen needles.

Tate had worn that blue jacket before. Why was he running around the woods shouting?

"Tate! It's Blanca. Where are you?"

A figure came crashing through the underbrush, stumbling into the clearing. Tate's wild eyes darted back and forth, the detritus from the forest clinging to his jacket and sticking out of his hair.

"Tate? What's wrong? Are you all right?" He looked like a madman with his head on a swivel.

"Did you hear it? Did you hear him?"

"Hear what? I didn't hear anything or anybody, except you yelling. That was you yelling, wasn't it?" She licked her lips.

Tate dug both hands into his hair, dislodging some of the leaves and dirt. "He was here. I heard him. I wasn't dreaming it this time."

She swallowed. "Dreaming what, Tate?"

"The whistling. I heard the whistling. The same song." He threw his arms out to his sides in a frantic gesture.

Blanca stared past him at the lone tree in the center of the clearing. She put her hand over her mouth. This was it. This was the tree where Tate had been tied up.

She'd meant to come here. It had always been on her task list, but after meeting Tate, she never believed he'd agree to join her.

"A-are you sure?" She glanced over her shoulder, almost expecting to see the whistling man behind her.

"You don't believe me?" His shoulders sagged, and he leaned against that very tree that had changed his life. "I'm sure, Blanca."

"I believe you, but why? Why would he come back to this spot with you here? Why would he want to remind you of what happened?" Did she believe him? It made no sense.

He flapped his arms, as if he intended to take flight. "What does it matter if I remember? I didn't see him. I can't ID him. That's clear, or he would've taken care of me years ago. He couldn't risk my memory returning and my pointing him out on the street. He's not worried about that."

"You think he'd be worried about you catching him whistling alone in the forest? If he is the one who stole the case files from my hotel room, he knows you heard whistling." She pulled at a piece of skin on the side of her thumb, the sting making her regret it immediately.

Tate bent forward and grabbed his knees so suddenly, she thought he was having a medical emergency. She took a step toward him, but he began talking.

"Maybe he didn't even know I was here. Maybe he's out trolling for another victim." He lifted his head as he continued to expel his breath in short spurts. "That's his precursor. His warning. The whistling."

Tate's words triggered something in her brain, and she gave voice to the thoughts that had floated through her head last night after she'd given up on the idea of seducing Tate.

"He wouldn't take another boy. It's too soon." Pulling up the collar of her jacket to cover her cold neck, she crouched on the ground. She picked up a stick and started stirring the leaves and dirt into a pattern. "Think about the incidents, Tate. Jeremy went missing in 2003, Andrew Finnigan in 2010. If you remembered correctly, Gabe disappeared in 2017, and now Noah Fielding. Notice anything about those years?"

Tate had finally caught his breath. Spreading his legs in a wide stance, he crossed his arms. "Those incidents are all seven years apart."

She nodded, glad he'd picked up her train of thought so quickly. "Seven years between each abduction. Why? What happens every seven years? Is there some event on the island or the bay that occurs every seven years?"

"Not that I can think of." His hands bunched the material of his jacket. "But seven is a notable number, isn't it? There's symbolism to the number seven in the Bible and in other religions, mythology, superstition. It could be anything."

"You're right, and it's his pattern." She tossed aside the stick and dusted her fingers together as she rose to her feet. "Now I'm beginning to wonder what happened in 1996, prior to Jeremy's abduction. Will we find another missing boy?"

"If this has been going on for the past twenty-eight years, we're not looking at a young man."

"Unless we're looking for more than one perpetrator. Maybe it's some kind of satanic cult. I'm sure they'd be interested in the number seven." She clenched her teeth to stop them from chattering. "It's cold, and we have a meeting with Isaiah Whitecotton."

"Right." Tate turned his head to glance over his shoulder at the tree before striding toward her. "Let's get out of here."

When they got back to their vehicles, Tate pointed up the road. "You can follow me, but if I see another car on this road, all bets are off. I'm stopping anyone in the vicinity."

"Got it." Blanca slipped into her car and gripped the steering wheel as she waited for Tate to lead the way. That encounter in the woods, whatever it was, still had him tightly wound. If he'd heard the Whistler for the first time in twenty years, that just might be it. Had he, though?

His Jeep pulled onto the road in front of her, and she pulled in behind him. They'd already passed the sign announcing they were on Samish land, but the reservation lay a few miles ahead. She had her DNA kit and hoped Gabe's cousin would agree to a buccal swab.

When she'd announced at the station today that the remains Tate had stumbled across during the forest fire cleanup belonged to Gabe Whitecotton, missing since 2017, she'd raised more than a few eyebrows and had elicited a venomous look from the usually friendly Sheriff Hopkins. If the bones did belong to Gabe, that news would put another nail in the coffin for Hopkins, even though he had agreed to reopen the case.

Tate made a turn off the main road, and Blanca followed him, passing the wooden sign between two columns of rock welcoming her to the Samish Nation reservation. Small, wooden houses scattered the landscape with mobile homes set farther back from the road. Tate drove past the meeting house in a log cabin, smoke twirling from the two chimneys. A red cross marked the medical clinic in a low-slung building, and Tate crawled past the nation's police station and jail.

After winding toward the edge of the reservation by the tree line, Tate pulled beside a children's playground. A man about their age, a long ponytail hanging down his back, pushed a boy and girl on the swings. When Blanca got out of the car, the kids' squeals made her smile.

Tate waited for her, and they approached the man, Tate's hand raised in greeting. "Hey, Isaiah. It's Tate Mitchell. This is Blanca Lopez with the FBI."

Isaiah ducked around the pumping legs of the children and stuck out his hand. "Good to meet you both. Jed instructed me to play nice, but it's better for me to meet with the FBI out here than in my house with my family around."

Blanca inclined her head. "I get it. Thanks for agreeing to see me."

"If what Tate said on the phone is true, that those bones he found are Gabe's, then there's nothing I'd rather do than to settle this." He stepped back behind the swings and gave each child another push. "Gabe was my little coz, you know? He looked up to me, and I never could figure out why he'd just take off like that without telling me."

Blanca asked, "You didn't think he ran away when he disappeared?"

"I don't know." Isaiah shrugged and tossed his ponytail over his shoulder. "Not like he hadn't done it before. Hell, not like I hadn't done it before. Plenty of young bucks on the rez itching to leave it. You know what I mean? But to leave without saying goodbye…"

He gave the kids another shove, and the girl's little feet reached for the sky.

Had Gabe played on this swing set? It looked old enough. She cleared her throat. "Did your family look for Gabe when he left?"

"All over Discovery Bay. I even went to Seattle."

"Did Gabe have a cell phone?"

"He had a phone. He'd turned it off, and nobody was ever able to trace it." Isaiah had stepped to the side, lost in thought while the arc of the little girl's swing dwindled, and her mouth formed a pout.

"Let me." She stepped behind the swing, pulled back on the rusty chains and let it go with a push. "I'm sorry, Isaiah."

Shoving his hands in his pockets, he asked, "What makes you think those bones are Isaiah's? Aren't you here for a DNA sample?"

"That was me." Tate raised his hand. "When Blanca told me the range of the disappearance and age of the bones, I put it together. Had to be Gabe."

"And you'd know, brother." Isaiah pinched his bottom lip with his calloused fingers. "What is going on? Now this tourist missing from the campsite. You think it's one person, or a series of coincidences?"

"That's what I'm here to figure out." Blanca patted her bag. "Can I get that sample now? It's just a swab inside your mouth. If you think the kids might be scared or bothered by it, Tate can take them to the slide."

"Yeah, yeah. Good idea."

Isaiah grabbed the chains of the boy's swing while Blanca stopped the girl. "Do you want to follow Tate to the slide? Your dad—" she glanced at Isaiah, who nodded "—is going to be right here."

The little boy charged ahead while the girl grabbed Tate's hand and followed.

Blanca covered her smile with one hand.

"He's pretty good with kids." Isaiah jerked his head toward Tate, climbing the steps of the slide.

"His nephew has been living with him recently."

"Right. His sister Astrid's kid."

Blanca clicked her tongue as she unwrapped the buccal swab kit. "These small towns."

By the time she finished with Isaiah and secured his sample in her bag, the kids had abandoned Tate at the slide and were barreling toward their father with demands for hot chocolate.

"Thanks again, Isaiah. I'll keep you posted." She wiggled her fingers at the children. "Bye, kids."

Tate took the bag from her. "I'll carry this for you. When do you think we'll have the results?"

"I'm going to send it to Gwen today. She'll put a rush on it for me. This is getting tangled." She popped her trunk with the key fob, and Tate loaded the bag inside.

"When are you going to lay it all out for your boss?"

"I'm on it." She hugged her purse to her chest. "I'm going to write up something for him tonight and send it off tomorrow, but I'll call first."

"Do you think he'll take you off the case? Add more agents?" Tate scuffed the toe of his hiking boot into the dirt.

"I don't know." She twisted her fingers in front of her. But she had a good idea.

"I mean, you're the one who uncovered links between all these cases. That has to count for something."

"You'd think so." She filled her cheeks with air and puffed it out. "Can I follow you out of here? Not sure I can get back to the bridge in the dark."

Tate tipped his head back, taking in the clouds that were speeding up the darkness of sunset. "At least it's not raining—yet."

Blanca climbed into her car and waited for Tate to make a U-turn back to the entrance of the Samish land. She knew in her gut the same person or group of people were responsible for the kidnapping and perhaps incarceration of these boys. She wanted to see this to the finish line.

As Tate took the curve in the road that would put them on a straight line toward the bridge, Blanca followed his taillights. A light sprinkling of water glistened like diamonds on her windshield, but she didn't know if the rain had come, or they'd entered the area called Misty Hollow by the falls. It seemed too early for Misty Hollow and the bridge.

The red lights in front of her had a hypnotizing effect until they swerved to the side. She slammed on her brakes, and her back wheels fishtailed on the wet road. What the hell was Tate doing?

She cranked up her wipers and squinted through the windshield. Tate had not only stopped his Jeep, but he'd also jumped out of it and had crossed the road into the forest. Had he been hearing whistling again?

She rolled up behind him, her head turned to the side, trying to pick him out across the road. Her palms got damp and her throat dry. She didn't see Tate, but she saw a light, like a flashlight bobbing in the darkness. Was it Tate's? Or did it belong to someone else?

She threw her car into Park and scrambled out the door, catching herself before falling to the road. For the second time that day, she rushed into the forest to find Tate. This time she heard the voices clearly—two men—and she followed the sound through the trees.

A light appeared ahead, and she ran toward it. Her eyes adjusted in time to see Tate take a flying leap at another man and tackle him to the ground.

Chapter Thirteen

Adrenaline pumped through Tate's system as he straddled the man beneath him, his fist drawn back. "What did you do with them? Where's Noah? Answer me."

The man sputtered, his mouth gaping open like a fish on a hook. "Wh-what are you doing? Tate? Tate Mitchell, is that you?"

Tate blinked. The flashlight that had been in the man's hand and now lay on the ground illuminated the area above his head, highlighting curly strands of red hair escaping from a black cap.

Tate ground his teeth together as he drove his knee harder in Porter Monroe's thigh. No wonder he'd been interested enough in the case to show up on the search and approach Blanca. Tate growled. "What did you do with him?"

"With who?" Porter coughed. "Are you talking about the missing kid? I don't know anything about that."

Tate's heartbeat had slowed down to a steady thump in his chest, and then he heard Blanca's voice.

"Tate, what are you doing? Who is that?"

"Porter Monroe. You were right."

Porter gasped. "Right about what? What is this? Let me up so we can discuss this like civilized adults. I don't have any weapons."

"I do." Tate patted down Porter's pockets and waistband. He rolled off him and reached for his gun. He held it on the crumpled form on the ground.

"Can I stand up?" Porter raised his hands. "Don't shoot me. I don't have anything. I haven't done anything."

"You were whistling." Tate ground out the words between his teeth.

"Whoa." Porter staggered to his feet, shooting a glance at Blanca. "Is whistling a crime now?"

Blanca moved to Tate's side, her breath creating puffs of steam in the cold air. "What were you whistling, Porter?"

Porter had gotten to his feet and now jerked his head between Tate and Blanca. "What? What was I whistling? Nothing. I was whistling for my dog, who I'm sure is now even farther in the woods than when I started looking for him."

Tate swallowed. His anxiety receded, making him feel light-headed. "Your dog?"

"What are you and your dog doing out here?" Blanca crossed her arms, bumping her shoulder against Tate's bicep. She had his back.

Pointing at a backpack on the ground, Porter said, "I came back to look for that. It's Zach Snider's backpack. He left it here after a hike. You can ask his parents. They called me to tell me he'd lost his pack, and I told them I'd go back to find it. I brought my dog, Frosty, and he ran off—probably after some critter. I thought he was coming back, too, until you tackled me, Tate. What the hell is going on?"

"Why were you hiking out here with kids?" Tate let his weapon hang at his side, as he took a step to the side and swept up the flashlight from the ground.

Porter narrowed his eyes against the light. "Oh, is that what this is about? A man can't enjoy the company of kids without being a perv? I went through this when Jeremy disappeared, too. Remember that? Of course you do."

"I—we're just trying to figure out what's going on out here." Tate shoved his gun into his pocket. Porter had been whistling for a dog. Had Tate even heard the tune? Had he heard it earlier? Was he losing his mind?

"Look, Porter—" Blanca put her hands out, palms first "—there was some…activity in this area earlier today. You can't blame Tate for suspecting your odd behavior."

"Whistling is odd behavior?" He doffed the cap from his head and used it wipe the sweat from his face. "You can check Zach's backpack, you can call his parents, you can even check on my alibi with Hopkins the day Noah Fielding disappeared—and yeah, he asked me."

"If you don't mind." Blanca walked to the backpack and picked it up. She gestured for Tate to shine the light inside, as she unzipped it.

She examined the typical contents for a kid's backpack. Of course, Porter could've just kidnapped Zach Snider, and then she'd feel foolish. She held out her hand. "Can I see your phone?"

"I should just tell you both to get out of my face, but I'll play along because that's what I always do."

Blanca snapped her fingers. "Enough with the pity party, Monroe. I'm an FBI agent investigating a cold case and current kidnapping. You can't tell me to get out of your face."

He dug his phone from his pocket, unlocked it with his thumbprint and handed it to Blanca.

The blue light of the display illuminated her face as she scrolled through Porter's contacts. She tapped the phone and waited a few seconds.

She said, "This isn't Porter, Mrs. Snider. This is FBI Special Agent Blanca Lopez, and I just have a few questions for you. Was Zach on a hike today with Porter?"

Her gaze darted between Tate and Porter as she said, "Uh-huh...uh-huh. I see... No, everything's fine, and Porter did find the backpack."

She ended the call after a few more pleasantries and held it out to Porter. "Thanks. That clears it right up."

Rolling his eyes, he pocketed his phone. "Is it okay if I keep looking for my dog now?"

"Go right ahead." Blanca waved her hand.

Porter shouted. "Frosty! Frosty!"

He turned to Tate. "I'm gonna whistle now. Is that okay with you, or is that gonna trigger you again?"

"Damn, Porter." Tate wiped a hand across his face. "Go ahead."

Porter let loose with a piercing whistle, which sounded nothing like the "Hokey Pokey" song. Several seconds later a dog barked. Then a white streak materialized, and a snowy white shepherd bounded up to Porter.

Porter pointed to Frosty. "Dog. Can I go now?"

Tate took a deep breath. "Sorry, Porter. It was just—"

"You don't have to explain, Tate. Even though you always try to pretend otherwise, I know you were traumatized by what happened to you. I feel sorry for you, and I feel sorrier for Jeremy."

When Porter stomped off, Frosty trotting at his heels, Tate covered his face with both hands. "God, that was embarrassing."

Blanca rubbed his back. "You don't have to feel embarrassed. Anyone in these woods is suspect at this point, especially if you heard another whistle."

He spread his fingers and peered at her through the spaces. "He was whistling for his dog, Blanca."

"You couldn't know that at the time. Honestly, when I saw that kid's backpack, something pricked the back of my neck." She hunched her shoulders. "The story he told could be true *and* he could be involved in Noah's disappearance. One doesn't necessarily rule out the other."

"You heard him. He has an alibi for the day Noah disappeared."

"So he said."

Tate widened his eyes. "You don't believe him after all that?"

"Let's just say I'm going to check his alibi with Hopkins and look into him a little more closely." She tugged on his jacket. "You're not losing it."

"It sure felt like it."

"Why did you stop your car and get out like that? You didn't hear the whistling from the road."

"I saw his light bobbing in the forest. I had to check it out. Then when I heard the whistle and saw a figure in the dark, all bets were off."

"Just get me out of here. It's giving me the creeps." Her hand slid to his hand, and she laced her fingers with his. "You're *not* losing it, Tate."

He led the way but kept hold of her hand, which seemed to anchor him in more ways than one. "Porter said everyone knew I was traumatized. That guts me."

"He didn't exactly say that." She squeezed his hand. "He said *he* realized you were—probably because he was part of the scene, maybe because he works with young people. Who knows? Maybe that's why he still works with boys—not because he's a perv but because he wants to help."

"But you're still going to check his alibi."

"Better to be safe than sorry." She looked down at the

phone in her hand. "Do you want to get some dinner in town after I drop Isaiah's sample at the station?"

"Sure." He opened her car door for her. "I thought you didn't want to be seen with me."

"I guess it's a little late for that now, especially if the FBI is going to send in more agents. We might not have another chance."

"Then, let's do it. You go to the station, and I'll head to the main drag and grab us a table somewhere and send you the address. Preference?"

She dropped to the seat behind the wheel. "I think it's apparent by now that I'll eat anything."

He felt a little stab in his heart. That married jerk had really done a number on her. He bent forward and placed a kiss on her full lips. "I think it's apparent by now that you're a bold woman who knows what she likes."

As THE CAR door slammed and Tate strode to his Jeep, Blanca put two fingers on her throbbing lips. That was maybe the best first kiss she'd ever had. It hadn't just warmed all her erogenous zones, it had also warmed her heart.

Maybe the event in the woods with Jeremy had traumatized Tate, but it had also taught him kindness and compassion. But he'd probably give up all those fine qualities to be just another guy without that experience in the woods.

She followed Tate over the bridge, and the spray from the falls sprinkled her windshield. A few miles later he stopped at a stop sign and stuck his arm out the window to indicate that she should go right to the station. She waved out her window and took the right, as he turned left to head onto the main drag of the town.

A few miles later on the slick road, she parked in front of the station and pushed through the front door. The desk sergeant was on duty, and the squad cars were in the field, which left the station mostly empty.

She greeted the deputy. "Did I miss anything on the Fielding case while I was out?"

"Nothing. Those poor parents and the little sister. Their vacation is supposed to be over in a few days. How do you go home without your boy?"

"I imagine you don't." She patted her bag. "I did get DNA from Isaiah Whitecotton, though. The more of these cases we can tie together, the more that's going to help the Fieldings."

"I hope you're right about those bones belonging to Gabe. You stirred up a ruckus here with your announcement. If you're wrong, you're going to have some egg on your face."

"I'm not wrong." She bumped the swinging door to the back with her hip. "Tell me something, George. Do you have any satanic cults on the island?"

His pale eyebrows shot up. "You mean like human sacrifice and boiling goats?"

"Human sacrifice?" She ran her hand through her hair. "Doesn't have to be that serious. Maybe just some goth kids or stone circles in the woods. Stuff like that."

"Yeah, there are a few kids like that. Dress all in black. The girls look like they have raccoon eyes."

"Yes, exactly like that. Do you know who the kids are?" She grabbed an overnight bubble pouch to send her sample to the FBI lab.

"Unfortunately, my girlfriend's daughter is one of them." He sat back in his chair and wedged one foot on the desk. "She's not a bad kid, just weird. You don't think they had anything to do with Noah, do you? They weren't even alive for Jeremy's disappearance and were little kids for Gabe's, if that's where you're going with this."

"No, I don't think kids are responsible, but I'd sure like to talk to your girlfriend's daughter about a few things. Just curiosity. She's not in any trouble." She put her hands together. "Please, George. You guys aren't gonna like it when several arrogant FBI agents descend on Dead Falls and start pushing you around."

"I can ask Felicity. That's my girlfriend. If it's okay with her, I'll ask Myra, her daughter. I'm sure Myra would love to tell you all about her Wiccan stuff, or whatever she calls it."

"I really appreciate it, George." She slipped him a piece of paper with her cell phone number. "Give me a call when you get the okay."

Blanca addressed the package to the lab and sent Gwen a message that it would be incoming in the overnight pouch. She waved to George on her way out and checked her phone in the station's small lobby. Tate had sent her a pin to a restaurant called the Bay Grill, and she tapped her display for directions.

Would this be her last dinner with Tate? The clock ticked in her ear. Even if she'd nailed it on all these missing boys being connected, *especially* if she'd been right, the FBI would be sending in a team. She couldn't remain the lone agent on this thing. She only hoped she'd get the credit due for blowing it wide-open.

She had a ten-minute drive ahead of her to decide how she wanted to handle her feelings for Tate—because she definitely had feelings. She peered out the glass door. The sprinkles that had started when she'd followed Tate into the woods had turned into a downpour.

George called to her. "You need to borrow an umbrella? We have extras in the back."

"I'm just running to my car. I'll be okay."

The short jog to her car soaked her hair, causing her curls

to spiral out of control. She cranked up the heater and shook out her hair.

The wipers could barely keep up with the water sluicing across the windshield, but she knew the way from the station to the heart of the town. She sat forward in her seat and squinted at the road in front of her. She kept her eyes on the white divider line, inching close to it to avoid the soft shoulder on her right.

She'd forgotten how curvy this road was, which she could navigate with no problem in the daytime with dry conditions. As she approached the next turn, she took her foot off the accelerator. The sedan sped up anyway down the grade, so she pumped the brakes.

The brakes squished beneath the pedal. They must be wet. She tapped the brake pedal again, and the car didn't respond at all. The next curve came up quicker than she had time to slow down, but she couldn't seem to control her steering wheel, which seemed to have a life of its own.

She knew enough not to stomp on the brake, so she eased her foot against the pedal. She felt for some engagement, a flare of panic leaping in her chest when she felt nothing but air. She pressed her foot to the floor, and the car lurched into the next curve, speeding up.

She tried to jerk the steering wheel to the left and felt her mistake immediately as her back wheels fishtailed and then hydroplaned. The car now out of her control, she could only hang onto the useless steering wheel as the car lifted off the road. As if in slow motion, the sedan landed with a bounce.

The last thing Blanca saw before squeezing her eyes closed to brace for impact was the shore of the bay rushing toward her.

Chapter Fourteen

Tate checked the time on his phone for the fourth time. Blanca should've been here by now. Should take about ten minutes from the station, fifteen for a tourist.

Rivulets of water streamed down the window of the restaurant, and Tate traced one with his fingertip. Okay, maybe twenty minutes given this weather.

He toyed with his phone. Should he call her? He shouldn't distract her when she was driving, especially in a downpour. He called the station instead.

The desk sergeant answered promptly. "Dead Falls Sheriff's Department, Deputy Vickers. Can I help you?"

"This is Tate Mitchell. I'm looking for Agent Lopez. She was supposed to drop off something there and meet me in town. Have you seen her?"

"Tate, this is George Vickers. She was here but left about twenty minutes ago. You try calling her?"

"Hey, George. Didn't want to disturb her driving. Just wanted to make sure she left already."

"She did." George coughed. "She probably made a detour to her hotel, maybe to change clothes. I offered her an umbrella, but she went out to her car without one. She probably got soaked."

"You're probably right. I'll give her a call." Tate ended

the call and drummed his fingers on the table. Blanca was an FBI agent. She wouldn't answer the phone if it weren't safe to do so.

"Did you want to order anything to drink besides water?" The waitress stood at the table, her tablet tucked under her arm.

"Not yet." Tate tapped Blanca's name from his contacts. The phone rang until it went to voice mail. Tate didn't bother leaving a message.

He left a couple of bucks on the table for occupying it for twenty minutes and ducked outside into the rain. He flipped up his hood and jogged to his car, a ball of dread forming in his gut. If he'd known the skies were going to open, he would've driven her to and from. Tourists got into accidents all the time on the island, and the road between here and the station posed problems even for the locals.

He took the drive slowly, his high beams sweeping the road. No other cars followed or came toward him. Just behind the station, the road meandered down to a boat dock, but nobody would be taking a boat out tonight.

As he fanned out on one curve, he noticed a glow of light coming from the bottom of the incline near the dock. Maybe someone did have a boat out tonight. He rolled into the next turnout and exited his car. He dashed across the road and peered over the shoulder where the grass had been flattened and deep gouges cut into the mud.

It took a few seconds for his eyes to adjust to the dark to figure out that the light emanated from a car turned sideways, wrapped around a tree but upright. It took him a few more seconds to realize the car belonged to Blanca.

He scrambled down the incline, using his hands to keep him from tumbling. Before he reached the car, he almost tripped over a body, stretched out in his path.

"Blanca!" He crouched beside her and felt for a pulse. It beat strong and sure beneath his fingers, and he released a heavy breath.

He ran his hands along the back of her head and felt a lump next to the smaller one she'd sustained the other night at the hotel. Otherwise, it appeared as if she'd decided to take a nap in the rain on the side of an incline.

"Blanca." He jostled her and dragged the top of her body into his lap to elevate her head. "Wake up."

A boom of thunder reverberated in his chest, and a flash of lightning opened the sky. An onslaught of rain inundated them, striking Blanca's face with large drops. That's all it took.

She groaned and blinked. As her lips moved, her eyelashes fluttered.

"That's right. Come out of it. You're okay." It felt like déjà vu, coaxing her from an unconscious state. But it could've been worse.

Now that he was closer to the car, he could see its smashed front end. Had she been thrown from the car, or had she jumped? Or maybe someone had pulled her from the wreckage before he got here.

He glanced over his shoulder as he pulled the phone from his pocket and called 911. Something told him this was no accident. He made his request for help and hung up.

"Tate?"

He brushed her wet hair back from her forehead. "It's going to be okay. I called 911. What happened?"

"Not sure." Blanca winced as she struggled to sit up. "I lost control of the car. The brakes, the steering wheel. Everything seemed to stop working."

"Did anyone…?" He gulped. "Did you see anyone? Any other cars on the road?"

"No, thank God, or I might've run into someone." She got to her knees, despite his suggestion to her to keep still, and crawled toward her open purse, the contents strewn across the ground. She pulled her phone from the mess.

"It's all right, Blanca. I called emergency services." He clambered after her and gathered her things from the rocky dirt. "This time, you're taking that ambulance."

The sirens drawing closer emphasized his point, and Tate stood up to wave his arms. He'd told the operator where they were, but it was still dark.

Blanca sat back down, holding her purse in her lap, looking lost. This time, she probably had a concussion.

He crouched beside her, rubbing her back. "How did you get out of the car?"

"I—I jumped." She cranked her head to the side and gasped as she took in the state of the sedan. "I thought it might go into the water, but it would've been much worse crashing into that tree. I just… I just closed my eyes and jumped."

"Quick thinking." He glanced at the EMTs making their way down the incline with a stretcher. "Were you able to send off the package?"

"The package?" She rubbed her forehead with one thumb. "The DNA."

"Yes, yes. I'm going to talk to Myra about witchcraft."

"Okay, okay." As the EMTs trooped down, Tate waved his arm. Even though a million questions crowded his mind, Tate stopped questioning Blanca. She needed medical care more than anything else right now.

When the EMTs reached them, Tate jumped up. "She evacuated from the car before it hit the tree, but she seems confused."

The first EMT, a burly guy Tate recognized from numerous fires, asked, "Any injuries you can see?"

"Bump on the side of her head. Scratches on her face and hands. Not sure what else, but she seems dazed."

"No surprise there. What's her name?" The other EMT dropped his medical bag on the ground.

"Blanca."

The EMT touched the back of Blanca's head. "Looks like you're doing just fine, Blanca. Good thing you jumped from the car. We're going to check you out down here first. Then we're going to put you on the gurney and take you for a little ride. Is that okay?"

Blanca glanced at Tate before answering. "Okay."

While the EMTs checked out Blanca, Tate talked to Deputy Fletcher, who'd been on patrol. "She said she lost control of the car."

Fletcher wiped the rain from his face. "Not hard to do in this weather. She's lucky she got out of that car. Wait, that's the sedan we loaned her?"

"Yeah, good job." Tate pinched the bridge of his nose. He didn't think for one minute that car was defective before Blanca started driving it. George at the desk seemed to think Blanca already put a pouch in the overnight mail basket, so what would be the point of stopping her now? If she died, the FBI would just send more agents. In fact, they were in the process of sending more people now. Taking out Blanca wouldn't stop that. How would the Whistler even know Blanca had taken Isaiah's DNA? Someone at the sheriff's department had loose lips.

Fletcher snapped his fingers in Tate's face. "Mitchell. Is Blanca okay?"

"Yeah, sorry." Tate sluiced his wet hair back from his forehead. "I think she's okay but probably has a concussion."

"She's been through the ringer since coming to the island, hasn't she?" Fletcher shifted from one foot to the other.

"You think it's related to your cold case and Noah Fielding's disappearance?"

"Maybe." Tate ran the tip of his finger along the seam of his lips. "Keep it quiet for now. Seems like there's a leak at the department."

"Wouldn't surprise me." He poked Tate's shoulder. "They're taking her up."

Tate strode to Blanca, strapped to the gurney, and took her hand. "You doing okay?"

"I'm fine." She squeezed his hand. "I did get the package into the mail. He didn't stop that."

As the EMTs hoisted the gurney over a pile of rocks, their hands disconnected, but there was no doubt in Tate's mind: they were on the same page.

AN HOUR LATER, Tate sat beside Blanca's bed in the emergency room. Her color had returned, her eyes looked brighter and her cuts had been dressed.

"Mild concussion. Otherwise, I'm okay."

"Can you tell me about the car?" Tate tucked one wild curl behind her ear.

"It was weird. I thought it was just the brakes, but the steering seemed off, too. And the display lights on the dashboard seemed to be flickering." She smoothed her hand along the white sheet beneath her. "I'd felt it before. I should've done something about it."

"Before? Before, when?"

"After our encounter with Porter, on the drive to the station. Something felt off. I just thought it was the rain."

"That makes more sense. Hard to imagine someone tampering with the car in the parking lot of the sheriff's station."

She picked at one of the bandages on her chin. "Which

means someone messed with it while we were in the woods with Porter."

"It could've been Porter. He left before we did. He was mad I made accusations against him."

"Now you're saying random residents of Dead Falls resort to violence over suspicions?"

"I'm saying maybe it's been Porter all along. Just because he was in the area legitimately looking for a kid's backpack and whistling for his dog doesn't automatically clear him."

"He does have an alibi for the time Noah disappeared." Blanca gave up and ripped the bandage from her chin, revealing some red road rash.

"You haven't checked that yet, have you?" He tapped his own chin. "Are you sure you should be tearing off fresh bandages?"

"It's annoying. I'm out of here as soon as the nurse returns with some instructions, anyway."

"I'll take you back to your hotel." He held up his phone. "I let the sheriff's department know that the car needed to be checked out. Deputy Vickers told me they'd do it anyway."

"I guess that's another black mark against me with this department." She held up her finger. "First, I lose their files, and now I destroy one of their cars. They'll be happy to see the others come in."

"What were you saying back there about witchcraft? It might've been the concussion talking."

She snapped her fingers. "It might have been, but remember we talked about the number seven and satanic rituals?"

He nodded.

"Turns out Deputy Vickers's girlfriend has a daughter

who's into that stuff. Maybe she can give me some information...or names."

"Myra McKay's a Satanist?" His eyes widened. "Who knew?"

"Not a Satanist, or at least I don't think so. More like a Wiccan."

"Oh, that's much better."

The nurse bustled into the room. "You're good to go, Blanca. If you get nauseous tonight or overly tired, you need to come back. Do you have someone who can keep an eye on you?"

Blanca said *no* and Tate said *yes* at the same time.

The nurse shrugged. "Would be better if you stayed with someone tonight, just to make sure you wake up tomorrow morning."

"That's comforting, Vi." Blanca rolled her eyes and winced. "Ow."

"What did I tell you?" Vi handed Blanca a clipboard. "You can sign yourself out. This guy giving you a ride?"

"I am, *and* I'm going to watch over her tonight. Anything amiss, and I'm taking her to the emergency room."

"Perfect." Vi patted his shoulder. "Listen to this guy. He has your back."

Handing the clipboard to Vi, Blanca murmured, "I know he does."

As Blanca hopped off the bed, Tate slipped a hand beneath her elbow. "Does she need a wheelchair out?"

Blanca punched him. "I do not need a wheelchair. Better get going before he has you committing to an overnight stay and room service, Vi."

Winking, Vi said, "I'm sure this hottie could convince me to do just about anything."

As they walked down the hall, Blanca nudged Tate with her elbow. "You have the ladies of every age swooning."

He rolled his eyes and punched the button for the elevator.

Tate had parked his car close to the emergency exit, and as he walked Blanca outside, he asked if she wanted him to bring the car around.

"Isn't that it there?" She pointed to his Jeep. "I think I can handle it."

He kept hold of her arm, anyway, just because it felt so right. When they were both in the vehicle, he jerked his thumb over his shoulder. "I retrieved the stuff from the trunk of the sedan and put it in the back seat. I'm glad you got rid of that DNA sample. Who knows where it would be right now if you hadn't."

"I know we're thinking the same thing about that accident, but why? Would the Whistler go through all that just to steal that sample? And how'd he know I had it, anyway?"

"It's what I told you before, Blanca. This is how small towns work, even during police investigations. You watch. By tomorrow, everyone and his uncle is going to know Myra McKay is a Wiccan. Vickers tells his girlfriend about the DNA, Felicity tells her sister, the sister tells her friend. Who knows who's overhearing this information?"

"So, the Whistler isn't a recluse." She rubbed her chin next to her injury. "Maybe it *will* get better when the rest of the agents arrive. The FBI is insular to a fault. They're not going to be sharing any information with the local sheriffs. Maybe this is why."

"Have you even gotten that report to your boss, yet?"

"Nope."

As they bypassed the center of town, Blanca put a hand to her stomach. "I'm starving. Why do forces keep conspiring to keep us from eating out?"

"Almost everything is closed, and I'm not taking you out like that." He flicked a hand at her.

She glanced down at the rip in the knee of her jeans and the dirt encrusted on her boots. "You're right. I'm a mess."

"But just right for my place."

"Your place?" She twisted a strand of hair around her finger. "I thought you were going to camp out on my hotel room's sofa again."

"Much better at my place. We didn't finish that lasagna, so you can have some of that. Not sure wine is a good idea in your condition, though."

"The last thing I want is a glass of wine, but food sounds good. In case you haven't noticed, food always sounds good to me." She snorted.

Tate put a hand on her thigh. "Why do you do that?"

Her head jerked to the side. "Do what?"

"Make remarks about how much you eat or how much you like food."

"Do I?" She glanced down at her fingers twisting in her lap.

"You do."

"Honestly, I guess I say those things before someone else can. You know…before someone tells me I'm eating too much or that I could lose a few pounds."

"Did your so-called mentor say those kinds of things to you?" Tate clenched his teeth.

"I—I suppose he did. Yeah, not a very nice guy."

"A manipulator. Clearly, you're beautiful and sexy and perfect the way you are. Any guy telling you something different is just pulling your chain." Tate huffed out a breath.

"Well, thanks. Let's go scarf down some lasagna and whatever else you have in the fridge."

Tate tipped his head back and laughed. "That's more like it."

When they got to his place, he pulled the food out of the fridge. "Do you want to wash any of those clothes? I'm sure Astrid has a robe you could wear."

Blanca plucked at the hole in her jeans. "I guess I'm trendy now. I'll dump them in the wash tomorrow."

He stuck the food in the microwave. "Do you want something to drink?"

"Diet Coke, if you have it. I feel like I need a little caffeine."

"Astrid drinks it, so we should have some." He ducked back into the fridge and grabbed a lone can from the bottom shelf. "Do you feel drowsy?"

"Not really. Could just use a pick-me-up."

He opened the can with a crack and placed it on the counter. After he washed his hands and grabbed some dishes, the timer went off on the microwave. With a pot holder, he took the dish from the microwave and hacked off half the lasagna. He slid it onto a plate and placed it in front of her.

He curled his arm around his plate. "The rest is mine."

She laughed and dug her fork into her food. "I forgot to tell you. I got a call from Dr. Summers, the former ME. He remembered me from the search, although he said he didn't realize I was FBI at the time. Anyway, he agreed to talk to me about Andrew Finnigan's autopsy and the marks on his wrist."

"That's good. Hopefully, he can shed more light on those marks and why the sheriff's department didn't pursue the matter." He crumpled his napkin in one fist. "I saw the televised appeal the Fieldings did for Noah. Gut-wrenching."

"I know. Nothing else found other than the beanie, and the blood is his. No trace of him." She jabbed her fork into a glob of cheese. "If they let me back into the station tomorrow after wrecking one of their cars, I'm going to look up any cases from about 1996. That's seven years before Jeremy's disappearance, and on this guy's schedule."

"If he does have a schedule."

"It sure seems like he does." She took a sip of her soda and crinkled her nose against the fizz. "Do you think the Whistler tampered with my car?"

"I think he did, but I'm not sure about his motive. If it was to snag Isaiah's DNA sample, I don't see the point. You'd just go back out and get another. It's just like the files he stole from your hotel room. It didn't stop the investigation."

"Slowed it down." She licked some tomato sauce from her lips. "Or he wants to kill me. It must mean I'm onto something. The Dead Falls Sheriff's Department and even the FBI think I'm flailing in the dark, but if I'm really on the right track, the Whistler knows it. The more he throws in my path, the more he distracts me, the longer it's going to take me to figure him out. Perhaps he's hoping I'll get yanked from the case, and new agents will have to start from scratch with my notes and without my secret weapon."

Tate jabbed the handle of the fork into his chest. "I'm your secret weapon?"

"Of course you are. You've been helpful—and you've saved me twice now."

"You saved me, too…from making an ass of myself with Porter Monroe."

"Unless Porter is involved somehow. Then maybe I stopped you from finding out the truth." Her phone buzzed with a text alert, and she wiped her hands before picking it up. "It's Vickers. His girlfriend and her daughter, Myra, gave me the okay to speak with Myra."

"I hope she can give you some insight into the significance of the seven-year gap—if it is a seven-year gap between the abductions. You're not going to tell her why you're interested, are you?"

"Not the details, anyway. It seems as if there's more than enough leaking going on in this town." She pushed her plate away and finished her soda. "Do you mind if I try to get a little work done on my laptop? At least the car didn't go into the bay and ruin all my possessions. Thanks for retrieving them, by the way."

"I have some work of my own to do." He stood up and stretched, all his muscles on display.

Blanca tore her gaze away and shoved back from the kitchen table, grabbing her empty plate. "I'll clean up."

"No way." He tugged the plate from her hand. "You suffered a concussion on top of a concussion. Find some place comfortable to work, or just go on up to bed and work there. I can grab you some of Astrid's things, so you don't have to go to bed in dirty clothes."

She glanced down at her ripped jeans and sweater with debris still clinging to it and grinned. "Yeah, I'm a mess. If you're sure."

"I'm sure. It's not like I'm not used to it. Astrid cooks, and Olly and I clean up. That's the way it is."

"Your sister is lucky." Blanca picked up her laptop case from the floor by the sofa and hitched it over her shoulder.

As she planted a foot on the first step, Tate called after her. "Let me know if you need anything. That toothbrush you used is still in the bathroom."

She made a quick decision before she could think about it too much. "If it's not too much trouble, can I take a shower? After that tumble down the hill and slogging through the mud, my body is probably as dirty as my clothes."

"Sure. In the hallway next to that bathroom there's a

closet with towels. There should be soap and stuff in the shower."

"Thanks, Tate."

She took the steps slowly, all her muscles beginning to scream at her. When she reached the upper level, she snagged a towel from the cupboard and went into the bathroom. She started the water to warm it up and shed her clothing. She peeked into the medicine cabinet and spotted exactly what she'd been looking for. She shook out two ibuprofen and downed them with a handful of water.

She stepped under the warm spray and closed her eyes. She'd never been on a case before where she'd been physically attacked. Was that a sign that she'd made it as an FBI agent or that she'd messed up the assignment? Had Manny ever gotten physically attacked on a case? He'd told enough stories, but he always came out the victor.

What an idiot she'd been not to see through his puffed-up hubris. Looking back, she'd realized Manny had been trying to get into her pants from day one. First, he'd started by telling her Latinos in the department had to stick together. Then after tooting his own horn to make sure she knew how wonderful he was, he'd offered to mentor her. It had worked. She got a lot of plum assignments from her association with Manny. She didn't realize until the end that other agents had assumed she was sleeping her way into favor.

She turned up the temperature on the water and stood with her back to the spray, letting the hot water pummel her. If she got yanked off this case, she'd prove them right.

She grabbed the towel from the rack and dried off, the ibuprofen already doing its work. Not wanting to cover her clean body with her soiled clothing, she wrapped the towel around herself and tucked her clothes under one arm. She opened the door and peeked into the hallway. Hearing Tate downstairs on the phone, she scurried to the bedroom and shut the door behind her.

She tripped to a stop when she saw a filmy baby-blue nightgown draped across the foot of the bed. She placed her own clothes on top of the dresser and rubbed the material between her fingers. Felt expensive. Astrid would probably kill Tate for loaning it out.

She dropped the towel at her feet and slipped the frothy nightgown over her head. She smoothed her hands over her hips, the soft material lustrous beneath her touch. Baby blue wasn't her color, but the nightgown made her feel like a sexy jungle cat.

Turning back the covers, she slipped between the sheets and pulled her computer into her lap. She had to finish that report to Crandall, and damn it, she could do it in a sexy nightie.

Her eyes felt heavy as she typed until her fingers refused to move across the keyboard. Seconds later, someone hovered over her, taking the laptop.

She jerked awake, and Tate froze, the laptop clutched in his hands. "I'm sorry. You looked uncomfortable. I just came in to check on you."

"I'm fine." Yawning, she twisted her head to check the time on her phone. She bolted upright against the pillows still stuffed behind her back. "I've been out for almost two hours."

He brought his face close to hers. "Widen your eyes a bit. Let me see if your pupils are dilated."

"I think it's just overall exhaustion and not the concussion." But she opened her eyes wide anyway, just to bring him in closer.

With his nose almost touching hers, his eyes shifted back and forth, studying hers. "They look okay. Did your shower help?"

"Helped me feel human, and the nightgown helped me feel—" Heat rushed to her cheeks. She'd been about to tell him she felt sexy. What an obvious, embarrassing line. But right about now, she could use it. She was desperate to make him stay.

His blue eyes shimmered like the bay surrounding this island. "I guess I'll never know how it made you feel, but it makes you *look* sexy as hell."

He still had one knee on the bed, leaning toward her. She grabbed the lapels of his flannel shirt and urged him closer. With the laptop still between them, clutched against his chest, she kissed his minty mouth.

She whispered, "It's not the nightgown. You make me feel sexy and beautiful."

"Because you are." He guided the laptop to the floor and brushed back her curls from her face. He cupped her chin with one hand and touched his lips to hers.

"I'm not going to break." Curling her arms around his neck, she pulled him onto the bed. "Kiss me hard."

He took her face in his hands and angled his mouth over hers, slipping his tongue between her lips. She drew him in, and their tongues did a sweet tangle.

When he pulled away, she gasped at the loss. She flipped back the covers, and in her best husky voice, said, "Join me."

He rubbed his chin. "Are you sure? You're injured, tired."

"And you're just the medicine I need." She patted the mattress. "Besides, I might be gone tomorrow."

He blinked. "This isn't… I'm not…"

She folded her arms over the low-cut nightgown, searching his face. "Did I read this wrong?"

"Maybe you did." He clasped the back of his neck with one hand. "I'm not interested in some one-nighter with you. I've had enough of that. I didn't ask you to spend the night to hit-and-run."

His words stung. Is that what he thought she wanted? "I—I don't fancy that, either, Tate, but what choice do we have? The agency might pull me off this case. I might be ordered home tomorrow. I want this with you before that happens. I want to feel what it's like to be with a man who values me, even if it is for one night."

He caressed her face, sending ripples of desire across her flesh. "It could never just be one night for us. I won't allow that."

She dragged his hand to her mouth and pressed a kiss on his palm. "Let's see where it leads us."

Already barefoot, Tate pulled off his jeans quickly, as if worried his brain might veto his heart. Blanca unbuttoned his shirt, and he shrugged it off.

Running her fingers along the warm skin of his chiseled chest, she said, "You wear too many clothes on this island."

"It adds to the mystery." He slid his hands beneath the filmy nightgown and skimmed them over her hips. "You feel as good as you look. And I'm sure you taste as good as you feel."

He pulled up the nightie and planted a row of kisses between her breasts and down her stomach as she wriggled beneath his attentions.

When he buried his head between her thighs, she curled her fingers into his shoulders to keep herself from floating off the bed. He brought her to climax, and as her body melted, she knew once would never be enough with this man. She'd need him over and over.

Chapter Fifteen

The following day, Tate scrambled out of bed before Blanca. If he stayed under the covers with her any longer, neither one of them would be able to leave. Even if this did end up being a one-night stand and Blanca took off today, it would be a night he'd never forget. He couldn't regret that.

By the time Blanca made it downstairs, Tate had showered, dressed and made coffee. She entered the room in the same clothes she'd worn yesterday, her hair scooped back in a ponytail, her face fresh and free of makeup.

She glanced at him from beneath her long lashes. "That was quite a night. Thank you."

"You don't have to thank me. You didn't exactly twist my arm." He raised the coffee pot in her direction, and she nodded.

"I know that, but you did have some reservations."

"The second my hand touched your skin I couldn't remember one of them."

"I do have reservations." She hopped up on a stool at the island. "I have a lot of work ahead of me today, and all I can think about is you."

"I can solve that. I'm off today." He set a mug of coffee in front of her along with some milk and sugar. "I can help you out. Myra? You're in luck. I know her mother. Dr. Summers? I sort of know him, too, although my mom knew him better. In fact, they both might be more open to talking with you if I'm by your side."

"You'd do that?" She glanced at her phone, cupped in her hand. "I'm meeting Myra at about noonish. Just enough time for me to get cleaned up back at my hotel and find out what Hopkins wants to do about loaning me another car."

He tapped his head. "How are you feeling?"

"Fine, except for some sore muscles." She quirked her eyebrows up and down. "But I don't know if those are from the car wreck or those hijinks from last night."

"Hijinks?"

She grinned and sipped her coffee. "Anyway, I could use an ibuprofen, if you have some."

He opened a cupboard where Astrid kept an array of vitamins and snatched a bottle of Advil from the shelf. He shook it before handing it to Blanca. "Knock yourself out."

Her cell phone rang, and she stared at it a second. "It's the sheriff's department. Hope the agency hasn't given me my marching orders."

She picked up the phone, and Tate left the room. If she were getting yanked off the case, he didn't want to be there to witness it.

Minutes later, he peeked into the kitchen. "Good news?"

"Not sure if it's good or bad. That was Sheriff Hopkins. He told me it looked as if someone had tampered with the electrical system in the sedan. So the crash last night was no accident."

Folding his arms, Tate wedged a shoulder against the wall. "That's good news *and* bad news. Good that our instincts were right, and bad that someone is definitely trying to get rid of you."

LATER THAT MORNING, Blanca parked her new loaner in front of his cabin for their meeting with Myra. He'd decided that he should play chauffeur for her around the island.

She walked across his driveway with a stiff gait, and he helped her into his Jeep. He knew that wasn't his fault. When he got behind the wheel, he asked, "Did you take more painkillers?"

"Just before I drove over here. They'll start taking effect soon." She smoothed back her hair, which she'd washed and styled to tone down her curls. "I didn't get a chance to check the database at the station for crimes against children in 1996, but Amanda gave me a token to use to log-in from my laptop. I'm going to want to look into that, especially if Myra confirms our seven-year theory."

"No news on Noah Fielding?"

"Nope."

He shot a sideways glance at her tight expression, as he pulled away from his place. "What's wrong?"

"I talked to my boss this morning, and he's sending in two more agents to look at the Fielding case. He thinks I'm spending too much time on the cold cases, even though technically that's why he sent me out here." She held up her hand as he opened his mouth. "He assured me it's not because he doesn't believe in my investigation. In fact, he was on board with everything I told him about the Ruesler, Finnigan, and Whitecotton cases. He's not convinced Noah's disappearance is linked...but I am."

He released a slow breath so she wouldn't notice. "That's a good thing, right? It doesn't sound like the other agents are going to drive you off."

"No, it doesn't. They'll be here in a few days, so I'm going to try to talk to the Fieldings again before the others arrive."

"You're meeting Myra at her house?"

"Yes, I got the feeling she didn't want Mom listening in, but I'll have to let her if she wants to."

Tate patted his chest. "That's why you have me. Felicity will feel more comfortable letting you talk to Myra with me there."

"Okay, I'll take your word for it." She took her phone from the side pocket of her purse. "Do you know the way? I have directions."

"I know my way all over this island, as long as she's still in the same place."

Blanca tapped her phone. "Riverbend Way. Does that sound right?"

"It does. I know exactly where she is." As Tate navigated their way to Felicity's house, Blanca hunched over her phone going through emails.

She finally looked up when he pulled into a housing tract with well-ordered homes, emerald green lawns and paved driveways. She blinked. "This is where the Wiccan lives?"

"Seventeen-year-old Wiccan. I doubt Felicity dabbles in the occult." He parked in front of a neat house with garden gnomes stationed in the flower bed. "Although, I don't know. Those little guys look creepy."

"Oh, look, a welcoming committee." She nodded her head at the windshield.

Myra, her black hair loose and hanging over her shoulders sat on the porch next to a young man, about Myra's age, with similar black locks and a sullen expression. "I think we found the Satanists."

"Stop calling them that." She poked his thigh with two fingers. "I think it's just witchcraft, not devil-worship."

"The intricacies obviously escaped me. I'll let you handle the conversation. I'll just stand guard in case they unleash the demons, or whatever."

She clicked her tongue before grabbing the handle of the door. "You're not going to be any help at all."

He followed her out of the car, and she raised her hand. "Hi, Myra? I'm Blanca."

The screen door swung open behind the teens on the porch, and Felicity McKay stepped outside, one hand on her hip. "Oh, hey, Tate. The kids aren't in any trouble, are they?"

Blanca tactfully allowed him to answer.

"Not at all. This is Blanca Lopez. She just has a few questions for...er, them. No wrong or bad answers, just information-gathering."

Felicity circumvented Myra and her friend, hand outstretched, a worried look on her fine-boned face. "Nice to meet you, Blanca. I don't have a problem with you questioning the kids, as long as this isn't anything official. They're just going through a phase."

"Mom." Myra rolled her eyes. "This is Jimmy Cervantes, by the way. He can help. He knows way more than me."

Blanca shook Felicity's hand and then nodded to Jimmy. "Good. Do you want to talk out here?"

Myra stood up, stomping her black Doc Marten boots. "You can go inside, Mom. We'll be okay out here."

"Tate, will you be here, too?" Felicity wound a strand of sandy blond hair around her finger, and he was pretty sure that had been the color of Myra's hair before the severe dye job.

"As long as that's okay with Myra and Jimmy. Blanca's fine with it."

"Let me know if you want coffee or anything. I'll make myself scarce." Felicity squeezed through the two teenagers on the porch and shut the door behind her.

Myra stretched and threw an arm at the chairs on the porch. "Do you wanna sit down?"

"Sure." Blanca climbed the two steps to the porch and claimed one of three chairs.

Tate waited until Myra sat in the other one and then looked at Jimmy. "You want the other chair?"

"Go for it." Jimmy shifted his skinny body, resting his back against the wood column to face the three chairs.

Tate took the last chair. He was finished talking for now. He'd done his part.

Blanca put her hands on her knees. "As you probably know, I'm here on Dead Falls Island to investigate the disappearance of Jeremy Ruesler about twenty years ago."

"Before our time." Jimmy smirked and stretched his legs across the steps.

Tate hoped like hell his sister and her kid weren't still living with him when Olly hit this stage.

"I realize that." Blanca pursed her lips. "But we're seeing some connections between Jeremy's disappearance and a few others on the island, and the number seven keeps coming up in weird ways."

Myra and Jimmy exchanged looks between their black-lined eyes.

"It occurred to me—" Blanca's gaze pinged between the two teens "—that seven is an important number in the occult, and it might have some significance to this case. When I mentioned that to your mom's boyfriend, George, he told me you might be able to help."

"Seven." Jimmy ran a hand through his greasy hair. "It's not just witchcraft and the occult, is it? Seven is important to a lot of religions, including Christianity, the seven deadly sins and all that. But for folklore, the seventh son of the seventh son possessed magical abilities. You get seven years of bad luck when you break a mirror."

"I always wondered about that." Blanca sat forward in her chair. "Why seven years?"

"Oh, oh!" Myra raised her hand, as if they were in class. "The Romans or someone believed that the human soul was renewed every seven years. So if you had seven years of bad luck, you could recover after the seven years."

Jimmy sat up straighter, pulling back his shoulders. "Seven levels of consciousness. The seven sacraments in Catholicism and the seven pillars in Islam."

"Don't forget tarot cards." Myra snapped her fingers with their black-tipped nails. "The sevens are for challenges, but good challenges. A chance to use creativity to solve a problem."

"Wow." Blanca reclined in her chair and clapped a few times. "You two know a lot. So seven might mean renewal instead of death or the end of something. Instead of the end, a beginning."

"Seven is a lucky number." Jimmy cracked his knuckles. "So maybe this guy is using sevens because he feels lucky."

"But why would he kill them?" Myra tilted her head. "For death, he'd use a different number, like thirteen or…"

"Or 666." Jimmy made a gargoyle face and grabbed Myra's ankle.

Tate quashed the smile tugging at his lips. Felicity had been right. Despite their goth appearance, these two were playing at being different.

Blanca said, "Maybe he's kidnapping them for a different reason. Do you two know of any occult groups or Satanists that might be involved in something serious like this?"

"In Discovery Bay?" Myra snorted. "The most dangerous people I know are the drug dealers. They do a lot worse than we do with our ceremonies in the woods."

Jimmy nudged Myra's foot and ran a finger across his throat.

Blanca flicked her fingers in the air. "Oh, I don't care about your rituals in the woods, as long as you're not killing animals or hurting anyone—including yourselves."

Tate cleared his throat. "And as long as you're not starting fires. Those can get out of hand faster than you might think."

Jimmy avoided his eyes, which told him everything he needed to know. Damned kids.

"Honestly?" Myra made a cross over her heart. "We mostly go out there to try to scare each other...and listen for the Whistler."

Tate's head shot up. "What did you say?"

"The Whistler. You know." Jimmy put his lips together and started whistling a tune that made the hair on the back of Tate's neck stand up.

Chapter Sixteen

Blanca's mouth dropped open. How the hell had these two known about the Whistler? He hadn't even been on the Dead Falls sheriffs' radar. She shot a look at Tate, whose face had blanched.

"Who's this Whistler?" Blanca kept her tone even and clamped down on her bouncing leg by gripping her knee.

Both teens gave identical shrugs. Myra said, "What do you call them? Urban legends? Except this isn't urban. It's a forest legend."

Blanca licked her lips. "What's the urban legend?"

"It's more for little kids." Jimmy chewed on one fingernail, painted black like Myra's. "Something like, *Listen for the Whistler or you'll get snatched.*"

"And he's supposed to whistle that 'Hokey Pokey' song?" Tate finally spoke up, his voice sounding rusty as if he hadn't used it in years.

"Yeah, but slow…and creepy." Jimmy clapped his hands, and all of them jumped. "When you hear that creepy-ass 'Hokey Pokey' song, you'd better run."

He and Myra laughed while Blanca tried a weak smile.

Blanca asked, "Do all the kids know this story?"

Jimmy lifted his bony shoulders. "I guess. We didn't make it up."

Tate jumped up from his chair and hovered over Jimmy. "Where did it originate? Where did it come from?"

Jimmy craned his head back to look at Tate, his lazy dark eyes popping open, his Adam's apple in his skinny neck bulging.

Blanca reached forward and grabbed Tate's hand. "Give him a chance to finish, Tate."

Tate backed off and dropped into his chair, as Jimmy eyed him from beneath a lock of dark, shaggy hair.

"I don't know where it came from. It's like any scary story. It's just there. Just like you don't go to that burned-out barn in Misty Hollow."

"I know I wouldn't." Blanca stretched her lips in an attempt at a smile. "Have any of your friends ever claimed to hear the Whistler?"

"I heard him one night." Myra lifted her chin with a side glance at Jimmy. "Nobody believes me, but I did hear someone whistling that song about a week ago. Freaked me out."

"A week ago?" Blanca counted back the days to Noah's disappearance. "You mean before that tourist boy went missing."

Myra's eyes widened. "Yeah, about then. And it was right in that general area. I was shook, so I took off running."

"Did you tell anyone about it?" The tone of Tate's voice had returned to normal, and his face had regained its color.

Jimmy thumped his chest. "She told me about it."

"Yeah, and you didn't believe me." Myra kicked Jimmy's boot.

"Why didn't you tell the police?" Blanca asked.

The two teenagers burst out laughing with Jimmy recovering first. "We're not gonna tell the po-po nothing. They don't believe us, anyway."

Blanca wasn't going to be the one to point out to them

they'd been talking to law enforcement for the past fifteen minutes. She raised her eyebrows at Myra. "Even George?"

"George is okay, but I'm not going to get involved in anything. Doing this—" Myra circled her finger in the air "—was just a favor to him because he's gonna help me buy a car."

"All right." Blanca rose to her feet and pulled her jacket closed. Dark clouds had started scudding across the sky and rain looked imminent. You didn't have to be a local to figure that out. "I appreciate your help, Myra, Jimmy."

"That's it? You're not going to arrest us?" Jimmy twisted up the side of his mouth.

"I told your mom it was nothing like that, and it isn't. Just some questions, and you were really helpful. You know a lot about that stuff. You're a smart kid. I hope you apply yourself at school." Blanca zipped up her jacket as the first drop of rain hit the steps of the porch.

Felicity poked her head outside. "Do you want to come in? It's starting to rain."

Tate answered. "We're done, Felicity. Myra and Jimmy were a big help. Thanks."

"Oh." Felicity wrung her hands in front of her, as if she were expecting an arrest, too. "I'm glad. You two, get inside, and if you're going into Myra's bedroom, leave the door open."

Myra covered her face with one hand. "Mom."

They all said their goodbyes, and Tate and Blanca ran, hunched over, to his Jeep. They sat in silence for a few seconds while he started the engine and cranked up the windshield wipers.

Blanca flipped back her hood, sprinkling drops of water onto the dashboard. "So all the kids on the island knew about this character, the Whistler, and none of the adults had a clue?"

"I never heard about him. Olly's too young to be part of that crowd. Something to look forward to. It's strange." Tate adjusted his rearview mirror and pulled away from the curb. "That got out somehow."

"And Myra heard him around the time Noah went missing, or just before. What are the odds?"

"The odds are someone's terrorizing the kids of Dead Falls and has been doing it for the past twenty years—and the adults and law enforcement have been in the dark." Tate waved to someone, as they left the subdivision and accelerated onto the highway. "What did you think about their number seven information?"

"I think if Jimmy puts that much effort into his school subjects, he's going far." The windows inside the Jeep had started fogging, and Blanca drew the number seven into the mist on the glass. "It fits what we've been thinking. The Whistler is not kidnapping kids to kill them. It's some sort of new beginning for him."

"He killed Andrew Finnigan."

"Maybe Andrew escaped." She circled her left wrist with her right fingers. "After being held. Look at Gabe—if those bones do belong to him—missing at twelve, fifteen-year-old bones show up. Where was he for three years?"

"After talking to Myra and Jimmy, we can rule out Satanists, can't we? You would think those two might know something about a group like that."

"Probably." She pulled her phone into her lap and plugged it into the charger Tate had snaking from the console. "But those two are babies. They can try all they want with the black eyeliner and the heavy boots. They're harmless."

"Don't tell Jimmy that." Tate snorted. "He sees himself as some kind of occult forest gangsta."

Blanca laughed. "I could send him to East LA where I grew up, and that muchacho wouldn't last ten minutes in the 'hood."

"News?" He pointed to the phone in her lap.

"Lots of texts and emails." She scrolled through the display with her fingertip. "The most important one to me right now is a firm meeting with Dr. Summers. Should I ask him if you can come along?"

"Yeah. As far as I remember, he lives on the other side of the falls, way past Misty Hollow and the Samish land. You don't want to get stuck driving out there in a rainstorm. Sometimes that riverbed floods and cuts off that area from the rest of the island."

She huffed out a breath as she tapped in the question for Dr. Summers. "And I don't think Sheriff Hopkins is going to trust me with another one of his cars in the wild."

"Nothing more about the sedan? Fingerprints? Witnesses? Special skills?"

Twisting her head to the side, she said, "You mean, did anyone need special skills to disable the electrical systems on that car?"

"Exactly. Porter Monroe is a handy guy."

"I read his alibi, you know." She drummed her fingers on the console, next to her charging phone. "For Noah's disappearance. He was on another island."

"We don't know precisely when Noah disappeared. He could've gotten lost first and then had the misfortune to run into the Whistler, who was out hunting."

Blanca's heart fluttered in her chest. "That's what he does. He gets this seven-year itch, or whatever you want to call it, and hunts for his prey."

"It's beginning to appear that way." He jerked his thumb over his shoulder. "Do you have your laptop in that bag? If so, do you want to do some research into 1996 at my place? Or I can take you back to the station."

"Now that I have the token to get into the DFSD's database, I'd prefer to work at your place instead of going back to the station. I don't get a lot of privacy there to work."

"How's that gonna go when the FBI sends more agents out here?"

"Most likely, Hopkins will turn over that big conference room to us. We'll take it over, put in our own computers and equipment and get all linked up to our resources in DC. That's how we roll." Her phone vibrated on the console, and she grabbed it.

"Dr. Summers okayed your presence but changed the meeting place to a coffeehouse in town instead of his place, so I might not need your chauffeuring services, after all."

Tate asked, "What reason did he give for the switch?"

She read his text again. "Said he's coming in to town for dinner with a friend, anyway, and wants to save me the trouble of hauling out to his place."

"If he means later this afternoon, I'll still join you. Maybe we can finally have dinner out ourselves." He cranked his wipers up further as the rain pelted the car.

A little shiver zigzagged down Blanca's back. She was glad she wasn't driving in this mess. She'd take snow with a good set of chains any day. "He wants to meet at four thirty. Is that good for you?"

"I told you." Tate turned his head and winked. "I'm all yours today."

Her mouth watered. "Don't tempt me, or I'll never get any work done."

He pulled into the driveway in front of his house, and

they clambered out of the car in the downpour. They stood in the foyer, dripping wet, shrugging off their jackets and leaving their boots by the door.

"Lunch? Soup?" Tate brushed back his damp hair.

"I'm good. I ate before I came over, but you go ahead." She patted the cushion of a sofa positioned in front of the big stone fireplace. "Okay if I set up shop here?"

"Make yourself comfortable. Would you like something to drink?" He crossed the hallway and retrieved a pair of work boots and a slicker. "I'm going outside for a while to make sure things are secure in case this storm gets worse."

"Do what you have to do. You don't have to…entertain me. I'll make myself some tea later."

When the front door slammed behind Tate, Blanca settled on the sofa, her computer in her lap and a pad of paper next to her. She accessed the DFSD's database using the instructions Amanda had given her and did a search on 1996.

A quick scroll-through showed no child abductions or disappearances during that year. She even accessed the years 1995 and 1997. Sighing, she slumped against the cushion. There went her seven-year-itch theory, unless the crime against Jeremy and Tate had been his first rodeo.

She shifted the computer from her lap, stood up and stretched. She strolled into the kitchen and made herself a cup of tea. As she dredged her tea bag in the hot water, she stared at the steam rising from her mug. She'd checked for kidnappings but hadn't looked at the runaways. Would the database contain runaways if the deputies never considered the incident suspicious?

She dropped the soggy tea bag into the trash and returned to her laptop. She did a search for runaways, but the database wasn't going to make it that easy for her. Unless that word was in the heading, the file wouldn't pop up in the findings. She'd have to dig deeper.

Lost in her research, Blanca jumped when the front door swung open, and Tate stomped his boots. "It's a mess out there."

Putting her hand to her throat, she said, "You scared me."

"Any luck?" After he removed his boots, he hoisted a canvas sack over his shoulder, shedding drops of water on her head as he walked behind the sofa. He placed a sack on the hearth of the fireplace and unloaded several piles of wood. "I'll light a fire later. It's too close to our meetup with Dr. Summers."

"It is?" Her gaze darted to the time in the lower corner of her screen. "That went by quickly."

"Did you find anything?" He stacked the logs in a heavy metal container on the hearth.

"It's slow going." She pinged her fingernail at her screen. "No abductions or missing children from 1995 to 1997, but Andrew Finnigan wasn't listed as missing, and neither was Gabe Whitecotton. So I'm going through again, looking for runaways."

"You should try checking into troubled youths, too. Why did the Whistler start abducting adolescent boys? There had to have been some inciting incident for him, some reason. Maybe some teacher got punished for inappropriate actions with a boy. He saw himself as innocent and then started lashing out."

She tilted her head. "You've got some imagination. Sounds plausible, but I hope you're wrong on that one. The principal of the elementary school on the island killed those two women a few months ago. If the Whistler is a teacher, the parents are going to storm the school board with pitchforks."

"Yeah, but maybe that's what you're looking at. Bryan Lamar, the principal, had a grudge…and he was a psychopath. It may be the same situation here—someone with a score to settle."

"And the seven-year pattern?" She pushed the computer from her lap and rubbed her warm thighs.

Crouching beside the fireplace, Tate clapped his gloved hands together over the pile of wood. "Like the kids said. He's trying for some sort of fresh start or renewal."

"You're good, Tate." She clicked on a tab in the database. "Here are a couple of accidental deaths in 1996. Ugh, a five-year-old drowned, and a toddler choked."

"Can you look at those later? We're going to be late for Dr. Summers. I already missed my window to take a shower, but I can at least change my clothes."

"You—" she kicked off the fuzzy throw blanket from her leg and sauntered toward Tate, placing her hands on his shoulders "—look like a sexy lumberjack."

In one movement, he got to his feet and wrapped one arm around her waist. He planted a chaste kiss on her closed mouth. "Do you want to make us even later?"

Her cell phone rang, and she placed her hands against his chest. "Saved by the bell."

As she grabbed her phone from the coffee table, Tate hovered over her shoulder. "Who is it?"

Glancing at the display, she raised her eyebrows. "It's the FBI lab."

She tapped the screen to answer. "Gwen?"

"I have some news for you on the bones."

"Go ahead. I'm putting you on Speaker." Her eyes met Tate's.

"Your hunch was correct. These bones are a familial

match to the DNA you submitted from Isaiah Whitecotton. They most likely belong to a fifteen-year-old Gabe White-cotton, and they've been in that grave for about four years."

Chapter Seventeen

Blanca chatted with Gwen for a few more minutes, and she assured Blanca she'd email the report to her this afternoon.

She dropped the phone on the sofa. "That's it. Your instinct was correct."

"Which means Gabe was kept captive somewhere before he was murdered. This is going to be rough on Isaiah and the family."

"On all the families." She gave Tate a push. "We need to get going. It's more important than ever to hear Dr. Summers's take on Andrew Finnigan."

Tate bolted upstairs, and Blanca folded the blanket and put her laptop on the coffee table next to her notes. She took her empty mug into the kitchen and rinsed it in the sink, feeling very much at home. Ever since last night, she and Tate had been tiptoeing around, trying to pretend they hadn't thoroughly explored each other in the most intimate way. This afternoon felt more natural.

As she freshened her makeup in the mirror at the foot of the stairs, Tate bounded down the steps wearing a pair of dark jeans and a plaid blue-and-green flannel, hanging loose over a blue T-shirt that matched his eyes.

She smacked her lipsticked mouth in the mirror. "Now you look like a sexy, *clean* lumberjack."

"I'll take that." He pointed to her laptop. "Are you ready?"

"Yes, I'm leaving that there, if it's okay with you. I'm still logged in and want to pick up where I left off. You're not expecting anyone to come into your house, are you?"

"I'll lock up, and I installed a security system a few months back after...an incident with my nephew."

She widened her eyes. "Your nephew's not twelve-years-old, is he?"

"Not yet, and it was nothing like that, but Astrid is a little jumpy."

"I can't say I blame her. Don't get me wrong. The cabin is beautiful, but it's still a little isolated."

"A lot of these places are. We have plenty of undeveloped land on Dead Falls. It's one of the least developed islands in Discovery Bay but the most populated because of its size." He grabbed his dried-off jacket by the door. "Are you ready?"

"I am." She patted the jacket she'd left by the front door, and hers had dried, as well. She zipped it up and pulled her gloves from her pocket.

When she stepped onto the porch, she tilted her head back to look at the sky. Despite the solid gray color, the rain had stopped for now. "Do you think the rain will start up again?"

"I'm sure of it."

Tate opened the passenger door for her, and she hopped into the Jeep. When he settled beside her behind the wheel, she said, "We're meeting him at Coffee Time in town."

"That's a popular spot, but it's close to some restaurants where we can grab a bite after meeting with Summers. In fact, it's near the Grill, where we were supposed to have dinner last night."

"Perfect." She adjusted her seat belt, nudging the bag at her feet. "I brought copies of the autopsy report and a few pictures of Andrew's body with some close-ups of his wrists. I hope he remembers after all this time."

"He was on the search with us. He didn't seem infirm or anything. I'm sure he'll have recollection of what he wrote at the time."

Raindrops started hitting the windshield by the time they rolled into town, and Blanca hunched forward in her seat. "Still pretty busy. The rain doesn't seem to stop people from going out."

"We have to adjust, or we wouldn't go anywhere. Plus, it's Christmas in a few weeks. People have things to do and places to go."

She slid him a glance. "Including you. When are you supposed to head out to Florida to see your mom?"

"Scheduled to leave in a little over a week, but I can always change that ticket." He parked the car and poked his head out the door, twisting to look at the sky as a flash of lightning cracked overhead. "Damn, this is bad news for the forest, even in the rain."

Blanca didn't wait for him to get her door. She landed outside the Jeep and flipped up her hood. She'd seen the sign for Coffee Time when they were driving up, so she hunched over and scurried to the sidewalk where the blue-striped awning shed fat drops of water.

Tate caught up to her and got the door.

The scent of coffee blasted Blanca as she stepped inside the warm shop. Even inhaling it made her feel warm inside. She flipped back her hood and shivered.

The spare, gray-haired man in the corner raised his hand, and she nodded in Dr. Summers's direction. Grabbing Tate's sleeve, she said, "He's over there at the corner table. I'm glad he chose a private spot for what I have to show him."

They hung their wet jackets on the pegs by the door, and

their feet squelched across the floor to the medical examiner's table.

Blanca stuck out her hand. "We meet again. Thanks for agreeing to see me, Dr. Summers."

"Happy to help." He slipped his bony hand from hers and shoved it toward Tate. "Good to see you again, Tate. How's your mother?"

"Mom?" A crease formed between Tate's eyebrows. "Oh, that's right. You two were friends. She's fine."

Dr. Summers tapped his coffee cup. "I already ordered, trying to stave off the chilly weather. Hope you don't mind."

"Of course not." Blanca settled her purse and bag on the floor, and turned toward the counter.

Tate touched her arm. "I'll order. You have a seat with Dr. Summers. What do you want?"

"Vanilla latte, please."

"I'll be right back."

As Tate made a beeline for the counter, Blanca took the seat to the right of Dr. Summers. "I brought the autopsy report and a few pictures to jog your memory."

"Good. I'm going to need that." He tapped his head. "The brain doesn't work the way it used to."

Blanca nodded, but her gaze took in the doctor's lean but fit form, his close-cropped gray hair emphasizing a pair of high cheekbones and light blue eyes. The man didn't look a day over sixty, hardly old and senile. Why'd he retire so early?

"I always heard it was a good idea to keep exercising your brain as well as your body in retirement, just to stay on your toes."

He slurped a sip of coffee. "I try to run, and I cut my own firewood. I even do a few crossword puzzles."

"Well, I'm going to try to give your brain a workout

today." She pulled the bag toward the legs of her chair and unzipped it. She pulled out the file and placed it on the table.

Tate returned with their coffees and took the seat beside Blanca.

Summers leveled a gaze at Tate. "I heard Ingrid moved to Florida. Divorced from your father?"

Tate raised his eyebrows, as Blanca bumped his knee under the table. "Yeah, she's in Florida. My sister and her son are visiting her now, and yes, she and my father are divorced."

"Damn shame." Summers scratched his sharp jaw.

Blanca drummed her fingers on the file folder. "So the autopsy of Andrew Finnigan."

"Accidental death from a fall." Dr. Summers leaned back in his chair, folding his arms. "He could've jumped, but we wanted to spare the family that torture."

"I know that, but I did see something curious in the photos of Andrew's body." Blanca opened the folder and with one finger pulled out a photo. She maneuvered it around so that it faced Dr. Summers, and she tapped Andrew's wrist. "Do you see something there?"

Summers pulled a pair of glasses from his front pocket and perched them on his nose. Even with the glasses on, he squinted through the lenses to study the picture. "No. What am I looking at here?"

Blanca bit down on her frustration and drilled her finger into the photo. "Right there. Red marks on his wrist. You even noted them in your report."

"I did?" He picked up the picture and gave it another look. "Yeah, I see it now. Significance?"

Blanca took a sip of coffee and licked the foam from her lips. She shoved another photo under Dr. Summers's nose. "Now, look at the other wrist."

Again he squinted, bringing the picture close to his face. "I do see that."

"Both of those marks look similar to me. They look like signs of restraints. Zip ties. Rope. They're the same shape and size. Surely, nothing in a natural fall—accidental or on purpose—would cause those marks. You even mentioned them in your report as suspicious."

"If you say so, Blanca." He massaged his temple with two fingers. "As I said, my memory isn't what it was."

She pursed her lips. She got it. Dr. Summers could claim memory loss now so he wouldn't be judged for not pressing the issue. "I have your report here."

Dr. Summers scanned the first page of the report with a slight quirk of his thin lips. "This brings back memories, for sure."

"Do you see what you wrote on the second page regarding the ligature marks?"

"Ligature marks?" His eyebrows practically jumped to his hairline as he turned the page of the report. "I doubt that I characterized these as *ligature marks*."

"Well, you did point them out as suspicious." Blanca jiggled her leg up and down, and Tate clamped a hand on her knee to stop it.

"You're right. I did." He ran his finger across the page. "I remember now. Yes, two red marks on his wrists, similar in size and shape, and no apparent cause for the injury, although a lot can happen in a fall."

Blanca blew out a breath. She finally felt as if she'd pulled the tooth. "You had that in your report, but there was no follow-up."

"That's right." He let the page of the report fall back onto the table. "I remember some kind of discussion with Sheriff Maddox, and the conclusion was accidental death."

"But you had your doubts." Blanca felt like a dog with a bone.

"I did, indeed." He skimmed a hand over his short hair. "Mad Dog Maddox was not someone who brooked disagreement. He wanted the case closed."

Tate cleared his throat. "Are you saying that Sheriff Maddox coerced you into that decision?"

"Coerced." Dr. Summers steepled his long fingers. "I suppose you could say that. He was a very convincing man."

Tate continued, "What about the lack of animal activity on the body, Dr. Summers? I'd always heard rumors about that, too. If Andrew's body had been out there for several days, there should've been more…degradation from animals."

"I do remember that. The boy could've been in the caves." He swirled the dregs of his coffee. "Where are you going with this, Blanca? You think this is tied to this current case with this boy… Jack?"

Blanca corrected him. "Noah."

Summers snapped his fingers. "That's right. Do you think there's a connection?"

Blanca planted her elbow on the table and sank her hand in her palm. "You heard about the bones Tate discovered last week."

"Of course." Summers glanced down. "I heard that might be Tate's friend gone missing all those years ago."

Shaking her head, Blanca said, "That's just it. Those bones don't belong to Jeremy. They belong to another missing boy. I just got confirmation this afternoon. I have a theory that these boys were being held."

Summers jerked back and grabbed at his hair. "Oh God, no. Whose bones were they?"

"There's a familial match to Gabe Whitecotton."

A furrow formed between Summers's eyebrows. "I don't know that name. Treated some Whitecottons out at the reservation before."

Tate said, "Same family."

"That's a damned shame. I can see why this has piqued your interest, Blanca. I'm sorry I can't offer much more. I did notice those marks, made note of them in my report, as you can see, and was probably bulldozed out of further inquiry by Mad Dog." Summers spread his hands. "You remember how he was, don't you, Tate? Ingrid never liked him."

Blanca kicked Tate's foot. "If the FBI reopened this case, Dr. Summers, would you be available for comment?"

"Absolutely."

They all jumped as thunder rattled the windows of the coffeehouse.

"I have another fifteen minutes or so before my dinner date. I'd be happy to skim through the rest of the report with you, Blanca. Can you give me a minute while I use the men's room?"

"Sure, that would be great." She turned to Tate. "Do we have some time before dinner?"

"Sure. Maybe the weather will settle down."

Summers excused himself from the table, and when he turned the corner to the bathrooms, Blanca laughed. "Does he have a thing for your mom, or what?"

"I know, right?" Tate tugged on his ear. "I kind of remember that. I'll have to ask Mom about him."

"Was he married, too?"

"Not sure. Divorced, I think." Tate put a finger to his lips.

The chair scraped as Dr. Summers took his seat. He rubbed his hands together. "Okay, show me what you got."

Blanca flipped over a few more pages of the report. "Can

you look at these findings? I think I know what they mean, but I could use some layman's terms."

Summers hunched over the papers on the table at the same time Tate's phone beeped.

Blanca put her hand to her throat. "What's that? I've never heard your phone do that before."

Tate had grabbed his phone and stabbed at the screen to stop the alarm. "It's a fire. Seems like lightning struck a tree and set it ablaze. The rain hasn't been enough to dampen the fire. Sorry about dinner, Blanca."

"That's all right. Get to work. Dr. Summers and I will finish up here and... Oh."

"Exactly. You don't have your car. You can probably get a rideshare to my place if you call now."

Dr. Summers looked up from his own phone. "Looks like the weather scared off my old pal. I'll take Blanca to her hotel or to your cabin, Tate. It's on my way home."

"If you don't mind, that's perfect." She flicked her fingers at Tate. "Go. I'll be fine."

He leaned in and kissed her on the forehead. "I'll meet you back at my place when I'm done."

When he left, Blanca and Dr. Summers continued reviewing the report, and the doctor really seemed to have changed his mind about the method of Andrew's death.

As she packed the file away, Blanca said, "I'm glad we'll have you on our side, Dr. Summers."

"My pleasure. You can call me Scotty. All my friends do." He pushed his chair back. "Now, do you want a refill, or are you ready to head out?"

"I'm ready. I hope Tate got out to that fire okay and that it's not too bad."

"He's a professional." Scotty pushed to his feet and said, "Oops, you don't want to forget this."

He bent over and picked up her phone from the floor.

She twisted her lips, as she took it from him. "How'd it land on the floor?"

"It was next to your purse."

"Thank you." She tucked the cell phone into the side pocket of her purse where she usually kept it and stood up. "Do you know where Tate's cabin is?"

"He grew up on that property, although the family home wasn't nearly as grand as what he has now. That whole family came into some money when the grandfather died. I think that's when Tate's parents divorced. Gordo, Tate's father, saw his chance and took off for Costa Rica or someplace like that."

Blanca put her hand over her mouth to hide her smile. Dr. Summers had feigned ignorance about Tate's mother's marital status, but apparently he knew the whole story. Knew more than she did about Tate's family.

They stopped at the door, and Scotty helped her on with her jacket. A steady rain accompanied them to Scotty's truck, parked on the street. He got the door for her.

When he got behind the wheel, he said, "Where to?"

She jerked her head to the side. "Um, Tate's place, right? Is that still okay? I don't want to put you out."

"No, no. That's fine. I just thought you might want to go back to your hotel first."

"My car is at his place. I had a little…accident last night, so he's playing chauffeur." How did Dr. Summers even know where she was staying? He was quite the busybody.

"That's good. Tate matured into a fine man, even though Ingrid had her hands full with him." As he started his truck, his phone blared an alarm.

Blanca jumped. "What is it with the phones out here? Doesn't anyone have a normal ring?"

"I have alerts from the DFSD." He cupped his phone in both hands. "Oh my God. There's been a sighting in the woods of Noah Fielding. They're calling on people to fan out and search. I... Is it okay if I just drop you off at your hotel? You can take a car to Tate's, like he said. I'm really sorry."

"No, no." Blanca snapped her seat belt. "I'm in. Let's go."

Scotty's truck lurched forward on the slick street. "I was hoping you'd say that, Blanca."

Chapter Eighteen

Tate tossed some gear in the back of the Forest Service truck, rivulets of water trailing down his uniform.

His second-in-command, James, swore beside him. "I was just getting ready to sit in front of the fire with my woman and a bottle of whiskey."

Tate smacked him on the back. "At least it wasn't serious."

Aaron joined them, piling more equipment in the truck. "I don't know about that, Tate. Someone purposely set this fire. That's pretty serious."

Tate shrugged. "Maybe some teens thought it wouldn't be a problem to set a fire in a rainstorm. Anyway, it all ended okay."

James shoved him. "Tate's anxious to get back to his FBI agent."

"And for that—" Tate slammed the keys against James's chest "—you're taking the truck back to the station, and I'll be in front of my fireplace before you will."

At the time of the alarm, Tate had gotten instructions to head to the site in his own vehicle, as others were coming from the station with the trucks. He'd been annoyed at the time, but now he was happy to have his Jeep to get back to his place...and Blanca. She should be there by now.

He punched on the ignition and let his Jeep idle and heat up as he texted Blanca. He stared at his message on the display, frozen in place. It hadn't been delivered. Could be his location. He flicked his lights at the boys, as he rolled away from the fire site.

His four-wheel drive gripped the road as he wound back to his cabin. He parked behind Blanca's DFSD sedan and jogged to his front door. He disabled the security system with his phone and slipped his key into the lock. A fire in the fireplace sounded good about now.

As he slammed the door behind him, he called out for Blanca. "You get here okay?"

The silence came back at him in waves, and he felt a prickle at the nape of his neck. He flicked on the lights of the empty kitchen. He'd figured she might've picked up some food or at least opened a bottle of wine.

He pulled out his phone, and his heart did a double thump when he saw his previous text message to Blanca still frozen in place. It had never gone through. He tapped the phone to call her and it went straight to voice mail.

"Blanca!" He took the stairs two at a time and veered into the empty spare room, the bed made and the night-gown he'd loaned to Blanca across the foot, just as they'd left things this morning.

He went back downstairs and sat on the sofa she'd occupied earlier. Maybe Summers had taken her back to her hotel and she'd decided to stay there. He called the hotel and discovered she hadn't been there all day. The clerk rang her room just in case but didn't have any more luck than Tate.

If she thought he'd be working all night, she might have gone to the station to follow up on something. Her laptop was still here, though. He called the DFSD station anyway, and the desk sergeant told him Blanca hadn't been in since the morning to pick up the new car.

Could she and Summers have decided to have dinner together? That seemed weird, but they'd appeared to be hitting it off when he left the coffeehouse.

He did a search on his phone but couldn't find a number for Dr. Scott Summers. The station might have it from the search the other night. The deputies had asked the volunteers to leave their phone numbers if they wanted to be alerted to new searches.

He called the sergeant back at the station, but he wouldn't release Summers's phone number to him.

He flipped open Blanca's laptop. She'd stayed logged in, so he was able to bring up a search engine. He did a search for Summers but found only out-of-date info about his practice.

He snorted. Maybe his mother had his personal number. The man's interest in Tate's mother was strange. Did she know Dr. Summers harbored some secret crush on her?

Maybe Blanca and Dr. Summers were having dinner together and Blanca's phone was dead or the storm had messed up her service.

He chewed on the inside of his cheek and navigated back to the DFSD database Blanca had been searching. She'd left the page up with the two incidents involving children from 1996.

He clicked on the first one. A five-year-old boy had drowned at a birthday party by a creek. As he skimmed the report, a name jumped out at him: Summers. Jackson Summers. Tate trailed his finger down the screen.

Jackson Summers was the son of Lydia and Dr. Scott Summers. He'd fallen into the rushing creek while the children were dancing to the "Hokey Pokey" song.

BLANCA PANTED AS she clumped after Scotty. "Hold up a minute. Are you sure you have the right location? I don't see any other searchers here."

"This is what they told me." Scotty stopped in the clearing and spread his arms out to his sides. "It always ends up being here."

Blanca had bent forward, hands on her knees to catch her breath. As she straightened up, her eyes widened. This was the place—the tree where Jeremy's abductor had left Tate.

"They told you to come here? Do you know what this place is?"

Scotty ran his hand over the trunk of the tree. "I do. Tate Mitchell was found here, tied up, blood in his shoes."

Blanca cocked her head. Did everyone know about the blood in Tate's shoes? "And the alert said to meet here? Was Noah seen here? Did he run away?"

Shoving his hands in his pockets, Scotty said, "Noah's safe, and he'll stay safe as long as you keep your nose out of our business."

Blanca massaged her fingers against the lump on the back of her head, which had started throbbing. "Wait. He's safe now? They found him?"

"He's safe with me. He's mine now."

The world tilted, and Blanca took a step to the side to regain her balance. "Wh-what are you talking about, Scotty?"

"I'm talking about my son." Scotty took a gun from his pocket and aimed it at her.

Her knees weakened, and she felt for her purse with her gun inside, which she'd left in Scotty's truck. She traced the edges of her phone in her pocket but already knew it would do her no good. She'd tried using it in the truck with Scotty, but it had been dead. He'd done something to it in the coffeehouse to make sure she wouldn't wonder why she hadn't received any alert about a search.

She choked. "The fire calling Tate away?"

"I set that fire on slow burn and phoned in the report when I was in the bathroom." He caressed the bark of the tree. "I knew Tate would go. He's a solid man now, but he wasn't always that way. He was trouble, unlike Jeremy. I knew I could handle Jeremy, but Tate would be a handful. Also, I didn't need two sons. Just one to replace the one I lost."

Blanca drove a fist against her mouth, and her lips cut the inside of her lip. "Where is Jeremy? What did you do with him?"

"I kept him with me. I kept him safe and raised him as my own."

"Is he alive now? Where is he?" She scanned the ground for a rock or stick she could use as a weapon. Against a gun?

"He got too old, didn't he? You raise a son and then set him free."

"The same way you set Andrew Finnigan and Gabe Whitecotton free?"

"Andrew was too much trouble. I should've known that. He escaped...and had an unfortunate fall. Gabe—" Summers practically beamed and puffed out his chest "—Gabe was a good son, but teenagers are hard to handle. If you ever have kids..."

Blanca gulped. She wanted kids right now more than anything in the world. She wanted a life. "Where is Noah, Scotty? Just tell me where he is. I'll let you leave. You can take off. Just give us Noah."

Summers chortled, an eerie sound out here in the woods, more animal than human. "You'll let *me* leave. That's rich, Blanca. I'm the one with the gun. Yours is in my car, and

I slipped the battery out of your phone when I took it with me to the men's room."

"You can kill me. It won't matter. I'm part of the Federal Bureau of Investigation. Agents will keep coming and keep coming until they find Noah and figure out what you did. When I disappear, they'll take over the investigation of the other two attempts you made on my life—at the hotel and the car. That was you, wasn't it?"

"Those weren't attempts on your life, Blanca. I wanted to put a little scare into you and get my hands on that case file at the same time. I have to admit, I rigged the car in the hope that you'd crash and get injured enough to get off the island. These other FBI agents you talk about won't be nearly as dedicated as you." He gave her an exaggerated wink that turned her stomach. "You have a personal stake in this now, don't you?"

She dug the heels of her boots into the mulch on the soggy ground. "Tate saved me both of those times, and he'll figure it out in the end."

He kicked the bottom of the tree. "You have such faith in Tate. Why? He couldn't save his friend, Jeremy, and he can't save you. He's off fighting a fire somewhere. He's not going to have any reason to think I killed you. Why would he? Why would anyone? I've been hiding in plain sight all these years, joining searches, performing autopsies. And I have my little family safe at home."

"Why are you doing this, Scotty? If you wanted a family of your own, you could have adopted a child." She suppressed a shiver at the idea of this man adopting.

He hissed between his teeth. "I had a child. A son. He drowned when he was five, playing a game at a birthday party, too close to the creek. I was working. It was my wife's fault. They never should've been there. So seven years after his death when he would've been twelve years old, I took another twelve-year-old boy to keep as my own."

"And seven years after Jeremy, you took Andrew, but that didn't last." She pressed a hand to her heart. "Why seven years?"

"Seven years is a time for renewal, for rebirth. Every seven years, I give myself a new son to replace Jackson."

"I'm so sorry for your loss, Scotty, but this isn't the way. You know the grief of losing a child. How can you take someone else's child from them? What about Birdie Ruesler? What about the Fieldings? How can you send them home without Noah?" The only thing that kept her hopeful was the belief that Noah was still alive somewhere. Was that why Scotty didn't want her to come to his place? He had Noah there?

He puffed out a breath from between his lips. "I never felt bad for Birdie. Her son was alive. Noah will be fine, too."

"Before…before you kill me, can you show me? Can you show me where Noah is and that's he's okay?"

"Oh, Blanca. You're just going to have to take my word for it. You're going to die right here, and poor Tate will have even more reason to avoid this part of the forest."

Chapter Nineteen

Tate navigated his Jeep through the road cutting through Misty Hollow. The rain pounded the hood of his car, and the windshield wipers kept his thoughts on track. *Find Blanca. Find Blanca.*

As he approached the road to Scott Summers's sprawling property beyond Misty Hollow, he cut his lights. Would Summers have some kind of security system? Booby trap?

He parked behind a copse of trees and slid from his car. He crouched low, his gaze pinned to the main house, low lights beaming from the windows. When he didn't see Summers's truck, he almost collapsed to his knees.

He crept to the house and peered into the windows. Through a few gaps in the drapes, he spied the rooms of Scotty's house: neat, nobody there.

He continued to slog through the mud into Summers's backyard. A few outbuildings dotted the property—dark, windowless structures that looked ready to fall over.

He rounded the corner of one and tripped to a stop. A building on the edge of the property had seen some improvements. As Tate stared at the structure, he noticed a glow of light emanating from the back.

He took out his gun and circled the building. The door had a padlock on the outside, and he grabbed a shovel and pounded the lock until it broke and fell to the ground. He kicked in the door, gun leveled in front of his body.

Someone yelped from the back of the building where he'd seen the light, and he crept forward. When he got to the end of the space, another door met him. This one opened to his touch.

It creaked as it swung open, and Tate held his breath. He sputtered as his gaze landed on a large cage, a dark-haired boy clinging to the bars with both hands.

Tate's heart pounded. "Noah Fielding?"

The boy's hands tightened on the bars. "Who are you? Are you with *him*?"

"I'm not with anyone, Noah. I'm Tate. I work for the US Forest Service, and I'm here to help you." Tate shuffled into the room a few feet. "Who is he? Who locked you up?"

"That old guy. That creepy doctor. He put something over my mouth when I was walking in the woods, and next thing I knew, I was in this jail." He shook the bars, which rattled.

Tate drew closer and surveyed Noah's prison. Summers had installed a toilet and sink, a cot, an exercise bicycle. Tate's stomach turned. How long had he held the boys here? How long had he held Jeremy?

As Tate strode toward the enclosure, Noah scrambled back. Tate grabbed the padlock on the outside of the cage and asked, "Where's the key?"

"He takes it with him." Noah edged closer toward Tate. "Are you gonna get me out of here?"

"Of course I am. I told you I wasn't with Summers."

"Summers. Yeah, he keeps calling me Jackson Summers. I told him my name was Noah. I—I tried to fight him."

"I'm sure you did, son. Did Summers…hurt you?"

"Nah." Noah puffed up his chest. "Only to get me to stop yelling or trying to escape when he brings food and stuff."

Tate scanned the rest of the building for tools he could use to break the lock. He didn't want to shoot at it. Too risky. "Where is he now?"

"He went to get some girl."

Tate froze and spun around back toward the cage. "What girl? A young girl?"

"No, some lady." Noah rubbed is nose. "He came in here all mad. Sometimes he does that. Comes in here all upset and yelling and stuff. He's not even yelling at me. It's like he's yelling at the wall. Walks around and grabs his head."

"What did he say this time?" Tate grabbed the bars. "Do you remember? It's very important."

"Said some lady from the FBI was looking for me. I told him they would. Said he was gonna stop her."

"When was this, Noah?"

"Like, I don't know. Earlier today after he brought me lunch." He aimed his toe at a tray on the floor and kicked it. "Hasn't even brought me dinner, yet."

"Do you know where he is? Where he goes?"

"Nah." He kicked the tray again, and it skittered across the cement floor. "Are you gonna let me out, or what?"

"Just hang on one minute. I saw some tools outside."

As he turned away again, Noah sniffled, his bravado seeping away. "Don't leave me here."

"I'm not going to leave you. I'll be back in a minute."

Tate ran back outside and found a pickax and a hammer. He came back inside with both, and a big grin spread across Noah's tear-stained face.

"I thought you were gone. Hey, I thought of something else he said."

"Told you I wasn't leaving." He hoisted the hammer. "Stand back."

He brought it down on the lock and hit a bar instead. The

cage rattled. He tried again and got a direct hit. Two more swings and the lock broke.

Tate yanked open the door and Noah flew at him, wrapping his arms around his waist, sobs racking his thin frame. Tate thumped him on the back. "It's okay. You're okay. I'm going to take you back to your parents. But can you tell me what you remembered, first?"

Noah staggered back, his cheeks red as he ran an arm beneath his nose. "Yeah, he told me he was gonna kill that lady back in the same place where it all started. I don't know what that means, though."

"I do, Noah. I know exactly what that means."

BLANCA SHIVERED AS the rain dripped from her hood down her collar. She pulled her jacket closed at the throat.

"Why did you let Tate live all those years ago, Scotty? Why not take him or kill him?"

"Why would I kill him?" He rolled his shoulders, and the gun wavered for a second. "He didn't see me. He fell off his bike after I already had Jeremy secured. I hit him on the back of the head to make sure I could get him away from the scene and tie him up."

"And the blood in his shoes? Why were the bottoms of his feet torn up?"

"He lost his shoes when his bike crashed, and then he ran from me." Summers hardened his jaw. "Troublemaker. That's why I hit him on the head, but he never saw me. When I tied him to the tree, I went back and got his shoes. Put them back on his feet."

She narrowed her eyes. "Why not just kill him? Why go to all that trouble?"

"Ingrid." He patted his chest. "I always had a soft spot

for Ingrid. I didn't want to take her boy away like mine had been taken from me."

Blanca's heart skipped a beat when she saw a light flicker in the trees behind Summers. Was someone else here? Noah? Maybe he could run for help. Porter Monroe? What she wouldn't give to have Porter crashing around the woods with his dog again.

Just when she thought she'd imagined the light, it came on again, as if in a pattern. Someone was here. Someone was listening.

"Tell me about your son, Scotty. Tell me about Jackson."

His head jerked up. "My son is with me now. I'm going to care for him. I'll convince him to stay with me like I couldn't convince Jeremy or Gabe."

"No, I mean Jackson, your five-year-old boy. Tell me about him, Scotty. Did he look like you or your wife? What was his favorite color?"

Scotty clutched his head with his free hand. "Stop. Jackson is gone now, but every seven years he's reborn in another boy. I don't want to talk about Jackson. I'm sorry I have to kill you. If you'd just left the island… Nobody cares about Jeremy Ruesler anymore. Tate doesn't care."

An eerie whistle floated out of the trees, behind Scotty. The slow "Hokey Pokey" tune wafted across the air, and Scotty staggered back against the tree, his weapon wavering at his side.

As someone came charging out of the bushes, Blanca dove for the ground and rolled away from the clearing. A gunshot blasted, the sound reverberating in her ears. Was Scotty shooting at her? She dug her fingers into the organic matter that carpeted the forest to pull herself farther along the ground behind a log.

When she heard grunting and scrabbling among the

leaves, she poked up her head. Two men tussled on the ground. Her eyes, already adjusted to the dark, picked out Tate straddling Scotty, a gun to his head.

He rasped. "I should kill you. I should kill you right now for what you did to Jeremy and all those other boys."

Blanca rose to her knees. "Tate, don't. They'll get justice, thanks to you."

Sirens wailed in the distance, and Scotty bucked beneath Tate.

"That's right, Summers. I already called the police, and I already have Noah, safe in my car. He's going home to his real parents, and you're going to tell me where you buried Jeremy so I can bring him back to his family, too."

Epilogue

Birdie Ruesler wiped a tear from her cheek and hugged Tate. "I'm sorry for all those years, Tate. I'm sorry I blamed you."

Tate held Birdie's thin hands in his. "You don't have to apologize, Birdie. I understood because I blamed myself."

"I know you did, and I had no right to add to your guilt. You were a child. I was just so angry, I had to direct it somewhere. I'm ashamed it landed on you."

"You lost your son. You don't owe anyone any apologies."

"And you lost your best friend and your innocence." She patted his arm and nodded toward a dark-haired woman with a baby in her arms walking toward them. "Did you see Celine before the funeral?"

"No." He held out his hand to Jeremy's sister. "I think I would've recognized you anywhere."

She kissed his cheek. "I don't doubt it, the way you and Jeremy used to bug me and Astrid all the time. Mom's coming to live with us in Idaho. She doesn't need to wait anymore, and I need her expertise with this one."

"That's a great idea." Tate tickled the baby under the chin, and she gurgled.

"He's a natural with kids." Blanca came up behind him and put a casual hand on his shoulder.

Birdie touched Blanca's face. "Celine, this is Agent

Blanca Lopez with the FBI. She's the one who helped Tate bring our Jeremy home to us."

Celine shifted her baby to the other hip. "Nice to meet you in person, Agent Lopez. I read all about you and how you were able to connect all the cases of the missing boys."

"Tate's the one who found Noah Fielding, rescued me from Summers and made him tell us where he'd buried Jeremy. If he ever gets tired of forest fires, he might have another career opportunity."

Squeezing Tate's arm, Celine said, "And Jeremy's up there smiling down at you, Tate."

Blanca took Tate's hand, and they wandered away from the rest of the mourners, who included Gabe's family, Andrew Finnigan's mother and the Fielding family, who'd returned to the island for Jeremy's funeral.

They sat together on a bench under several towering Douglas firs. The sun shifted through the branches, creating a dappled pattern across their laps.

Tate traced one of these patterns on Blanca's thigh with his fingertip. "I still can't wrap my head around the fact that Dr. Summers fed on his own grief to destroy so many other lives."

"Look at Birdie. Grief makes people react irrationally—oh, and Dr. Summers happens to be a psychopath. The point is, you brought peace to a lot of people…and indescribable happiness to the Fieldings. Noah worships you." She rubbed his back and kissed his jaw. "You also brought peace to yourself and that twelve-year-boy you used to be."

"I may have done the heavy lifting, but you're the one who thought out of the box and linked all those cases together. None of the other law enforcement officials who looked at these abductions brought the same insight that you did. You're a rock star, Blanca Lopez. Does the agency know that now?"

"I think they're catching on to my brilliance. They have an assignment for me in DC, some analyst work." She tucked her arm in his. "That means I have to go home, but there's always face-to-face on our laptops. We can get kinda kinky online."

"Yeah, about that." He pressed his lips to the side of her head. "I put in for an assignment that's going to take me to DC. Do you think you can show me around when I'm there?"

She squealed and grabbed his face with both of her hands. "No way. Are you serious? I mean, I know we talked about taking this relationship further, but I thought that was just you sweet-talking your way into my bed."

He eased out a breath, not wanting to show her how relieved he was at her response. "Ha! I told you I didn't do one-night stands, not with you."

She put her luscious mouth on his. "That's not what I heard around here. Small towns, ya know?"

"Ah, that was before. Before you helped that skinny twelve-year-old boy find peace and redemption."

She kissed him again, and he didn't feel guilty at all about his happiness. In fact, he had a feeling that Jeremy was giving him a wink.

* * * * *

COMING SOON!

We really hope you enjoyed reading this book.
If you're looking for more romance
be sure to head to the shops when
new books are available on

Thursday 4th
January

To see which titles are coming soon, please visit
millsandboon.co.uk/nextmonth

MILLS & BOON

Introducing our newest series, Afterglow.

From showing up to glowing up, Afterglow characters are
on the path to leading their best lives and finding romance
along the way – with a dash of sizzling spice!

Follow characters from all walks of life as they chase their
dreams and find that true love is only the beginning...

Two stories published every month. Launching January 2024

millsandboon.co.uk

OUT NOW!

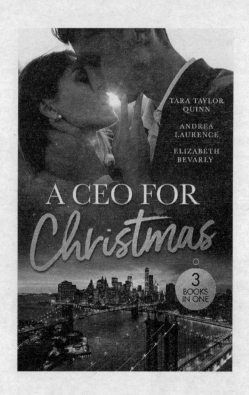

TARA TAYLOR
QUINN

ANDREA
LAURENCE

ELIZABETH
BEVARLY

A CEO FOR
Christmas

3
BOOKS
IN ONE

Available at
millsandboon.co.uk

MILLS & BOON

OUT NOW!

3 BOOKS IN ONE

A Christmas Fling

THERESE BEHARRIE   SARAH M. ANDERSON   CAROL MARINELLI

Available at
millsandboon.co.uk

MILLS & BOON

OUT NOW!

**Available at
millsandboon.co.uk**

MILLS & BOON